MAGGIE GEE

Virginia Woolf

in

Manhattan

TELEGRAM

First published 2014 by Telegram

This paperback edition published 2015

Copyright © Maggie Gee 2014

ISBN 978 1 84659 199 0
eISBN 978 1 84659 189 1

A full CIP record for this book is available from the British Library.

Printed and bound by CPI Group (UK) Ltd, Croydon, CR0 4YY

TELEGRAM
26 Westbourne Grove, London W2 5RH
www.telegrambooks.com

Maggie Gee is the author of twelve acclaimed novels, including *The White Family* (shortlisted for the Orange and IMPAC prizes) and *My Cleaner*, and a memoir, *My Animal Life*. She is a Fellow and Vice-President of the Royal Society of Literature, and Professor of Creative Writing at Bath Spa University. Her work has been translated into fourteen languages. Maggie Gee was awarded an OBE in 2012 for her services to literature.

'Audacious, playful and dazzlingly written' *The Herald*

'Maggie Gee has pulled off a remarkable feat ... She has made Woolf abundantly human once more in this exhilarating novel, with its passages of lyrical beauty and its passionate defence of imaginative writing.' *Virginia Woolf Society of Great Britain Bulletin*

'Gee does a terrific (and puckishly poetic) job with Woolf's wit and acuity, her hoots of laughter and sudden fadings of joy ... wickedly funny ... this novel contains lines that sparkle' *Sunday Telegraph*

'Brilliant ... Moving and funny ... Gee writes about Woolf with wit and affection, and has crafted an amusing and clever novel' *Shiny New Books*

'This giddily playful novel from Maggie Gee is a cunning what if: what if Virginia Woolf were to suddenly reappear in a library in modern-day Manhattan? ... It's a gloriously funny, fleet-footed novel about the relationships be... ways literary heroes live on in ...

740006927029

*For Mine Özyurt Kılıč, with love,
and for my friends in Istanbul*

PART ONE

London–New York

There is thunder as Angela flies to New York with Virginia Woolf in her handbag, lightning crackling off the wings of the plane.

Bad karma – not that she believes in it. The flight is delayed and the pilot greets them with a warning. 'We're expecting a little turbulence today so if the seat belt signs go on, we'd ask you to return to your seats and keep your seat belts fastened ...'

Electricity flashing on chemical–rich pools 3.5 billion years ago started life, Angela reads. The power of lightning. She snaps her book closed at once. *Life on Earth*, it's called. *Death in the air*, she's thinking.

Taxiing, now. Too late to leave the plane.

The passport in her locker says 'Angela Lamb'. Place of issue, London. Date of birth, 20 May 1966. There are many stamps on its pages, she's a Frequent Flyer, she should be accustomed to storms.

The contact name at the back is still Edward Kaye, because she doesn't know how to change it. (In any case, is she ready? They're married. She's in her mid-forties. Too late for another child, with another man.) Angela has one child: an only child: Gerda.

Life must have started in lots of different places, she decides as the honeyed arpeggios of the safety film unfurl. Many organelles – was that the word she liked in the book? – many cells, many pools, times, universes, lightning streaking through it all. Strong enough to spiral through billions of

years, splitting and changing, unstoppable, playful.

Life! (Is it a waste to marry only once?)
What will life do next? Where are they going?

Angela's itinerary's crazy: London–New York–Istanbul. Angela will fly direct from New York to Istanbul, nearly eleven hours. There are easier ways of doing it. Still Angela's diary is demanding, geography must bend to accommodate her – the curve of the earth is certainly not going to stop her. New York for the New York Public Library, where she will read Woolf's manuscripts in the private Berg Collection. Then Istanbul to give a paper at a big international Woolf conference, 'Virginia Woolf in the 21st Century: Cross-cultural and Transformational Approaches', at Istanbul University. She's not an academic, not really, she tells people, but yes, she does a few 'university gigs', she has an 'attachment' (a Visiting Professorship).

Her real work is writing novels. She's published by Headstone Press, recently subsumed into the gigantic Haslet group, who also make large profits from chopped, reconstituted meat. She's popular, yes, she's won prizes including the Iceland Prize, but she craves more: respect. To be counted as literature, which she loves – though she also likes money.

Now she's picked up, as an alibi for take-off, Virginia Woolf's 'Professions for Women', written in 1931, a human life time ago. It's a brilliant essay, but she's reading the same sentence over and over. Something about Woolf's difficulties with sex and the body. 'Telling the truth about my own experiences as a body, I do not think I solved. I doubt that any woman has solved it yet ...'

Roaring down the runway!

And, as ever, part of Angela thrills to the speed as, at the

last moment, the bullet full of people noses up, up, into the air. She's flying!

And a thought out of nowhere floats across the cabin, light as a mosquito, and lands, invisibly, on her: if I'd met Woolf, if she had met me, on the same loop of the ribbon of spacetime, what would she have thought of me?

Would she have — *liked* me?

— *Would I like her?*

Charged with electricity, the thought darts onward.

Around them, around all the silver planes in this part of the air, lying this way and that below the stratosphere like so many unmagnetised iron filings, the weather systems surge, gigantic, careless, throwing off sparks from tremendous anvils fifty thousand feet up. Most jets fly at thirty-five thousand feet, so everyone's under the cosh. The pilots are not so much tense as alert.

The chief steward of Angela's flight is chatting to the pretty new flight attendant as she does her checks. He's stimulated by her frightened eyes with their brown Bambi lashes. 'There's no danger from lightning as you know,' he tells Neela, trying not to look too directly at her breasts. 'The fuselage acts like a giant Faraday cage.' Her pupils are blank, unfocused, she has no idea what he's talking about. 'If we take a strike, which we won't, it would exit near the static wicks on the wings.' 'Wicks,' she says, clutching at his words, 'on the wings,' and she sets down her pen very carefully. 'There was something about that in the training sessions,' but she's thinking *the wicks of candles, burning, blazing, if it happens, I hope I'll be brave.*

Still climbing.

Everyone's hoping they'll break into sunlight soon, but they don't. They continue to shudder through cloud, and the seat belt signs remain on. Outside the window, the streaming greys are uneasy, with distant flickers that may not be flickers at all,

they hope, just minute changes of light or viewpoint.

Some haul the Safety Instructions from the pouch in front of them and stare at the cracked plastic with pictures of blank little humans doing the right thing and surviving. It doesn't show what to do if there's lightning.

A loud creak and all the video screens come down from the roof of the cabin, stay blank, go back up. Uneasy laughter. It happens again. They laugh less, look around, not long enough to meet other eyes. Have the plane's electrics gone wrong?

For some reason, Angela is thinking of Edward. Gerda and Edward. They have been the twin pillars of her world, but now it's all up in the air.

Then the PA crackles into action. 'Will everyone please remain seated with your seat belts securely fastened.' The pilot's voice sounds urgent. 'We are about to go through a period of turbulence.'

Now the plane starts to jerk like a conker on a string. There's a loud crack, some enormous force that's indifferent to them, they are tiny and nothing and someone is sobbing.

All bets are off: Neela screams as the plane falls through space-time: thoughts collide,

Mum told me not to do this job

 Edward *Gerda* *love*

Virginia Woolf goes flying through the air

 and lands somewhere else entirely

Yes, it's begun.

I

VIRGINIA

Suddenly there's time again; & I'm in it.

Plenty of time.

 (Is there? – or just a bright gap in the night of unknowing?)

I spent … *seven, eight decades* … in the dark – a normal lifetime.

 And now I am here – am I? Back on the blade of the here & now.

Will I leave any mark when I write? Will this new world read me?

 Its unending light, which they all take for granted, cuts orange slats in the blinds of my room at night. Past two, three, four in the morning, the light streams on, and my head strains away like a land-locked sea lion.

 I used to live, long ago, in a low quiet house, which had darkness at night & smelled of the garden, lilacs & roses, cut grass, cheroots … Leonard. June nights: him safe in the house nearby. Bats & owls, my brain racing, sometimes, but often calm – knowing I was home. One doesn't notice how sweet … (Who was it that said 'Observe perpetually'?)

 Somehow I slipped a century. Stones in my pockets weighted me down – I sank, bursting – Then nothing. So many years in the dark. It seems I was not forgotten.

 Someone longed for me, here in New York where I never went – someone híngered, and hauled me back up,

protesting, yanked me through hedges & gates of dreams, and untidy, sleepy, stunned, I was suddenly half-awake in Manhattan, Virginia Woolf in Manhattan, and it is – can it be, really? – the twenty-first century. You see, I wanted –

ANGELA

I wanted to sound up to date, that was all. Because my Istanbul paper was called 'Virginia Woolf: A Long Shadow', and I decided to look at the primary sources. I'd forgotten a lot since I first read her. So I booked a last minute package to New York, where Woolf's manuscripts are kept.

She did mean so much to me back when I started. Yes, she was a talisman.

Something more fundamental than the paper. Where was my life, and my writing, going? I thought it might help to be close to her.

Perhaps I should begin with my daughter. (V. never had children, of course. There I've done better.) Gerda is thirteen. I have kept her alive! And she's newly away at school. A rather good one, Bendham Abbey, though no-one in my family had ever been to public school before. Hard, very hard for me, sending her away, and Edward protested ... *don't think about that*. Second term, Gerda would be fine. Mobiles were banned – it's archaic, but apparently, problems with theft, concentration in lessons. I told her we could email every day ...

-ish. So that was fine. In theory.

Of course, I am busy, as I explained to Gerda.

Odd thing – Virginia's the quintessential English writer – but there they all are, in the New York Public Library, all those famous manuscripts, *Orlando, The Waves, To the Lighthouse*. In the Berg Collection, the dim red leather comfort of the Berg.

14

I suppose in the UK I've got used to being treated with a certain – not deference, no, but people have been nice to me, since I won the Iceland Prize. And the Apple Martini Prize. My name has become quite well-known. The Apple Martini shifts a lot of books, and actually made me money. Me and Gerda and Edward, that is. Holidays in Egypt, Australia, Jamaica. A new, better house. I'm a success. Success, success, that shiny slippery word, which I hope will never slip away from me.

Once people I met on planes or trains would ask 'Will I have heard of you?' and I would say, 'Probably not.' But now they say, with a dawning smile, 'Oh yes, you're quite famous, aren't you?', and ask if I'm going to write about them, and I smile at them politely, thinking 'Not a chance.' Then they ask me if I know JK Rowling, and I say 'I met her at a party once, but really she was talking to Philip Pullman,' and honestly, they still get quite excited.

I am successful, and I'm still quite young. Though not as young as I used to be.

VIRGINIA

She ran after me as if I were a brigand. Once I saw it was a middle-aged woman, I let myself be caught. But it unsettled me, the way she said my name. Not 'Mrs Woolf', 'Virginia'.

She knew my name.

ANGELA

To be honest, in New York my name means very little. Whereas Virginia Woolf was huge here in her lifetime – *New York Herald Tribune* No 1 best-seller with *The Years,* on the cover of *Time* magazine, etc. And afterwards, she did cast a long shadow.

Growing bigger and deeper in the seventies and eighties as all the other women were eclipsed. On every university women's

studies literature course, first and dead centre: *Virginia Woolf and this*, *Virginia Woolf and that*, *Virginia Woolf and the also-rans*. She's special, clearly, but all the same – isn't it just easier to fetishise one person? Then you don't have to think about the rest.

I'm certainly not jealous.

In her best work, she wrote for everyone. The clarity, the astonishing reach, the perception.

VIRGINIA

When I died I thought I was almost forgotten, gone.

ANGELA

So this is what happened, as I understand it. (Only Gerda will believe me. She stares right through me with those pale blue eyes half-hidden by long thin red-blonde lashes, and then she shivers and hugs herself and says, sing-song, 'Re-ally, Mummy?' Gerda was raised on fairytales.)

New York. No pickup at the airport. When I called the hotel to remonstrate, they said there was no record that the plane had landed. Sleepless night, glaring orange hotel sign outside my window. Everything felt frazzled and burnt out. Yet underneath, something itching, energetic.

I slept. And woke: to a new beginning.

A new day, after all, in New York! One of my favourite things, a New York morning. So what if the breakfast room was overcrowded? A fat man shouldered his way out and I nipped into his seat by the window. Sun on my eggs. Outside, the wide street streaming with purpose. I'm a positive person, it's one of my virtues – Edward was a bit of a moaner. The gorgeous light scored straight to the park. The hotel was a dump, but near Central Park.

I love it all. The skating rink, the joggers, the lake, the spring

trees, that delicate yellow – the zoo. Oh yes, I love the zoo. It's a play zoo, really, tiny and lovely. Monkeys, bears, in the heart of the city, so alien and mysterious. Alive in the moment, so different from us.

But first of all: work to do. Off to the New York Public Library.

(Inside, part of me was still shaking. I'd felt shallow or hollow, ever since that terrible blaze of white light.)

The woman in charge of the private Berg Collection where the Woolf manuscripts are kept gave me an oblong yellow reader's card: 'ANGELA LAMB is hereby admitted to the BERG COLLECTION (Room 320) for research on VIRGINIA WOOLF. This card is good through 27 NOV 2020 unless revoked.' I like membership cards. They make me feel entitled. I haven't always felt that way.

Virginia, of course, was born entitled. But part of me is still the daughter of Lorna and Henry, born in Wolverhampton.

Statutory humblings. Abandon your coat, your briefcase, your camera, your pens, your phone before you can enter. I didn't mind. I was excited. I couldn't wait to get my hands on her!

Then the librarian explained.

There's a rule that only applies to Woolf, because she is so valuable: no original manuscript material can be accessed. 'I'm afraid you have to read her on microfilm.' But it's hardly the same, is it? She hasn't breathed on that film, or used it, or touched it.

I was muttering furiously under my breath, head down because I didn't want to be evicted from this submarine, cosy, womb-of-a-room where only the two librarians and I were working. At least I was *near* those manuscripts. At least I sat two feet away from the heavy glass case where the walking stick she carried on that final day was lurking, a horrible thing of

dark, hooked cane. It looked – cursed. I'm allergic to suicide. And yet, it was a link to her.

Who has more right than me to read her?

All the senseless 'No's of my life jostled and surged in my head as I sat there. Virginia, I thought, Virginia, I crossed an ocean to get close to you. Can't they let me reach you somehow? I sat there and longed: for her elegant angular writing, her amused, classic face. English! She was English, but these rich Americans had filched her!

Then the pleasant girl brought me one article, a strange piece Woolf had written for *Hearst Magazine and Cosmopolitan* in 1938, a carbon copy on thin onion-skin paper, with a few corrections in ink. The title was 'America which I have never seen interests me most in the cosmopolitan world of today'.

And at once I was enjoying the dance. 'Cars drive sixty or seventy abreast,' she assures us (though she never went there!). 'While we have shadows that walk behind us, they have a light that dances in front of them, which is the future.' I was smiling as I read. I'll take you home to Europe, I silently promised, if I can get to you I'll slip you in my bag and take you back to Sussex, to Leonard, to Lewes ...

Perhaps I had spoken aloud – 'I'll take you back to Leonard, to Lewes' – for one of the librarians was staring at me fixedly.

Or not at me. No, behind me.

I heard, or half-heard, a croaking sound. Half-human. Distressed. Straining. And I turned in my chair. And saw.

VIRGINIA
Did I hear 'Leonard'? Did I say 'Leonard'? Can I now even remember how it was?

Suddenly from nothing
 was I something again?
My own voice waking me from too far away –

hearing my own voice rather deep and tremulous, I thought
 & almost – *old* –
 (for inside I was still young, a girl, when I died)

I followed it up
 from the depths of cold watery sleep
 into the warmth of a small dim room I did not know

a woman breathing as she read, lips half-moving, very serious,
 a sigh a small smile

She was reading me with such strong desire and I wondered
 'Who is she?'

she has blonde hair but she is not young

I am on the threshold I'm too tired I don't know
 a fish jerking it's me that she's reading yes, it's my soul
it's me –

And she reeled me in, hauled me up. A strain like a tooth
being pulled.

ANGELA
This woman. This strange woman. That was all I thought. Tall
and dusty in bedraggled green and grey clothes. A suit. The
librarian said, 'Excuse me. May I help you?' Then closed in on
her like a gaoler.

VIRGINIA

Stirring and gathering myself too late to go back –
 an ache coming together
puckering a long fall of satin curtain
 a wavering
a pulling together not wanting
to be seen

 exposed

her eyes, their eyes

 but *oh* –

the waking of the light

in the dark so long lost in my own crushed rib-cage
 weighted with mud and slime though dying was no
worse than the terror nothing
 is worse than the terror

Here, I am suddenly here.

Warm wood. Women. Electric lights. A strange room.
 Two books in my hands. Yes, they're mine. Hold them close
to my body, hide them. Mine.

And, as if new-born, no fear. Was it over?

ANGELA

Almost before I knew what was happening, she was gone. In a
pincer movement, two librarians hustled her out of the door.
'If you don't have a need for access to original material …'
one was saying, and the strange woman gaped like a fish, while
the other librarian intoned, 'The librarians in the *open* reading

rooms will be happy to help you.'

The door swung shut. There followed a hubbub of librarian excitement, which is quiet, but the first words I could make out were 'Who was THAT?'

And as soon as I heard it as a question, I knew the answer, and made for the door.

Out on the landing, a gaggle of Japanese tourists with cameras, a big-nosed man in a red woollen hat – but not her. So I ran down the stairs, and there, on the last flight but one, by a seat where a black boy in shades was sleeping, there she stood, yes it was her. A tall angular shape from the back, not going forward, hovering, leaning, like a tall-masted sailing ship. Her white fingers trailing on the balustrade, then touching two books, which she clutched to her ribs, shyly, as if in wonderment.

My breath caught. I slowed down, and came to her step by step.

Step

by

step.

I was afraid. I kept walking, I drew abreast.

I was any fan, any groupie, suddenly. I could see her face. Her great globes of eyes, darting down, away: hunted.

Perhaps I should have left her. But how could I have let her stumble out on to the streets of Manhattan on her own?

I had to say: *'Virginia?'*

VIRGINIA
She said my name, that first time, as if I belonged to her. They

shan't have me! She said 'Virginia?' and I was off like a hare. There were red ropes, I went the wrong way, a man in uniform stopped me & asked to look at 'those books', I had two of my own & he looked at me hard and said 'Ma'am, are these from the library?' – but I said 'No' & rushed on, with her after me. And then –

ANGELA
Half of me was laughing, half of me was shivering, nothing like this had ever happened, not to me. But I couldn't let her go.

It was brilliant; it was impossible; it was so thrilling I could hardly breathe. It was Virginia Woolf in Manhattan. And I reached out my hand.

VIRGINIA
She *touched* me. It felt – electric. You see, I wanted –

ANGELA
It was like dipping my hand in water.

VIRGINIA
I wanted to come back.

2

ANGELA

I loved my life: I was in the thick of it. Things I had earned by writing my books. Yes, I've earned them, and I enjoy them. Films, travel, clothes, chocolate. I loved my daughter – I love my daughter. (It seems a long time since I emailed her.)

I love good food, and taking out money, nice thick chunks of it out of the wall. And no, I don't have to feel defensive. My parents were poor, and my mother couldn't cook. I like the sunny side of the street, because when I was a child, days were darker. When I was a child I was often afraid. And of course, more recently, problems with Edward. Eco-heroes are hard to live with.

It was more a question of living without. Edward was on an expedition to the Arctic, financed by a cat's cradle of grants. I hadn't wanted him to go. There were a series of explosive rows before he went. I told him, if he was leaving me, he needn't bother coming back.

I hadn't expected to be alone. But who wants to be with the wrong person? I knew my life was about to get better.

And so I paused before pushing onward. A dark smudge on the event horizon. Something brief as a fin surfacing.

(Because reading Virginia Woolf isn't simple. I love her, but parts of her make me shiver. And sometimes – yes – she creeps into my head, a pale bony version of the woman she was, and she's pointing to places I've never been, tunnelling away from air and sunshine. Although of course she can be very funny.)

In that instant the universe split, and I was sucked into this particular story.

There she was, white, in front of me.

'Virginia?' I sighed, a second time.

3

VIRGINIA

A yellow-haired female was gaping at me. Not respectable. Primped & painted. Yet her demeanour was kind enough. All around us, more painted women. Everyone smelled of chemicals. There were many Africans and Chinamen.

Was it Wolstenholme's laudanum? How had I lost myself again?

The world whirled round me, I had no centre, perhaps the voices would begin.

Yet part of me was still, quiet. A child, watching. Was I reborn?

ANGELA

Then, too late, I remembered my manners. We stood in the foyer of the library, the great loud streets roaring past outside, but there was still glass protecting her — I felt from the start I would have to protect her. 'Mrs Woolf?' I corrected myself. 'Mrs Woolf? May I help you?'

'I think,' she said — such a beautiful voice, but absurd! If she tried to give a reading today, people would laugh out loud at her fluting vowels, her long 'I's like 'A's, her 'a's like 'e's — 'I may perhaps need help. I seem to have forgotten where I am.'

And I stammered, 'The New York Public Library.'

'A library?' Large eyes, grey-green, puzzled. Blurred or misted with age or doubt. Blinking out from caves of bone. 'Perhaps there is a telephone?'

'Use my mobile,' I said. 'But we must go outside.'

She stared, then continued as if I had not spoken. 'Is there a telephone I might use?'

So many things to explain to her. But first I must get her to some kind of shelter. Virginia Woolf on these blaring streets … 'Come back to my hotel. It's not far.'

On the other hand: Woolf in my modern room – modern to her – small, slightly seedy, the radiator humming, my shabby 1970s Waddington Hotel?

Her voice became more imperious. 'I'm so sorry, I don't know your name, but I really must telephone my husband.'

And then I was overwhelmed with pity. She did not know that he was dead! But I said – that temptation to show my knowledge – 'Leonard.' There must have been something in my tone, for she looked back at me, alarmed. 'Are you an acquaintance of my husband's?'

'I've heard of him. Everyone has.'

And her long, almost equine face relaxed. Those mournful, haunted eyes sparkled, her full lips lifted in a sweet, shy smile. Yes, a chalice of happiness. 'Do you think so? Mr Woolf will be amused to know that.'

You love him still, I thought with pain, pain for her and then for me – Edward said he loved me, but he still walked out. Had I ever been loved as Virginia was?

'You'll have to come with me,' I said, almost brusque (people were starting to stare at her). And then, as kindly as I could, 'Come with me, I'll look after you.'

And yes, that's what I tried to do.

4

GERDA

My mum picked up this weird old woman. That's what I thought till I googled her. For a bit, Mum thought about nothing else. She claimed this person was 'very famous'. Mum didn't bother to explain to me. I just thought, 'Yeah, she's got a loony in tow.'

She should have told me. I would have believed her. And in the end – but that's much later.

ANGELA

Virginia smelled. Of mud, and roots. People were pausing and sniffing the air as they pressed through those great library doors. I wasn't able to be objective. I thought, it's a dream, of course it's a dream, but please don't make me wake up until –

I needed to learn what she had to teach me. Maybe everything. About life, and writing. She had the secrets. She'd reached the end. The hard truth people can never tell us. At least, that's something I've always thought. Not till the end is the pattern complete. But then they slip away through the gate. They can't come back, we can't ask questions.

Yet here she was. Virginia.

VIRGINIA

Have I slipped my leash?

I think that's it.
I've made it through to the other side, the place I never
 believed could be.
At first I thought, banally, I was dreaming.
Now, all round me, this dream has flesh
 bars bricks towers trees tall silver-grey trees
beside the library crows yes flown out of my past
 friendly crows '*Kaar, Virginia*'
& now I have to find the others.

(I don't think everyone is here. No matter, so long as Leonard is.)
 He must be here. He wouldn't leave me.

6

'This is Fifth Avenue,' Angela says, as Woolf steps tremulously along the pavement. 'Incredibly famous street, Virginia.'

Yes. The greatest, straightest avenue in one of the greatest cities in the world. Shining street surfaces, traffic lights, pavements without cracks or pot-holes. City of dreams: city of films.

'Yes,' Woolf says, 'I'm not a bumpkin.' She looks to her left: streaming ribbons of cars, and windows as far as her eye can see. Rare yellow-green trees wave messages; there's a faint green fingerprint, Central Park.

And back to her right: more towers, more cars, the blinding glass of skyscraper windows. She turns, like a horse fretting in its collar, to the left again, irritable, hoping against hope for something different. How can buildings have grown so tall?

Her great eyes search for that slim glimpse of green. There, yes. Still yellow with spring.

I could go there and be happy.

A half-thought forming: *Alive again.*

But they're both hemmed in with right-angles.

Two lost ants. Tiny nets of nerves. Glittering scraps of spider's web.

ANGELA

She was like a trapped animal.

Of course, they have built over the past. Once Manhattan must have had fields.

And then – oh shit – she launched herself forward.

VIRGINIA

It was the noise, roaring, blasting. And sun on a thousand surfaces. Shards of sky, elbows of trees, clouds leaping out at me from strange tall buildings. The sky and the city had been smashed together, with jagged pieces thrown everywhere. I thrust the books deep into my pockets, I would need my hands to protect myself, my head spun, I walked forward, blind –

'What in hell are you DOING! Madness! *Beyakoof!*'

A yellow car had almost hit me. The wind knocked me sideways, and I saw the furious face of the driver. He had small wire glasses under his turban. Where was this place & who were these people? I stood quite still in the middle of the road & cars screamed past me & I wasn't afraid.

I had been changed, because I wasn't afraid. Perhaps the darkness had finally left me. Wherever I had been – for however many years – I had left my fear behind like a parcel, & something began in the midst of my confusion, although I was dazed, something started – a jolt of joy, which could not be stifled, small as a child set free in a hayfield, stunned for a

second then gathering pace, dancing across, the yellow dust flying –

'*Kaar, Virginia.*' A crow welcomed me back to the pavement where it pecked at a crack, pecked at the gap between the worlds.

ANGELA
She almost died before her new life started!

VIRGINIA
She dragged me – pulled me hard by the arm, I nearly struck her for her impudence – into a place that smelled of fried meat. I have always hated restaurants. Music I had never heard before – loud drumming & someone shouting – I placed my hands over my ears & said, 'Where is the telephone?'

ANGELA
'Please sit here, where you are safe. There are things I must explain to you, but first I will get some coffee – I don't remember if you drank coffee?'

VIRGINIA
The woman spoke as if she knew me!

ANGELA
I mean, there's been coffee since the eighteenth century, but God knows which modern kind she'd like, latte, cappuccino, Americano … Expresso seemed like the safest choice. Was there anything about it in the *Diaries*?

VIRGINIA
'Yes, of course. I *adore* coffee.'

I came back from the counter balancing my tray and saw her, for the first time, clearly, from a distance.

First, though old, she was beautiful. Very pale, drawn like a bow. Thin and tall. Her eyes, avid.

Second, she was extremely odd. Two small children were staring at her, American children with little round bellies. She was like a great mayfly, long neck poking forward. Straggling limbs, her knees jutting out. Then two long feet like heavy boats that might float away from her altogether. Greasy grey hair pulled back in a knot at the nape of her long column of neck. She wore a long woollen suit that might have been tailored, but didn't fit, as if she'd tried to shrug it off but then given up in embarrassment. Yet her long white hands and blue-white wrists had escaped, and couldn't wriggle back in again. She didn't look unhappy, but intensely self-conscious. At the same time, she was curious. Her eyes flicked up, her eyes flicked down. Her eyes went swooping round the room, hungry to see everything. I thought, what will she think of us? – Plastic surfaces, harsh colours, half-dressed people celebrating New York's unnatural spring heat-wave.

I brought back an expresso for her, and my normal creamy half-shot latte, which came in a rather attractive tall glass. Without hesitation, her starved bony hand reached across the table and closed on my latte.

She left me the small, bitter cup.

She got the cream, and I the grounds. Her tall angular shape between me and the window, a cone of darkness drinking my prize.

Yes, I thought, we are in her shadow.

I watched her grey-green orbs dipping and sweeping. She was almost in a trance. What was she learning?

I saw she didn't want to talk to me. Her mind was working

on its own, and her bony hands like sea-creatures scampered across the table-top, climbing the curve of her narrow glass (*my* narrow glass, I reminded myself), skating down to the base again, twisting the metal frame that contained it, lifting her tea-spoon, putting it down.

And suddenly I remembered *The Waves*. 'Let me sit here for ever with bare things, this coffee cup … things in themselves, myself being myself.'

'Myself being myself.' I knew what she meant. It was why I fled home and its social duties – why I fled Gerda, which makes me ashamed. Because I wanted to be myself. Was I myself in my writing, at least?

Was I good enough to stand naked?

She was good enough. God, she was good. She even managed to write well about coffee.

I watched her swallowing my latte. Yes, of course, she was ravenous. She was sucking it down in great raw gulps, as if she was trying to drink the world. She hadn't eaten or drunk for decades!

She said 'Could you bring me another, please? Then I will telephone my husband.'

Bring me another! Did she think it was free? Unlike her, I did not inherit money. She spoke to me as if I were a servant. Of course I would try not to hold it against her, but well – my grandma *was* a servant.

Still – 'I will telephone my husband' – annoyance yielded to a surge of pity.

How could I possibly begin to tell her?

Everyone she knew was dead.

8

ANGELA

Safety. I still hadn't got her to safety. That was the mantra in my brain. Through a blur of noise, speed, fear I guided her back to the Waddington.

Virginia Woolf, that leviathan! How lucky I was to be in this dream — or was she lucky, to share *my* dream? Did the dead get holidays?

Briefly, I moved through space beside her, and every step felt dangerous. Thank God it wasn't very far. The Waddington, Seventh Avenue. The last hotel I would have chosen.

Perils of last-minute internet packages. Flights were cheap, but what a dreadful flight!

The lift. I do remember that. She cowered from the walls as if they were shrinking. I slipped my keycard across the room door and saw her eyes fixate, briefly. Then we were in, and she saw the phone. 'No, Virginia, wait a moment.'

I expected the dream to fall apart. I think I hoped that waking would save me, but the unspeakable silence extended — she was still there, and I was still there, and the room was as constricting as before, like the small-sized room where everyone dies, for I had looked after Henry and Lorna, and once you have seen your parents die, nothing is quite as it was before.

Somehow she'd have to be told about Leonard.

And I began to try to explain.

'The twenty-first century,' the woman said, for the second time, patiently, slowly, as if I were a child or an idiot.

And so it all started to scream in my head, the noise of the traffic five floors below us – the moans & gurgles of the radiator – this yellow-haired woman who looked so hard at me, & took my arm, & told me lies – this strange small room full of ugly furniture, the pale telephone like none I had seen that squatted on her bedside table like a sickly, sleeping, dachshund pup, & this dyed stranger did not want me to use it –

I must wake up *It's time to wake up*

'You can't call him,' she said to me. 'I'm so sorry, he – can't be called. As I said, it's the twenty-first century.'

 'Of course, *of course* I must call my husband – '

I MUST WAKE UP IT'S TIME TO WAKE UP

I strained to wrench myself out of the dream –

 The detail felt too sharp for a dream. This box-like, tiny, oblong room, the ugly bed with its poor, bare, bedhead – the square black screen staring out from one corner, some awful cinema machine – the cheap brocade curtains, the poisonous smell this woman said I was imagining.

 Could it be true that I had jumped a century?

 Could I be ... back?

 I stared out of the window. A strip of sky. A ray of light.

 A sudden jolt of absolute beauty. Through the mean window it signalled to me a world of new signs, flashing, glowing.

 But Leonard. *Leonard*. Was he here too?

 Odd that I can't remember how I left him. I can't remember

yesterday. And yet I surely spent it with him. My mongoose love, my beloved mate. With whom I've had such happiness. They underrate the joy in marriage. No-one could be happier than we have been –

I don't think two people could have been happier

Stare at the floor, the yellow walls, the painted-over wallpaper. The nameless spots and spills and smears. The human body, leaking stains

No, look away, that air, that sky

'Virginia do you want some water? Virginia? *Virginia?*'
 'Leave me alone. Please be quiet.'
 For I heard a voice of terrible clarity, reading the note that I had written, picking me up by the scruff of the neck and shaking me with guilt and horror –
 (Somewhere in the room, a loud bell shrilled. The woman started patting her body frenetically, up and down, like a meaningless dance. Then she dragged a small box out of her pocket. Now she was talking and smiling to herself.)
 I understood. Another telephone. In this strange world, some did not need wires, some slept like dogs on bedside tables. I would make her give it to me, and ring Leonard. 'Sorry,' she muttered. 'Sorry, Gerda.'

GERDA

I sneaked to the village before detention and called my mother from a phonebox. It smelled of London: smoke and old wee. London! Where I wanted to be. She didn't sound at all happy to hear me, and she was talking much too quietly.

'Sorry I haven't been in touch. There's someone here. Sorry, Gerda – '

'Who?'

'Someone who is *right beside me*. Someone very famous I'm having to look after. Someone special. I'm *busy*, darling.'

'How about looking after your daughter? Aren't I special? I hate you, Mummy.' I banged the phone down, though it missed the cradle and swung there, hopeless, like a baby on a cord. Banging its head against the glass. Just for a moment, I felt powerful, but it was raining outside the box, there was nothing I knew, just the horrible village.

I was the baby, swinging, hopeless.

ANGELA

She knows she is not supposed to call me. But that's children: they choose their moment. They ask a lot. Though one gives it gladly. I had told her never to hang up on me.

Virginia, too, was like a child. She showed no interest at all in me. Yes, I pitied her pain over Leonard. But I had worries of my own. I had no clue what was happening to Edward.

However much I tried not to care, I didn't have a heart of stone. Some of the time they would be using huskies, but

some terrain would be covered on foot. Edward had done special training for months – I should know, I had complained enough when he didn't do his share of the household chores – but he was also accident-prone, and health and safety were not his forte. He was cavalier about equipment, and frostbite, and when I fretted, called it 'fussing'.

What if I just read about his death in the papers? Did he, or his team, know where I was? I'd left my new mobile number with the neighbours, but had Edward actually noticed our neighbours? Men could be impervious. I didn't want to hear the news from strangers. How could I ever tell Gerda?

It would break her heart. She loves her father.

VIRGINIA

1941. I am back in the gyre, water corkscrewing towards perdition. I am fifty-nine. I will never be older.

The thing I wrote before I set out. That day in March. I remember it.

The skies were clear, blue and bright, a great blue blank bearing down on me, dazzling, blinding, and naked terror, everyone would know, everyone would see me

everyone would say the book was no good

The day before, I had seen the doctor. Octavia asked me to take off my clothes take off my clothes so she could see me what did she know? too young to be a doctor!
I told her no, there was nothing wrong.

Why did Leonard make me visit her? sharp eyes peering at my nakedness that terrible look of pity, kindness, yes yes Octavia, yes, *thank you*, thank you, my hands are always cold (*thank you, that hardly proves your brilliance*)
 (I didn't say it, I was polite) Leonard had told her to ask me to rest I saw his careful hand behind it now they would all gang up on me

she asked me to 'Try, try for Leonard'

That night I could not sleep at all

The morning, clear everything clear it was very cold
I fetched my fur I needed one last touch of comfort
flowers in the garden were too bright fat yellow daffodils,
harsh, triumphant

Yellow varnish this yellow room

cruel that Octavia asked me to try 'for Leonard', as if I had no
care for him, and she, a stranger, knew everything

I have tried so hard. I can try no longer

The Furies waiting where the path disappears

*The hideous old women bare their claws at me, wet-mouthed,
whispering as they crawl towards me, brown scaly talons and hanging
flesh*

I could smell their furious iron-rich breath, the great blades of
their scissors wet with light, the hellish light of the blue spring
sky, gnawing my fate before I was ready
 I loved my life but I had to go, once the Furies smell you
you can only flee. I knew that day I could not outrun them, the
sky was cloudless, they had me at bay –
 I wrote to Leonard & I wrote to Vanessa. Words I had
practised many times. With the breath of the Furies hard in
my ears & their split yellow nails, like torn bamboo, sharpened
ready to gouge my eyes out.

In this hostile, stinking, yellow room the dreadful words return
to me, words that can never be unsaid, the deed, once done,

that can never be mended
 the wound I dealt him, the grief I gave him

darling Leonard how I struck at his heart

knowing I must hurt him, I pulled on my coat, thrust my
hand deep into the pocket as I almost ran down through the
meadow, it was ready now for the fate it must carry, yes, I had
gone too far to go back,

a tiny voice like the voice of a child that wanted to be born
 was crying Stop *a tiny part of me cried in the night*
 small, stubborn, a scintilla of light
trying to escape me, trying to get out

but the path led straight to the river bank the Furies
behind me every step of the way behind me, ahead of
me, snapping at my ankles, tearing at my stockings like vicious
brambles, battering my ears with icy hatred, whipping me
onwards, *flee, flee*

this time I knew they would never release me

the river roaring
 full of crazed blue light Omega chunks of blue and brown

feel certain I am going mad again

 can't go through another of those terrible times
begin to hear voices *can't concentrate*
 I am doing *what seems the best thing to do*
You have given me the greatest possible happiness · *I don't think*
 two people could have been happier

could have been happier

this terrible disease
> *I can't fight any longer*

ANGELA
After a long silence, her voice came, hoarse. 'I did it, didn't I. That terrible thing.'

VIRGINIA
Sitting on the woman's ugly bed, which was broken-backed under a yellow-gold cover, with nameless shadows, wine or blood – it groaned beneath me like the sea, as if my grief was too heavy for it, & I groaned louder, I groaned like old metal, I groaned like banks of black stones on a beach, moaned in pain like a wounded beast

I remember

the clumsy walk at midday with the voices shrieking and baying behind me, the yelps of the Furies hounding me down through the meadows I had loved for so long, the skin on my back crawling with terror, *Virginia, you're mad again*

I remember

thrusting the stone in my pocket
large, heavy, waiting for me, the stone like a toad on the river-
 bank
I held it weighed it in my hand
blind, brutal *I choose you*

forcing the stitches of my pocket apart and as it started to tear,

as I heard the silk split, I stopped myself, gently, be gentle with it, yes, I controlled it, the heavy bludgeon

remember

the brute knocking hard at my flank as the Furies reached me and I jerked away, their black hide blotting out the sky, great shrieks of raucous joy as they pawed me, knowing my fear would drag me down and hold me under the green tangled water — but a voice in my head still whispered *Leonard*, a woman's voice said *how can I leave you?*

Leonard, Leonard. Yes, again. *Leonard my love. I can't leave you.*

But it was too late for him to save me. Or my dear sister who was so patient, with her stooping head and steady eyes.

Yes, it was true. I left him behind. I loved my husband but I left him behind, & slipped through the door where none can follow.

Two o'clock in the afternoon, though several lifetimes have slipped away. Two fragile organisms, blown together. Dandelion clocks on a dirty bedstead. Angela, Virginia.

She was washed downriver like a broken doll. He had to identify her three weeks later. Children thought she was a log in the water. They stoned it, hard, to make it sink. The happy bird-calls of adolescents. Then one boy realised it was a body.

Down in the street, the cold is beginning a slow fight-back against the spring heat-wave. The dark, repressed, pauses, alerted. Soon it will be able to creep back into the gullies. Then it will climb up the buildings again.

Angela looks around her and shivers. 'Mrs Woolf, are you all right?'

VIRGINIA

I suppose he had to identify me.

After that, did the horror start to eat my face? Did the sight erase poor Leonard's memory of what he once thought beautiful?

Wracked on the bed, I remembered my crime.

ANGELA

She was pale as wax, and sat there trembling.

'Mrs Woolf? Virginia?'

She shook her head, again and again, like a dog shaking water away.

VIRGINIA

'I don't know you. Why are *you* here? Why won't you let me use your phone?'

ANGELA

Her breath rasped like an old man's.

'It's the twenty-first century. Some way through. My name – I've told you several times – is Angela Lamb. And I'm alive. It feels to me as if we're both alive. But Leonard – well, he died long ago. You can't call him. I'm so sorry.'

She stared back at me, blind with anger. Her hand still stretched towards the phone.

I spoke more brutally than I intended. 'The world you knew is – everything's gone.'

'Gone? What are you talking about?' But her arm drew back, her shoulders bowed.

For a minute she sat there saying nothing, kneading the bed-cover with big white hands. She looked — epic. I will never forget it. I did feel pity, but also … the writer in me was trying to record it. How could I ever describe this moment?

I was there. I was — *chosen* to see it. Somehow I had to find the words.

The tears began to roll down her face, bright ropes of water on her dry white skin. She cupped her hands, and her head dropped into them. The clever long skull with its silver hair. She sat, a dead weight. A broken statue. A water-streaked monument on a stained bed, in the wrong room, in the wrong century.

I was there, myself, with Virginia Woolf. Later, much later, I am writing it down.

Neither of us spoke for a long time.

'I know this is hard. I'm so sorry to tell you … But you see — we're in the twenty-first century. Leonard would be what, well over a hundred. He had his life. It did continue. After you — '

And there I fell silent. 'I mean. It's seven or eight decades since you — '

But I couldn't say to her 'since you died'. I couldn't say 'since you killed yourself'. That phrase is an impossibility. It can never be said between two human beings.

We sat there, two tall, solid women in a room that felt too small for us, a banal, real, insect-sprayed room in Manhattan where no-one cared if they poisoned the guests so long as the bed-bugs didn't survive, and the radiator hummed, and the traffic roared, and everything was as real as this table.

I knew too much, and she too little. By suicide, she had lost the right to know about the man she loved. She had turned

her back, gone on alone.

(A stab of pain. Was it what I had done? The last thing I'd shouted as he strode down the hall: 'Don't come back. Don't bother to phone.' And then he didn't. He didn't phone. He thought I meant it. He was a man. I dragged my thoughts away from Edward.)

I, a mere stranger, knew more than Virginia. That Leonard had managed to write again, loved again, been happy again.

I thought: I can't tell her he was happy.

(And what if Edward is happy again? What if he has another woman?)

'I say, Virginia – Mrs Woolf – let's go out, before it gets cold.'

VIRGINIA (*angrily wiping her face on her sleeve*)
'It's all my fault. I left him alone. I thought he would be able to work, without me …'

ANGELA
'This is too much for you. And me! You like walking, don't you? I need some air. Perhaps you would come for a walk with me?'

VIRGINIA
'I must go home. I need to go home.'

ANGELA
Desperation makes you creative. 'The zoo. There's a zoo. You would like the zoo. A zoo in the park you caught a glimpse of. Central Park. It's beautiful.'

VIRGINIA (*pulling herself together*)
'Of course I have heard of Central Park.'

ANGELA

'Would that be – agreeable?'

 She gave an almost imperceptible nod.

VIRGINIA

'Better than staying here, I suppose.'

ANGELA

'That's settled, then. Rest, then a walk. First I need the bathroom. Oh, perhaps you need the bathroom?'

VIRGINIA (*coldly*)

'I bathe in the morning.'

ANGELA

'Lavatory. Closet. Oh, I don't know. I will leave you to it.'

 I couldn't bear to be inches away when Virginia Woolf was – no, impossible. I took my phone out into the corridor. It was ridiculous, of course.

 (For several days that's what I did, and for my own needs ran down to the lobby and queued behind the departing guests, tripping over their long mule-trains of baggage.)

 When I came back, she was emerging from the bathroom. 'All right?' I said. 'You – push down the handle.'

 She looked at me, indignant. 'I'm used to water closets,' she said. 'We had one installed at Monk's House. Yours is rather … *elaborate*, of course.' I glimpsed something scarily like contempt, and banned myself from noticing.

 'Virginia, you'll need a coat.'

 Now I was glad I'd brought too many clothes, with a view to impressing American men (small chance of that with her in tow.) I beckoned her over to look in the wardrobe and indicated my second favourite, a smart narrow coat of merino

wool, black and slick as a liquorice stick. She shook her head.

No, she was stroking, with her long, sensuous, lingering fingers, my favourite Stella Maris trench coat, beautifully, generously cut from blue mohair. The yoke floated out like a sail at sea. It had sharp reveres and an indigo belt, such a beautiful belt of shiny blue snakeskin, *no-one* should wear that coat but me ...

I never learned to say 'No' to her.

Soon we were tensed on the brink of the street. I caught our reflections in the lobby mirror. I was sombre, invisible beside my companion, the ivory oval of her face suspended over her long blue body, fabulously winged like a Morpho butterfly. Everyone turned to stare at her.

(She couldn't have done without me, though.)

GERDA

So Mum stopped answering my emails. I hated this school. I was furious. Then she sent an email that explained nothing.

> I am having to take care of Virginia Woolf. That was the person I was talking to. Am sending this email while she is resting. You can't imagine how demanding she is. I don't suppose you'll have heard of her, but if you had, you'd be impressed. She's really *very* famous. It's wonderful, but it *is* a pressure. I am her ONLY living friend. Love love love, coochy-coochy-coo, strokes and hugs from your loving mother. PS hope school is fabulous. PPS She's a genius.

I thought 'Who IS this Genius?'

Next day I googled Virginia Woolf. Fuck me, 5.9 million results.

Then I found out she was actually dead.

I really started to hate my mother.

ANGELA

Was it a kind of celebrity worship? Virginia was one of the first celebs, with her background and her beauty. Let's face it, it wasn't just raw talent. It must have helped her, knowing everybody (which certainly couldn't be said of me).

Privilege. It can make you hate them.

This isn't really what I meant to say. Because yes, she was the daughter of Leslie Stephen, the most famous Victorian man

of letters, yes, she was friends with EM Forster and Maynard Keynes and Lytton Strachey, yes, she had a small private income and looked like a clever, dreamy angel – but she wrote like an angel, as well. A pinioned angel, not the household kind.

Delicate, witty, brutal. Woolf does it all, at the speed of light. Each time I read her, I admire her more. I try to be critical. But she's just ... good.

And if she was privileged, I accept it. Because she did it for all of us. Showed she was cleverer than the men. Showed what we were capable of. I told Gerda, 'She's a genius.'

All the same – she was privileged.

GERDA

I hated the idea of Virginia Woolf. I mean, my mum was a writer herself. Why did she have to be obsessed with this Virginia? Why's *she* s'posed to be such a genius? I might be a Genius myself one day.

But mum didn't care, she just ignored my emails, or sent back three lines about her own life.

I felt so lonely in that phonebox. Geniuses need encouragement.

ANGELA

What hope is there for the rest of us, who don't have Woolf's advantages?

GERDA

Then I remembered Hans Andersen. He had to leave home when he was younger than me. His parents were actual *peasants*. I don't suppose anyone encouraged *him*.

He just ran away to Copenhagen, and became a great writer all on his own. His *Fairy Tales* is my favourite book. No wonder, I was named for one of them, Gerda, the hero of 'The

Snow Queen', who was brave and went off On Her Own around the world

So that encouraged me in my plan.

ANGELA

I had more advantages than my own mother. Which is partly why I've done better than her. Of course I've passed them on to Gerda. That child doesn't know how lucky she is.

I suppose she might actually do better than me!

I couldn't be jealous of my own daughter.

GERDA

These girls at school started calling me fat. I was going through a sturdy phase. They can all shut up, I like my food, and I know I'll be beautiful in the end. My mum and dad always told me I was, and two boys fought over me at St Mark's. But then these girls did something really bad, and I had to pull one of them's hair quite hard, and two of them fell in the swimming pool, after I gave them a tiny shove.

I may be fat, but I'm quite strong. I'd forgotten one of them couldn't swim.

So then I was in a lot of trouble. But it wasn't fair to call me a bully. I tried to tell my mum what had happened but I know from her emails she didn't take it in – 'Marvellous, Gerda, I'm glad you're having fun.'

I love my mum but she's slightly defective. Which is a word she uses for Dad. Or men in general. My mum is Sexist! Although she tells me not to be.

I am recording criticisms, in a notebook I aim to leave in my room in the holidays, so she can read it.

In fact that wouldn't work at all, because I don't think Mum's a sneak. In fact she couldn't be arsed to sneak.

Meaning, she isn't that interested.

Only because she has so much 'Pressure'. She talks a lot about 'Stress' and 'Pressure'.

Being successful is a 'Pressure'!

She should go back to being poor again.

(I take that back, she needs money for ME.)

So I will have to read my list aloud. Possibly at bed-time, when she's tired. She gives readings, so will I.

Later I'll be more famous than her. Har har har on Mum.

I do love her though. I don't mind admitting it.

I like her when she tickles me, and when I lie down and she pulls my feet, which sounds perverted, but is Normal. I liked her to do that since I was a baby, and when she hasn't got Pressure, she will.

Mummy. Mum. She's in my heart. But the words have started to feel weird and echo-ey. As if she's floated off somewhere, or both of us are floating away.

(Maybe I'll start to call her 'Mother'. That word's like an enemy.)

14

ANGELA

Zoos are always remarkably expensive. I don't want to sound mean-spirited, but it didn't seem to have occurred to Virginia that someone was having to pay for it: $40 is not nothing!

I'm not asking for much, just a 'thank you'.

VIRGINIA

The zoo crouched close to Fifth Avenue. A short walk across a burst of green. The architecture was … suburban. Some of those people were staring at me.

It was frightening to see how much things cost. I pretended not to notice her paying. I had no money, no money at all.

This expensive zoo was small and old. This couldn't be the future, surely? London Zoo was so much larger. Those iron cages looked Victorian. Again I thought 'It's just a dream.'

But the American voices were so loud and real, and the light was sharp in the woman's wrinkles. Her mouth was tight as she searched for the dollars. There were fat children eating coloured ice creams. One of them looked at me and giggled.

I liked to know what I earned, as a writer. But when we went out together, Leonard paid.

ANGELA

'Poor polar bear. So huge and yellow. It looks sort of … left behind. I can't help feeling sorry for it.'

VIRGINIA

The woman was jumping to conclusions.

'It would devour you. One swipe of its paw. *Pif, paf!* You would be gone.'

ANGELA

Thank you.

VIRGINIA

A second later, it had slipped into its pond, and an African keeper said 'Hurry downstairs,' where we found a wide window under the water, and almost before we had got used to the dark and the bright blue oblong of glass beside us, a massive turbine of white and yellow erupted against the stillness, and two pink paw-pads pressed at the window before the bear forged back up to the surface – immense power, effortless – a swirl of bright bubbles like a cape of minnows. I felt to my marrow the thrill of life. I was there, I saw it. I was alive.

And yet, that wall of glass between us. A line where two universes collide. The bear was totally indifferent to us.

Of course, I wanted to tell Leonard.

ANGELA

She was enjoying herself, I know. Her eyes brightened. She was walking fast.

We loved the underground viewing window for the penguins! I had only ever seen them above ground. Hobbity creatures with a comic waddle. Swimming, they were unbelievably swift – straight as an arrow, aerodynamic. So fast that when they shot up to the surface they took off out of the water like birds!

The first time it happened Virginia hooted, we stood there together and laughed with pleasure – a line of tiny planes

taking off, kids shooting off the end of a slide. I thought, Gerda would love the penguins. And as I thought it, my iPhone pinged.

Guilt. Of course it would be Gerda. The email was short and to the point. 'What are you DOING? I miss you, Fish Face.'

Darling Gerda. I emailed back, 'Doing my duty. Are you in a lesson?' I was going to add more, I really was, but when I looked up, Virginia was gone.

I found her outside in the late sunlight, watching a rocky island in a lake where two blond monkeys were pressed together. Delicate ears, bright pink faces. One moment wrestling, the next caressing. Maybe they were lovers, or brother and sister, or both, but they lived in a world of two.

Virginia didn't acknowledge my presence. She watched the monkeys, far away.

VIRGINIA (*still not looking at Angela*)
'I blame myself. I abandoned him. I thought he might work better without me.'

ANGELA (*too quickly, wanting to help*)
'Leonard did work. Don't torment yourself.'

One monkey leaped on the other's back, mounting it, briefly, then stroked or cuffed the underling's head. For a while they nuzzled and licked each other. All the time Virginia was watching them. Two strands of grey hair whipped across her face, blowing across her wounded mouth.

I felt protective, but her eyes flashed back at me.

VIRGINIA
'What do you mean? What do you know? Why are you calling my husband "Leonard"?'

(The woman dares to know more than me, she knows everything about my husband —

I'm a wicked woman. I left him, left him)

ANGELA
'I know — Mr Woolf — wrote many books. And — people loved him.'

VIRGINIA (*sighing*)
'So he did go on. He did his work. I wanted nothing more than that.'
 (And yet, that furious stab of hurt.)
 This stupid, unfamiliar place. The poor monkeys, on their barren island. Yet they are happy because they are two. Grooming each other, chattering, tickling, playing at tag — so once did we.
 If only you were here, my love. We could walk out and face them arm in arm. He would take my hand, if we were alone, and we would walk under the elms together. Somewhere, perhaps, we are walking still. If I had woken before he died, I know I could have found him again, just a little older, a few years sadder ...
 I will not deign to ask her about him, this yellow-haired, vulgar-looking, fat-breasted woman with her harlot's painted lips and eyes. How did I get trapped with her? She has nothing to do with me!
 Where are my friends, who understand? Who would have helped him after I ...
 But they are gone, if he is gone.
 And oh, Vanessa. Lytton. Vita. Even poor old Ethel, and Clive. Dear familiar names and faces. Must I be thrown among common strangers?

Another, separate, point of pain. For oh my Angelica – beloved niece, fairy child with a mouth like your mother's – it is not bearable if *you* are dead.

When I left her she wasn't even a woman. Pixerina, with her fairy kisses. Angelica. Are you gone, my dear? Just for a moment she's here beside me, sunlight on her cap of pale hair, blue eyes wide and far away, she could never sit still, she's tugging my hand.

Child, did it go well for you?

The pain again: that her life should end. That girl in white, dancing in the garden. Running to me in my chair for a hug. Her arms round my neck like a wreath of pale flowers. We threw sugar lumps down for the big-rumped horses from my balcony in Gordon Square ...

No, every fibre of my soul refuses.

'Why did I come back? Couldn't they leave me be? I want ... I want ... I want to go home – '

ANGELA

'Let's just see the sea lions. Then, I promise, I'll get you home.'

I only meant 'to our hotel'. But as I said it I remembered my promise, my foolish promise in the Berg Collection. The thing I had whispered under my breath, and the next moment, she was there. 'Virginia, I'll take you home ...'

Was that the hook that had hauled her up? Had I just wanted to feast on her?

'Please come, honestly, you'll like the seals.'

She didn't say 'Yes', but her shoulders sagged and the wild look vanished from her eyes. She walked beside me to the sea lions' island, a barren rock in the middle of water. Close up it was entirely artificial, a man-made hill of fake golden-brown sandstone, built with a spiral track to the top.

Did they keep two different species of sea lion together?

We saw one massive yellow–gold gleaming creature, a bit like a legless elephant. It sat on the shore, unable to move. Then there were two slick dark ones – no three slick dark ones – streaking like submarines through the water, slim and playful, black princes of speed. The light dripped off them as they climbed from the water, muscular flippers scything the sand.

We watched, Virginia and I, as the sun began to leave the hill. We watched the seals climb after it. Soon the black princes had outpaced the band of shadow that seeped up to eat the sunlight, lolloping up like three black rubber brackets, squeezing, unsqueezing, unstoppable. Now they were performing yoga twists to a clapping human audience, necks swinging round like oiled silk, heads pointing back to the dark behind them. I was excited. I joined in the clapping! Then I looked at Virginia, my own neck turning a little stiffly – I'd been neglecting my personal training – and saw her face was strained and grey. I stretched my hand out without thinking, I'm almost sure I didn't actually touch her –

VIRGINIA
'Get away from me! You've – kidnapped me.'

ANGELA
American heads stopped watching the seals and turned to stare. She had really shouted. Some of the faces looked accusing. Instantly I too got angry. 'It's not my fault. You just – *appeared*. You just *showed up* in the Berg Collection. It's actually a restricted library. You didn't even have a ticket.'

Absurd of me, of course, to reproach her for intruding in a library that's mostly famous for having her books. Hers and Nabokov's.

'Sorry,' I said. 'I didn't mean ...'

Then something quite surprising happened, as if she realised

I was all she had.

'I too am sorry. I should not have shouted.'

There was a pause. We both breathed deeply. The sea lion acrobats were still performing, tireless, youthful, competitive.

VIRGINIA

'The library – yes, I remember that. But there's something before. Long years of – something. Everything's dark. I can't focus.

'And suddenly, you're always here. I do not mean to be ungrateful. But I never knew you, did I, before?'

ANGELA

Now Virginia's voice was low, and her lips (so beautiful, that sculpted curve, and she, unlike me, was not wearing lipstick) were almost back to their normal colour. The look she turned on me was beseeching. Yet she was saying she didn't trust me.

'I'm just a reader. I was in the library. Your manuscripts are there, for people to study. I was reading you, or trying to – ' (when I said I was reading her, Virginia looked up) – 'that library doesn't make it easy. I wanted to read you so very badly – '

VIRGINIA

'People still read me? You still read me?'

ANGELA

'And then you just materialised. And the librarians threw you out.'

It sounded brutal. She looked offended. I changed the subject, hastily. Perhaps it was time to talk about me. An enormous man in an anorak had planted himself in front of me, blocking my view with his wide grey back, his fat pink

neck, carroty curls.

'I'm not just a reader, in fact. I'm a writer.'

Was Virginia listening?

The man walked backwards to take a photo, planting his elbow in my stomach. 'Excuse me, ma'am.' His face was unlined, genial.

VIRGINIA

'People still read me in the twenty-first century?'

ANGELA

'I was just saying, I write too. Of course, you won't have heard of me …

'Never mind. I read you, yes. You ought to know that everyone reads you.'

VIRGINIA (*not listening, turning away*)

'My last book was a failure, a disaster.' Leonard denied it but I saw it in his eyes. I knew that my worst fears were true –

ANGELA

'*Between the Acts*. Of course I've read it. Generally considered a masterpiece.'

And her eyes brightened. Such beautiful eyes. The afternoon sun intensified the colour: grey and green, green and gold –

VIRGINIA

'*Between the Acts*? A masterpiece? How strange. So – it *was* published.'

(I loved that book when it was just an essence, a wisp of pale silk, frost on the downs, their long spines reddened by the sunset. A pageant … something as light as its name, Poyntz Hall. I wanted to stipple it like Seurat, make it short & musical,

& the world could be distilled in the gaps, aerations between the bright points of the brush-strokes.

But then it grew long & dragged at my heart & I knew the execution couldn't match the first image. And then the clawing fear began. And darkness ate in around the edges. Then they started to lie to me, telling me it was good enough to publish — I knew it wasn't. And so did Leonard. Although he denied it, his face declared it

the strain puckering his dear deep lines

How often I gave poor Leonard worry.

— Is it possible that we were all wrong?

'Did you say they are calling it a masterpiece?'

ANGELA
'Some people say it's your best book. I think it brings all your themes together. '

For the first time, then, she looked at me. It was a long, assessing stare.

She looked at me. I looked at her. I dared to meet those startling eyes, their shocking hunger, their intelligence. Around us other beings surged. Families wailing like cats mating: hordes of busy animals. But we were human. We saw each other.

With one accord, we looked away.

I fixed my gaze on the narrowing band of sunlight on the sea lions' island. While we were distracted, everything had changed. Unnoticed, the great pale sea lion elder had heaved its vast yellow bulk up the mountain, pushed past the black balletic young and surged on rolls of fat and muscle up to

sunbathe on the very summit. Old, solid, surprisingly strong. Late sunlight gilded her.

VIRGINIA
'Of course I don't care at all about the critics.'

ANGELA
'Of course.'

VIRGINIA
'I never gave a fig for their opinions.'

ANGELA
'No.'

VIRGINIA
'What kind of thing exactly do they say?'

ANGELA
I tried to give her what she wanted. 'That you were trying to link art to the people – ' But a little devil made me go on. 'Whereas Bloomsbury became a byword for, you know, snobbery. Art for art's sake, and all that stuff.'

VIRGINIA
'Snobbery? Bloomsbury? We are socialists! Leonard is always out canvassing!'

ANGELA
'Sorry, sorry. Yes, I know. Your husband was remarkable.'
 I watched that past tense give her pause. Her long arms wrapped around her body, her head went down, then up again, her eyes burned, she was formidable.

VIRGINIA

'Did you hear me? *We were socialists.* Anti-imperialists through and through!'

ANGELA

I wouldn't let her hector me.

'Perhaps that message didn't reach your public.'

VIRGINIA

'The public can be ridiculous ...' (*Brightening*) 'But I have a public? – Still? – Now?'

ANGELA

'You do.'

There was a pause. Something shifted between us. For another brief moment, we looked at each other. Sunlight, or hope, gave her skin a faint flush. Yes, she was very beautiful. (But Edward called me beautiful, too. I was still young, and she was old.)

Her brows lifted. A secret smile.

VIRGINIA

And in that moment, life poured through me. My new 'now'. My American now! The particular. That apricot sunlight. It was just on the point of leaving the island, intensifying as it yielded to night. The vault of the sky was indigo violet, making love with the apricot. The animals straining up into it.

And I am here. Life has come back.

Indigo, violet, the pigeons circling, each vane of their wing-tips sharp on the glow.

The electric shock of life thrilled me, shivering in an instant across the tiny stalks of hair on my skin, the back of my neck, my hidden places. I was alive. And I had a public.

ANGELA

A low whoosh, then another, and another. And finally something like a *thwack-whoomp*. All four sea lions were back in the water.

VIRGINIA

'Let's go back out on the streets and walk. You say we're in America?'

ANGELA

'New York. But it will soon be dark.'

VIRGINIA

'Of all places. I never went there! Never went to America. I never cared to, I loved Europe ...'

I did want to go. I was afraid. Part of me wanted to stay in my room, never going out, writing, writing. Another part longed to see the world. I loved our car. I was safe inside. Leonard, me, and Mitz Marmoset, and Europe floating past outside the window ...

We knew Europe, all our friends went, but America seemed a world away. I imagined the cars in endless ribbons, dozens abreast, streaming into the future, indifferent to me, a vast indifference ... Terrifying. I would not exist.

In this American *now*, was I a different person? The night was coming, but I wasn't afraid.

On the other hand, I had no luggage. What did they wear, these new ... New Yorkers?

'I have no clothes. Just these old rags. More to the point, I

have no money – '

ANGELA
'Nothing at all in your pockets?' (I had seen it, clearly, a bulge in her pockets.) 'Alas, I'm not exactly rich.'

VIRGINIA
' – and nowhere to live. Where will I live?'
After all, one had to live somewhere.
Just for a moment, I felt simple pleasure. Somewhere to live. A new place. The fun I had had at Monk's House. Finding the perfect bentwood chair, glimpsed through the window of an antique shop. Yes, I would have to find somewhere to live!
But is anyone allowed those pleasures twice? Would they suffer me to … begin again? Whichever hell-hounds had let me go.
Maybe I was just released for the day.

ANGELA
'As I said, I'm not rich. Not *rich* rich. But maybe I can tide you over.'
Virginia was staring at the gravel. We followed the thinning crowd through the gate. The sun had slipped behind the towers that ringed the park like gate keepers. Would it be fun to walk through the park?
Very soon we were just two shadows, silent companions in a world of shades. Every now and then she stepped off the path to touch a plane tree. Her fingertips lingered, digging her nails into the bark. Once, I noticed she wasn't there and saw her clutching the ordinary black railings, clinging on as if she'd never let go. She came back making small contented noises, tilted forward, smiling and nodding. But not at me. She was on her own.

I thought, if only the others knew – the tired humans walking home, the writers, students, advertising people, eyes on the path, shoulders hunched – that this tall shadow is Virginia Woolf. And she's with me! I breathed in deep.

We were only five minutes from the gate when she suddenly said 'I'm tired.' She stopped. A light through leaves made her face cavernous. She was surely paler than before. She tried to say some more, but couldn't. I found a seat. It felt cold to the hand, the wooden slats uncomfortable. She sank down with a muffled groan.

'Virginia, are you all right?'

But she didn't answer. She gathered herself, as if she was bringing herself back from the darkness, pulling her shoulders back like a soldier. With the faintest sigh, she was on her feet. And in a second, she'd set off again.

'Virginia, you're going the wrong way.'

Back on Fifth Avenue, the headlights had come on and the shop windows glowed like stained glass. Every so often she stopped and gazed. Those features, indescribably familiar, suddenly grown intimate. In lit close-up, astonished, pleased. How could it be – it *couldn't* be – that face shone out from my own blue coat, those white hands gestured from its wide blue sleeves? Above my collar, the mauve veins of her temples. I thought my eyes would eat her up.

(They hypnotise us, those images. Woolf, Auden, Nabokov. Monumental, moonlit, deaf. Now she had come to live amongst us.)

VIRGINIA

'So much electricity.' We had paused in a wash of lemon light from a window where giant pastel easter eggs circled the air. 'It's dazzling. My eyes are tired. This city must be very expensive ...'

ANGELA

After all, she did write *A Room of One's Own*. She knew you couldn't live without money.

VIRGINIA

'Every so often, I'm tired to death. '

ANGELA

'Virginia, we're nearly home.'

ANGELA

Back in the room, I ordered tea; luke-warm water and teabags arrived. The lack of competence invigorated her.

VIRGINIA

'Tea was always appalling abroad. France, Germany. So nothing's changed.'

ANGELA

I felt defensive about my century.

'Actually, this isn't typical. It's just a rather poor hotel.'

VIRGINIA

'Is it poor? *Really?* Then why did you choose it?'

ANGELA

Virginia was sitting on the bed. Her long elegant frame made it look short and narrow.

I contemplated the difficulties of explaining the perils of internet deals. First I must explain the internet. No, put it off until tomorrow. 'Because it's cheap,' I said

She had draped my coat over the single armchair. I sank down beside her on the same twin bed, leaving a respectful gap between us.

VIRGINIA

'Oh. Are you poor?'

ANGELA

I was furious! 'Certainly not.'

Her interest was anthropological: I was just a human from another era. No, I wasn't real for her.

But I *was* real. Money is a touchy subject. If she was going for frankness, so would I. 'You ought to be massively rich by now. Royalties, and rights, and so forth.'

VIRGINIA

'If so, they certainly haven't told me. Possibly I was hard to contact.'

ANGELA

I tried not to think she was mocking me. Something to do with the class difference maybe. The elongated vowels of her 'really'. The accent of someone who had never had to work.

All very well for her to time-travel and end up here with no means of support.

VIRGINIA

I was chortling with pleasure at the nerve of this woman. I loved the fact that she could talk about money. So many women are incapable of doing so. Brazen, yes, but invigorating. All the same – did she think they'd been sending me cheques?

ANGELA

I blushed with shame. She was definitely laughing. I wanted her to think me intelligent. For one second I almost felt – hatred.

'So you don't have any money at all, Virginia?' (Why should I pussyfoot around with the 'Mrs'?) 'That's rather – inconvenient.' I snickered, mirthlessly. Two could play at that game.

I poured myself another cup of tea, without looking to see if she needed a refill.

VIRGINIA

She had gone too far. She was a vulgar woman. But I could wipe the smile off her face. 'I didn't take any money with me – on my last day.'

ANGELA

I did feel bad.
 'Sorry, Virginia.'

VIRGINIA (*severely*)
'Mrs Woolf!'

ANGELA (*taken by surprise*)
'Sorry.'
 No, it was absurd, I would not – kow-tow. 'But you know, we are in the twenty-first century.'

VIRGINIA (*not understanding*)
'Surely good manners are still important.'

ANGELA
'Yes. My name is Angela. Just in case you want to use it.'

(*Pause.*)

'Wait a minute … what's that in your pocket?' (*Disappointed*)
'Oh I suppose it's just a *stone*.'

VIRGINIA
'There is nothing of interest to you in my pockets.'

ANGELA
I saw from her face she was *lying* to me!
 Hauteur punctured by childish guilt, a smidgin of fear mixed

with laughter – she looked like Gerda aged one and a half, hiding her banana under the sofa. Which must explain what happened next. Looking back on it I can hardly believe it, but this is what happened. We had a fight!

'There *is*.' I reached for the bulges in her jacket, she tried to turn her back on me – we had a brief tussle. *I was tussling with Woolf.* I was stronger, of course – she had been dead for a while! – yet something had changed since she first arrived, when I had touched her hand and there was nothing there. Her body no longer felt liquid, boneless. She was panting a little. No, she was laughing.

There was a hard object in each pocket, straining the frayed tweed of her suit.

VIRGINIA

'They're books, that's all. I like to keep them with me.'

(Oddly, the struggle made me giggle. I had not been touched for such a long time. I played with my brothers, long long ago. When I was a child, and things were easy, before Mother died and the house went dark.)

'I mean, they are mine. I did write them. I even published them. I have a right.'

(Why was I justifying myself to *her*? She was becoming a parent figure. Poor Dr Freud would have something to say, in his flickering, subtle, shrunken way –

– How very late I came to love him. Like fathers, only after they die … I loved my father, but the noise, the groaning, the hurricane that shook the doors. Then, when he'd gone, I could think, in the silence, I could feel for him, I could dare to love him. After Freud died, I began to read him.)

ANGELA

'My God. *To the Lighthouse.* What a glorious copy.'

I could hardly believe what I saw on the bed. As she pulled it out it had fallen open. I gazed at the print, the Hogarth typeface, the fresh, dense cream of the pages. And then I closed it, and it really sank in.

'Virginia! It's a first edition.'

There it was, Vanessa's lovely design, the grey swirls of the waves below, the few plain strokes to denote the lighthouse, the black dots swarming in different densities to show the light blazing up in a fan. All around it, the lighthouse wall. 'It's worth a fortune. What's the other one?'

VIRGINIA (*stays silent, lost in thought*)

ANGELA
'Virginia! Show me the other one! I am excited! It's incredible!'

VIRGINIA (*starting, and staring hard at the book before handing it over*)
'Somehow my books came to find me.'

(*Angela opens some pages, amazed.*)

VIRGINIA (*dreamily*)
'They were waiting for me in this strange world, new as the day when they came from the printers. We have other lives, I think, I hope …

'*Orlando* was a joy to write, like a wild gallop across strange country … such a happy autumn till my pen rebelled. But somehow, yes, one finished things …'

ANGELA
'*Orlando!* Sorry, this is overwhelming.

Could I take a photograph? Just this once? For the books, not you?'

I was a tourist! I did, right there, with her perched on the bed, *Orlando* on her lap, *To the Lighthouse* beside her. Virginia Woolf, with two first editions!

The balance of power had shifted between us, with the fight – the fight! – and now the photograph. But one long white hand went over her face. And I saw her gather herself. Her force.

(I must have somehow pressed the wrong button, because when I looked later, there was nothing there.)

VIRGINIA
'Kindly never do that again. I cannot, will not, be photographed.'

ANGELA
She was furious. She stood up tall. She blocked the light. She detested me.

'Sorry,' I said. 'I knew that, actually. It's in the – '

I stopped. It was in the biographies. She didn't know the biographies. So thick, so intimate, so many.

'Sorry,' I said, again. I stretched out my hand, palm up, placating.

VIRGINIA
'Let's talk about more interesting things. Did you say – these – were valuable?'

ANGELA
'Immensely. Of course, you might not want to sell them.'

We looked at each other, and it was decided.

VIRGINIA (*hand half-extending*)
'You said your name was … Angela?
 – You want me to call you Angela?'

ANGELA (*still slightly wary*)
'As I was trying to explain to you, no-one says "Mrs" in the twenty-first century.'

VIRGINIA
'I see. Then you may call me Virginia. I had a niece called Angelica.'

ANGELA
'My full name is Angela Lamb. That's the name on my book jackets.'

(I say this automatically now, having noticed that often, when I meet a stranger – an *un-literary* stranger, that is to say – they ask 'Do you write under your own name?'

Virginia was hardly un-literary.)

VIRGINIA
'I think I shall call you "Mrs Lamb".' (*Slight smile.*)

ANGELA
'Please don't!'

(*They turn slightly towards one another.*)

VIRGINIA
'Angela.'

ANGELA
'Virginia.'

VIRGINIA (*with gaiety*)
'Let us go out and make some money!'

(*After a second, they shake hands.*)

GERDA (*reading in a loud voice in front of the mirror in her room at school*)

'Crimes By Mum
1) Sending me away to school
(Though I admit I was bored at home. But only because she goes out so much.)
2) Bad cooking. One day I'll be a BRILLIANT cook
3) Forgetting to buy chocolate logs
4) Going on about cleaning your teeth
5) Going on about Dad, even if it's his fault. Breaking up with Dad, who is my dad after all, and it would be convenient to have two parents. In the same house. Or at least talking to each other.

Why didn't they think about that? And me?

6) Not realising I am a Genius
7) Obeying the rule about phones. Amina Sharif's mother didn't. Of course she is a Princess.
8) Not getting me a better phone
9) Having boyfriends – YUCK – and disgusting ones
10) I'm sure she does. Yuck Yuck Yuck
11) Going on about HER in general
12) Talking though I told her not to
13) Taking back the one jacket of hers I would EVER borrow, and refusing to lend it again just because it had a teeny bit of sick on the pocket – doesn't she want me to look nice?

14) NOT READING MY EMAILS PROPERLY'

I think when I read this to her at home, I shall deliver Point 14 in a deafening shout, because she will have stopped listening by then.

 – When is my mother coming home again?

ANGELA

Our brief *rapprochement* could not carry us through. I ordered sandwiches from room service, she did not like them and asked for more. I confess I grew irritable – 'You did choose BLT, Virginia, I warned you it would be disgusting.'

I was exhausted, and doing my best, and her BLT cost $20, and she ate the fries, so we couldn't send it back. I needed her to sleep so I could catch up with email.

I tentatively offered to lend her some pyjamas but she just shuddered and shook her head. So I went to the bar for half an hour, telling her she might like to take a bath, and came back to find her standing at the dressing table, jacketless, shoeless, quivering with energy, her hair a thin mermaid screed across her shoulders. She was trying to open my computer! Instinctively I moved to stop her.

'No, Virginia, it's a machine. It's complicated. I'll show you tomorrow.'

She definitely had *not* taken a bath.

She told me 'she wanted to see how it worked', but why was she prising it open with a fruit knife?

Then I retreated into the bathroom, and when I came out she was dead asleep – asleep not dead, I checked from her breathing – stretched out stiff as a religious relic on the twin bed I'd slept in the night before, her handsome head smack in the middle of the pillow under which my sleep socks and radio were hidden. The night was chilly, but I tried not to blame her. It was a relief to put the light out. I thought, 'In the morning,

she'll be gone.' I had started to hope it was a dream.

Alas, I woke almost hourly to hear her snoring, and she was up before I opened my eyes in the morning, standing four-square staring out of the window. She had put her jacket and shoes back on. I thought, I am going to have to crack the washing problem, and swung my legs straight out of bed.

'Morning, Virginia,' I croaked. 'Would you like me to run a bath for you? A nice hot bath, you know, before breakfast?'

VIRGINIA

She talked to me as if I were a child. Quite soon I found she was obsessed with bathing. She seemed to do it nearly every day! Perhaps she perspired more than normal.

Ignoring her was the best policy.

ANGELA

She turned, briefly, from her brown study. 'The towers,' she said. 'So beautiful.'

She breakfasted quite docilely on toast, staring round the room at the other guests and for the most part ignoring me, but once she had finished, she became impatient. We got back to the room and she went to the cupboard and without a by-your-leave, started to put on my blue coat. My blue coat. The coat I loved.

'Virginia, I'm not ready yet. Also, you won't need the coat today. It's not that cold. I will put it back for you.'

I needed to do a little research before we set out to make ourselves rich. I switched on my laptop. The room was so small I had been forced to put it on the dressing table. Writing is the space where we try to escape our real-life names, our familiar faces – but here I was forced to stare in the mirror.

That day, however, it was an advantage. I used the mirror to keep an eye on Virginia.

(What if she suddenly tried to climb out of the window? I had only just got her, I mustn't lose her – though part of me already longed to be free. The physical presence of the twentieth-century's greatest female literary icon, with her faint sour smell of earth and pondweed, wasn't so easy to get used to.)

I could see her sifting through my things, lifting and fingering my possessions. Death seemed to have removed her inhibitions. I understood, but it made me feel anxious. Would she judge me by my reading matter? *Eminent Victorians* would make the grade, but what would she think of my bedtime reading, snatched up at the airport to help me sleep? The *OK!* Special on Jordan's surgery, 'Step-by-step: How Jordan Remade her Body?' I supposed she would scarcely understand it. But no, she was leafing through it fascinated, chuckling from time to time. 'Do you like pornography?' she asked. 'In my day, one would have hidden it.'

'It's not pornography, Virginia.'

She waved a photo at me triumphantly: Jordan's gigantic, conical breasts.

'No, Virginia, it's normal. Women just make their breasts bigger.'

'Women make their breasts bigger? What do you mean? Have you made *your* breasts bigger?' She came round to stare at my chest, avid.

'*No*, Virginia, certainly not, I really can't explain this now.'

My life had become her research project, a kind of reverse archaeological dig. I tried to ignore her and get on with my mission.

Now she had dropped *OK!* on the floor and was stood transfixed by the window again, staring out at the bright buildings, their white cliffs pitted with thousands of windows. Her wattled neck smoothed out like a heron's as she peered over at the street below. Then she hunched her chin upon

her chest and squeezed her forehead against the glass. Urgent, anxious, inquisitive; a monkey, now, pressed against the bars. She was full of new, restless life, making sounds, low hungry murmurs.

I googled 'rare books Manhattan'.

But there she was, peering over my shoulder, her shadow darkening the screen. 'What kind of typewriter is *that*?' she asked. 'May I?'

Before I could stop her she was pressing the keys, her heavy arms displacing mine, that cloying odour of weeds again, pale lizard fingers slow and clumsy – I tried to remember, had she always written longhand? Yes, but she had typeset for the Hogarth Press. She was supposed to be good at that. The comfort of metal letters in rows.

The text in Google was gibberish. Maybe Leonard corrected everything. She threw her arms up in frustration, long heavy wings of an albatross.

'These keys don't work. Where is the paper?'

'There is no paper, Virginia.'

'How can it work without paper?'

She looked at me, stubbornly uncomprehending, then pounced on the tiny hotel pad which lay by the TV remote control. 'This is the paper. But where does it go?'

'It doesn't. Writers don't write on paper.'

'There cannot be a world without paper.'

'Well there is still paper, but' – I tapped the machine – 'not here.'

We stared at each other across chasms of time. 'I promise I will explain later.'

But she sat there on the bed, directly behind me, watching every move with distrustful eyes, as I clicked on the website of Goldstein & Sons. Rare books, Madison Avenue. Pictures of a book-filled gallery came up.

'So the film you are watching is connected to the keyboard?'

'It isn't a film, Virginia.'

'We had cinema, you know, in our day. Leonard and I were fond of films. I am perfectly acquainted with cinema.'

'Virginia, it isn't cinema.'

'It's this stick that makes those pictures, is it not?' And before I could stop her she had snatched the TV remote control that lay by the pad and was pressing buttons at random.

And then the yellow room became bedlam, for the TV suddenly blasted out full volume, and it was the news from Afghanistan, a deafening stutter of machine-gun bullets, the dead booms of bombs exploding, buildings black against crackling orange, and she made a choking, inchoate noise and in her panic must have pressed again, for now we were watching a black-and-white Second World War film, and planes were whining down overhead, a swarm of planes with Nazi markings, and I heard a howl, she was actually howling. I wrestled the controller away from her, and the room was quiet as death again, except for the traffic and her breath, tearing.

'Virginia? Are you all right?'

She crouched in a corner by the door, a tangled, darkened, thing from the river, her elbows raised to protect her head. It took twenty minutes to comfort her.

I had to explain it, bit by bit. I showed her the TV, I showed her the remote, but I saw she couldn't take it in. I went to the bathroom, leaving her alone, and came back to find her peering round the back of the laptop, her hand exploring the reverse of the screen.

'Virginia, what are you looking for?'

'The opening for paper to come through.'

'I said, no paper.' I had to distract her. 'But look, we'll do an internet search on you.'

I typed 'Virginia Woolf', and then showed her the figures – 5,900,000 hits.

'That means nearly 6 million references to you. And look, those are just some of the pictures.' I showed her a jewel-like line of images.

She stared away into the middle distance, her eyes sharp and then unfocused. 'So really, this is a kind of book? And this keyboard is to search the index?'

'In a way,' I said. 'Look, it shuts like a book.' And I made to close the lid, but her hand stopped me.

'Leonard,' she said. 'Is he in your book? Will you type "Leonard Woolf" into the index?'

I did. 'One million three hundred and eighty thousand hits', I said. 'That means, nearly one and a half million references. And look, there are the pictures again.' A line of bright thumbnails like the ones of her.

'Why are they so small?' she said. 'I must see him!'

Three of the six thumbnails showed them together. The first one I clicked on was a wedding photograph, sepia. She was so different! A full-bodied woman with a fresh, round face, looking slightly too hot, febrile, female, in an elaborate, patterned, ankle-length dress. A deep soft flounce over the bosom, and a wide-brimmed hat laden with flowers. But under the half-veil across the forehead, two large, naked, pale-lashed eyes gazed off to the side away from Leonard, a narrow youth with thin sloping shoulders and a full, melancholy mouth like hers. He did not look like a jubilant bridegroom. I call him a youth, but he did not look young. I had never realised he had jet-black hair – in the photos I knew, he looked grey and dusty. Virginia was larger and heavier than him! Such a weight of worry he was taking on ... yet everyone said he was deeply in love. And there was her mouth – that sensual mouth, hard to attach to someone virginal.

And because I had read the biographies, which told us more than anyone should know about another human being unless they are their parent, sibling, child, I knew what years were to follow the wedding – descents into madness, violence, depression. Her new husband struggling to cope.

(She was also saner than anyone. The cool intelligence of most of the *Diaries*. Pages bubbling with happiness.)

Virginia gave a small 'Oh' of longing. Old, she reached out, and touched the screen, the space where they were alive and young, illuminated in my machine, the time capsule I took for granted.

They looked so alive, but they were unresponsive, the sepia couple who long ago were totally taken up by their moment.

She pressed the screen and I pulled her back.

'Will it move?' she said. 'Can you make us move?'

'Sorry,' I said. 'It's not like that. It's what it is. It can't be changed.'

'I wondered … if it could be changed.'

She wasn't just talking about the image. She knew too well what lay in their future.

I said, as gently as I could, 'Would you like to look at the other photos?'

Leonard alone. He was forty years older. His long thin face engraved with lines. Those eyes, intelligent, used to sorrow, deep-set under strong grey eyebrows. And the mouth still full, a young man's mouth – a foreign face, not an English face, that was my instinctive judgement. But that was how Bloomsbury thought of him: 'Virginia's marrying the Jew.' Both a joke and not a joke.

'Mongoose,' she said, almost inaudible.

This time I refrained from showing knowledge. What would she have thought if I answered 'Mandril'? His name for her.

His beloved baboon.

I knew too much, we knew too much. Their secret bestiary of names.

'It's enough,' she said, and turned away. 'Perhaps you would save that page number?' Her back was rigid, her voice formal.

'Mrs Woolf, it would be an honour.' I didn't correct her idea of the computer. 'I can find it for you whenever you want.'

'Please,' she assented, still turned away.

I went back to my search for a few moments, checking that Goldstein was what we wanted. 'Goldstein & Sons, Rare Book Dealers. Madison Avenue. Shall we walk?'

And so we did, an incongruous couple flashing past the Easter windows; Virginia, though stooped, inches taller than me. To my surprise, after a shaky start, she began to lope two paces ahead, a steady, strong, athletic walker despite her grey hair and unnerving pallor.

I had to half-run to keep up with her, though every so often she would stop dead and stare at something I would never have noticed – I no longer saw the advertisements like acid flowers bursting from the pavements, I didn't notice the fetish shoes, six inches high with inch-thick platforms; I took the display of wealth for granted. I actually had to pull her away when she shrieked with laughter at two women, obviously well-to-do, walking arm-in-arm against the sunlight, perfectly outlined from loin to ankle, the shapes of their hips, their crotches, their thighs, in skin-tight black leggings and ankle-boots, and above the waist, boxy expensive jackets, ropes of pearls, vast sunglasses and artfully streaked hair falling below their shoulders.

'They go out without skirts,' she hooted, happily. 'What fun to see New York prostitutes! Leonard would laugh.'

'Virginia, they're not prostitutes. It's just the fashion of the day. I agree it's strange, but they don't feel naked. Everyone pretends not to notice.'

'But I could see *everything*,' she insisted. 'Of course they can only be prostitutes.'

'You're going to see lots of women like that.'

'And no-one laughs? No-one says anything?'

'Not in New York, Virginia.'

She was pounding along like a racehorse once more, but I saw from her furrowed brows that she was thinking. And then she stopped and smiled at me, her head tipped bird-like to one side. 'It's Hans Andersen's story, the one I love.'

And I said, as we started to walk again, past a mirrored building that showed us, large, shivered into two rivers of fragments, as a bird flicked over our reflected heads and blinding sunlight made us blink at each other and think for a second we could be friends: 'Yes, it's "The Emperor's New Clothes".'

GERDA

I do have a lot to tell my mother. Failing that I shall write it down.

𝕸𝖞 𝕭𝖆𝖙𝖙𝖑𝖊 𝖜𝖎𝖙𝖍 𝖙𝖍𝖊 𝕱𝖚𝖗𝖎𝖊𝖘, Part the First

(I have decided to write it like an epic. I have chosen an epic typeface. Just seeing those letters cheers me up. I do need cheering. I am *On My Own*.)

I know it isn't good to get into fights. But I also know that you have to be brave. It's like in that enormous great book, *Cat's Eye*, which I liked a lot until it got too long, where the girls start doing mind games on each other.

No-one was ever going to bully ME. My mum taught me that, which I'm grateful for, because my mum was bullied at school.

So I knew I had to stand up for myself. Anyway, why should they call me fat? Ayesha was ugly, but I didn't complain, and Linda had big pink ears like a monkey, but I had never mentioned it, and Cindy had skinny legs like sticks and I'd seen her breakfast: like, ONE cornflake.

I mentioned it *all* after they started on ME. But then they got madder, and things got worse.

Cindy, the skinny one I called Anna, which I also told everyone was short for Anna Rexia – (I know that sounds bad, but I never did it till after her friends started calling me 'Greedier', which was her 'witty' pun on 'Gerda') – was not as stupid as the others. I admit she was good at English. In fact she was second best to me, which is one of the reasons why she hated me, and besides, she was jealous because I could eat food, lovely chips and jelly that she just glowered at.

In any case, Cindy is a feeble name. It's a Princess name, and she'd like to be a Princess, whereas I am trying to be a Hero.

Probably to date I have fallen short.

So this Cindy – 'Miss Anna Rexia' – thought she would play a good joke on me. All of a sudden she started being friendly. She came and talked to me in the library (we were the only two who read books in the library, which everyone else probably thought was sad.)

And I was dim, and thought she meant it. And I was too soft, and was nice back, because really, I wanted to be friends with them. In fact, I don't like quarrelling.

So for a bit, I went around with them, but only because I didn't have many friends, so I missed my old school, and missed London, and if you want to know, I missed my mother, though I knew why she had to send me away, I understand she has to do her work –

I'm crying now, which is pathetic. I won't let ANYONE make me cry.

It's just that sometimes I miss my own bedroom. My own things. And my friends from home.

But I'll be OK, because I'm Gerda.

And I want my mum to be able to work – she has a right to, and she's a writer, and I do love her, and I don't want to stop her, like my dad did, she says, because he was a Bastard, though he definitely cooked, when he was at home, and shopped and

brought her cups of tea. In any case I wish Mum wouldn't call him a Bastard. If I stop her writing, perhaps she won't love me, though she claims to love me most in the world.

And like I said, she needs money for me, or I will never get my new iPad, or my new bike, and my phone is CRAP – she promised me a new one, but then she forgot and went away.

One day I'll be a writer too, and I won't want anybody to stop ME. So fair enough, I had to go to boarding school, but why did it have to be this horrible hell-hole, Bendham Abbey, which is s'posed to be the best, but is full of bitches?

I meant to say 'Wankers'. 'Bitches' is sexist. I'm against sexism, like Mum.

I'm tired now so I'm going to eat Jelly Beans. I saved my favourites, which are Pomegranate.

To be continued in

My Battle with the Furies,
Part the Second

ANGELA

Goldstein & Sons, rare book-dealers. We hurried towards it through a shoal of banks, huge blank corporations, auction-houses. Along the cold black gullies, past cliffs of black glass, the cars came streaming and honking past us. Fast, deadly, not seeing us.

The towers there always strike me as satanic. Darker, more hulking than over on the West Side, and the shadows they cast are cold and solid, as if spring could never creep in here. She was shivering, drawing her shabby tweed jacket closer. I thought, we'll have to buy her more clothes, and I will take that smelly suit to the cleaners – 'Do the best you can, someone drowned in it!' – (Yes, Virginia's presence was wearing, and yes, sometimes I fell back on cheap jokes.)

I remembered from the *Diaries* her unease at buying clothes.

VIRGINIA

I wanted to go straight into the shop with her, but she insisted on leaving me round the corner in a cafeteria. As if she didn't trust me. (Anyone would think they were *her* books we were selling.) As soon as I got there, I was ravenous. I had only eaten two slices of toast, after not eating for many decades! There was a delicious smell of fried potatoes. She found me a table by the window and made me promise not to wander off. Of course, that was ridiculous. She sometimes reminded me of Leonard – he, too, often sounded like a gaoler.

I admit the last day I went out on my own I did not prove I could be trusted.

ANGELA

'Virginia, what would you like to eat?'

VIRGINIA

She was earnest and sensible: not playful. Something to do
with not having servants – the business of life, the workaday
duties, had ground her down.

I tried for lightness, (*Laughing*) 'Oh, soup and salmon and
ducklings …'

ANGELA

'You won't find that on the menu.'

VIRGINIA

I wanted to know if she had really read me.

'Partridges?'

ANGELA

She could be a show-off. 'Virginia, you've got to order,' I said.

VIRGINIA

'Sprouts foliated like rosebuds?'

ANGELA (*still not impressed*)

'I see, it's the food from *A Room of One's Own*. You're quoting
yourself. Or testing me? I promise I've read it half a dozen
times. It's a great text. But leave that aside.

'Here you'll get sandwiches or salad or a burger. Fried beef
in a bun. With chips.'

VIRGINIA (*enthusiastically*)

'That sounds delicious. Beef and potatoes. Nothing beats a
good *boeuf en daube* … Yes, I'll have that. Go and sell the books.'

ANGELA

She was definitely used to having servants!

'Will you be all right, Virginia?'

(I thought, 'How will she manage? She won't understand a word people say!')

WAITER

'Burger and fries, Ma'am?'

VIRGINIA

'Well, that's – just the ticket.'

ANGELA

So that was that. I parked her there. I didn't know much about rare books, so I expected a learning curve, and I didn't want her there mucking things up.

(*Quietly*) 'Virginia, *please* remember not to leave. Because you haven't got money to pay with. So you will be pursued and arrested. I won't be long.'

But she was lost in thought, staring happily out at people on the pavement. One hand waved vaguely as I walked away.

ANGELA

Goldstein's was staffed with polite, good-looking young men who hovered purposefully in pale suits, gracing the customers with discreet smiles that hinted at shared passions. The shop was so beautiful I felt rather shy. It wasn't like English second-hand bookshops with piles of dusty books in corners. It was high and airy, with a gallery, a large dark table in the middle of the room for customers to inspect the books, and display cases around the walls. They showed exquisite single copies, dotted in careful asymmetry, like blowing leaves in a Hiroshige print.

And what did I see, on the right-hand wall, winking at me from behind the glass? A copy of *To The Lighthouse*, with the familiar Vanessa Bell book jacket. The lighthouse tower, the radiating beams, and Virginia's name in capitals. (How different it felt seeing it now. Of course I had read her name on book jackets hundreds of times, but never before with this intimate jolt of recognition – the woman was waiting for me just around the corner!)

My heart lifted, then my heart sank – of course it was good to see it displayed among the jewels of the collection. But if they had one copy, would they want another?

She was next to *Frankenstein* by Mary Shelley. And there was *Orlando* on the other side!

A clean-cut, shiny-haired young man wavered closer.

'Good afternoon, Ma'am. May I assist you?'

'I'm interested in Virginia Woolf.'

'We have a quite good collection, as you see. And over here, there's a nice copy of *A Room of One's Own.*'

I trotted obediently after him. There was yet another first edition, sporting the original dust jacket, slightly browned at the edges but the colours still bright, a clock on an ink-blue background. Perhaps the clock meant the time was right for women to have money and a room of their own.

Now once again, Virginia needed money. And a room of her own in New York, which I was sorting. Mine was much too small for us.

(Too small for me, as well. I had left it too late to book my flights and then BA Business Class was £4,000! I was haemorrhaging money for Gerda's fees, so I'd suddenly thought 'Oh, sod BA' and booked a package through lastminute.com. Unfortunately the hotel was the Waddington. OK, it got full marks for location, but it hadn't been renovated in decades, no mini-bar, no desk. I wasn't too bothered, I would be in the library. But when Virginia came along I suddenly saw it through her eyes – a yellow, chemical, ugly box. Yet she'd stared out of the window as if she was in heaven. Is all life heaven, compared to death?)

Would her opinions unsettle my life?

Would she always, somehow, make me feel a failure?

I dismissed the thought. I was a best-selling author, with two degrees – she didn't have one, though they called her 'the cleverest woman in England' – and I went to the gym and looked after myself. Whereas she looked as though the only exercise she did was dragging herself through a hedge backwards. I had good hair. Ok, this was shallow, but – I had a daughter. She did not. Leonard had forbidden her to have children in case it drove her mad again – though I knew my daughter had kept me sane.

A pang of love: my darling Gerda.

I remembered I hadn't emailed her.

'... Ma'am?'

'Oh, sorry, I was day-dreaming.'

'*Room of One's Own* costs – let me check. Cinnamon boards and the Vanessa Bell jacket – you are aware she is Woolf's sister? Yes, it's not cheap, because it *is* quite unique – $12,800.'

'*Excellent*,' I said, and he looked at me strangely, but of course I was deducing how much her books might earn us. And 'quite unique' was not English, but this wasn't the time to point it out.

'You're interested?'

'How much is *To the Lighthouse*?'

'First trade edition with a pristine dust jacket, $28,000. Four hundred and somethingth of eight hundred signed copies. You really couldn't hope for a better copy.'

'Could I actually have a look at it?'

His movements brisker, he went to the case and tenderly removed the book, then led me over to the big dark table, seated me with a small flourish, and placed the thing reverently before my chair.

It was a clone of Virginia's copy, though her jacket was un-yellowed by time, her colours truer, the pages whiter. And on the inside fly-leaf, his tapering finger pointed to her signature.

I had seen photos, but never the real thing. It was smaller, quieter than I imagined.

'I thought she signed in violet ink?'

'It is purple – but the years fade it.'

The writing was – what? Business-like. The opposite of bohemian. Slanting, clever, fluent, neat. (Of course, I would have to get her to sign them! Why hadn't I thought of that before?)

'Would you like to hold it? It's quite exciting. Part of literary history.' I thought, I've touched enough literary history today

to last me for a while, young man.

'So $28,000 is the top price a copy of *To the Lighthouse* would fetch? I mean, it seems to tick all the boxes – signed, first edition, book jacket.'

'Well – unless someone found a personalised copy. Not that it would, as you say, tick boxes.'

The merest hint of professional disdain.

'What would a personalised copy be?'

'I don't think this is likely to happen – most Woolf first editions are accounted for, and something like this would already have surfaced – but if someone were to turn up with a book she had signed for a friend, rather than a signature done to order – you know she pre-signed for her American publisher? – that would be something very special. Signed copies were more unusual then. Especially if it were something meaningful. Best of all, a message to someone famous – Lytton Strachey, for instance, are you familiar with him? – Vita Sackville-West – or, best of all, Leonard.'

'I *see*.' And I was starting to see. How we could actually make ourselves rich. My expectations had been too modest. 'Great! Well, thank you for showing me that.'

'You don't want to look inside?' He was taken aback – but he couldn't know that I had to think about the actual author, sitting round the corner, Virginia Woolf in her slightly smelly glory, eating a hamburger with fries. I had to keep her off the streets of New York until she had money, and knew how to behave.

I am a socially anxious person. Because of my background, which was working-class, despite my profession and education, despite my accent, despite my money, my house in Hampstead and daughter at the Abbey, I try to behave, I try to fit in.

Virginia was never going to help that happen.

I would need a contact here at Goldstein's. 'I'll be returning

tomorrow or the next day,' I called to the young man's slender, faintly affronted back as he walked off to return the book. He closed the case with a definite 'click'.

'Uh … Sir?' I tried, emollient. 'I have a friend. She has some books I think would be of interest to you.'

His smile was automatic, with the briefest eye contact. 'Perhaps she could submit the details by email? I'll give you my card.'

He gave me his card. (Of course they must have heard it all day long, people coming in or phoning up, making coy, slightly vain allusions to books they were sure would be 'of interest' to Goldstein's, and when they saw them, most of them weren't.)

'She's an old lady,' I smiled at him. 'She doesn't use the internet. I think she would like to drop by in person.'

'As you like,' he said, with the faintest shrug, and his hair was so tidy, his shirt so white, I did wonder what he would make of Virginia.

We would have to deal with the pondweed odour.

I found her sitting good as gold in her café, investigating a tomato-shaped squeezer of ketchup, a quarter of which she had ejected on her plate, a dense, blood-red, viscous hillock of sauce. 'Have you seen this?' she inquired, gaily.

The burger had been a great success! She told me Angelica would have loved it.

Virginia ate six burgers in the next week.

GERDA

𝔐𝔶 𝔅𝔞𝔱𝔱𝔩𝔢 𝔴𝔦𝔱𝔥 𝔱𝔥𝔢 𝔉𝔲𝔯𝔦𝔢𝔰, Part the Second

So there was Cindy, being all friendly, and so were her mates, Linda and Ayesha, and I actually did, sort of, enjoy it, although obviously Linda and Ayesha were dim. Ayesha had big eyes that stuck out of her head and giggled with her teeth showing like a Rabbit, and Cindy was only friends with them because she was too weird for other people, but I'm weird too, so I didn't mind that. And even though Linda and Ayesha were boring it was nice for a bit to go round in a gang. Safety in numbers.

Except it wasn't.

So after we'd been friends for about a week and I had started telling them some of my secrets, not my real secrets like Mum and Dad quarrelling or me having a Genius IQ, which I know makes some people go off me – why? It's obvious I'm a Genius – but just ordinary ones like Mum being a writer or us getting a whacking great house in Hampstead (before we had a normal one like everyone else, in fact our first one was just a terrace) after Mum won the Iceland Prize. I wasn't boasting, I was just saying. There's nothing to boast about in things like that. One day I hope I'll have things to boast about.

I did say one thing that was a mistake. They were all going on about how ugly they were, how thin fat spotty bandy big-nosed

et cetera. It was a competition, how ugly you could be. They were sort of waiting for me to join in. I expect they thought I would say I was a Ginger, oh tragic tragic poor me poor me, or maybe moan that I was too fat, because it's true that I'm not skinny. But I didn't. I told them what I really thought. 'I like my hair, because it's me. I have to eat lots, because I'm always hungry. I'm just not bothered how much I weigh.'

'Why not?' Cindy asked. She looked really angry, as if I had cheated, and Linda and Ayesha stared hard at me. 'If I was your size, I'd kill myself!'

And then the others fell about laughing, but then they went, 'Oh Cindy, that's rude, I'd never say that, did she hurt your feelings? Of course you're not fat, not REALLY fat, oh Gerda, you're fine, really, are you all right?'

So then I said, 'It's different for me. I know one day I'll be tall, like Mum. I think I'm going to be beautiful.'

So then they all went very quiet, except Cindy, who said 'You can't say that.'

And although I was already regretting it, I was brave, and said 'I just did, so what?'

Quite soon after that the three of them began to talk about how they were going to give me a present. It started one Saturday, which is the day some girls have parcels from their parents. A lot of girls, in fact, so it gets a bit competitive. Some mothers don't have to work, like mine does, – (lazy!) – so they spend their whole time making great big parcels with chocolate bars and *Heat* magazine and Bobbi Brown liquid eye-liner, which we're not allowed to wear, by the way, but the girls who get them go *Ooooh* and *Aaaah* and *Oh, my mother is such a sweetie, look what she's sent me this time, everybody!*

As it happens I haven't had a parcel yet. I know it's because my mum is so busy. And so I am Mature about it. I've decided I'm not a Materialist, except I really want that phone.

So apparently Cindy, whose mum hadn't sent one either, had got it in her head I wasn't happy because I was stuck on a table of show-offs. (In fact I wasn't bothered, they can all fuck off with their Stupid Idle Full-time Mothers.)

So later that day she came in with Linda to C13 where I was doing prep and said 'We've decided to do something nice for you, because we like you, but it's a secret.' So I said 'It's not my birthday yet,' and she said 'It doesn't matter, we just want to do it.'

And then for two weeks the three of them were talking in whispers about this Secret Present, and laughing a lot, and not explaining, because they said then it wouldn't be a surprise. And they said 'We're going to give it you on Saturday morning, because that's the day it's nice to have something special.'

And when they said that, I started to hate them, because I could see they felt sorry for me, and no-one needs to feel sorry for me, because I am really a Strong Person, but another part of me which is soft and weedy enjoyed the attention, and feeling special, because they kept repeating that I was 'special', so they had this 'special' gift for me. And everybody wants to be special.

And whenever I came into a room where they were, they hid whatever they were doing, and giggled a lot, and were all simpery-smiley, *Ooh Gerda, how are you, lovely to see you, your Special Surprise is nearly ready.*

And I hate to admit it, but I got quite excited. I thought I was popular at last. Not that I wanted to be popular. Heroes don't need to be popular.

But deep inside me was a kind of Gollum, a slithery Gollum like in *Lord of the Rings*, which wanted everyone to like me, because that had never happened before, because of my weirdness.

So for a bit I was almost Obsessed, and thought about it when I was in bed, because I need to have good things to think about before I can get to sleep in this place. Because I seem to have lost my dreams. My Wonderful Dreams that I've had since I was a baby.

(I do believe they'll come back one day.)

So the weekend arrived when they were going to give me this Special Present they'd made all the fuss about. Saturday breakfast was the same time as usual, i.e. too early – these posh schools have normal lessons on Saturday morning, which is outrageous. (Because lots of girls are so thick that they need them.) I don't need them. I prefer to read books.

I admit I might not have been looking my best, because I had got up in a hurry, and had not combed my hair, and had sleep in my eyes. I was sitting at a long table facing the window, because I love spring, and the trees were coming out, and the tiny green leaves made me feel happy, because the same tiny leaves would be unfolding at home, and so I hadn't lost everything. And the same sun shone in a bar on the table, a bar of gold that reached out to me.

And I thought, 'Tonight my dreams will come back.' And then I thought, 'Maybe Dad will come home, and he will save me from this Dump,' and that thought was happy and sort of heroic, I saw him striding into Maths looking handsome and saying 'My daughter is coming with *me*,' but then I found I was almost crying, which shows I was being Sentimental, which Dad is always very down on, and also, that day I wanted to be happy, and so I stared back at the sun on the trees. Trees would be budding all over England. And Scotland too, but I've never been there, because Mum always says 'Oh, *Scotland*, boring boring, why don't we go to Egypt?' The buds were bright, like dots of green glass, and the sun lit them up so they were like a necklace.

And I was glad when my 'friends' arrived, because I enjoyed it when they called out 'Gerda, Gerda how are you, how are you today?'

(I know it wasn't really that I liked them so much, just that the Gollum inside me felt all smiley-wiley because it thought other people would notice and think, 'Oh Gerda's popular.' And I agree that that's pathetic, but I am still young, and Will Get Better.)

And so I sat there smiling at them – and partly because of the leaves, and the sunlight, and suddenly feeling it wasn't so bad, this Hell-hole which my dumb mother had chosen.

Then Cindy produced something from behind her back, with a silly flourish like a waiter. 'At last it's finished, it's from all of us, we really hope that you will like it!' Her face looked peculiar, sort of partly nervous, but at the same time she was laughing so much that I could hardly hear what she said.

The Special Present was an envelope, quite fat, with 'Gerda Lamb-Kaye' in capital letters. I like my full name but at primary school a boy called Darren teased me because it sounded like Manky, or Monkey. Darren was bright but drove everyone mad, and he was also a Total Div. Two nice boys who loved me punched him by the fish-tank and he got a nose-bleed all over his T-shirt. That stopped the bullying! Yay! Besides, the teachers at primary school definitely didn't allow bullying.

In any case, there was my Special Present.

When I think about it, my cheeks get hot. I actually got up and hugged the Bitch (or Wanker as the case may be.) Though I have nothing to be ashamed of.

And the others all giggled, they were so excited, and I thought it was because they had done something nice. Because some people laugh with happiness. When I am happy, I laugh all the time. But since I came here, I haven't laughed much.

I am going to send Mum another email.

What's the matter with her? Why isn't she answering? She can't have much to do, in New York. She must have got rid of that woman by now.

Maybe she's started another novel. I shall finish **𝕻𝖆𝖗𝖙 𝖙𝖍𝖊 𝕾𝖊𝖈𝖔𝖓𝖉** here, and email her.

ANGELA

Virginia was hyperaware of odours. Chemical odours, not her own. She found the interiors of buildings stifling. I took her for a walk in Central Park. She became so elated I started to worry.

VIRGINIA

Free at last! We had been walking for an hour and still not reached the northern tip. It was almost like being in the country. (Not quite: running people kept passing us, covered with sweat, attached to machines.) Spring had scattered the park with beauty – as we entered from Fifth Avenue, the sun on the plane trees was fresh & bright, each tiny leaf was blowing, dancing – the stuck traffic had turned to a procession, yellow taxis played their horns, blinkered horses shook coloured plumes & even the plastic flowers on their carriages shone with life, quivered like feathers – sea-winds had blown the grime away – everything looked crystalline. A fur of tiny yellow-green crystals electrified the outline of branches, mauve and white crocuses starred the grass, there were dazzling mirrors of silver-blue sky on the frieze of pale towers around the edges.

ANGELA

She knew about plants, much more than I do. 'Oh, look at this darling maple,' she cried, pointing to a gnarled, slightly stunted tree that in close-up was covered with vivid red-yellow flowers that burst straight from the wood, small tufts of tassels.

VIRGINIA

So fiercely young. A wrinkled black tree bleeding bright blossom before it had leaves. 'It's an old tree that can't wait to be young.'

ANGELA

So many things made her laugh with pleasure. Her teeth were bad, grey-blue and yellow, but her face was still astonishing, transfixed with joy in this New York morning –

Why did I feel – excluded?

Perhaps I was losing my joy in living, the magical thing that Gerda has. Was it because I was responsible, and always thinking about someone else? First Gerda, of course, but now Virginia.

I worried about her, so very happy, too soon after being so sad.

The rest of that day went on practical matters. We needed violet ink and dip pen. Virginia simply could not comprehend that a pen and ink might be difficult to find.

'It won't be a problem. Everyone needs pens,' she kept insisting, obstinate.

'Actually, Virginia, no, they don't.'

'But *children* can't use those electric writing-books' (at first she called my computer that, because to her it was a book on which one wrote.)

'Actually, Virginia, yes, they do. It's a laptop, as I said. A laptop.'

'Laptop,' she said. 'Yes, I like it. Short, and final, open and shut. Like "lapwing", yes, a bird on the lap. A flap of the wing, it's done. Laptop.'

'Nice, Virginia, yes. To us, though, it's just – functional.' It was slightly annoying, the way Virginia arrogated to herself the role of poet. I could have thought of all those things. But

because she got there first, I didn't.

In Bloomingdale's, though we were looking for ink, Virginia was constantly distracted, astonished by the wealth of the twenty-first century. 'The colours are so – dense and deep,' she said. 'So bright as well. You're *drenched* with colour.' She kept crying out and pointing: curtains of peacock-blue moiré satin, piled cushions of crimson devoré velvet, pale lemons, terracottas, all peculiarly bright and clear against Bloomingdale's sharp black-and-white floor-tiles. Crystal, silk, soft leather. Gleaming porcelain, gold and silver. The blaze of electric light dazzled her. 'How do they make the lights so *bright*?' Of course, her last memories were of the war, the browns and greys of the austerity years. Her eyes widened further when she saw the prices.

'Is everyone in New York a millionaire?' she asked.

'Manhattan is mostly the rich and their servants.'

(Perhaps no world should have so much money? The bit of me that grew up working-class still had an appetite for more. New York – the city with everything. Things were less comfortable when one was with Virginia.)

And could we find pen and ink? We could not. It was as if our world no longer needed to be written. It was simply *there*, solid, confident, lush.

We tried in Sachs, we tried Bergdorf Goodman – everywhere we went, the idea of 'pens' was met with polite astonishment.

'We used to stock them, but not for years.' There was a tacit comment: *you're out of date,* and of course, Virginia *was* out of date, it was one of her plus points, really, being vintage –

But had *I* become vintage without noticing? I had a pen in London, I used it for signing, a beautiful Waterman with a gold barrel that Edward gave me for a wedding present – and for heaven's sake, I was not exactly old.

I was only forty-nine, and on Facebook and Twitter!

Going round with her must have made me seem older. I suppose, age-wise, she looked like my mother, but in some respects she felt like my child. I was her midwife in the twenty-first century.

After hours of searching and repressed irritation, – why did she never stay where I left her? – we found the pen in the oddest place, thanks to a recommendation from the Waddington doorman, who bought razors there. It was a first-floor business up a dark stairway on Fifty-seventh called 'Shaverland', which had a sideline in antique pens. An old man who introduced himself as Moshe nodded and frowned when we told him what we wanted. Sighing, he got up and stood on a chair, huffing and puffing alarmingly, to pull out drawer after drawer of pens. Each time he heaved himself up, swearing, lurched perilously back again, then finally laid down the drawers side by side, with a triumphant crash, on the glass of his counter.

'Dat's all I got,' he lamented. 'Once I had ten times more of dese things. Take your pick lady, just take the lot. It kills me getting up dere after them.'

'I don't care to write with fountain-pens,' said Virginia, unmoved by the effort he'd made. 'I have used them, but they make a mess.'

'Well fountain-pens is what I got,' he said. 'You want computers, you go elsewhere. De udder lady asked me for antique pens. Course all pens is antique nowadays.'

Not hoping for much, I explained what we wanted – 'Dip pens.' His eyes lit up behind crusted spectacles. Wrapped in a soft, ink-stained pink cloth he kept half a dozen old dip pens, which he spread triumphantly in front of us, then limped off to fetch a big bottle of black ink, an aged, moth-eaten piece of blotting-paper, and a lined notebook. 'See, lady?' he said to

Virginia, who was still looking sceptical, 'we got da lot here, we got it all.'

'Choose, Virginia. Try one out.'

Sulkily she chose two or three. She had evidently taken against this process. I was so looking forward to seeing her writing, but she dipped the first pen, scratched it on the paper, frowned, dipped and dipped again, an irritable bird bent over the inkwell.

'Your ink has run out,' she said crossly.

'It ain't!' he protested. 'You're doin' it wrong.'

They glared at each other over the counter. 'She is a professional writer,' I put in.

'If ya don't want it, don't take it.'

'Take it, Virginia. Choose one or two.'

'How can one choose when one cannot test it?'

'It's OK,' I told the man. 'These will be fine.'

'Your friend don't know how to use a pen.'

'I most certainly do!'

'Ya don't.'

'She is actually a very well-known writer.'

'Yeah? What's your name?'

She stared at him, then with deliberation enunciated 'Virginia Woolf.'

'Virginia Who? I ain't heard of you. You're not Jackie Collins. You're not Stephen King.'

'Well *I* have never heard of *them*.' Thank God Virginia started laughing.

I mollified him by paying – though it was an absurdly small amount. We left with directions to an art shop selling coloured inks.

By eleven that night I had diluted half a bottle to a shade resembling the Goldstein signatures. It took me hours of trial and error, and the floor of the shower was lavender. Virginia

wasn't helping at all, flipping through shopping channels on the TV, exclaiming softly, clutching the remote.

'No, nothing like it,' she said, at last, glancing briefly across. 'I'd never choose a colour so anaemic. And the books have been away from the light, so the signatures would be bright, surely?'

Why hadn't she said that in the first place? Lost in her novel dream of shopping.

We used the untouched half. A clear light purple.

'Better practise first,' I told her. 'Your hand might be shaky after all this time.' I tore out a page from the hotel pad and left her alone while I rinsed the shower and then myself.

What happened after that was rather odd. I came back refreshed to find her sitting there frowning. 'It's the pens, not the ink. The ink won't come out,' she said.

'Right, Virginia.' I wanted this finished so I could settle down and email Gerda. (That nagging awareness: I kept forgetting her. Luckily she was a self-sufficient child.)

'Let me try.' I tried. The pen worked perfectly. I signed my name with a flourish. 'You're just not pressing hard enough.'

In the end we had to do it together. I sat beside her on the bed, with the books open on my bedside table, slipped my hand over the back of hers – cool, bony, the veins making ridges like water-contours in hard sea-sand – and with my hand pressing hers, it worked, the familiar writing, clear and bright, and my heart jumped as I read what she'd written.

In *Orlando*, she wrote 'For my sweet Vita, to travel centuries and worlds with you – Virginia'.

In *To the Lighthouse*, she excelled herself.

For Leonard, always and only Leonard.
Your V.

'Well *done*, Virginia. I think they'll love it.'

It turned out to be an understatement.

But I woke up at three in the morning, the anxious hour, with Woolf snoring beside me, and all I could think about was Gerda. In the end everything was for her, for Edward didn't love me any more – (it was partly why I changed my number, because he had it, but never called; I refused to blame reception in the Arctic.) Now there was only me and Gerda. 'For Gerda,' I thought. It was all for her. Everything I did would be for her.

'Dearest Gerda, I'm thinking of you. It's gone 3 AM in NYC and I miss you so badly my sinuses ache. It's getting tiring, looking after Virginia. Soon we'll be moving to another hotel …'

I planned the email in my head, I thought of the loving things I would say, but my thoughts kept creeping away to Woolf, what on earth I would do with her in the long run. Since I was the only person she knew, just one lone person in the whole modern world – how would I ever get rid of her?

Sleep stole back and dragged me under.

First thing next day I went down to Reception and booked Virginia her own room. I had to pay for two nights in advance, which would give me time to find somewhere else. It was worth it to know I could have my life back.

Could I? Would my life ever recover?

GERDA

I sent 𝔓𝔞𝔯𝔱 𝔱𝔥𝔢 𝔉𝔦𝔯𝔰𝔱 and 𝔓𝔞𝔯𝔱 𝔱𝔥𝔢 𝔖𝔢𝔠𝔬𝔫𝔡 to my mother, but still the woman did not respond, just sent me bulletins about what SHE was doing, and then I began to feel worried, because although Mum could sometimes be forgetful, she didn't usually forget me for *weeks*. She claimed it was all because she was looking after this ancient freak (I admit that is what I thought about Virginia, mostly because I hadn't read her) – but I knew she didn't love Dad any more, and I thought she was probably having an affair. She had bought a lot of new clothes since the break-up, and started wearing very bright orange lipstick, which of course did not suit her Big Orange Face.

She hasn't really got an orange face, I said it because I am angry with her. Har har har on Mum.

Things were still not going well at school, either. Nor did I feel quite ready to put my Great Getaway Plan into action.

For a start, since my mother was in America, I didn't want to give her worry, not THAT much worry, in any case, and although she knew I was brave, and a mensch, (as Dad said when he first saw me ride my bike no-hands), she would certainly worry if I ran away and some idiot teacher from here rang and told her, and they would be shrieking, which is what they do whenever something slightly out of the ordinary happens, like two girls falling in the swimming pool and one of them, Linda, who was a non-swimmer (but I didn't know that) losing her specs (har har har) and having to be life-saved by the other, who did it badly and nearly strangled her, and all

the shouting got a lot of attention – so although I was sitting in the library by then, reading a book about Manhattan (to see if there were dangerous beasts in Central Park, since that was near where my mother was staying, and I thought that might explain her silence, if she had gone walking and got a bit Gored) – my house mistress came and hauled me out and shouted loudly in the corridor.

'Why did you push those girls in the pool? Gerda I will not tolerate bullying.'

'Then why did you let those girls bully me?'

'Don't answer back!'

'That's not an argument.'

I had taught my mother that 'Don't Answer Back!' wasn't a valid argument – it's something that grown-ups always say when they can't come up with anything better – but evidently no-one had told Ms Cannon.

I accept that wasn't the right time to try, and soon I was waiting to see the Head Teacher.

But I had better go back to the beginning, or actually we had got to the middle, and I will write down my side of things, which none of the teachers has bothered to hear, and then I will email it to my mother. In the end, sheer volume will wear her down. There will be room for nothing else in her inbox.

Gerda and the Furies,
Part the Third

I am falling asleep, I will write it in the morning.

VIRGINIA

Angela fussed about the smallest things. The trip to Goldstein's would be an adventure! I had carried off impersonations before, of course, when we were all young, and afraid of nothing. If I could play an Abyssinian prince with a flimsy false beard and burnt cork on my skin and convince the whole crew of HMS *Dreadnought*, fooling Goldstein's would be perfectly simple. One just needed confidence, a sense of fun.

I wish she were a woman of one's own type. I am not a snob, but perhaps she lacks breeding, and many situations make her anxious. After all, we were only going to a shop.

Yet after she found me a room of my own, she virtually demanded that before we go to Goldstein's, I use the peculiar shower attachment in my bathroom, which she explained in tedious detail. I didn't listen. I soaked the floor! –

I think it was the same neurosis about hygiene that made her insist on new underclothes even before we bought skirts and blouses. She kept saying 'shush' like some wretched governess when the brassieres made me hoot with laughter. They were called things like 'Lilyette' and 'Bali'! To think modern women should wear contraptions that make their bosoms stick up like hay-stacks! – and some of them make them bigger with plastic, like that funny Mrs Jordan in the magazine! – and the knickers covered nothing, they were strings with lace. 'I draw the line at buying these.' 'Then you'll just have to wash out your own each night,' she said rather strictly. (Why? are they mad with cleanliness, today's

humans?) So I asked if they had some not made of string, and chose some French knickers in pink satin. I think it was malice that made her ask for 'large'. She herself is on the large side, but I am not.

New outer garments were more of a problem. There was really no necessity, my suit would be good for several more years. I did not want to be obliged to her, and of course she was using her own money until I had managed to get some of my own.

I resisted, but she insisted, so we ended up back in Bloomingdale's.

And then my mood underwent a sea-change, for oh, the glory of Bloomingdale's! One particular colour called to me; one particular part of the spectrum. I wanted to be warm again. I think I had been cold for such a long time. I wanted to be in summer, although of course this was still only spring. Anything from yellow through orange to pink. The sunshine colours. An Italian wall. A street of Spanish orange trees. Angelica's cheek on a July afternoon. Apricot: marrying pink and gold. It called to me from a satin hanger. Golden blush on a warm pink silk that glowed in their white extravagant light. A shirt, long-sleeved, with curved reveres that had something dashing, something dry about it – I tried it on last of a pile of things, I was about to take it off and leave, but at the last second I turned up the collar in the mirror of the changing-room – and in that instant, looking back at me, boyish, over my shoulder was the ghost of a self I had been once, witty, wide-eyed, mischievous, young. I peered through the curtains and summoned Angela.

'I want to keep this,' I said, and laughed.

'Why are you laughing?' She sounded suspicious. 'Did you choose the most expensive one?'

It wasn't her fault. Though she had good points, she

constantly showed a side that was – common. I don't like to use that word, of course one's egalitarian, but Angela was obsessed with money. Perhaps she could not sell her books. When I inquired, she got rather angry & claimed she was actually 'a best-seller'. I was fifty before I started making money, so I tried to judge her less severely.

Today I will have money of my own! One does need money – I'll try that again. We all need money and a room of our own – I must remember not to use the 'one', I have noticed it's fallen out of fashion, as if no-one wants to be singular now. Everything is 'we' – they feel things in herds, the citizens of the twenty-first century.

Regrettably, her guess about the blouse was right! 'That will be $400, Ma'am.' '$400?' Angela stared, her mouth tightening like the mouth of a purse.

I didn't actually see her pay, she just gave him a small plastic card on which I suppose her address was written. The man put her card into a tiny machine that must have printed her address for their records. I would learn to do all these things in time – one would have to learn, if one was to stay.

To me, the prices made no sense at all, they were all unimaginably enormous, but she acted as though I had done it on purpose. For some reason I found that amusing, as if I were a young girl laughing at Nurse, so we left Bloomingdale's with her in bad humour and me snorting quietly behind her.

But for me, the shopping trip was a success. I had a new skirt as well as the blouse, quite hideous but serviceable, in olive-green wool, which had the advantage of covering my knees, & it did go well with the apricot shirt, like leaves and fruit, like a late warm summer –

(if I were with Nessa, it would have been fun –)

This morning, the woman was annoyed again. Apparently I'd 'spoiled the effect of the new clothes', by snatching up my old tweed jacket at the last moment as a cover-up. I don't know why, I suddenly felt naked, as if I might be laughed at in my brand-new get-up. With my tweed jacket, I had an old friend.

She sat as far away as she could on the seat of the yellow taxi. Because I knew she was trying to help me, I turned to her as we stopped at the traffic lights – curious traffic lights they have, bright yellow, suspended from blue sky, thin air – and said 'You see, this jacket is moral support. Because I'm going to lose my books. They're all I have left from – the old world. My jacket keeps me company.'

And at once she melted, and smiled at me kindly, and said 'Of course, I understand. It's just, that blouse cost $400. I've never spent that much on a blouse. I suppose you can't understand our money. Perhaps you will, when you have some of your own. Before you know it, it will be gone.'

And then she said something more interesting. 'You don't have to worry about losing your books. You'll be able to buy copies in any bookstore. Lots of people read you, as I said, Virginia. At least, those people who still read. We'll go and buy you new books today.'

America wasn't as I had once imagined, cars streaming smoothly to their destinations – 'seventy abreast', I think I wrote – no, they all cut across each other, and every ten minutes they all ended up in a blank stand-off of honking metal, noise I had never heard or imagined, the driver of the taxi-cab was swearing loudly and I said we should get out and walk, but Angela told me it was perfectly normal, 'Sit tight, Virginia, it won't take long. New York is like this every day. I don't want you to get there looking wind-blown.'

It seemed I had to play the lady.

I didn't want her to look like a loony. Getting a great writer into the shower is not the easiest thing to do, but I had managed that semi-successfully – her hair looked sweet and fluffy at breakfast, and without the odour, her beauty shone through – then at the last moment, what did she do? She only snatched up her pondweed jacket.

Yet I was growing fond of her.

The trouble was, she took up all my time. I was busy with her from morning to nightfall. I vowed that day I would update Gerda. I hadn't been reading her emails properly. Not that I needed to worry about her. She had been so happy at all her schools, whereas other mothers had been through hell.

I said, 'Virginia, about my daughter – '

But at that moment, the taxi stopped, I saw the dark towers, we were there.

GERDA

Gerda and the Furies,
Part the Third

Childe Gerda to the Dark Tower Came

(This is a quote I have borrowed from Byron, which is one of
the Best Bits in English.)

So we've come to the part where Cindy and her sidekicks gave
me the 'Special Present' at breakfast. And I was confused about
what to do, as they seemed to expect me to open it at once,
with everybody looking, but I felt embarrassed, and besides I
wanted to save it till later when there wasn't so much to be
happy about.

I did feel happy that Saturday breakfast. It was just because
they'd taken trouble. Someone had really thought about me,
though Mum had vanished across the Atlantic and Dad was
working at the North Pole (this isn't a joke, he's a climate
scientist, quite famous actually, Edward Kaye).

You could see from the envelope that they'd taken trouble
with my name, written in beautiful lettering, probably by
Cindy, who is artistic, though the art teacher hasn't noticed it.
So I thought that what was inside could only get better, and I
always save the best till last.

So I just got up and said 'Thanks a lot, I'll open it after morning lessons,' and they looked disappointed, but that seemed normal.

But actually I couldn't wait. Only Cindy was in my set for English and she stared at me through the whole lesson. I thought it was a look of adoration, and I kept on waving and smiling at her (I am a Dimwit. I AM A DIMWIT! WRITE THAT OUT FIVE THOUSAND TIMES).

But I'm not a Dimwit, remember. They are.

Because when I finally got to my room after lunch, I couldn't bear to wait till bedtime, and besides I wanted to tell them I liked it, because that would make them happy too.

So I carefully tore the pretty envelope open, without damaging the lettering. I thought I would stick it on my cork-board, which hadn't got enough things on it yet. Then other people would be curious and I would say 'Oh my friends did it for me,' and they would know that I had good friends.

I couldn't take in what I saw at first.

Mummy, this is a **Cliffehanger**.

VIRGINIA

Loping in to Goldstein's out of the brightness, I felt half at home for the first time since I had woken in this new world.

It was shady, and cool, and full of books, and the furniture, when I looked quickly, seemed familiar, dark and sober like my parents' house, though soon I saw it was all artifice, smooth modern copies of teak or mahogany.

It didn't feel like a bookshop to me. It called itself a 'gallery', with books displayed like jewelled objects. As if they were not to be used every day. Part of me liked that, part did not.

(At the Hogarth we made our books beautiful too. When we first started, we knew nothing about business, but we knew what we wanted; Vanessa designed all my dust jackets, & minded about each tiny detail. We came as near to a quarrel as we ever had since the smoothing away of childhood hatreds when she didn't like the final version of *Kew Gardens*. An hour of torment as she talked to me with terrible calm reasonableness that was worse than any rage could have been.

After that, Leonard and I were even more careful. Our books were not *éditions de luxe* – we had a horror of Victorian ornateness, of gold-tooled curlicues and pompous typefaces – we wanted simple, beautiful things.

Nessa's drawings were just a few strokes, almost child-like – nothing to the untrained eye – but those few strokes made something perfect: a bowl of flowers on an empty stage for *Jacob's Room*, the novel that ends with emptiness – Nessa understood without being told. For *The Years*, that cursed brute

of a book that weighed on me like an overstuffed sofa (though Americans all went mad for it!) Nessa made something that ached with lost time, a pattern of repetitive, cycling suns getting smaller and smaller, going on for ever, and just one cut rose, dark as blood. For *The Waves*, she drew shell-shapes of light and water and two figures standing for all my characters, one rushing forward into the water, the other hanging back, turning towards us.

Of them all, one cover was probably my favourite. *To the Lighthouse* has a bright tower – masculine, powerful – that somehow holds within it a female form, her arms lifted. The gesture of a powerful mother, not the angel in the house but someone stronger, tall and courageous, a light-bringer, a light-giver – Grace Darling, perhaps? Florence Nightingale? Yes, a brave, strong, luminous angel. All my life I had looked for such a figure.

How lucky I was to have such a sister – how cursed she was to have one like me.

Though once at least I could be of service, when Julian died and she needed me.

I had loved my nephew always, even when we quarrelled. But perhaps I liked being, for once, a mother – for a while I was a mother to her …

'May I help you, Madam?' a young man said. He startled me; I was daydreaming. And I found myself saying something quite unexpected, for Angela and I had discussed it all and I had learned my words off by heart, I was supposed to tell him I had some books that were left me by a great aunt, a writer – but suddenly something different escaped me.

Because I was drawn back into the past, and forgot the part I must play in the future. I thought, I have never seen *Between the Acts*. My last novel that I thought so bad. That the Furies took and tossed in the air till all I could see of it was failure and

darkness. In the world I lived in, it was never born. Never born, like my own children.

I couldn't bear to stay alive to see it. By the time it was published, I was dead.

Did Leonard ask poor Nessa to do the cover?

(It was I.

I.

Who asked it of her. By slipping away, while they had to continue. How she must have suffered, doing that task.)

'Are you OK, Ma'am?'

'Perfectly, thank you. I wonder … do you have a copy of Virginia Woolf's *Between the Acts*?'

Surely he would know me, recognise me. But he smiled at me with bright, neutral eyes and said 'I'm happy to say we do.'

Angela looked at me accusingly but I mouthed 'Later', and followed him.

Almost at once, I glimpsed my name. Suspended in a glass case on the wall, I saw the copy of *To the Lighthouse*, which Angela had told me they had. I felt a brief, intense uplift of pleasure to see how it sailed there like a pale ship, safely afloat in the twenty-first century.

The boy meanwhile had taken a slim volume from a bookcase and, holding it like a precious flame, lightly cupped between both hands, said 'This is our copy of *Between the Acts*. If you'd like to sit down, you can inspect it.'

Inspect it! As if it might be defective! Now the moment was here, I became afraid. I felt an almost religious dread – not that I have ever been religious.

Like the Ancient Mariner, my blood thicks with cold

as if I was daring to look behind the curtain
 & see something I should never have seen
as if I had forfeited the right to see it, because of the terrible
 thing I had done –

'Forgive me,' I said, & looked away for a second before I could
bring myself to focus.
 'Sorry, Ma'am?'
 'Nothing. A slight headache.'

And then I looked, and saw in a flash how perfect it was.
Perfectly simple. Yet everything was there. All the unsayable.
Only Nessa … only my sister.

After the finale of the village pageant, the actors go home to
the drama of their lives. My last page ends with the actors
starting to play their part in this bigger pageant. From their act
of love, new life will be born

I could not do it the doctors stopped me
 could not make life as other women did
 this mystery that was all the world needed

Nessa had drawn a stage with theatrical curtains – a graceful
bow to the theme of the pageant. Closed, as if for an interval,
when the curtains come together and the cast disappears so the
audience, briefly, may come to life and chatter.

But these still curtains had another meaning. The show was
over. I had slipped from the theatre.

And garlanding the curtains she had drawn roses, prodigal roses, country roses, and I knew the roses were thrown there in mourning, her wreath for the sister who had gone away.

'Sorry,' I breathed. 'Forgive me, Nessa.'

Her cover wrung my heart, yet it couldn't be bettered. The artist in me bowed to her. It was her goodbye, her delayed reply to the terrible note I left for her.

The artist bowed, but the sister howled. The sister in me was wrenched with pain.

She who had known me from the start
 she had slipped away, she was lost in time
the emptiness the blind, mute ache
 she had to die without my comfort

Where were her ashes? Where did she die? She was older, I should have sat by her bed. With my act I had lost the chance to accompany her through the only life we had, the life we had shared since we were children, scene by scene, side by side.

Nessa must have been lonely without me. Duncan would have been off with boys, and what use to her, really, was poor red-faced Clive?

I do not know if she grew old. This thought transfixed me, a nail in my forehead.

Why had I never understood? Why did the thought of their pain not stop me?

Was I as selfish as Leonard once said, in one of the worst arguments we had? Afterwards he told me it wasn't true.

(I did care for him, and petted him, in ways that no-one else can imagine. He was wonderful, but he wasn't a saint. I mothered him sometimes. I cared for him.)

But no, I had to save myself, because the Furies were after me. When the Furies claw you, there is no more reason. I knew that only my death could stop them, make them hang, slavering, over the water, shrinking and dwindling as the day grew darker and the last bubbles rose to the surface. They lost their power. I drove them away.

I am many things, but not a coward.

ANGELA

Of course, she isn't like other people, and naturally I shouldn't expect her to be, but it did look odd, the way she sat there staring. A great teardrop rolled down her cheek, and she shook her head so it jerked to the right, like a stray raindrop on a train window flying through the dark woods of the past ...

We had urgent business to attend to.

'Are you all right?' I touched her hand. To my surprise, it was warm and firm, and in that instant her posture changed, she sat up in her chair, she gathered herself.

'It's hot in here. I must remove my jacket.' It wasn't hot, but I was relieved, until she folded the smelly thing and dumped it, without ceremony, on my lap.

'*Thank* you.' My ironic tone was lost on her, but I did not mind because without the jacket, she was a different woman. In her apricot silk, she looked old but immaculate, a woman of distinction, fine-boned, aristocratic, exactly the right person to deliver our script. I still wished the jacket were less smelly (I was getting the hang of her subjunctives), but dropped it on the floor beside her chair.

She said 'Thank you, young man, for showing me that. It brings back memories of my past. I may be interested in purchasing it, but first I have some books I think will interest you. They are Virginia Woolf first editions.'

(I remembered in a flash we had forgotten one thing – I

obviously couldn't risk calling her 'Virginia'! But we hadn't arranged an alternative name.)

Another bland young man was summoned. 'Ah yes, Madam, you came in the other day.' He recognised me. I realised I was sweating. We surely wouldn't get away with this. Yet the books themselves could not be more authentic, we had not stolen them, what had I to fear?

I think I was frightened it would all melt away. That we'd look in the laptop case which held the books and find there was nothing there but air. All morning I had been oppressed by fear of the dark towers of Madison Avenue (I'd seen her shiver, and closed the car window to protect us both as we rode through). I was afraid our dream would shrivel. And yet her hand felt warmer, sturdier.

I snapped back from my brown study, sitting where I was at the great dark table, to hear Virginia halfway through her script on the other side of the shop, at the desk! The staff were attentive.

'Bring the copies, Angela,' she commanded. She seemed to have got used to calling me 'Angela'. I obeyed – yes, I had got used to obeying.

I handed her the laptop bag. *One at a time*, I prayed. Spread out your jewels for full effect. She did.

In fact, she was masterly. A sort of hush fell when they saw *Orlando* really was a first edition – 'May I, Ma'am?' – and wondered at the fresh bright orange boards, the ruler-sharp edges of the photographs, the unchipped, unmarked transparent dust jacket. 'The glassine is in remarkable condition,' one of them said, aside to the other.

'Glassine?' I said.

'Oh, a technical word.' He smiled at me with a new deference. They were handling it like a votive object.

'I have something else,' Virginia said. Her long white hands

dived into the bag and pulled out her pristine *To the Lighthouse*. 'I see you already have a copy of this, so perhaps I should take it to another dealer?' She feigned hesitation – was she going to put it back? The woman was a consummate actress!

'We'd very much like to see it,' one said, and the other said hastily 'I'll go and get Alex.' Yet another member of staff was fetched, an older, grander man in a suit, and as they came back in whispered conclave, I caught the word 'exceptional'.

'Do you mind me asking where you came by these?' the older man asked, clutching *To the Lighthouse* with a covetous hand.

'Yes, they've always been in my family,' Virginia drawled, in her most patrician accent. 'We are actually a distant branch of the Stephens. Some people say I resemble Virginia. My great-aunt Theodocia' – *Theodocia!* Surely she was over-egging it, but no, they were hanging on her every word – 'was not a reader, and kept them in a locked cupboard, but then she left me her whole estate, and of course, when I saw them – one knew they were of interest.'

And then she played her master stroke. 'Oh, you might take a look at the title pages. She's written personal messages.'

'Virginia?' they asked in unison, and just for a moment I thought she would answer, I saw her clever lips poised to respond, but I broke in to stop her, 'Yes, that's right. Inscribed by the author. One is to Leonard. And the other, to Vita.'

And then an atmosphere of celebration broke out. Soon the whole staff were crowding round the desk, smiling on us like lottery-winners, then staring at Virginia with – awe? Suspicion?

'There really *is* a family resemblance,' said one of the young women who had joined the crowd. 'I think there's a news story in this,' said the first young man I had spoken to. 'Would you mind if the media wanted to take your photograph with

your great aunt's books? They will love the fact you resemble the author.'

'My family has always avoided publicity,' Virginia intoned with queenly calm.

'There's no need to be anxious, Ma'am,' the older man said repressively. 'My younger staff sometimes get over-excited. May we offer you a cup of tea? Perhaps we could find something stronger?'

I wasn't sure how Virginia was with drink. Doubtless there were mentions in the *Diaries*, but without being able to check up on it, I feared alcohol might bring out her inner truth-teller. 'My friend never drinks before lunch,' I stated.

'By the way, you have not mentioned money,' Virginia said to the senior man. 'What would you be able to offer us?'

I looked at her open-mouthed. Virginia Woolf had hit a home run!

'Of course these are difficult times for the book trade,' he began, with the pat-ness of a man who had been saying it for years. Virginia just smiled and said 'Of course'. And then she pulled *Orlando* back towards her across their desk where it glowed in the light and started to get up, saying 'I wasn't sure this was the right moment to sell. I'm in no hurry, we can sell these in London.'

I'm in no hurry, we can sell these in London! I was still laughing in the middle of the night.

VIRGINIA

I haven't enjoyed anything so much in ages (well, of course, I haven't enjoyed anything in ages).

We came away from there with mountains of money!

They rang the accountant for permission, then somebody was sent to the bank for dollars – Angela explained we could only take cash.

She took charge of the last stage of negotiations. I nearly spoiled everything. When they offered $50,000 for both books, I said '$15,000?' in astonishment, meaning '$15,000 is a great deal of money,' and Angela said, with a meaning look, 'No, you misheard, they are offering us fifty, fifteen would obviously be absurd. But I'm afraid you'll have to offer rather more than that.'

Then the older man made a phone call to a 'private client' he thought would buy. He came back all smiles and said he was now able to offer us $80,000, since he had a firm offer from 'a keen collector. Someone who will give the books a very good home.'

Eighty thousand dollars! It was unbelievable! More money than the Press earned in a decade – more money than I probably earned in my lifetime, though in those last years we felt ourselves rich!

But Angela just said 'Thank you. My friend and I will have to think about that. I'm sure you have made a decent offer, but in fairness to her – she's not *au fait* with New York prices – I

think I must encourage her to see what other dealers' prices are.'

And then someone materialised with tea, and we sat there not quite believing our luck but trying to frown and look undecided while they all went into a huddle at the back, and within ten minutes, silver-haired Alex had returned with their 'best offer', '$90,000 if we can agree this on the spot.'

We looked at each other. We nodded 'Yes'.

Ninety thousand dollars is a great deal of money. Thousands of fifty, twenty and ten dollar bills take up space. They counted them, lengthily, in front of us – sorted them into thousand-dollar wedges – then made two parcels of forty-five wedges, neatly wrapped in plastic & firmly taped, and put each parcel in a carrier bag, chattering and laughing – immensely complacent, & so were we, we were all happy – and all this joy was the result of money! I didn't try to lift the bags, but Angela did, and put them down, surprised. 'They're actually quite heavy,' she said. Unlike the joy we felt, which was weightless.

The young men carried the bags to a taxi. Handshakes all round. Jubilation.

One did feel slightly self-conscious, however, in a taxi loaded with bags of money. Angela and I were both over-excited, my cheeks were hot, I was gasping with laughter, we kept replaying our best moments and saying 'I can't believe it worked', 'Did you really say that? It was priceless' – when something happened to dampen our mood. We started to hear a low buzz of voices, growing slowly louder, through the windows of the cab, which had slowed down to a walking pace.

'Sorry, ladies,' the cab driver said. 'Looks like the kids are at it again. Not too many, we'll be through in no time.'

At the next crossroads, a blockage. A mob of people, a

straggle of tents, bright pink, bright yellow – whistles, singing – a forest of signs like bristling scales. The noise they were making was more jolly than angry. Some of the signs were incomprehensible, but others, one could read without difficulty: 'OCCUPY WALL STREET', a big banner said, crookedly supported by two young women, chewing, laughing, with an eager look. Another – oh, and then several the same – claimed 'WE ARE THE 99 PER CENT'

'We've read about this in England,' said Angela. 'They're anti-capitalists, Virginia.'

'One has always felt like the one per cent.'

What if they guessed what we had in our taxi?

'Yeah, they've been doing it for years,' said the cab driver. 'Cuts no ice with the money guys, but maybe it makes the kids feel better.'

'They're not all kids, are they?' said Angela. Certainly some were middle-aged or older, though they wore what looked like childish clothes – romper-suits, pyjama trousers. As we jerked along past the surging pavement, a thin old man with furious eyes was suddenly pushing too near the car, waving a sign that said 'GIVE BACK OUR MONEY' – red-rimmed eyes, a jutting chin.

It felt a little personal. 'It's the banks they're demonstrating against,' said Angela. 'Look, behind them, that vast building.'

Yes, I could see it, a cliff of dark glass. And a line of sinister figures in helmets between the plate-glass and the rag-taggle protest – dark uniforms – and carrying guns! In front of them, a long white banner – a sheet? – bore accusatory black spiders: 'Banks, You're Busted'. Americans had poor handwriting. 'Don't worry, ladies, the cops will protect you,' the driver said, turning and smiling.

'Those helmets look like German helmets,' I told him, but he just laughed and grunted.

It took an age for us to creep past them. Plenty of time for us to look at them, plenty of time for them to look at us and see the evidence at our feet, though none of them showed the slightest interest. 'GRANDMOTHERS AGAINST GREED' – a tanned, lined woman sat cross-legged on the pavement and waved at passers-by, her long white hair blowing out like Medusa's. What if she caught my eye? I looked away. I felt like a criminal, caught red-handed. One was not used to having so much money.

One felt – at fault, with the mob outside, this cheerful mob of bright-coloured people. Perhaps there was a feeling that we should have been with them, for one or two of them were sitting down, their signs propped beside them, reading books, & the tents were like strange, fluorescent life-forms on these rigid streets where nothing was growing. 'QUESTION WHAT YOU KNOW' was like a thought that had skipped into life from my own pages. Yet soon their noise became tiresome, a cacophony of whistles scraping at our eardrums.

We had to get the loot back to the hotel.

Yes, we were there. 'Hurray!' said Angela. We forgot the demonstration and enjoyed the money.

VIRGINIA

For the first time I felt this writer who came from the future was pleased with me. Pleased with the real Virginia, not the dead Virginia she knew from the writing.

I was not my everyday self in my novels, because they rarely allowed me to be funny.

In life I was always hooting with laughter, people were ridiculous, life was absurd. And so was I, and Nessa, and Leonard, and all my loves, Lytton, Ottoline, Roger, old Ethel Smyth like a charging shire-horse ...

Of course I was myself in my diaries, but they were my secret, and never published. By now they are destroyed – I asked Leonard to do it. He would never reveal me to the eyes of others.

The diaries were the place where I laughed, and examined myself, and found myself and others wanting. And learned my craft. Most days I wrote something. Except when the shadow came upon me, and even then, I tried to track it, tried to record my fight to stay sane. Hundreds of thousands of words I wrote.

Was it a waste, since no-one ever saw them? There in the diaries, I captured my world. The texture of the hours and minutes: the shining lawns between day and darkness.

Sadness brushes me – lost, forever.

Would I re-read it if I could?

No, no time, I am a new person. When I'm less tired, I will write all this newness (I've tried, as it happens, a couple of times, and I don't want to upset Angela by complaining, but

the pens she bought from that huckster are useless.)

'We're changing our hotel,' Angela announced. 'You have no need to economise, and I'm only at the Waddington by accident. I suggest a little place called the Wordsmiths Hotel. Though I've only got four days left in New York.'

She only had four days left in New York!

I thought, what will happen after she's gone? Will she take me with her? Where is she going? What will happen about the money?

Wherever she goes, I must go.

GERDA

Gerda and the Furies
Part the Fourth

(This is the part after the **Cliffehanger**, which is where I was
going to open the envelope that had the special secret surprise
that my friends who were really the **Furies** gave me.)

I did open it. This is what happened.

I couldn't take in what I saw at first.

There were two squares of cardboard, one pink, one
pale blue. Each of them had a tiny photo of me, which they
must have taken off my Facebook site. They looked like
membership cards.

They were. One said:

PRIVATE MEMBERSHIP: FAT FARM

This card admits one severely overweigt person to the
Bendham Abbey Weigt Loss Club.

(Cindy was bright, but couldn't spell)

Catagory: Ginger Mingers (G.M).

Name of Member: Gerda Piggius.

Duration of membership: Lifetime.

The other one said:

PRIVATE MEMBERSHIP: LOONY BIN

This card admits one severly loony person and her mother to the Local London Hampsted Loony Bin.

Catagory: Big Heads, Showoffs and Raving Mentalists.

Name of Members: Gerda I-think-I'm-a-Genius Lamb and Call-me-Mummy Lamb.

Duration of membership: Lifetime.

I stood there staring in absolute rage. Then I took the envelope and tore it in two. But I kept the cards as Evidence, and later I would be glad I did, though I shoved them at the back of the deepest drawer in my room. Even there they still managed to eat my brain. Like actual Devils, a pale pink one, a pale blue one, jeering and sneering till I took them out again and read them half a dozen times, and my blood was boiling, and I was crying, but I wasn't sad, I was just making plans. To kill all three of them, of course.

I didn't wonder why they did it. I knew straight away. My deepest instinct had always told me that even when they were being nice, those three girls actually hated me. But my Gollum-y side wouldn't listen to it, because I wanted it not to be true. (And maybe Cindy didn't totally hate me, but when she did, she knew how to hurt me.)

And it wasn't just the insult to me. It was the insult to my mummy. (Too late now to wish I had never told my enemies I still called her 'Mummy'.) Maybe I talked about her too much, but I had less family than they did because I'm an only child, which I like, as I don't have to put up with brothers and sisters stealing all Mum's love and attention. (If there were

more of us, she'd NEVER email.)

And so I sette off in search of the Furies, who hadde pursued me so pitilessly, hunting me with laughter and with kindnesse. And what I dydde to them will be in Part the Fifth.

(I just remembered I told you already.) (I nearly drowned them in the swimming pool.)

So this is

𝕿𝖍𝖊 𝕰𝖓𝖉𝖊 𝖔𝖋 𝕲𝖊𝖗𝖉𝖆 𝖆𝖓𝖉 𝖙𝖍𝖊 𝕱𝖚𝖗𝖎𝖊𝖘

Honestly, are you reading this, Mummy? Do you care that it actually happened to me? And I was brave? Are you proud of me?

ANGELA

Things got better for us at the Wordsmiths Hotel. She had plenty of money in the purse I gave her and thousands in the hotel's deposit room, an absurd amount to keep in a hotel, but I couldn't come up with anything better. She had no passport or driving license to open a deposit account at a bank, and I was uneasy about her putting such a large amount into mine. If journalists ever got wind of this, I wanted to come out – smelling of roses (does money ever smell like roses?).

Yet I was doing her many favours. How would Virginia have managed without me? It's true my time is valuable, too. My workshops cost $1,000 a day.

Perhaps she should have offered me a small percentage?

Five per cent. Or maybe ten. Nine thousand dollars would have been most helpful, but obviously it was up to her to suggest it. I could hardly ask her directly, could I? The Wordsmiths Hotel cost a lot of money. Without her I would have stayed on in the Waddington, ghastly though it was, and got on with my paper.

Which would have been about Virginia, true, and for which the Turks would be paying me. But the Virginia Woolf I was writing about was so much less trouble than the one I was with. The first earned me money, the latter cost me.

VIRGINIA

I wonder how much of the money is mine? After all, without Angela I would have nothing. So far she's given me $500, and

told me to be careful with it.

I think it would be fair to split the money in two, but she might not agree to that.

So I'll ask her to work out today's equivalent of £500 and a room of one's own'. Then I will request it, bold as brass.

ANGELA

We took the largest rooms on the 'literature' floor (the entire hotel is literature-themed, and we found ourselves in two 'queen-sized' rooms nestling alongside each other, named 'Hemingway' and 'Scott Fitzgerald'). We told reception we had two bags of valuable books to keep in their strong room. (Well, the money was the fruit of her books.)

Would my books be valuable, a hundred years later?

It didn't matter, I was a best-seller. She seemed surprised when I told her that. Only one of her books was a true best-seller, and that was probably her worst, *The Years*.

– I'm not quite sure what that has proved.

Sometimes I felt almost hostile to her. Worrying about her well-being was distracting me not only from my paper, 'Virginia Woolf, A Long Shadow', but also from the answer to my problem: what should my new novel be about?

– That sense I was on the brink of something.

Edward had a gift for discouragement. When pressed, he would say, 'You're a really good writer, but I preferred your early books.'

'Don't you like what I'm writing now?'

A short pause before he answered 'Of course.'

Before leaving London, I'd had lunch with the new editor at Headstone. She looked about fifteen years old in her orange jacket and plastic shorts, and assured me she was a 'fan' of mine.

I tried to explain what I was feeling. 'But you're a success,' she said, surprised. 'We love what you do. Everyone's happy.'

I wasn't totally sure she had read me, but she knew the sales figures were good and said my work was 'wonderful'.

'Believe me,' she said, with an earnest expression, 'very sadly, we're having to shed some of our – more mature writers. But Angela Lamb is a brand!'

From that I learned only that she thought I was old.

I tried my agent: we had a coffee. She talked about my foreign rights. 'I want to feel passion,' I interrupted her. 'I want to write something I feel passionate about.' She was a nice woman. She said, 'You should.'

Which was why I had set off for New York and Istanbul. I could have written another novel in my study. But I was looking for something else. The common life I once shared with Woolf – when 'inspiration' meant 'breathing her in'. Her daring, her certainty that anything could be written. Her sense of wonder at all of life.

Well, I had certainly got close to her, even if the novel was still under construction.

In the Wordsmiths Hotel, everything was new. I carefully explained to her the taps, the safe, the television, the elevator, the CD and DVD player, though she only pretended to understand me, as I learned quite quickly from the men in the lobby after 'your wonderful mother' – I soon disillusioned them! – broke the TV and jammed the aircon. But she'd learned to work the hotel telephones, thankfully, which meant she didn't always come to me when she had a problem with reality.

She marvelled at her elegant sunken bath, the soaps and oils, the high-speed lift. Especially the lift, which Virginia played in for a whole morning. I heard her laughter in the corridor.

'Virginia, what have you been doing? Where have you been? You're all flushed.'

VIRGINIA

'Up to the roof-top bar and down to 'Literature', down to the 'Reading Room' and up again, down to the lobby to talk to the porters (they're charmers), up to the top again to take in the view – you get there in seconds, it's terrific fun! I shall write an essay on the high-speed lift!'

ANGELA

Later I knocked on her door to go to supper and found her seated at her desk, the hotel notepaper in front of her. I tried to get a glimpse of what she was writing, but she must have just started a new blank page.

The lobby staff seemed to adore Virginia. They obviously thought she embodied Olde Englande, and bathed her in courtly bows and beams whenever we left the hotel together.

(Yes, very sweet, but Virginia milked it. Sometimes I felt I hardly existed.)

She was learning to do things solo, thankfully. Which was a relief, since now I had only two and a half days left in New York. The conference was preying on my mind. I still hadn't finished revising my paper, though I was getting my quotes together. The hostile critics could be so savage! Sometimes I found that rather bracing, and allowed myself a horrified snicker. Of course I didn't say a word to Virginia.

As things were, would I be able to leave her?

'Virginia, we must make a plan.'

GERDA

I have received an email from my mother. I am obviously Concerned about her, which is what she sometimes says about me, when she is on the phone to other mothers, but she doesn't mean it, she is just getting in on whatever they say they are worried about, eg. Drugs, Sex, Boys etc., though I have never done any of that.

I WILL FIND A WAY TO WORRY HER LATER!

Hallo Sweet Pea! (It's what she calls me, I TOLD her not to)

Thank you for your lovely story which I read quite quickly – I will soon re-read it but life is rather rushed just now. I read all three bits and it's really funny. How ever do you think it all up? You really are a genius.

(But she doesn't mean it, she's just saying it, whereas I AM a Genius, with a Genius IQ. My old school told her, but she forgot. I TOLD HER THE STORY REALLY HAPPENED TO ME. SHE REALLY IS UNSATISFACTORY. Or perhaps she has lost her glasses again, and I'm not there to help her find them.)

How's school? Now I have to explain something very important and peculiar which is happening to me. Only you in all the world will believe me. Please do believe me, darling, I'm counting on you.

(Yes, but she didn't believe MY story!)

You did know who I meant by Virginia Woolf? Or possibly you've googled her? The most famous woman writer of the last century, she's brilliant, I've always admired her, she's said to be a snob but she's beautiful and clever and her face is all over twentieth-century university literature courses, as you will find if you decide to do one. I don't really know what to say about her except every sentence she writes is poetry! But she went mad and killed herself. I am shorthanding, of course.

(She made Woolf sound like a total mong. The writer who I love at the moment is Kurt Vonnegut, because he is funny. And great. He's dead like her, but he didn't kill himself, in fact he fell over and hit his head and died despite not wanting to. I thought, 'He's loads better than that old woman.')

Virginia has come back to life. She just appeared one day in the library. I was reading her, for the conference, an important, international one as you know, where I have been invited to speak

(That's the first time she's mentioned it. My mother may have Alzheimer's.)

(She has NEVER told me. I would have remembered. I know I have to keep tags on my mother. I have always instructed her to tell me her movements, and now it's more important than ever, with Dad not here, and Possible Boyfriends. She's out of practice, she will choose the wrong ones)

(at least I hope she is out of practice)

and Virginia walked in. She isn't a fraud. She's the real deal. But now she's lost in the twenty-first century. She had no money, she was totally helpless, and obviously I had to take care of her.

(Has my mother been spending my inheritance?)

I don't know what I will do with her when I have to go and speak at the conference

(or to be fair, she may have told me at Christmas, I was mostly in a rage with her at Christmas because she had bought all the wrong presents, so it's possible I wasn't listening, and in any case, Mum talking is boring)

and in fact I am one of the plenary speakers. By an irony, the conference is all about her – 'Virginia Woolf in the 21st Century: Cross-cultural and Transformational Approaches.' I can hardly take her to her own conference!

(why not? Wouldn't it be helpful to have the actual writer telling all the academics and people like my mother where they are going wrong? Surely it would be good for them.)

(Still I do feel proud to think of my mother addressing an International Conference, in New York or Harvard or wherever it is, with all the academics listening to her, which never happens to her at home ... I do remember about the conference. I do remember that Mum was thrilled.)

So I've been working out where I can park her safely. Imagine, she had been dead for *decades*. There is so much to explain to her. It's very like having a new baby.

You are my baby and my best-beloved. I do hope you've made some nice friends at school. Why don't you write and tell me all about them?

(I did tell you. They are horrible.)

I can't send many emails just now, I'll be busy with Virginia for the next two days and then I am rushing off to the conference – I am *dying* to ring you, but the school does ask us not to disturb you in your first two terms, I suppose they think you are all weeds and might beg your parents to take you away! But I know you always love your schools.

(stop talking)

The biggest hug in the world from your mother.

(who is useless)

PS. Don't forget to brush your teeth.

(SHUT UP Bum Face)

To write back properly would have taken me two hours, and I had some important plans to carry out, involving running away from school, so I kept myself to a single question.

Dear Bum Face

Why can't Virginia Woolf go to her own conference?

Yours sincerely,

Gerda Lamb-Kaye, Genius >:-(Etc

(You may wonder why I wasn't more surprised about Virginia Woolf coming back to life. It's because people come back to life all the time.

My grandma talks to me in the night. Grandma Lorna who looked after me, and so did Grandpa, until they died. Sometimes she gets in the bed and cuddles me, which is also something she did for Mum when Mum was little and had asthma, and Grandma would come to her bedroom in pyjamas and tell Mum stories till she went to sleep, and when I was really upset about the Furies, Grannie crept back, quite shyly, after a long while, and got in with me, and held me tight, and slipped away before it was light.)

Dear Gerda,

IN HASTE.

I'm not totally taken with the name Bum Face.

Yes, I could take Virginia to the conference, but the complications! She's – difficult.

You haven't told me any names of your friends. I do care, you know. I am a loving mother. Perhaps you would like to ask them to stay? I'll look in my diary and see when I'm there.

Lots and lots of love

Mum

PS. It's OK about calling me 'Bum Face'. I take it as a badge of honour. Did I remind you about cleaning your teeth? Xoxoxox

ANGELA

Serving Virginia. It was endless! I'd spent what seemed like hours on the phone trying to get Virginia a passport. Some proof of identity was bound to be needed once I was no longer on the scene to help her. She might decide to go back to Europe; in the long run she would need a bank account. I'd been dealing with the UK Borders Agency. When I saw the forms, I wanted to laugh. 'Free for those born before 1928' – if only we could reveal her real birth-date! '*Purpose of your visit to the USA.*' I put 'Tourist'. She was a tourist – a time tourist. I said (with truth) that her old passport was lost.

But no, the agency could not be appeased. They required documentary evidence that she existed. Stubbornly, blindly, the bureaucrats refused to believe in Virginia's reality.

I wanted to go through the proper channels. But when I told Virginia, she arched her brows, and her eyes danced, and she said: 'I think I will talk to my friends in the lobby. And one friend in particular. How much are we prepared to spend?'

(She has picked up the habit of sitting in the lobby and – what I can only call *holding court*. It seems they can't get enough of her. Whereas I have had a basinful.)

Two days later she was laughing on the landing. I opened my door to see what was up. She was brandishing a red UK passport. 'Look at this, it is REMARKABLE! I could leave tomorrow for Samarkand!'

I opened it. It was astoundingly good. Not a crease in the plastic over the photo. Virginia's face, skilfully tinted. She said

'They took the photo off the internet.'

'Yes, Virginia. That's all very well. But what will happen to the person who owned it? How did your friend get hold of this?'

'*Obviously* it's stolen, Angela. And then they adjusted some trifling details. One regrets the necessity, but there we are. You weren't getting anywhere by being straitlaced.'

At least she had identification, of a kind. I went back to writing the list of things we could do together in my last few days.

(I'd asked her to jot down what she wanted to do, but nothing appeared on the piece of paper I put in front of her in the lobby, probably because she never stopped talking.)

'She's a riot,' the oldest porter said to me as I stood waiting while she fetched her bag.

Yes, she could easily cause a riot.

Here is the plan I made for her.

1. Find Bloomsbury painters in New York galleries

2. Buy V.'s books from New York bookstores

3. Another walk in Central Park?

4. A drink in the Algonquin Hotel, where Dorothy Parker and her circle met

5. SEE STATUE OF LIBERTY

The sixth item only exists in my head.

6. *Sort out what happens to V. after I go. Who can I find to look after her?*

This question has become more urgent since Virginia started going out on her own. She's been back to Bloomingdale's and bought more clothes. I hypothesise that they were very expensive. A coat, yellow cashmere, the colour of sunlight. She sits in the lobby in various outfits, coral silk, turquoise shantung, topped this morning by a navy cartwheel straw hat of staggering dimensions.

VIRGINIA
I bought a hat. It's almost a poem. A cloud-dark disk like a storm at sea. With a dotted veil like small bees blowing. Very satisfactory, yes.

ANGELA
10 AM in the lobby. We were meeting for items 1 and 2 on our list.

And there she was in her extravagant hat, perched like a blue and gold bird-of-paradise landed here from far away. She must have seen me raise my eyebrows. I didn't mean to, but I never got used to her. At once she looked defensive, suddenly elderly, beak thrusting forward, awkward, anxious.

'Virginia!' I hope my tone wasn't chiding. 'I thought we were doing museums and bookshops this morning?'

'I hope so.'

'You seem to have dressed for a wedding.'

'The hat is not appropriate?'

'You look beautiful. Of course you do – ' (she straightened up, she expanded, blossomed) – but, well, things have changed since the 1930s.'

'When one went to galleries, one tried to look smart. We tried to look smart,' she corrected herself. 'But possibly I'm overdressed?'

And instantly she was deflated, her spine crumpled, the hat

looked silly, her long white hands began kneading each other, her eyes crawled nervously across the floor.

Of course I didn't want to upset her. 'I would be proud to go out with you' (I meant it) 'and all the bookshops would be impressed, but we did think we'd go to Central Park afterwards, and Central Park is very windy, famously windy in fact – '

'It ain't – ' (laconic interruption from her friend in the lobby, but fortunately she did not hear it) 'your girlfriend just don't get the hat, Ginny – '

' – so I suggest, we come back after the park and pick up the hat before we go to the Algonquin. There it'll be just perfect.'

'Yeah, the Algonquin's kinda elegant,' her pal behind the counter added.

So that was decided, and off we went. But the hat came with us. She stood beside me, waiting for the taxi on the narrow pavement. The angle meant I couldn't see her face, but out in the sun I couldn't deny it: the indigo hat was a glorious presence, a dark pavlova full of air and light, poised on a long-necked porcelain cake-plate.

'Virginia, we're going to have fun.'

GERDA

Mum's 'In haste' email was the final straw. She was having fun, half a world away! She hadn't a clue what was up with me! She thought I would invite those Monsters to stay!!!!!

(I know they weren't Monsters really, just girls. But I needed someone to take my side. I needed Mum to understand. In person, I could sometimes make her listen. Her not understanding was an actual Crime, not a Misdemeanour like most of what she did.)

I thought, 'I'll have to kill myself if I can't get away from them. Mum isn't listening. No-one cares.' Then I thought, 'No, I'd rather kill *them*.'

At school that day we read Sylvia Plath. I don't think she's so marvelous. But the teacher said, in a special solemn voice, 'She is a great poet, who took her own life,' as if the two things were actually connected.

And afterwards everyone went online and googled images of her. I had to hang back, because since what happened with Linda and Ayesha and the swimming pool, the word had gone round I was a Maniac, and I couldn't be bothered to tell them I wasn't. (Maybe I am a Maniac.) There were thousands of photos! 'She's really pretty,' Cindy said, looking at one of her with long blonde hair in a blinding white dress with frills and lace that I would never be seen dead in, which Mum would say is 'an unfortunate choice of words', but still, and then they found another one of her in an itsy-bitsy bra-top and skirt and Anna sighed, 'And she's so thin,' and everyone

went on about her waist till I wanted to throw up and said 'She's cross-eyed,' although I knew they would say 'You're jealous.'

To me she looked old-fashioned and mad. Her face is puffy, like a squinty-eyed goldfish. What sense does it make to kill yourself? If she'd stayed alive, she'd have written more poems. So even if I want to kill myself, I won't, because I am going to Have a Life.

If you ask me, suicide is Pants.

This is a point where Mum would say, 'There are things you will not understand until you're older.' But actually, I understand now. Maybe later I'll understand less. I might get worn down by other people's thoughts, all the ideas that everyone shares, like all of them thinking Sylvia's great, pouring into my ears like sand till it's blocked solid and I'm shut out. Then I'll be old like everyone else.

My grandpa once said 'Don't cry, Gerda. You don't have to believe what people tell you. And you don't have to be like everyone else.' And I always remember what he said.

I moved slowly away from the swarm round the screen, like a gang of weak moths, fluttering and struggling, who couldn't get free from the Poison Light that came off her dress, her face, her waist.

That settled it then. I would go and find Mum. I would not be a victim. I was on my way!

Very early next day, while the Monsters were sleeping, faint Snurds of death-breath spoiling the morning, I slipped out of bed, picked up the small backpack I'd stuffed with things the night before (I was Dick Whittington, on the road to London), crunched down the gravel, hearing every footstep – what if a teacher was walking early? – looked back at the Abbey, which was red as blood, and saw for the first time it was full

of eyes, cruel glittery windows in its greedy body, which had swallowed me up with so many others. Would they catch me and bring me back again?

(I suddenly remembered arriving hopeful – how *sad and pathetic* that I'd hoped to be happy. Oh woeful, woeful, I had dreamed of having friends! I AM A DIV! I AM A DOUBLE, TREBLE DIV!! I started running till I got to the corner but I had to stop because the bag was heavy.)

And with my face scrunched up against remembering I hurried on down the torturous drive, under Spiteful yew trees and monkey puzzles, but as I crept out on to the public road, the bus arrived, we zoomed on to the village, and my heart lifted, back among Normal People, cheery women taking their kids to school, and I used my last cash to get a ticket to London, and before midday, I was home again.

ANGELA

Sometimes New York felt – alien. The streets so hard and straight and bright. The traffic on Fifth Avenue was stalled again.

VIRGINIA

The store-fronts stared at us, flashing in the sun, blank-faced, clean, a line of giants, and insect people streamed into the dark, then out again clutching tiny parcels; it seemed both communal and purposeful, as if they were under orders from afar.

(When I was shopping, had I looked like that? But no, I chose things, I improvised. Shopping, for me, meant freedom – did it?)

ANGELA

Virginia had removed her hat. 'I love it even when it's on my lap!'

And then she began to talk about the money.

'What would £500 a year in the 1930s be today in dollars?'

'I don't have a calculator in my head,' I said.

'What is a calculator?' she asked.

'It does our maths for us,' I told her. 'No-one today can do arithmetic.'

'Is there one in your laptop book?'

She's learning, but she's not there yet. 'I have a calculator in my phone.'

But when she got too much information, she simply ignored it. Her mind was on its own thermal.

VIRGINIA
'About the money. If I stay here a year – if I am allowed to stay here a year – I'll be able to live by writing, I suppose. But it will take time to write a novel.'

ANGELA
I was taken aback. Of course she was a writer, what else would she do? But I hadn't considered what would happen next. Because Virginia Woolf had done her writing – Virginia Woolf the historical figure. There it was in the university libraries, the rows of volumes, the critical editions. It must be over; she had entered the canon. How could it all begin again? Would she be Virginia Woolf Mark 2? Of course, she couldn't change her name, because her name was everything. This would be, what, her Late Period? 'Posthumous Period' was too weird. Would she write a novel about New York? Publishers would fight over it.

I felt suddenly, sharply territorial. Writing about our world was, well, my job. Though of course her observations were – of interest.

VIRGINIA
'I will need a safety net.'

ANGELA
New York, outside the window, looked very expensive. I got out my phone and googled the money.

First 'inflation rate since 1930'. There were two different ways of calculating: one retail prices; the other, earnings.

The first result was surprising enough. Using retail prices,

£500 a year would now be £25,000 a year. Above the average UK national wage. In New York, $40,000, which sounded like more. So to bring Virginia's dictum up to date, the 'Shakespeare's sister' of today would now need $40,000! Suddenly it sounded a lot less modest, Virginia's prescription for what a writer needed.

Then I tried the same things using the 'earnings' index, which I thought would come out less. But here the results were truly spectacular. A wage of £500 in 1930 would be £76,000 today – which translated as $123,000!

Suddenly I worried about why she had asked me. Of course she was thinking of the money in the strong room; $123,000 was more than we had!

The relevant measure clearly had to be prices.

I told her 'Virginia, you won't believe this, £500 a year in today's money is $40,000.'

Her beautiful, full lower lip dropped. 'It's not possible. Is it? Such a lot of money.'

'It is a lot of money,' I said, relieved.

'I was hoping – that is to say I hoped – I wondered if I could draw a year's income from the money that we made selling the books. But I can't take $40,000. Because it was you who came up with the plan.'

And then I felt ashamed, of course. Because Virginia asked for so little.

(Yet I couldn't forget the $400 shirt, and that hat *had* to have been awesomely expensive.)

VIRGINIA
'Oh I do so love my navy-blue hat.'

(Its spotted veil, light as a breath; sea-mist dotted with tiny swallows.)

No, I couldn't begrudge her it. Though I half-remembered something from the *Diaries*. Leonard had called her 'extravagant'. Was she unworldly but extravagant?

'Virginia, if you liked – I could look after the rest of the money for you. We can't leave it here indefinitely. I can just open a new account. I don't want any of it, honestly. It's your money. It's a pleasure to help.'

So that was decided, and I felt better, though I knew I might regret the decision later.

(There was a discrepancy in one of my accounts, the so-called joint account with Edward, my debit card account, which I myself had never used abroad since a lot of trouble with a fraud in Paris. I'd looked online a day ago and it seemed to be several hundred short. I suspected Edward might be drawing funds, though he'd told me, when we opened it, after he made all the money from *The Palace of Ice*, that he wanted it to be 'my little hoard' – yes, he did sometimes put money in, but all the same, it was meant for me.)

But no, I didn't take Virginia's money. I hope I did my best for her. I tried to be a daughter, not a jealous sister.

Even though, at close range, she was exhausting, it was like being eaten alive by an emu, the long neck always turning on you.

'Is all of history in your computer? The history of money, and peoples, and wars, and clothes, and food? It's impossible.'

Of course, it seemed impossible to those who came before the internet.

'It's a kind of net … that trawls for fish … every kind of fish, and shell, and coral, and millions and millions of grains of sand, and old rubbish, and plastic bags … it misses things, but it's not selective.'

'But every book must be selective.'

'That's the trouble. On the internet, it's the reader who has to be selective. '

'How can you choose if you don't know what's there?'

'You enter a search – something like a fishing-hook – and a huge rush of material comes up. Then it's over to you to pick what you want.'

'*Caveat emptor*?' she said, nodding, her big grey eyes alight with interest. '*Caveat lector*, I mean?'

'Virginia, I don't know Latin.'

'But you went to the university? Well, it means, 'Reader beware'. I never went to the university, but all of us knew Latin. My sorrow was that my Greek is second-rate, whereas my brothers all learned Greek from the nursery. Girls didn't go to school – '

'I actually went to a rather good school.'

'Then I don't understand why you don't know Latin. And you write books – you're an author? *Auctor auctoris.* You must know *some* Latin.'

'It's a different world,' I said, despairing.

It was a phrase I grew tired of repeating. She knew so much – had read so many books, though some of the authors meant nothing to me – read literature in Greek and Latin – yet knew so little, because time had moved on, shouldering past her, greedy, brutal, chewing up names, forgetting faces, spewing out new things to bury their tracks.

The pace of change had doubled, quadrupled since she wrote about time in *To the Lighthouse*. In the novel's central section, 'Time Passes', the years crawl by in a gradual erosion of surfaces. In the far distance, the great war thunders. Entropy is slow as flowers.

Whereas now time was just a kaleidoscope of earthquakes, everything collapsing and starting again, names and technologies jumbling to rubble.

Home, I thought. My home, my family. Where were their faces in that blur of dust?

But another part of my brain was whirring. Could there be a twenty-first-century 'Time Passes'?

Lo and behold, we were at the Whitney.

GERDA

Home.

It was empty and echoing. The house felt – cold. But it was OK. I had plans to make, now I had Mum's money. No, I would not be staying long.

Should I have felt guilty about using her debit card to book my ticket to New York? Of course I shouldn't. She had left it there, in the usual place under the Jeff Koons clock, with the PIN number she was always forgetting. She used a credit card abroad – something about security, but she clearly hadn't thought about security at home, which was her fault, really, it was 'asking for trouble', as she said to me when I took my iPod to school, and even more careless, she had let me know where she kept her emergency stash of cash. Yay! Twenty-five crisp twenty pound notes tucked inside the paperback of Vita Sackville-West's *All Passion Spent*.

'Gerda could you listen to me for once? GERDA PUT THAT BOOK DOWN AT ONCE AND LISTEN!! I'M TELLING YOU THIS FOR YOUR OWN BENEFIT,' she had shouted, one hot June afternoon when I'd just got home, and then I put on my Special Listening Face, so she stopped shouting and did her Extra Meaningful Voice which she used for sad things, 'just in case something happens to me and your father.'

Well something *did* happen. My parents split up, and sent me away to boarding school, bastards, and no-one was here to care about me, and so I was forced to take care of myself.

And yes, I felt weird about it, but so what? In lots of adventures people Actually Kill People. What I did was not even theft.

She *said* it was 'for my benefit'. She meant me to do it. I took the money.

ANGELA

First stop that day: the museums. Looking for Virginia's old coterie.

But they were her friends, her sister, their lovers, so nothing was simple, and she was abstracted.

We tried all the museums where there might be a chance.

First the ones where I was sure we would find them.

Vanessa Bell: one painting in the Whitney. *Not on show*.

Duncan Grant: two paintings in collection. *One on show*.

And there it was. A small oil of a vase. To me, it looked at best mediocre. But Virginia lingered in front of the small grey thing for ten minutes, fixed, staring, until, gently, I pulled her away. 'There are lots of his paintings in the Tate, London,' I said to her, but she hardly heard me.

I was sure we'd find work by Roger Fry – Roger Fry, the man who brought modern art to London with the two postimpressionist exhibitions. Roger Fry, who Virginia had been in love with as a very young woman, the subject of her only biography. Roger Fry, once a young prince in New York, chief buyer for the Metropolitan Museum.

But he had disappeared without trace. In the Met, no-one had heard of him. I had to repeat his name several times, but was met only with polite blankness.

We had lunch in the Met's self-service restaurant, a cavernous yellow-lit purgatory, where unreal tourists flitted by, passing grim-faced with water-glasses. There was a vague air of disrepair, as if the money had run out. The floors were

cracking. There was mould on the wall. She hardly touched her greasy food, just sat there playing with it, pale and silent.

Then 'We are near Leafy, and the Sticks,' she mumbled.

I thought they must be parts of New York she had learned about from her new friends in the lobby. 'I don't know where you mean,' I said.

'Lethe,' she said, this time more clearly, yet her great eyes were staring through me again. They looked vitreous, cloudy, impossible to plumb. 'The cup of forgetfulness. I am trawling for their faces. Roger, young – his mane of hair, his eyes glowing … You must know Lethe, and the River Styx, which all who die must cross. Perhaps you don't, if they no longer teach the classics.'

I hastened to tell her I knew both names. I felt offended that she thought I might not, and I was exhausted from all those museums, and the weight of her sadness – and my own. I couldn't help thinking, 'This will happen to me. This is what happens to most of us. After we die, it's as if we never lived.' And the Bloomsbury Group had been so famous!

(In one small island, for one or two decades.)

As the spectral tourists processed with trays, she asked 'Do you moderns understand death? In New York, everyone's trying to be young, and fifty-year-old women go out without skirts, and remember those creatures I kept seeing on the street who I thought had been burned, but you explained they had just had plastic surgery, and their features were smudged … Do Americans think they will live forever? Do they think they will just continue to get richer?'

I batted the question away with facts. 'Maybe they did, but I don't think so, now. There was an attack on New York. At the beginning of this century. It changed the way Americans thought about themselves. Three thousand people died in one day.'

'Three thousand people? Here? Why?'

How could I explain? Impossible. 'Partly religion. Partly power. The two things have got confused. Rich countries are hated by poor ones because they seem impervious. There's always a struggle over resources. And as you have seen, there's so much wealth.'

I fell silent, then tried again, but I couldn't explain the whole of modern history, not that I understood it myself. It was complex and stupid as the Treaty of Versailles, which she had been talking about last night. It would go on forever: war, hatred, 'I want it', 'No, *I* want it.'

'Death was suddenly right here, in the middle of the city.'

She looked tired, and shook her head. 'Leonard would know,' she said. Now she was pouring sugar on the table, the sands of time from her bony hands. 'But I wasn't asking about politics. I was asking about … What was I asking about?' In the yellow artificial light, she looked jaundiced. A long cobweb trailed from the lampshade.

'I think we should go,' I said. 'Time to visit the bookstores.'

VIRGINIA
'I was asking about …'

ANGELA
Her voice trailed away.

VIRGINIA
about forgetfulness

the forgotten

a fin crossing a blank horizon
something darting a small skimmed stone

stitches on the edge of vision

ANGELA

I couldn't see what she was staring at. Then I did. There were ants on the table, carrying grains of sugar home.

They moved with blind, silent purpose, doing the thing they were born to do, one after another, an endless succession.

Virginia stood up without a word and stumbled back out into the daylight.

GERDA

When I opened my eyes I tried to be happy. Home. I'm home. Except it isn't.

How can it be home if I wake up on the sofa, because there weren't any sheets on the bed?

My mum didn't leave any food at home. Or milk or even cereal. It's vile being home without any breakfast. Mum can't be arsed to look after me. She should have guessed I would run away. I truanted from my other schools.

(I can't blame Dad because he's in the Arctic. Otherwise I would, don't worry! When dads feel guilty, they spend money.)

What they don't realise – splitting up parents – is that it splits *us* up as well. There's a feeling, non-stop, at the back of your brain. A sort of numb feeling that all you have to do is run it all backwards, and maybe you'll get back to a year ago, or two, or three, or whenever our family was last happy – (I want to cry when I think the words 'our family', because 'family' used to give me a warm feeling, and my parents were special, which made me proud) – but this time around I would make it better, whatever I did that helped it go wrong. Yes, I admit I sometimes made trouble.

And the place you went back to, without cracks or splinters, that would be home, for all of you, and you'd never have to leave, unless you chose to.

Though of course, one day, I would, and I will.

It's children who should leave, not parents. So there's always

someone for us to go home to.

As things are, I can't ever go home. I've got here, haven't I, but everyone's gone.

My family. Which was once complete.

A little island where I lived with them.

Now I look back, it's gone small and misty. I peer like a div but I can't see our faces.

I think about now, and everything's bad.

Dad's in the middle of the Arctic circle. Teeny little matchstick man. Maybe he's shouting, I can't hear him. Maybe he's trying to shout my name.

Mum is swanning it in Central Park. She and Virginia, both Being Famous, neither of them thinking about me for a moment.

I'm coming to get you, just you wait.

ANGELA

I had thought we would stroll through Central Park, thus crossing item 3 off our list – it should have taken half an hour or so. But as soon as I looked at Virginia in the daylight, I saw she would not be able to do it –

It was a cool, cloudless spring day. The glory of above-the-ground. I was relieved to be out in the light, and surely the walk would be good for her?

But something had happened to her in the Met, or perhaps in the other museums that morning.

Hard to remember, hard to describe. I was never clear about what I saw.

Virginia had chilled and faded. She had hesitated on the wide flight of steps that leads down from the portico of the Met, and I took her hand, and it was very cold, as cold, or nearly, as that very first time, when it felt like trailing my hand in water.

VIRGINIA

Something came up from the ground, a deep shudder

yes, they were calling me down to them
 darling Nessa *Roger* *Duncan*
reaching out beseeching me *no, I was not ready*
 to join them

dead deep cold of a place without sun

but a hand her outstretched hand touched me

ANGELA

Her light had gone out. Her face was grey. She was smaller, slighter than before.

I dropped her fingers, because I was afraid, but I tried to smile at her, I spoke to her urgently, '*Virginia?* Let's get a taxi to the bookshop.'

She didn't answer. She was suddenly stooped. She clutched her turquoise shantung against her, the curve of her collarbone sharp in the light, wrapping her rich shot-silk around her as if she was trying to hold the heat in.

'Cold,' she whispered. 'Cold as winter. I didn't know New York was so cold.'

But there by the pavement stood the line of yellow taxis, a chunky string of cheery toys, waiting for life, movement, money. Avoiding her hand, I pushed her towards them.

She was in the taxi, I slammed the door. Concentrated sunlight poured through the glass. It soared, in that small space, like an anthem, and she sat and slept for a while, which scared me.

But as she slept, she relaxed, expanded.

A flush of colour returned to her cheek.

We were heading for the big Barnes and Noble that took up five floors of the Lincoln Center. My first intention was to impress her. It was a wondrous bookshop that I knew well, with classical music in the basement and a café with a view on the fifth floor. My original mission had been rather gung-ho: to show her what my century could do. Choice! Speed! Image quality! Tables groaning with glossy hardbacks, international art books with colour photography she and her contemporaries

could only dream of, swathes of foreign languages, psychology, philosophy, politics, economics. But after the sadness of the art galleries, I was focused on showing her her own books.

We would find her in depth in the Literature section − I had no doubts; I'd bought her books there before. After that, I decided, tea and cakes. Perhaps in Le Pain Quotidien? A little bit of Europe on the 72nd, yet with a certain homespun rigour; plain wood tables, good-for-you bread. That would put life back into her veins. She could sit and drink tea and enjoy her book jackets. Nourishing titbits of critical praise! (And if my books were there, she'd be able to see mine. The critics had been kind to me. At least, the ones we selected for the jacket.)

If only it had happened that way.

Barnes and Noble's flagship store had closed. There was a small, legal notice on the central doors. The last book had been rung through the tills the week before. Soon a discount clothing store would take its place. Where once there had been five floors of books, there were now five floors of emptiness. It had gone dark, my beautiful building.

The palace of books. While my back was turned, there had been a violent overthrow. I peered through the glass and at first saw nothing, then less than nothing − empty shelving, crumpled bits of paper, a SALE sign lying at an angle to the wall.

'Oh, Virginia, I'm sorry. It's closed down. I don't know why.'

'But you said it was the best bookshop?'

'Yes. Did I? No − there are others.'

I wanted to protect her from the blow I felt. We were both authors. Authors need bookshops. Tunnels of ore waiting to be mined. But no, the canaries were dying in their cages. The human customers had rushed for daylight. I took a step back, and turned away.

The space outside the Lincoln Center was too wide, too

windy, the polished stone reflecting sky, blank, stupid, and nothing was written, and maybe one day there would be no more writing. Only images. Only surface.

'It's rather a shock to me. Everything's – gone.'

And suddenly Virginia was comforting me. 'It's just a shop,' she said. 'Don't worry. Bookshops closed down in our day too. They are only businesses, my dear. The books themselves will live elsewhere. Maybe they are going to live in your … laptops? *We have other lives, I think, I hope* … I know I wrote that somewhere. Yes, of course, *Between the Acts.*'

'But you despaired,' I said to her. I realised I was leaning on her, slightly, her triangular figure in its gorgeous clothes suddenly taller, steadier, sheltering me from the blaze of sky.

'Yes, I despaired,' she said. Briefly, her voice was rough with sorrow. 'But never about a business, dear. I thought I would go mad again. I thought my writing was a failure – '

'Yes, sorry. Stop, Virginia. What I'm feeling is trivial.'

'Sorrow is sorrow. We all despair. But now we must find another bookshop.'

'There's another good one: *Borders.*'

The next second, she left me there and struck out boldly for the kerb, where her turquoise arm with its long white pinion waved at the sun for a yellow taxi. One veered towards her and she turned to me, elated by this new success. Inside the taxi she chattered gaily about the book business in the 1920s and 1930s, the risks they took with the Hogarth Press; how they taught themselves to print with a pamphlet – 'The printing press cost us less than £20!' – the pleasure of selling 134 copies, 'but all the same, we made a profit – and then later, of course, we published Tom Eliot!'

But I still felt the cold of the shop window, the moment my eyes got used to the dark and focused on the emptiness.

There were plenty of people on the pavement outside Borders. But something strange was going on. The windows were in the grip of some fever. Garish red and yellow notices, ugly as a municipal flower-bed, pushed up brutally across the glass: '90% OFF!', they shouted, '50% OFF!' Black on yellow, fighting a glaring scarlet background. People were pouring through the doors. Virginia and I were carried in with them. Inside, though, we all paused, puzzled. You couldn't see the books behind a forest of signs, all of them shouting percentages at us.

'It's a New Year sale,' I said to her. 'Sales make a lot of money for shops.'

But then I thought, it's not New Year, it's far too late for a January sale. And '90 per cent off'? How can they make a profit if everything is 50 per cent to 90 per cent off?

My eyes were hurting. The figures were jumping, 50!, 90!, inside my head.

A plump young woman in a too-tight overall was hurrying through with a pile of books. I stopped her and asked, 'What's going on? It's a strange time to have a sale.'

She looked at me, dead-eyed like a fish, too fat, too hot, on the point of expiring. 'It's a sale,' she repeated, stubbornly.

'But is it a ...?' No, I could not say it.

And then she said it. 'A Closing Down Sale.'

'Why are you closing down?' She said nothing. '*Why are you closing down?*' I insisted, hearing my voice shoot up an octave. But I must be nice, it was not her fault, she was only a few years older than Gerda.

'Is there a Literature section?' I asked.

She looked as if she didn't know the word. Perhaps it was my English accent, for after three seconds with her brain ticking over she suddenly said, 'Oh, *literature*. Like *criticism*. That'd be in Academic. But I'm not sure there's anything left.'

We stood for a second and stared at her, and she at us,

uncomprehending. Should we have tried to bridge the gap? But she had turned and gone, it was already too late. Virginia and I stayed still for a moment, two authors becalmed in a flood-tide of panic.

'I shouldn't have brought you here,' I said. 'We're going to look for a real bookshop.'

'Could we try a smaller one?' she inquired. 'In my time, we never had such — *monstrosities.*'

'Maybe we should never have had them either. Maybe they're dinosaurs who grew too big.'

They had swallowed up food, coffee, cards, events, readings, signings, music. The books grew worse, and the choice less, 2 for 1 on celebrity memoirs, dreadful novels by chefs and actors. Till the customers noticed they were being sold rubbish.

And then, basically, we were all fucked. Not that I would ever say that to her.

But then I did. 'So we're all fucked.'

She froze for a moment, looked at me doubtfully, and then exploded into peals of laughter, rocking about in her turquoise shantung, shoulders shaking in the harsh fluorescent light — morning sunlight on a beetle's back. I thought for a moment she would actually take off! Her smoke-blue hat was whirling, spinning, and her laugh rang out and everyone was staring, and I was laughing because she was laughing ... then her hat fell off, and both of us stopped.

I had to find a place where books were still sold. I asked, on impulse, a thin elderly couple, the man silver-curled, with intelligent spectacles, reading outside a café near Borders. He gave Virginia's hat an admiring smile. Too late I saw his book was on accountancy. But he listened to me and answered eagerly, '31, West Fifty-seventh Street. Rizzoli's bookstore. It's a jewel. Honestly. You'll love it.'

We did. From the moment we saw the shop front, an arch of glass and stone and behind it, not SALE notices, but rows of books. They were playing Mozart softly inside. The galleried floors were Victorian, detailed. I went to the till on the ground floor and asked the smiling youth for Woolf. 'Virginia Woolf.' He nodded, eagerly, his long hair shaking like a spaniel's, and sent us up to the third floor.

But Third Floor was 'European Languages'. A thirty-year-old woman sat by the till, engrossed in reading. 'Excuse me. Virginia Woolf?' I asked, doubtful. 'We were sent up here.'

'Ah yes, Woolf,' she said, without surprise, eyes still on her page, and checked the computer. 'Yes. We have her in Spanish, French and let me see, yes, Italian.' Virginia's face rearranged itself, she had been afraid there would be nothing here either, but now she was uplifted, her eyes brightened.

And there they were, her boats, safe home. Sheltered in the harbour in their different liveries. 'There you are, Virginia. *A Room of One's Own* in all three languages. And several copies,' I said.

'*Una Habitación Propia*! It sounds like "Clean your room, young lady",' Virginia exclaimed, plucking out a copy, but I could see that she was pleased. 'I like the Italian title better, which makes it sound so delightfully selfish – *Una Stanza tutta per se*. Oh, and I love *La Signorina Dalloway*, so sinuous and silky … So these are the books they prefer,' she mused. 'But you said *Between the Acts* is thought my best?'

'By some critics. And some writers. Like me,' I said, shyly, for I did admire its spare certainty. 'But everyone likes *To the Lighthouse*,' I said.

I left her crouched like an awkward cormorant, bent over the books she was feeding upon, and went downstairs to find her books in English. Perhaps she would like to re-read her work. Perhaps, after I'd left for Istanbul, someone could

organise some readings – performed by a 'Woolf look-alike!' She would play Virginia Woolf to the life!

I returned to the original polite young man. 'Were you lucky with your search?' he asked me.

'Yes, thank you. But of course they were translations. I'm eager to find the originals.'

He looked slightly blank. His skin was flawless.

'In English.'

He tried his computer again. 'I'm sure we would usually have her in English,' he said. 'Perhaps someone has just bought them.'

I thought I would push it a little further. 'Have you read her yourself?'

'Oh yes, I've read her.' His voice was charming, educated, light. My liking for him grew apace.

'She's taught on university courses?'

'Yes.' He was giving me everything I asked for – except, of course, the actual books. But the bookstore was Italian, they specialised.

I should have left it at that, and we'd have been ahead. But because I was in charge of Virginia's possessions, the gloves and umbrella she handed to me (though I too am absent-minded! I too am a writer! Usually, others look after *me*), I had stopped to stuff them safely in my hold-all, which delayed me enough for one more bit of conversation. Three floors up, I heard her feet coming down, her large feet in the metal-tipped shoes that must have been standard in her day.

The young man said, with gathering confidence, 'I associate her poetry with Sylvia Plath.'

'With Sylvia Plath?' I said, puzzled. 'Her poems?'

'Yes, I suppose because they're both a little dark. Woolf's poems are dark, wouldn't you say?'

Dark, not to say unknown, I thought, but I just smiled and nodded, and the feet clumped nearer, and she was suddenly

right with us, Virginia Woolf, solidly real, smiling, clutching a carrier-bag of her books, the real author, back from the dead. Back from the mists of oblivion which swirled around us even here, blurring the angles of names and faces, unpicking carefully-worked sentences and knitting them all into a matte of grey weed. Sucking us all into a vast indifference, where Plath and Woolf could be confused, two strange women who killed themselves.

'Do you have anything by Angela Lamb?' I asked suddenly. Yes, I had been self-denying, I'd only thought of Virginia, but at the last moment, my ego woke.

Polite puzzlement: the expression I dreaded. 'English novelist, contemporary, winner of the Iceland Prize,' I gabbled. 'She isn't so well-known over here.' (I said that because Virginia was listening.)

'L-A-M-B?' he asked. He pretended to look on the computer. 'No, I'm afraid we must have sold the last copy.' He smiled at me and in his expression I read the faintest hint of pity. How many other authors went into bookshops and innocently asked for their own work?

I saw Virginia was watching me. In those luminous eyes, mixed emotions. She was sorry for me, that I could see, but there was also a fleeting look of triumph she didn't entirely manage to hide, a quirk of the lip, the briefest smirk. I didn't even hate her for it. We were trodden like grapes, we went down into mulch, only a few names got on to the wine-bottles.

I couldn't bear to meet her gaze. 'Come along, Virginia.'

Just as we were going through the door, the nice young American voice hailed me. 'Ma'am? I've found something here. Forthcoming. The paperback of *Lost Children*. By Angela Lamb. That was the name ...? Says here it won the Caffe Nero Prize (we're not familiar with that over here) and is the book of the upcoming movie. With Brad Pitt and Angelina Jolie. In

any case, we've got five copies on order. If you like, I will set one aside for you.'

I beamed upon him. Yes, exactly, Brad and Angelina, take that! Gerda had been insane with excitement, it seemed more about Angelina than Brad. Only I and a few other people knew that the film, in fact, was not a goer. Scripts one to four had all been crap. But I wasn't going to spoil his illusions.

'Don't worry, I'll be in Turkey,' I told him. 'But really – you've been most helpful.'

Together we practically sailed down the street, ready for our drink at the Algonquin. We had both survived the waves of destruction!

I said, 'Virginia, I'll drink to you.'

(I tried to forget that before my reprieve I had felt a moment of temptation to tell Virginia that the assistant had confused her with an American poet ...)

She said, 'Angela, I'll drink to *you.*'

GERDA

Would she still be with the mad old woman? (Which is what I still thought Virginia was, because I hadn't yet gone to my mother's bookshelves and borrowed her books to read on the plane, in order to find more reasons to hate her.)

They were probably getting pissed together!

I've decided NEVER to drink wine. Mum gets Idiotic on wine, and talks a lot about herself. (Except when she's with Dad; they just quarrel.) (Well, to be fair, they SOMETIMES quarrel, and now of course that's the bit I remember. Sometimes it made them all lovey-dovey, and sometimes Mum could be quite funny, though I did not encourage her.)

All right, I couldn't bring my dad home, but at least I had Mum's address in New York, not that she gets any credit for that, when she said she and Virginia were moving I nagged her to tell me, in case I needed her, obviously, and she emailed back 'Don't be silly, Gerda, you are so wonderfully self-reliant! But you'll like the name, it's the Wordsmiths Hotel.'

Mum had the conference to go to, too. The diary said she would be back in a week, and obviously I couldn't wait till then.

Staying in the house-which-was-once-my-home was like being the last bit of coke in a can. Poked back in the fridge, with the bubbles gone.

'Self-reliant'. It sounds OK. A bit like 'valiant', a word I like. Everyone should rely on themselves. Nobody does that more than me (though this is an Assertion, not a Fact, as my

History teacher is always saying.) But it's not enough to have ONLY yourself. My namesake, Gerda, in Hans Andersen, was helped by a lot of different people on her Great Journey Round the World to look for Kay (who despite his girl's name, was a boy, of course. Cool for a girl to save a boy, but she still needed help from the Sorceress and the woman of Lapland and the woman of Finland and best of all, the Little Robber Maid, who kept a reindeer, and lent him to Gerda, and gave her berries, but stole her fur muff, and had a knife, oh the Little Robber Maid is TOTALLY cool. She is my favourite character.)

I have been self-reliant about going to New York. I booked my own ticket, I packed my bag, I printed off maps from the internet. Such a sensible city, so clear and straight! I went to New York once with my dad, when I was seven years old, and kept a diary, which I realise now is excellent, though when I was eight I thought it was pathetic. And although I don't really remember it, there had been ages when he wasn't at home, and I only vaguely knew I had a dad. Mum does remember and it makes her cross, when she feels like having a go at Dad. 'You were never around when she was little.' But then they fell in love again or something, and Dad came back from Denmark or wherever and lived with us, and of course I thought it would be for ever ...

Still best of all was having Dad to myself, so I loved our trips, with Mum Not Nagging. And America was our first Big Adventure, so sometimes I replay it all in my head.

Dad bought me striped cutoffs and expensive rollerblades, which caused a row after we got back from New York because Mum insisted they were 'dangerous'. (I love my dad. My dad is − my dad. He is always doing 'dangerous' things. And he took me to FAO Schwarz's toyshop, even though it was 'not ecological', as Mum pointed out, which was mean of her.

And later she relented and let me go rollerblading, as soon as she saw I was good at it. She even got some herself, and fell over, and Dad said 'You're too old for that,' and she went red in the face, and silent, though later she pretended she thought it was funny.)

I won't go to FAO Schwarz this time, because I am almost too old for toys. I do remember it, though, being happy. Why must being happy make you sad?

Being with Dad was more exciting than anything, just on our own, har har on Mum, so I got all the treats, and Dad was mine. But we knew we'd go home, and Mum would be waiting, and she would hug us, and tell us off, and make us have baths and proper meals. We knew we would all be together again. And home was home. But that was then.

VIRGINIA

Oh, the Algonquin was marvellous. The silky calm after the blaring streets.

Yet, oh, the Algonquin made me sad!

ANGELA

I loved it as soon as we walked inside – it still had that feel of the 1930s. High ceilings, elegant lamps. Red, so red, with satin-striped armchairs and rose-patterned carpets. Cool and quiet.

VIRGINIA

Just a hint of the brothel about it; which, for writers, is appropriate.

This was the New York I might have visited with Leonard if we had said 'yes' to that vulgarian. The American woman who came to see us and offered to display us like monkeys in a cage. The money was extraordinary, so we listened. 'You will give some talks and answer questions.' I did admire her brazenness. The profit motive was all there was to it. She wanted to make money to buy more of the food and drink that had made her skin so shiny and pink, stretched tight over mounds of flesh.

I don't know why I hated her.

She was a different kind of woman, one who made me feel … insubstantial. Both superior and inferior, for I couldn't understand any world she lived in. (I was different now. I wanted to know.)

We said 'No' to her, so we never saw New York, though

every time I had a book published we sent over hundreds of special copies that I'd sat for hours patiently signing. I wouldn't have bothered, but Leonard insisted. 'America is an important market.' He was practical, Leonard, as well as clever. If he were here, he would know what to do, I would not be dependent on her ... But Angela tries to be kind to me.

The voices in the Algonquin were a low, polite murmur, and the music played in the same gentle register, so it took a few minutes to separate the two. We sat at a table at the back, in shadow.

As we got used to the dark, cream lilies bloomed like small pale faces from vases in corners. Writers met here, the Algonquin set; we knew about them in England of course. Dorothy Parker was a name on our horizon, a little danger behind my back like a wasp buzzing & fizzing at the window – but she was a journalist, not a real writer! – (I never strove to be a wit) – and the more friends urged me to read her stuff, the more I knew I never would. She was far too young! These clever young women ... Hadn't she been unhappy in love?

'When did Dorothy Parker die?' I asked Angela. I wanted to be sure.

'Oh ages ago. Before I was born.'

'Did she have children?'

'I don't think so.'

A tiny surge of satisfaction. 'She was very funny, but she wasn't happy?'

'How would we know? She was really funny. And good, Virginia. Really good. I am surprised you never read her. She's the only one whose name has survived. Of all that circle. She eclipsed them all.'

Ah, so Angela admired her. Why should I feel jealous? A thought struck me. 'Did she – she didn't – kill herself, did she?'

ANGELA

There was a half-hidden note of longing. She didn't want to be the only one. It shocked me, but I told her the truth. 'In the end she died of a heart attack. But you're not far wrong. She tried four times.'

VIRGINIA

I pitied her then. To have gone through the horror. To try and fail so many times. I envied her, too, because she beat her Furies.

Now I knew she was dead, I wished I had read her. I no longer needed to be – jealous. The ugly thing I felt for Katherine Mansfield, and she'd died too, and I was sad.

And then I wanted to write about my feelings, as I had long ago when Katherine died. To wield the delicate tweezers of words; to pick up the sentiment ready for dissection; to hold myself under the pitiless light. That urge to write, the pleasure-muscles tensing ...

Before they could move, the new fear pounced. The novel sense of helplessness. I had started to flinch away from the attempt, in case a series of accidents – yes, I was sure, they were just accidents – my weakened hand, the hopeless pen – should harden into a change of state. In case I could not – simply could not –

Like the young man who happens to fall; has another fall; so many excuses. So many good reasons why it should happen. But he falls again; he falls again. Until the inevitable diagnosis.

I dared not voice it to myself.

Could I survive, mute, diminished?

Each time I tried, the void had yawned. The paper seemed to eat my words. It stared at me: a terminal blankness.

Terror winked. I had to write. Don't think about it, think about it, think.

(Was it because of my decades of silence? Had my voice dried, constricted?)

ANGELA

'Dorothy Parker's like you, Virginia. She's survived as the others fade. In Britain, no-one still remembers, I don't know, Marc Connelly or Robert Sherwood. Everyone knows Dorothy Parker.'

VIRGINIA

'Maybe the others weren't any good?' I needed to believe it happened for a reason.

Yet, surely, Duncan and Roger had been good. That feeling of emptiness in the Met, the sense of bodies being washed downstream ...

They can paint no more. Have no more chances.

ANGELA

'Alice Duer Miller was part of the circle, a gifted poet, but she's disappeared. I'm afraid it's just what happens, Virginia. History has to simplify things. And someone vivid like Dorothy Parker – or you – well, you throw the rest into shadow.'

VIRGINIA

'Vivid. Yes, I like that word.'

She thinks me vivid.

Yes, I was good.

There was nothing to be frightened of, then, was there? The small white faces, the Algonquin lilies, bloomed round the room, peering towards us, wanting to be with us. Longing to be vivid, out in the light, talking, writing, shining with luck, the luck we have.

Yes, I had everything, because I'd come back. That was the

luck. To be here in the moment …

But if I couldn't … of course I could. I was a writer. Writers must write.

Something dislodged inside my brain. I looked at Angela, hating her. I must not hate her. I was slipping, falling …

'I'm hungry,' I said. 'I'm thirsty, too. Will they bring us some, what do you call it, nibbles?' (It was a vulgar word she used.)

ANGELA

'Bring us some nibbles, waiter, please. And tea, Virginia? Or something stronger?'

VIRGINIA

'Wine, please. I need a drink.'

ANGELA

'Perhaps champagne? Or a nice red?'

VIRGINIA

'I'll have champagne. A vat. A bucket.'

Angela's painted eyes flicked wide with shock.

ANGELA

She hadn't had a drink for over half a century. Is it surprising that it went to her head?

We toasted each other. As I chinked her glass – she recoiled minutely, as from a *faux pas* – the volume of the music rose to meet us.

VIRGINIA

Jazz standards of the 1930s. Sadness blew across the sands. A cold sea-mist. The room was thinning …

ANGELA

Her pupils widened, and she was lost. I watched a veil come between us. She put down her glass and played with her hands, one clutching the other, wringing and squeezing.

'Virginia?' She looked at the floor. 'Virginia, are you all right?'

She picked up her glass and drank deep before she answered.

VIRGINIA

'Yes. No. I'm not sure.'

ANGELA

Her champagne flute was two-thirds empty.

VIRGINIA

For a moment I felt cold as death. But as I drank, the bubbles expanded, blood came coursing back through my veins. Briefly, I felt warm towards her, and yes, I had to talk to somebody. 'You see, I have been trying to write …'

ANGELA

'Trying to write? Yes, I saw you. That evening in your room at the Wordsmith. Have you been writing every day?' At last, the longed-for conversation! Might we talk, one writer to another?

Her beautiful mouth twitched at the corner.

VIRGINIA

'Something's … amiss. Things keep going wrong.'

ANGELA

'You mean, with the writing?'

VIRGINIA

Something in her eyes: an avid glint. A dog scenting a whiff of death.

'I didn't say that.' But the drink drove me. 'It's not easy to talk about. I'm not, it isn't, it isn't getting done.'

ANGELA

'Virginia, I'm all ears.'

VIRGINIA

I saw ears bursting from her face, fat and shiny and obscene. Budding from her pouter-pigeon chest, rose-pink fungi on her arms, her hands. Yes, all ears. Was she leering at me?

ANGELA

'If anyone can understand it, it's me.'

No answer. Virginia leaned back in her chair.

Two twins walked past, with identical frowns, heading over to the table at the back where there were booklets of Algonquin history. Their hair fell straight in long fringed bobs, heavy as rulers, a style they were too old for. Matching suits. Combative heels. I thought, they will never escape one another.

Virginia had finished her champagne. Maybe I should have sat and waited. But how was I to contain myself? *Now, at last, we could talk about writing.* What I had longed for from the very start, when she appeared, like an answer to my prayer –

I summoned a waiter to play for time. 'Two more glasses.'

'No problem, Ma'am.'

I had to grope to find the words. Yes, I was shy, but I was excited. Our drinks were delivered, I raised my glass, she looked away, but I plunged in.

'I'm not surprised you find writing hard. This world's so new and strange to you. I myself have been blocked of late. I

mean, I published only last year, the reviews were fine, the sales were great, but it's not like turning on a tap, is it?' (Virginia twitched slightly. I hoped we'd connected.) 'There've been the problems with, you know, Edward … And you and I have been quite busy.' (I meant: 'I've been busy looking after *you*.') 'I'm not totally sure what to write about, though something, somewhere, may be coming together … You get to a certain stage in your career – you haven't read me, Virginia, that's fine, but I am quite famous, and it *is* a pressure – didn't you find? Was it true for you?'

Her eyes were fixed, cold and still. A distant pool I could not see into. 'It's even harder for you, of course, because in a way, this would be your comeback novel!'

Her fingers clenched on the stem of the glass, her great lids dropped. What was she thinking?

I wondered, *is this going well?*

But I took a gulp and pressed on regardless. 'That's partly why I came to New York. And why I wanted to write about you. I thought, get back to first principles. Why, you know, is your writing so – great? What is the point of – what we do?'

I found myself blushing. Had I been clumsy?

VIRGINIA

I wanted to spit. Did she think we were the same? Did this woman presume to share my feelings? She thought she saw into my soul. She thought we would share 'confidences'. She thought I was 'blocked', like any novice! Soon she would be giving me 'advice'. I held my lids shut for a long, long time, and hid inside my world of darkness.

ANGELA

Was it possible she had gone to sleep?

Very slowly the anger drained away. Foolish of me to confide in her. Foolish to let the world peer in. Yield a chink, and they forced one open, left one wet and crushed on the sand.

I did not believe she was a cruel woman.

Nor, indeed, completely stupid. I had never read a word she had written. Now I vowed I never would.

'The pens,' I snapped. 'Those stupid pens.' I had decided not to complain, but the words leaped out of their own accord. 'That old man sold us defective pens.'

'Pens?' she said, puzzled. 'Oh, the pens from Moshe … The one I used was quite OK. Here, borrow my biro. It's a pen, Virginia. Just so you have something. Just for now.'

I took the thing. It looked cheap and synthetic. I held it firmly away from me.

No, I was growing angry again. I put the biro in my bag, breathed deeply, managed to say 'Thank you.' Let it all leak away into the music.

My fault, mine, to have shown my wound.

That terrible feeling of nakedness, akin to what I once felt with Gerald, when I was a child, helpless, small. Or that terrifying sense of being undressed when I sent my first novels to publishers. It was why we started the Hogarth Press, so that never again — never again — would I feel I had been passed around among strangers, naked as a baby from the waist down, to be judged and prodded, discussed, handled.

I drank down the wine, and became the jazz.

Angela sat beside me looking worried, her stupid frown, anxious mouth, as if she knew things had gone astray.

Yes she should be nervous. True, she admired me. She was big and awkward and unhappy.

Yet she was the only friend I had.

ANGELA

'They have obviously forgotten the nibbles. I think I'm pissed.
Are you OK?'

VIRGINIA

Saxophone, piano, a blue swell of memories. It was the music
of the past. 'A foggy day … in London town …'

ANGELA

'Virginia? Do you want to go home? Is it the music? You look
so sad.'

VIRGINIA

'Partly sad … also happy. The music makes me think of
Leonard.' I could share my heart, perhaps, my woman's heart,
but never, never would I share my writing.

ANGELA

'I hope I didn't offend you, just now. Talking, you know, about
the work?' I hated myself for sounding meek.

She shook her head in a definite manner that closed the
door upon that room. It was unspoken, but I understood. She
would not talk to me about writing. It hurt me, but I had to
accept it.

VIRGINIA

'It's all forgotten. I wasn't even listening.'

ANGELA

Why did she have to humiliate me? No, I wouldn't let her make
me angry.

Probably she was just unhappy.

I thought, I told her I published last year. She hadn't written

a book in decades. Was it that – Virginia was jealous?

Yes, of course. She was jealous of me. My mood picked up. I could afford to be generous.

'More champagne?' She didn't answer. 'Two more glasses.' I made myself smile. We were getting into a drinker's rhythm. Thank God, some canapés arrived. Both of us fell on them like gulls, our fingers stumbling together on the plate. Soon we would be holding hands.

VIRGINIA

'Something I've been meaning to ask you. Something about – about – Leonard.'

I had tried to ask her many times before. My tongue tangled; my tongue tumbled.

But all round the room, the flowers helped me, the white faces, the white hands, the writers reaching from another world. Don't abandon us. We need you. Tell of your love. Remember us. Mention our names, or else we die. The lilies and I became pure longing.

'I hope Leonard wasn't alone, that's all. I hope he did not live alone. You won't tell me – will you tell me, please?'

ANGELA

The question I dreaded and expected.

How could I tell her? That he loved Trekkie Parsons, that they lived side by side for much of his life. The thing he'd said that saddened me, even though it was in another lifetime, with Virginia dead and long past caring: 'Knowing and loving Trekkie has been the best thing in my life.'

I mumbled my way out of it. 'I think he was all right.'

VIRGINIA

'Isn't it in your – laptop? You said that everything was there.'

ANGELA

Her voice was sharp, her eyes suspicious. I did not want to lie to her. 'You have to search. There are millions of words. Sometimes you cannot find the answer.'

VIRGINIA

As if I were a child to be lied to. There must have been another woman.

But Leonard loved me. His wild monkey. I know he found me beautiful.

Yes, I was loved. That I never doubted.

In any life there are losses, sadnesses. Nessa loved Duncan more than he loved her. But Leonard loved me while I lived, as I loved Leonard. Equally.

Dearly, deeply we loved each other; lived for each other in our moment.

They thought I was cold, but what did they know of the way my love and I lay together? On summer nights. Those summer nights … even if I failed him. In the ultimate place. He was my love. We lay together. Is one caress better than another?

Because I was clever, they had to gloat that I was not a proper woman.

Yes, they were glad I could not be a mother

 grim old men, refusing me
Leonard's young face mimicking theirs

 'Virginia, it's not sensible we must refrain
 you are too fragile'

I could have been a mother too
 could have been loved as Nessa was

but they all refused *'the Goat is mad'*

 'everyone knows the Goat is mad'

No, I must not go down that track

 the more I drink, it surfaces

 fin like a blade black, flashing
 dark water beside the path

under the weed, the arid rock

 (the pen-nib breaks, my fingers bleed)

shrunken shapes at the turn of the road

 beckoning me to confide in them

rope ready to slip round my neck

 stopping me writing staring, pointing

'Can't you write, Virginia?'

 'Oh, so sorry to see your pain'

'Maybe we could talk about it?'

 holding their sides and cackling

Get away, run, while they are still distant,
 cartoon enemies, weak and small,

hunkered down to wait by the roadside

'Tell them to turn the music up!' I heard my own voice, loud, confident. Angela went to do my bidding.

Dance me away into this tune Take it away, Snakehips Johnson
 Oh dear yes, I will conquer this mood

it doesn't matter
San fairy ann

A foggy day in London Town

They bombed the Café de Paris *No-one can say we were not happy ...*
 We will defeat them England will win

I won't be beaten I'll write again

ANGELA
'Virginia, you're not drinking your champagne. You asked for that last glass. Don't waste it. Virginia? – oh, well done!'
 Suddenly she had tipped it down.
 'Something very practical – our trip to the Statue of Liberty.' (Those 's'es came out thick, slurred.) 'If you want to go, must be tomorrow. My last day.'
 She looked at me and repeated it blankly.

VIRGINIA
'Your last day.'

(*my last day I must not think about my last day*)

ANGELA

The drink had lessened my inhibitions. I reached out and stroked her hand. 'Virginia, dear, are you all right? Still on for the Statue of Liberty tomorrow?'

VIRGINIA

'I like the sound of "tomorrow".'

A beautiful word, so sweet and light. I used to be afraid of tomorrow.

At the corner of my eye, those three tiny figures.

No, I have left them behind in hell.

ANGELA

'What time shall we go? Late morning? Virginia? *Virginia?*'

She slow-danced a spoon around the table.

VIRGINIA

'Yes, it will have to be tomorrow.'

I let myself be lifted by the music. *I was a stranger in a city ... I had a feeling of surrender ... the outlook was decidedly blue ...*

And happiness was suddenly stirring, the music was yearning for its major key and I was on the pavements of London with Leonard, we saw two magpies, the sky was bright blue, I drank the rest of my glass in one, and inside my bloodstream there were dancing bubbles.

ANGELA

'So are we on for tomorrow? No hats, Virginia, it will be breezy. Please bring that nice yellow coat you bought. If you don't mind, I'll wear my blue one. We will both look beautiful!' I found myself giggling inanely. (I must get home and drink strong coffee.) She might have a hangover, but what the hell? 'We'll ask a tourist to photograph us. I do want

a record of us together.' In her weakened state I thought I'd risk asking.

VIRGINIA

'I am a little afraid of boats.'

Absurd, I have already drowned. Yet here I am, still 'a little afraid', as I was always a little afraid when my father took us out in the boat …

ANGELA

'Must get the bill. Virginia – '

VIRGINIA

'I might just sit here a while longer.'

ANGELA

'How will you get home?'

She didn't answer, she was deep in thought, but when she spoke, her voice was calm.

VIRGINIA

'I'll sit here for a while, with Leonard.'

They were playing 'Just one of those things'. One of our favourites. He sat there beside me.

I needed Angela to go away.

'How will I get home? In a taxi, of course. I can command New York taxis.'

ANGELA

Normally I wouldn't have left her, but I was in no state to take decisions.

'Virginia – I believe you. See you in the lobby, 10 AM.'

Angela is walking briskly through the sunlight near Battery Park towards the ticket office for Liberty Island, but Virginia is lagging.

VIRGINIA

'Yes yes I admit it, you're right, I shouldn't have had those extra glasses.'

ANGELA

'My fault. I shouldn't have left you there.'

VIRGINIA

'I enjoyed it.' (*Pause.*) 'I am an adult.'

ANGELA

'A policeman found you sitting on a fire hydrant. You're very lucky he brought you back.' (*She walks even faster.*)

VIRGINIA

'I wasn't sitting.'

ANGELA

'What were you doing?'

VIRGINIA

'I had attempted to leapfrog it. That is why I cannot keep up this pace.'

ANGELA (*laughs, slows up*)
'All right, Virginia. I hoped we would get the twelve o'clock boat ... but maybe time doesn't matter.'

VIRGINIA
'No, time matters, don't be absurd.'
　　So hard to understand while you're in it. Only when you're near the end ...
　　(*Suddenly striding out*) 'Yes, we must catch this ferry, you're right. You see, I don't want to miss anything. In case ... they take me back.'

(*Pause.*)

　'I do so love it, in the light.'

ANGELA (*puts her arm round her for the first time*)
'I hope you had a good time last night?'

VIRGINIA
'They have little books of quotes at the back. I tore out a poem by Dorothy Parker.'

ANGELA
'You tore the book?'
　　She looked ashamed.

VIRGINIA
'All right, I admit it. I tried to copy it, but the stupid biro didn't work. The one you gave me. It doesn't work.'

ANGELA
She was suddenly annoyed, her cheeks flushed with blood.
　　'Well I'm sorry the biro didn't work,' I said. 'But for

goodness sake, Virginia, we'll buy another.'

Her frown relaxed. 'I suppose we can. It will be all right, won't it?'

'Of course it will.'

Then she showed me the poem and I nearly fell over. It was 'Resumé!'

'I love that poem!'

VIRGINIA (*cheering up again*)
'Let's read it aloud!'

ANGELA
And we did, badly, both holding the paper, when we got to the quay, panting and laughing –

'Razors pain you,
Rivers are damp ...'

Then we decided to write our own version. It was such fun! We made up the lines together, and I wrote it down in my notebook.

Shavers cut you,
Streams are muddy,
Poisons gut you
And jumping's bloody.
Shooting's noisy,
Hanging's a dive,
Gas is queasy –
GIRL, STAY ALIVE!

It's not every day you get to write a poem with Virginia Woolf and Dorothy Parker.

43

ANGELA

We missed the ferry, not that it mattered. I teased Virginia a lot – I think she half-enjoyed being treated as a wicked woman of the world. 'Leonard used to monitor my drinking,' she said. 'He didn't like me to get too excited. It was nice to let go, just once in a while. I felt – careless. I just didn't care. And because he's not here, I looked after myself. I had to get myself back home.'

The strange thing was, she was looking younger, despite the headache that creased her forehead. Her cheeks were pinker, her jaw-line firmer.

And then there was her *joie de vivre*. Her endless curiosity, which made her seem twenty years younger than she was. Wherever we were, her eyes swooped around like birds skimming back from a long migration. On the boat, she bought herself two packets of biros: she seemed ridiculously pleased.

I liked her company.

I liked Virginia.

Even when we had to wait for forty-five minutes, snaking in line through the sun and wind with hordes of heavy-legged tourists in shorts ... no, probably they were Americans. Why did Americans always look like tourists?

Perhaps because they wore so few clothes, though this was only a faint spring heat-wave, with wintry breezes still blowing off the sea and a crisping of small white curls on the water. As if they'd thought: Spring! Time for a sun tan. As if they did not understand weather, or seasons, living as they did in airconned homes. Why should I be snippy? They were bent on fun.

That day felt like a holiday. Everyone was there, waiting for the voyage, the world and his wife in sunny mood. Dreadlocked young African Americans gyrating their hips to the rhythm of their iPods. Half a dozen Muslim youths in white tunics, clustered together in a laughing murmur, but every so often looking around them, their black beards jutting defensively forward. Later I saw the grim body-search as they went through security for the ferry. Three elderly, masculine, English women, two of them in nautical caps and blazers, speaking in voices nearly as fluting as Virginia's, shouting about *Fidelio* at the Met. And, of course, the children – the children. The children, so much lighter than us, doing handstands and cartwheels, running about. Except the ones who were too fat to run, standing with stout knees pressed against one another, their cheeks churning secret comforts against the gum.

And with me suddenly were two Gerdas, the red-haired child of five or six who used to dance like an elf in the sunlight and the Gerda of today, heavier, steadier. How my girlie would love to be here. She had always loved holidays, travel, adventure. I suppose in that way she resembled her father, though of course he took everything much too far …

My dearest daughter. My darling girl. Late at night, when my chaperone duties were over, I started so many emails to her, falling asleep with them still unfinished, the drafts a layer-cake of good intentions.

Not that I should wholly blame Virginia. Sometimes I had certainly put work first. But that was nothing to feel guilty about. Someone had to think about the bills. Her father had contributed almost nothing during the first few years of Gerda's life, and now he swanned casually off around the world, but he never seemed to worry, he never felt guilty!

But maybe all of us should have felt guilty, in our tiny, fractured, nuclear families. Yes, Mum and Dad had helped with

Gerda, but of course they grew old, and of course they died, and a working mother must sustain a career, so the children never get quite enough care – not even with the most responsible parents. I had tried to be responsible, from the start.

Lucky Virginia. Poor Virginia. Nothing to feel guilty about. But no small hands around her heart.

As we filed on to the boat and climbed the steps to the viewing deck, I said to her 'My daughter loves boats. Gerda would really enjoy this trip.'

But the wind took my words, and she didn't know Gerda, and in any case, the boat was leaving the quay and her eyes were already fastened on the view, the dazzling expanse of blue water, the skyscrapers diminishing into the distance, grey and blue and bronze and pink, and there across the bay, the pale grey-green lady, bleached by distance and the sun. She held up her torch: her arm looked white. Still far away, she looked small, hermetic.

Still far away, but growing by the minute.

I had loved the Statue of Liberty since my first trip to New York, ten years ago, when I first got an American publisher. I felt she held that beacon up for me. Her stone tablet became my book. That vision of a welcome to America.

Today, she was waiting for Virginia and me. I fixed my eyes and my hopes on her.

Yet none of it was personal. She was beautiful because she welcomed us all. The 'huddled masses', the refugees … even if their children were those fat adolescents sulking with popcorn in the queue for the ferry.

(I knew that Gerda had put on weight, most of it in that first term at school. Was even that going to be my fault?)

Virginia practically ran round the boat, this morning's stiffnesses forgotten. I followed the yellow of her coat as she jostled boldly for the best view among the batteries of clicking

cameras. As the statue hove huge out of the sea, the battle for the side of the boat grew fiercer, but somehow Virginia was holding her own.

Perhaps she was so eccentric-looking that no-one bothered to object – of course I had got used to her, but her lambent eyes and full tremulous lips, so classic, so Victorian, looked even more astonishing above her brisk yellow twenty-first-century trench-coat. I watched her changing sides of the boat with a great sliding 'Whoop!' as it veered around the approach to the jetty of Liberty Island, her hair flying free from its normal bun, laughing happily into the wind as the horn of the boat played a great trombone –

The Statue of Liberty towered above us.

Then a crush of people fought to be first off the gangway, and I watched her anxiously from the back, her slim yellow back marking her tracks, her wild grey halo bobbing up and down, while the boat docked, and I saw, amazed, she was making progress, she was pogo-ing through, she was burrowing headlong towards her goal, now she was almost at the front of the line –

They opened the gates.

Virginia stormed it!

She was off over the grass ahead of all of us.

I was left panting far behind.

VIRGINIA

Once one's off the boat, one approaches from behind. I was desperate to get ahead of the mob. She loomed ahead of us, too big to take in, planted on her big cairn of brick. I was panting, half-running, to stay ahead and I could not hurry while looking upwards, so I saw her in snatched glances, like a Wyndham Lewis drawing, her back, her huge foot, her tremendous arm, the strong, groomed hair, so different from mine ...

Then I rounded the corner, came out on the green foreshore, and faced her at last. I saw her whole.

Yes, I saw her clear for a second. I wept.

For there was my fond, foolish dream. The model of the just female warrior. Tall, kindly, an amazon. The mother brave enough to hold up the light — Vanessa's dust jacket for *To the Lighthouse*. Her strong, bent arms, her intent gaze, the way she stoutly faced the sea, searching out those in need of her, the storm-tossed ships from all over the world —

(not turning inwards as poor Mother did, reading the Bible, mending the sock the servants were too tired to darn, polishing the hearth that was 'not polished properly' — 'Sit down, Julia, you'll exhaust yourself' — visiting the sick and caring for little ones, not her own little ones but those of the benighted, chastising herself for what she had not done, rebuking us mutely for our failures of duty, driving herself onwards, always on, her cheeks growing hollower, her face falling in, her eyes flaming brighter as they sank into their sockets, her whole body burning up from within like a narrow white candle stuck fast on a table, flaring up, finally, then fading out. That terrible attrition behind closed doors. Only terror for us, locked outside, whispering children without understanding. She grew weaker, finally, until she died. How did that help us? We were left lonely.)

Here she was, now, my Liberty. No-one could interfere with her. Her body was formed from massive blocks of limestone, her crown an immense defence of green metal. She did not worry. She did not fret. Her strong calves walked. She was marching on the future.

I stood in her shadow, near her huge feet. I was ahead of the crowd, alone with her. Her head was hundreds of feet up in

the air, her massive eyeballs scanned the horizon, looking for those who needed care.

I felt I was with Mother, too. That she, and all the suffering, were here. That with Liberty, mothers could be tired children. That they could rest, and she would care. Julia's head leant upon my shoulder.

The air was cool, but the wind had dropped. I realised how exhausted I was. I had been dragged through time, summoned into this world like a book requisitioned from a distant library ... A great ache of weariness wrapped my body. Sleep drifted up and took me down. I was safe to fall, I was coming home ...

ANGELA.

'Virginia? *Virginia?*'

I couldn't see her, but I knew she was there. A huge crowd circled the monument. The twenty-first century having fun: taking photos, playing loud music, wrestling, shrieking, eating their picnics, cross-eyed boys playing video-games, three Japanese girls in pink trying to break-dance, a Chinese teacher with terrible acne shouting and sweating as he marshalled the children, two tall blonde sisters – northern Europeans? – doing double-jointed yoga near the foot of the statue, a circle of well-behaved primary school children cross-legged on the ground around their leader, each with their different-coloured lunchbox, a roundel of plastic flowers on the green – I hurried through them – where was Virginia?

Then at the centre, a huddle of people, a cage of figures bending over someone.

For a moment, as I pushed my way through to her, I thought that she – that she was gone. But just as I got there, the cage-bars loosened, the bent figures straightened, I saw Virginia – stretched on the ground – but yes, she was moving. As I called

her name, she began to sit up. I could see in her eyes, small-pupiled, stunned, that she felt overrun with people, pressing all round her, blocking out the sky.

'Could you give her some air?' I asked them, brusquely. 'Let her breathe and my friend will be fine.' There were offers of help, which I rejected. They drifted away, disappointed.

She leant on me as we went back to the boat. Her face was pleated, drained and grey. I said 'What's the matter?' but she couldn't speak. I sat her beside me on one of the long seats, settled her head against my shoulder.

It was the closest we had been. Through my warm blue coat I could feel the heat, as if her brain were burning her. I did not dare to move, or disturb her, though part of me wanted to stroke her hair, her grey-brown hair, more flyaway than ever since I had prevailed upon her to wash it – I suppose I longed to smooth it, tidy it. Yes, there was still some brown in there. Gold strands gleamed in the afternoon sunlight: had I noticed that before? (And of course I thought of Gerda's hair: her beloved head with its hanks of bright chestnut. Such beautiful hair, though when she was little, she had been bullied as a 'ginger'. No-one would dare bully Gerda now!)

The siren sounded to warn us we were sailing. Virginia stirred and sat up straight.

'It's me, Virginia. Are you all right?'

'Yes. Don't fuss. Of course I am.'

But she sat and shivered, almost silent, as the boat wheeled round to cross the bay and the life of the boat blared on all round her.

'Shall I get some tea?'

Virginia ignored me. But when I brought her some, she began to recover.

VIRGINIA

'Thank you. Thank you for your trouble.'

I think she must have thought I fainted. At the feet of the Statue, the great bronze mother. I know that I was safe with her. It felt like sleep, perfect contentment. Sleep, yes, or something deeper.

But when I woke, I was no longer alone. I was being eaten by the twenty-first century. The smell of these people, fatty, cheap, a mixture of sweat and something synthetic – in my day people didn't smell like petrol. They swirled around me like a poisoned sea.

Then Angela came and took me away. I don't remember getting back on the boat, but when she brought me tea, sips of life returned to me.

ANGELA

'Look, you can still see the statue.'

VIRGINIA

I turned for one last look at her, my grey-green statue with her fine Greek profile. By now the contours of freedom had blurred. Against the light, she was just a stick, a stick surmounted by a needle. But if I screwed up my eyes at the sun, I could make out the line of the arm in the centre, reaching up, up, holding the beacon skyward. Straight and strong against the blaze of day, tiny and brave on the expanse of sea.

I still felt the thrill: she still moved me.

Yet somewhere, the stone of disappointment.

Freedom had come, to some at least. Freedoms we never thought possible. It was ugly: it was beautiful. I had not understood, in *Between the Acts*. Freedom for the masses is not aesthetic.

Everyone was free – 'But what does it mean? How do they

use their American freedom?' I didn't realise I had spoken aloud.

ANGELA
'That isn't the point. Everyone is free. *Everyone*. That's really something.'

VIRGINIA
Yes, everyone was free, from the women milling around me on the boat in their trousers and shorts, their cheap necklaces and unflattering brassieres, shouting at their husbands in loud coarse voices – to the Africans, who were everywhere, chewing toffee and nuts, throwing the wrappers on the ground, laughing with their children, who had sticky faces, no longer in chains but out for the day, talking louder than everyone else; here were the servants, out with the masters: there was no distinction between the two, those women carolling about the opera and the big-thighed, ignorant working class; half of these people were hooked to machines, little white ones that hung from their ears or bright-coloured boxes in their pockets; homosexuals were free, for couples of men were holding hands quite openly, and when we got to the Statue, two men embraced and pressed their lips together and laughed – and how is it possible – part of me flinched, when Bloomsbury was full of buggers like Lytton?

This was freedom: we had longed for it.

I had seen it all: it was done; it was finished.

Yes, I thought, and now I am tired. Tired to death of what I have seen, and what has been lost, in this dazzling new century, with the masses forever pressing forward till those like me will be trampled underfoot – we have been trampled, for they are all gone, Desmond and Lytton, G. E. Moore, Maynard, Leonard and all the others, those wry, clever faces, those cultured brains

with their subtle cargo of Latin and Greek, their skilful phrases, their philosophy, their discriminations, their subtleties in art and life – all of it discarded and out of date, their names forgotten, the velleities lost that they argued over till the morning hours; the bookshops are gone, the books are gone, the crowd round the Statue hardly used language – and who will I write for, if I write about this?

Maybe the past can never write the present.

Long strands of grey hair blew into my mouth, perhaps I should get it shingled, like hers, my spine ached, my feet had swelled … I felt I might die of extreme fatigue. The moment swelled and receded all round me. I'd come too late. I could see nothing.

Yes, I had had my vision. But that was decades, a life, ago. I had my vision in my own century.

Angela understood this world. I did not envy her for belonging.

But oh, she must not leave me here. Angela was my only hope. 'Angela, please, I want to come with you.'

ANGELA
'Of course, we're going back to the hotel.'

VIRGINIA
'No, you must take me with you tomorrow.'

ANGELA
'Tomorrow?'

VIRGINIA
'To Turkey.'

ANGELA

'I can't, Virginia. You're joking, of course.'

VIRGINIA

'No, I promise, I am not joking.'

ANGELA

'Virginia, you know it's all arranged. All sorted with your friends in the lobby. You'll be perfectly safe at the Wordsmiths Hotel. They will look after you beautifully.' (I could hear I was doing my annoying voice, the voice that you use to bear children down with extra-determined cheerfulness.) 'You have a special deal for the next four weeks. And I must go home and spend time with Gerda. It's her birthday, you know, at the end of term. Then after her holidays are over, I will try to come back for you. By then you'll have decided where you want to be. I'll take you there. That is a promise.'

I felt – panic. I had to escape her.

And yet, I did not feel easy in my mind. Virginia was always so up and down! (Which was fair enough, being a manic-depressive, but her behaviour was so hard to predict.) However understanding last night's policeman had been, she had jarred herself on that fire hydrant.

VIRGINIA

'I've been to Turkey before, you know ...'

ANGELA

'Remind me, where did you go?' I asked. I was playing for time, my mind spinning.

Could I conceivably take her with me?

Could Virginia fly on a plane?

So far as I remembered, she never had.

And what on earth would she make of the conference? I thought of the email from Gerda. 'Why can't Virginia Woolf go to her own conference?' As usual, Gerda had a point.

VIRGINIA

'We sailed to Constantinople. Of course, the Turks re-named it Istanbul. It was terribly hot. My brother had gone home ... we knew nothing. We had been to Greece, really. That was the aim. Very early in the morning, we approached by sea ...'

And I was young, so very young. It was the morning of my life. Nothing was fixed. It was marvellous. Later we looked down on the sea from Pera. From east to west, everything was on fire, rose and blue, above, below. I watched it side by side with Nessa. This was our world, stretching out for ever. No-one could grow old, or die. Those were the last days of being invulnerable, perfectly young, perfectly hopeful. I will always love Constantinople.

'... and every window and roof was shining.'

ANGELA

Of course. The first volume of the *Diaries*. Her beloved elder brother died. And yes, years later, just across the sea in Bursa, Vanessa had a miscarriage.

'You might not want to go back, Virginia.'

'I miss Europe,' she said, matter-of-factly. 'I like Manhattan, but everything's new. I would be nearer to ... *my country*.'

That 'my country' harrowed me. Of course, without me, she would be lonely. Istanbul would be nearer home. Old Europe, old Asia, not new New York.

'You would have to fly. On a jet plane. They go higher and faster than your planes did.'

'Can one still see the ground?' she asked me.

'Sometimes, yes. Through gaps in the cloud. It's like looking

down on a map of the world.'

She clapped her hands together, perfectly happy.

VIRGINIA

'I would love to fly, of course I would. And Angela – I have a passport!'

ANGELA

Thus, in a single conversation, it was settled. From those few moments, the whole mad chapter. Her friends in Reception helped with Turkish Airlines; there were still a few seats on the morning flight.

'You know we probably can't sit together?'

'I am an adult,' Virginia said.

We bought a cheap suitcase in downtown Manhattan, a padlock and a packet of address tags, hurried back to our rooms and packed.

'To Hotel Golden Horn, Istanbul.' She laughed with joy when I wrote our address.

GERDA

To the Lighthouse, Gerda reads, with cynicism.

Then she leans back and closes her eyes. She's on the plane, she's off to New York, she's got her mother's stupid book ...

Time for a little self-congratulation.

1. She has escaped her terrible school without being spotted.
2. She has replied, in a masterly fashion, by email, to the increasingly urgent phone messages the head has been leaving for her mother. 'Gerda is now safe with her parents. We are removing her from your school because you have failed to deal with Bullying. Gerda as you know is a gifted child ...' Gerda had fun for another paragraph or two before ending, 'Yours Truely, Professor Angela Lamb.' No-one would guess it was from her! (Normally, Mum never used the 'Professor', but this was a moment when it might be useful.)

3. She is finally about to read a book by her mother's new girlfriend, so soon she will know how crap she is, from the point of view of a Genius (Gerda), and she will enjoy telling Mum that, and it will be great, in any case, to sit on a plane reading a book and eating airplane food, which is superdelicious compared to the nutritious rubbish school served up. Or dry cereal, which she's been living off (much too busy to go to the shop.)

To the Lighthouse. Gerda unfastens her seat belt, looks at the book jacket and considers. As a title, it's a bit shit, which is what

she had hoped and expected to find.

To the Nuthouse, she re-titles it.

But then she remembers Wikipedia said that Virginia Woolf had gone mad in real life, and she remembers the Bullies, at school, who gave her a ticket to the Mental Hospital, and starts to feel a bit ashamed.

Maybe she should give the book a chance. Soon, after all, she'll be back with Mum, and everything will be all right. She imagines the first enormous hug.

To the Mother, she thinks. To Mummy. To Mum. To New York and my defective mummy. She slips off her shoes, smiles out of the window at bright blue air, and sneers joyfully down at her pages.

Within twenty minutes Gerda is gripped.

PART TWO

Time Passes:

London-New York-Istanbul

ANGELA

The taxi crawled towards the airport. With luck – and Virginia certainly had luck, coming back from the dead is virtually unheard of! – we might make the plane, despite the coincidence of two horrendous traffic accidents. Both the usual exits from Manhattan were blocked.

Stop, start. Stop, stop.

'What will happen at my conference?' Virginia asked.

I pretended not to hear. At moments like this, I couldn't deal with it. I had specific worries, like her fake passport. Missing our flight, getting arrested.

Wherever we got stuck, that late afternoon, horrors. An old woman vomited by a wall against which a line of carrier bags slumped like drunks. LAST DAYS, said a small forest of signs on a corner. A group of people, eyes half-closed in the sun, faces blank and blissful, were waving to and fro in unison. Their lips opened and shut like happy goldfish. One sign, black on orange, shouted KINGDOM, another one, PRAISE. The believers faced inwards, and pointed upwards.

Virginia said 'Is that a cult?'

'Oh – they're just evangelicals.'

'Missionaries?'

'Protestants.'

'Protestants were never like that in my day.'

'Well – it's an anti-hierarchical thing.' I couldn't be bothered to explain.

'Meaning?' she said. I looked out of the window. 'Angela,

please, I need to understand.'

She knew how to make me feel guilty. Sighing in the heat, I set out once again to explain the madnesses of my world.

'People seem to want to shake up religion. Go back to the beginning. Be passionate. Radical Christians, radical Muslims, even Buddhists are getting het up. It's a rebellion against – '

'Rationality?' she interrupted. 'I hoped you'd be growing more rational.'

She had a way of blaming modernity on me. 'We seem to be going in the opposite direction.'

The taxi wasn't moving in any direction. The lanes ahead were chockablock. In an hour and twenty minutes, the gate would close.

'Sorry,' she said, 'I interrupted.'

'Virginia, I'll explain later.'

We were in gridlock. The fumes were acrid. I shut the window, and the heat was intense; flies in a box of glass and metal. Manhattan was not so safe after all, so radiantly open, so transparent, with its lattice of streets laid bare to the sky. I was suddenly glad Gerda wasn't here. Edward had brought her here, when she was little, and they both insisted she'd enjoyed herself, but it wasn't really a city for children – it felt like a blocked sink.

We had to get out: we couldn't get out. The traffic was stifling, the noise was thick, like a badly made, scratchy blanket. Being locked in made us vulnerable, as if we could be crushed by a single blow.

New York became a trap. Not right at the core of things after all, not the place where everything important happened, fame, money, publishers.

It made me long for – Istanbul. City of a thousand entrances. She was talking again. I zoned back in.

'What will happen at my conference?' she repeated.

'You'll see,' I said, turning my gaze away from the eagerness in her great orbs. (I had forebodings. What would she make of Bakhtin? *Derrida*?) 'Perhaps you shouldn't call it "my conference", Virginia. Even though it is, in a way. The organisers won't understand … I honestly can't think at the moment, I just want us to catch our plane.' Oh dear, I was sounding irritable. Perhaps she was traumatised by fear of flying. 'Are you OK, Virginia?'

VIRGINIA

I was fine, not grumpy and nervous, like her. Raring to climb the steps of that plane.

All day, my companion had been pale and grim, and snapped at me when the cab was two minutes late, and when I protested, said 'It's all right for you.' She was using that expression a lot, and sighing. Perhaps she found travel stressful.

I'm sure I'd done everything I could to help. Except for leaving my handbag in reception, but they managed to locate it without too much trouble, only then of course I had to tip them again, and Angela looked 'stressed' as the moderns say, when they gave me their addresses, one by one, and we exchanged politeness, and the 'guys' made me promise to write to them, and she suddenly shouted, out of the blue, 'The fucking cab will get tired of waiting!' which certainly cast a pall over proceedings, even though she was soon saying 'Sorry, sorry' – it was only the third time I heard her swear, and the first time it had been directed at me. Though now she was being quite lax with the driver, who could surely find an alternative route. 'Why doesn't he go faster? Should one suggest it?'

ANGELA

'What you mean is, "Will *you* suggest it." New York cabbies don't like suggestions.'

That sulky face, like an aged adolescent. I forced myself to sound maternal. 'Let's just wait for the future to happen.'

In the early evening, the lights were coming on. As the outlines of buildings blurred into darkness, the solid traffic liquefied, the city was stirring, unlocking itself – it would let us go, we would be on the plane. New York was beautiful again.

We passed the suburbs, lower, smaller, neither of us talking, in this thinning dream. When we stopped at the airport, we heard people shouting, and on the roof of the taxi, a cool rain drummed. I sat there for a second, adrenalin draining, then hurried her out into the night.

Just over our heads, a plane was landing, a graceful, steady-winged, jewel-eyed moth. I imagined young faces pressed against the window, excited by the lights of New York, and we couldn't wait to get away from it.

At check-in I had a lot of talking to do. Virginia, I claimed, was a much-loved relation who had never flown, and must sit by me. She might have tried to support my story, instead of standing at an angle looking sceptical, but, hot and blustery, I managed it.

Then I had to sweat blood at the passport check. Virginia, however, became glowing and excited. She grew in stature: she was suddenly an actress; held out the passport like a hand of cards in a brilliantly exciting game, laughing 'Good *evening*' in her resonant contralto, while the voice in my head said 'Oh keep it *down*, oh don't draw attention to yourself.' But in minutes she was through, waving her aces, though the man stared after her, shaking his head, as if she was familiar. He spent much longer frowning over mine.

We ended up seated side by side in the middle section of the plane. I had sacrificed my extra-leg-room seat at the front of the cabin, but was she grateful?

No, she didn't even notice. I told myself, 'Don't expect

gratitude.' She was turning the pages of the in-flight shopping magazine, slow and reverent as a medieval monk.

And then she looked up. Her radiant smile. 'I'm so excited,' she said. 'Thank you. Thank you for everything you have done.'

By the time we took off, the rain had stopped, it was dark outside, but Virginia was buzzing, bolt upright against the seat belt. She left on the reading light above her head, an eye of gold in the darkened cabin.

ANGELA

Once we were up in the air, the lights flicked back on, and I
fully took in what I had noticed at the gate –

VIRGINIA

'Jews. That is not what one expected! This whole plane is alive
with Jews.'

ANGELA

I have to teach her not to talk like that. All the same, she is
factually correct.

It was a party of Hasidic Jews. Who would have expected
that on Turkish Airlines? The full malarkey, black clothes,
frizzed sideburns, the young women in nun-grey head-scarves.
I asked a disgruntled English-speaking steward and he said
there were thirty-two of them! End of the Jewish holiday in
New York and all the planes back to Israel were full, so a whole
crowd of returning Israelis had decided to fly back via Istanbul.

VIRGINIA

It was – archaic. Medieval! Binding their arms, wielding their
Bibles, standing up praying to the east in the aisles – so irksome,
surely, for the Mohammedan aircrew (or at least I assumed they
were Mohammedans, surely most Turks were Mohammedans?),
bob bob bob, mutter mutter – and those thongs cutting off the
circulation to their arms. They actually produced thin leather
thongs, rolled up their sleeves, and bound their left arms in

front of us all! I had wondered for a second if they meant to whip their wives, those devout young Jewesses with their heads tied up in bundles of grey and their unpainted faces – (I have seldom painted, but I'm not a modern woman) – suckling lines of beatific Jewish babies while gazing across in adoration at their long-headed husbands, with those foolish curling brown sheep-ears of hair. When the latter weren't binding themselves or praying or gazing up, rapturous, at nothing, they read, while the women cared for the children. (And the girl with the baby who sat next to me couldn't read her prayer-book without moving her lips.)

What would Leonard have said? He'd have detested it. He was rational, he disliked excess.

Angela thought I would be frightened of flying, but actually I felt more alarmed by the Jews.

ANGELA
I see this journey is going to be hell.

VIRGINIA
I am not a snob, I am curious. Although the girl next to me was obviously a peasant – she looked like a farm girl in her grey head scarf, and she breast fed from her great healthy breasts, two secretive mounds that made me blush – she wrote in a notebook once the youngest child slept. I asked her what she was writing; she smiled, and suddenly looked less bovine. Her eyes were very blue: her husband's, brown.

'I'm a playwright, Madam. I write plays. For young people in schools, mostly.' Accent: American, and something else.

I asked her what the plays were about? She said, her lips beaming upwards, eyes ardent, 'Follow the ways of the ancestors. No, I think I'm translating that wrong. "Follow the ways of your forefathers." It's what we all believe,' she added.

If so, how on earth could we talk to each other? My life was founded on reinvention, I fled the cobwebs of Hyde Park Gate and my father's terrible groans in the night …

'Your forefathers,' I echoed. 'What if they were wrong?'

'We have survived for over a hundred generations. They cannot be wrong,' she said, with an air of reproof, not unfriendly, but − tinged with pity. She was sorry for me because I was not one of them, not one of the self-elected, the saved. Such radiant belief in the hands of children! Remember I lived through the pre-war years.

1938. When we drove through Germany, Leonard and I and Mitz Marmoset. We were uneasy about being English, we wondered if we would be attacked, but the Germans we met made a pet of Mitz, and that fat man who gave us two free beers in Munich assured us we were 'blood brothers'. *Brüderschaft*, that terrible, bludgeoning word.

They too were following their forefathers, searching for heroes in the ruined state. When they talked of the future, they had the same glow. Like those radiant Christians on the New York pavements. Wherever it shone, wars would follow.

But maybe I was wrong. She seemed sweet, and simple, and she laughed into the eyes of her babies, and doted on her poor hairy-eared husband.

In any case, it was very late. The lights were going out all over the cabin. Now only the stewards trudged up and down, leaning over one passenger, smiling at another. For a moment they reminded me of my mother.

Caring for others I suppose I shunned, because I had to live with a virtuous woman, because I had seen where her virtue led: poor Mother, who worked till her knuckles were red, sewing, visiting, noting, sorting, till her mouth pulled grim and thin as a thread … all my life I had avoided that path.

Beside me, all round me, the babies were fed by very young women desperate for sleep. I felt a sudden compassion for my neighbour, not so much older than Angelica had been, but her flushed pink cheeks were already worn, her eyes were straining to read the prayer-book in the short gaps when her baby was happy; her drive to write was chained to duty. There must be a way we could talk to each other.

ANGELA

In a way they were very like Arabs. Being covered and so on. The men and women with their demarcated roles. I said so to Virginia and she yawned. She said 'Of course, they're all Semites,' in her most superior way.

I wasn't putting up with that. 'We don't use language like that anymore, it's considered anti-Semitic.'

VIRGINIA

'We were never anti-Semitic. Never. One is allowed to detest one's own in-laws.'

ANGELA

'There are famous synagogues in Istanbul, you know.'

VIRGINIA

'But very few Jews.'

(*Pause.*)

ANGELA

'How do you know?'

VIRGINIA

'Because I've been doing it too. The thing with the ... thing.'

ANGELA

'What thing? No thank you.' (The flight attendant was offering coffee, but I never drank it after 3 PM)

VIRGINIA

'Yes, please. Strong. The thing, the thing, the modern thing, the … computer. I've been internetting. On the computer in the lobby. There are only 17,000 Jews in all Turkey, in a population of 80 million. Or should that be eight hundred million? That's about point something per cent.'

ANGELA

'I say, Virginia. I'm impressed. Nevertheless, statistics aren't the whole story. There are thousands of, um, Jews married to Muslims, or secret – Jews – from centuries back. (*Sotto voce*) By the way, do you mind not saying "Jews"?'

(I mean, it was obvious. We were *surrounded*.)

VIRGINIA (*blankly*)

'Not saying Jews?'

ANGELA

'It might sound silly to you, but we prefer "Jewish people".'

I knew it *would* sound silly to her.

VIRGINIA (*hooting with laughter*)

'Why on earth?'

ANGELA (*irritated*)

'Oh, you wouldn't understand. It's about … respecting difference.'

Even as I said it, I knew it sounded weak. But my diaphragm tightened with embarrassment when she used these terms in

her ringing tones.

(The other one was 'Africans'. That had taken half an hour to explain. Virginia would not let it drop. 'I don't understand how it can be an insult when Africa is a continent. Why are they ashamed of a continent?' 'That's not the point, Virginia, they're not. It's about what people choose to be called.' 'That's idiotic. It's … unphilosophical. A table can't choose to be called a chair.' 'A table doesn't have feelings, Virginia.')

Though famously sensitive, it seemed Virginia was only sensitive to her own feelings. Whole categories of people didn't count for her. Me, for example. Did she see me as human?

Yet she made my judgements feel less secure. 'Aren't you tired, Virginia? I'm not up to talking. I thought that I would watch a film. Look, the controls are in your arm rest.'

VIRGINIA
'Thank you, no, this is too exciting. The plane is a film, and we are in it.'

They were addicted to cinema, these modern people! At home, at table, or on tiny machines on the streets of New York — now even on a plane they couldn't do without it. We were flying headlong through the air, ten thousand metres up, according to the pilot, surely that was excitement enough? But no, they were all glued to their films.

They were so much lonelier than we had been, each lost in the story of his own choosing. Even the children were attached to wires, laughing and gasping to their solitary rhythms as we sped above whatever ocean it was, Atlantic, surely, or possibly Pacific.

(Except the Jewish children, that is. They looked — livelier, talking and playing, hugging their parents and each other.)

Back in the 1920s, 1930s, people were rooted in reality. Loyal to reality, one might say. True, sometimes Leonard and

I read through meals. Were we addicted in our own way? But – ordinary people weren't, one thought. Meals got cooked, dishes got washed.

In this new century, it wasn't so. The whole populace was lost in fancy.

Angela was putting her headphones on. They made the shape of her head like a monkey. 'If you don't mind, Virginia – '

Two seats away, a fierce little boy was twitching in time to gun-shots. Martial music swelled from his screen. Part of me was curious to share his excitements – but no, like 'TV', I would find it a mixture of soporific and overwhelming. Better to live on the wave of the moment.

An American was talking in the row in front. He had a lot of opinions about Turks. 'You see they have a different sense of morality. They love their Allah, I'm not saying they don't. But they'd cheat you as soon as look at you …'

I was – completely in the midst of life. Partly because Angela was rather stout, so I felt the pressure of her arm, and the Jewess with the baby had sharp elbows which she waved around as she fed her child, and we all played bit-parts in the comedy above the clouds as the Jews performed their primitive rituals –

How agreeable to feel relatively modern, for once!

But as I watched the couple to my left I started to like them, for they loved one another. It was unmistakable, their tenderness; and the same was true of the wider group, who constantly made contact with each other; they almost seemed like one family, and not Leonard's squabbling, divided one. Maybe religion did unify people. Like the New York Christians, bobbing in bliss. Maybe believers were happier than us.

Until, that is, the Christians fought the Jews, the Jews the Mohammedans, the Mohammedans the Hindus …

And the rhythms started to become soothing, till in the end,

they smoothed me to sleep.

I laid my head on the breast of the night.

ANGELA

When she put out her light, it was gone midnight.

(Gerda, also high in the air, flying in the opposite direction to New York, was trying to balance her book on her tray while eating the extra chocolate mousse she had persuaded her neighbour to yield. Gerda was happy. On her wrist she was wearing Mum's gold bracelet, which had magic charms of animals, deer, pigeons, a friendly dog. 'That's a nice bracelet,' the woman said; she had a daughter around Gerda's age.

But Gerda hardly noticed. 'I'm reading,' she said, which was just a Fact, and not Bad Manners. She was far away, in a world of crowing cocks and candles, and faint green stains on the waves at daybreak.

Here Mr. Carmichael, who was reading Virgil, blew out his candle. It was past midnight.

… But what after all is one night?

Still Mum always told her to be polite, and with a sigh, Gerda briefly stopped reading the 'Time Passes' section of *To the Lighthouse* to say 'Excuse me, thank you for my pudding.'

... what after all is one night? A short space, especially when the darkness dims so soon, and so soon a bird sings, a cock crows, or a faint green quickens, like a turning leaf, in the hollow of the wave.

Night, however, succeeds to night.

ANGELA

And only when Virginia was asleep – I was afraid she would read my secrets on my face – only then did I do what I wanted to do.

For among the films on offer that night I'd seen one choice I never expected.

A film I knew all too well, though even three years ago, hard to watch. *The Palace of Ice* was a documentary made to raise awareness of global warming, starring a father and daughter who sleighed across the Arctic.

So long ago. Or so it seemed. But what is three years, after all? Is it possible that then we were a close family? So recently, such an ache ago.

Three years. Gerda was, let's see, nine or ten. Edward must have been forty? It was Edward's idea. They made the film together.

But who had to deal with all the problems? With the furious school, who never accepted that travels in the Arctic were educational, with tracking down extra-warm thermals for Gerda, and patient lists of everything she needed – all right, to be fair, *she* made the lists, but I found it all, I ticked it all

off! Who had to extract school-work for her to do on the trip from the self-righteous primary school teachers? 'She may be bright, but she does need to work. It's not good for children to feel exceptional.' But even as they said it, I knew that she was, and I knew they knew it, for they let us go.

(Let *them* go, I mean. No, not me. I was never invited on their adventures.)

So who was left crying at Heathrow Airport when they went through the doors of the departure lounge? – I can see them still, I love them still, for all my hurt do I love him still? – two backs disappearing, one small, one tall, unnaturally inflated by the blue duck-down parkas they could not fit into their luggage, going away from me into nowhere, but his hand, his dear big hand, on her shoulder, and her round face turned up to his, as usual. I could only see part of her cheek, her eyes, but every particle of it was smiling, she was totally happy, alive with laughter.

I could never love my own father like that. But Edward was Gerda's role model. I think she wanted to be him, not me. That wasn't easy for me to see.

(And now I wonder: who did the leaving? Did I go away too much myself, to write? Did *I* leave *them*? What was the truth? Flying through the air, so far above the earth, our story fell apart, my role became less certain.)

And now it was here, the film they made, *The Palace of Ice*, and to be fair, I knew how much it had cost Edward as he struggled to keep the backers on board, to balance the books and appease Channel 6, who veered from one mad suggestion to another as different editors tried to make their mark. He had to keep believing it would happen. It was one of the ways he gave Gerda confidence, his buoyant belief in the next new thing. He always worried less than I did. (Of course, he could leave the worrying to me.)

I paid the price. For I did the dull things once her Grandma and Grandpa were no longer around, homework, bedtimes, early mornings – so yes, I was the dull one, and yes, I felt resentful.

When she came back from the trip, she was so round and rosy, so sturdy and so full of – yes, joy. She had had her father to herself, she had been round the world, why shouldn't she be happy? And besides, she had been off school for five weeks. 'Mum! Mum!' She rushed straight in and hugged me. 'I've never been so happy in my whole life!'

I was happy for her, I was happy for them, I was happy for Edward, but of course I felt – lonely. There is an arithmetic of happiness: other people's doesn't always add to your own, sometimes there is only so much around, and if you see too much of it has gone to others –

I looked at them, radiant, framed on the doorstep, his tall form outlined against the light behind her, and his hair was long, and his beard was long –

What I saw was duty. A lot to do. They would come in laughing, not wiping their feet, and their bags would be full of dirty washing.

'That's great, Gerda. Tell me all about it. But first, to look at you – you need a bath. Did she wash her hair *once* while she was away?' I turned to Edward, behind her in the doorway.

'What kind of welcome is that?' he asked.

'I'm only joking. I'm so happy to see you.'

But they had been so long away …

I would not think about that day. The precipitous decline into actual screaming.

Gall and wormwood rose under my ribs.

No, press the button, the film had begun. Great sheets of ice: aerial footage shot with a hand-cam from a small plane, and as I looked at it, my bitterness went, and I saw how wide,

and how beautiful, and how little we human beings mattered, and I wept. Nothing, nothing but love for them.

Then Edward turned the camera into the cabin, and there was Gerda, three years younger. My child, who will always be part of me, and I of her, though she will have to forget me, at least enough for her to shine.

In our short, human lives, three years could be everything. Everything could change. From a child, to a woman, an angry young woman, a teenager sent away to school.

I had only done the best for Gerda. The best for her – and the best for me.

I stopped the film for a moment, and breathed deeply.

(Another Gerda, on her own trajectory over the ocean, under the stratosphere, went on reading *To the Lighthouse*, unknown to Angela, far away. Only two hours until she landed, only two hours to reach the lighthouse, no-one must interrupt her now.)

Round Angela, Virginia, and all the sleeping bodies on the Turkish Airways plane, the semi-night of an enormous machine. The engines must always go on turning, the electricity can never go off. The flight staff are doing their calculations: how many vegetarian meals had been eaten? Maybe Yasemin had not cleared the rubbish away, or Emir was taking his break early. It didn't matter, someone must bring aspirin to that mother with four children and a terrible toothache.

All right for the pilot: gallant at the helm, he could trust his computer to carry them onwards, over the Atlantic, above thousands of feet of ice crystals and roaring air currents, with his coffee beside him that someone else had made; eagle-eyed, erect, the brain behind the beak, thinking, perhaps, of his garden in Denizli, if the lilies would be standing when he got home, if his beloved *zambaklar* would have survived the winds,

and whether that heron would have taken his carp: his duty is simply to be a brain, while the flight attendants, most of them, fortunately, women – he considers it more natural than having men, though sometimes the families made terrible trouble (it was easier for women to look after people, even these new feminists could not deny that) – the flight attendants care for the great bird's body, the bodies of the passengers, the body of the plane.

Angela jerked awake in dreadful anxiety. A dream of the day after Gerda started boarding school (the child was very brave, she had barely cried, perhaps she didn't really mind leaving home?) Angela, too, was perfectly calm, yet she woke in the night and stumbled down the dark landing to go to the bathroom, Gerda's light was showing, she walked in, unthinking, to switch the light off as her daughter slept, and stretched out her hand to feel the warmth of her cheek.

But Gerda having left the day before, she reached further, and further, touched nothing and no-one. She clutched at the duvet: her arms remained empty.

ANGELA

How long, after all, is five weeks? – I think now. That was all the filming took. Not so very long to be apart. Though I had to live it day by day, and every day they were together. It was nothing, a breath, in the life of our marriage – we had been back together for half-a-dozen years. Yet it caused a little crack, and then another crack showed, and the ice that we lived on started breaking into pieces.

Now we were all so much further apart, and neither of them knew what flight I was on, those sweet, banal ties of everyday knowledge, tender, restrictive, were long gone. I didn't notice them passing, forgot to regret them. Now, too late, I felt the loss.

At least I knew Gerda was safe in Hampshire, that was what one paid for, at that type of school, the knowledge that people would look after one's daughter.

(At Bendham Abbey, Bendham, Hampshire, the Head was reading Gerda's email, livid. 'The arrogance of these ghastly parents! She doesn't have the courtesy to pick up the phone ... And she may be an author – have you read her stuff? – but she can't spell "Truly". Ah well, that's that. I had hopes for that child. In six years, we'd have made something of her. Now, of course, the mother will spoil her.'

Three thousand miles away, 'that child' is swooping, motherless, towards New York.)

Edward had been gone now for over three months. For two of those he had been back in the Arctic. That terrible last scene when he told me he was going, and I said, in that case, don't bother coming home ...

No, I refused to think about that.

Compared to five weeks, three months was a lifetime. (Though Gerda's school terms were twelve weeks long, which I had promised would be over in an instant –)

I hoped, suddenly, piercingly, that Gerda was all right, that she had not been lonely without us, but the pain was too much, and I pushed it away. If she wasn't happy, she would tell me about it. *She'll be surprised how fast time passes. The young are different: they feel things less. I managed to find her an excellent school.*

All around me, sleep and stillness. In the half-dark, they were all connected, an arm flung out, a leg, a foot, sleeping forms turned to one side or another, some with dropped jaws and open mouths. Business people at the top of their game, temporarily soft and boneless as children. Hands curled loosely, wavering outwards – unprotected, entirely themselves. Virginia – I hardly dared look at her –

I risked it. She lay there, marmoreal, grave, a life-mask of the famous face, no longer disrupted and humanised by little throbs of need or humour. As at the beginning, I was moved, awed.

Nothing, it seemed, could break that image, that pale, silent, Olympian stillness which, second by second, in the sleeping cabin, seemed to fold our stories into itself. I looked away, afraid. I resumed my film. (Could I even exist, so near such greatness?)

(But 'What is smallness, what is greatness?', Virginia had written.)

Once in the middle of my film, just once, a man at the front

of the cabin had a nightmare and there was a roar, a rupture of the calm, and a flight attendant came rubbing his eyes, his shirt loosened at the neck, and hovered above him till he slept again. Then again peace descended; I watched the film until 3 AM, I became part of it, I sleighed with them, their dear warm bodies inside layers of furs, under ice-blue skies and long-set sunlight, across the endless fields of white, I smiled to myself to see them laughing as Edward tried to push Gerda's shoes on over layers of socks and they both got the giggles, or Gerda shouted with triumph when she managed to get the fire to blaze up, and their fire-lit shadows wavered on the snow; then there was the dazzling light of morning: all over the ice figures were stirring ...

But no, I had slept through the end of the film.

A white scimitar of light had pierced the cabin.

A baby mewed briefly, then another, and another, and the mothers were stretching and enfolding their young, and the flight attendants, smiling and tidy again, came down the gangway with a drinks trolley – 'Sir? Madam? Tea? Coffee?' – and everywhere people were raising their blinds, round lids over a line of bright blue eyes.

Now the morning light became a brilliant white sheet and all the little creatures were waking quietly, bleached out by a night of excessive activity: the praying, the reading of old testaments, the caressing and dressing and undressing of babies and toddlers and their passing from loving hand to hand over seat-arms and across gangways. The crew (Turkish Muslim and one Armenian Christian) try to wheel their breakfast trolleys up and down, their demeanour as polite and cheerful as ever, 30,000 feet above the sea.

ANGELA

The American in the row in front had started talking to his bouffant wife, who was coming to Istanbul for the first time, and a student with long straight pale caramel hair unlucky enough to be sitting next to him. Was she married? he had to know. Why not? Actually, she was studying Islamic art at Columbia University. 'I thought art was forbidden in Turkey!' he roared, over the top of her explanation. 'So that'll be a short thesis, right?' 'Well – ' 'The men don't understand our women, honey. So dress modestly, especially being blonde, or they'll be all over you like flies.'

'Really?' The student's voice was American too, but her 'really' could not have been more cynical.

Virginia's first remark, which came 0.5 seconds after she had said 'Good morning' to me, reverted to the Jewish question.

VIRGINIA

'Is it that Jews don't like to be Jews? Is that why they prefer to be called "Jewish people"?'

ANGELA

'Actually, I don't even know. I don't think it's that, in this case. It's different when they're among themselves, I believe that then they do say "Jews" ...'

I wished we had never started this.

VIRGINIA

'They are among themselves, Angela, there's at least two dozen of them, look.'

ANGELA

'*No, don't point, Virginia.* It's too complicated. Take my word for it. It is my century, for heaven's sake. Just wait until we're off this plane.' (But I felt – mealy-mouthed and uncertain, suddenly.) 'Look could we not talk about the Jews – Jewish people, I mean, could we stop? It isn't relevant to Istanbul. It's mosques we're going to look at. And churches. The Aya Sophia, the Blue Mosque and so on.'

VIRGINIA

'Aya Sophia. Is that ... St Sophia? I went there. We went there. Vanessa and I. People stared at us. Back at the beginning of the century.'

ANGELA

'Back at the beginning of your century: 1906, I think it was. You wrote about it. You were very young. Of course people stared. You and Vanessa were both so lovely.'

VIRGINIA

'Twenty-four. I would love to go there again.'
 Everything was ahead of me then.

ANGELA

'Ten years older than my daughter. I wonder if you will ever meet her.'

VIRGINIA

'We went there in the evening. We were curious. I wasn't afraid of anything ...'
 The lights came on slowly – candles. We women were upstairs, we went up a long ramp, you could hear children calling somewhere like birds. It was ... dim, when you looked down, dim murmurings, amber air and shadows, people kneeling and rising in long lines like waves on the sea, and the world going on indifferently around them, the business of the world. I was impressed, but it was all a mystery, it was so other, such strangeness.
 'I thought: we can never meet, Christians and Mohammedans, we are as different as – well, as different as you and me.'

ANGELA (*hurt*)
'Are we so different?'

VIRGINIA (*pealing with laughter, then stopping, genuinely surprised*)
'Don't you think so? You're so ... tidy. And of course, so ... modern. Whereas I am ancient, a dinosaur. I never had children, you're a mother, I was an old wife, and you're divorced – '

ANGELA
'No!'

VIRGINIA
'Of course we're different.'

ANGELA
'I'm not divorced.'

VIRGINIA
'Separated?'

ANGELA
'Nonsense!'

VIRGINIA
'You said – '

ANGELA
'Nothing of the kind. Edward's away. In the Arctic. It's true that we quarrelled. But I think he still loves me. Not that it's relevant. But as it happens, we're not formally separated.'

VIRGINIA
'Sorry. (*Pause.*) You are lucky, then. I will always miss ... Always.'

ANGELA (*watching her rapt, tender face*)
'You quarrelled too. In the *Diaries*.'
 Damn. I had given it away again.

VIRGINIA
'Did he say that in his diaries? And publish them?'

ANGELA

'Maybe I've got that wrong.'

I couldn't tell her that I'd read her diaries. That everyone at the conference would have read them. Or perhaps I should. Perhaps I should warn her. Her clear instructions: destroy my papers.

VIRGINIA

'All married couples sometimes quarrel. After all, two worlds are forced together. As different as, well … I don't know.'

ANGELA

'New York and Istanbul, perhaps?'

VIRGINIA

'But Leonard and I were both very English. My brothers were his friends at Cambridge. It was inevitable that we should meet. Yes, he was a Jew, but – '

ANGELA

'*Jewish*. But yes, I see, it was different for you. Edward and I were from different classes. His family were Danish, though they'd anglicised their name, he had gone to Cambridge, he was middle-class – '

(*Pause.*)

VIRGINIA

'And your family?'

ANGELA

Her tone was kind, encouraging, yet in it I detected a hint of malice.

VIRGINIA

'Perhaps they were from the lower orders?'

ANGELA

'We don't use those phrases.'

VIRGINIA

'Have I offended you?'

ANGELA

'It's not your fault, but you're – just as you said, a dinosaur. And now I am going to read my book. Which is by a modern novelist. You don't seem anxious to learn about those. You might like to read my newspaper. It's *The Times*, and I bought it at the airport, so it's two days old, but all the same, it might help you – catch up, Virginia. With the modern world. Really, you could update yourself.'

She saw I was annoyed, and took the paper, but when I looked across two minutes later, she was sound asleep, as if it was bedtime. But then, we were soaring across time zones

and she, after all, was from another century

time travel

could it really happen?

(*Angela's eyes blur over her pages.*)

(Gerda is landing in New York. The woman next to her sitting by the window who gave her the chocolate mousse earlier points out Manhattan as they fly overhead. So many tiny towers

that they seem like a life-form, bristling like crystals alongside the blue water, and down the middle, the great crack of green. 'That's Central Park.' 'I know,' says Gerda. It looks amazing in the morning sunlight. 'Isn't that gorgeous?' the woman says. Then 'Your mother will be so happy to see you.'

'Yes,' says Gerda, in a slightly strange voice, not adding 'Although she doesn't know it yet.')

VIRGINIA

I had slept like a child, and when I woke, the life of the plane was in full swing.

'Where are we?'

'Somewhere over the Balkans,' said Angela.

'The Balkans? Is there still fighting there?'

'Well, there was … quite recently. If a decade ago is "recently". People thought there would never be fighting in Europe again, after your war, you know what I mean.'

'They said that about the Great War, too. The war to end war. The Great Lie. Fortunately Leonard was too blind to fight. So there's no fighting in Europe now?'

'There is trouble in Iraq,' said Angela, 'and Afghanistan. And Syria. And Palestine. We are up to our necks in it.'

Where were these countries? I was slightly vague. Leonard would have known, of course. Somewhere in the Middle East, I was sure, somewhere near the cradle of all mankind, the Tigris and Euphrates. How beautiful our language is.

The Assyrian came down like a wolf on the fold …

Why were men always fighting each other?

The cabin girl – no, what did they call them? In my day, of course, they had cabin boys – came down the corridor with difficulty, 'Excuse me, Sir,' 'Excuse me, Miss,' using her trolley like a slow, polite chariot, and lurched to one side as she bent over me, trying to proffer a plastic tray that held some kind of

packaged fodder, with a sidelong glance at the stubborn man who, evicted from the gangway by her mission, was making her roll like a ship at sea as he strained to stay standing and praying in his seat.

The rosy-cheeked young woman beside me was suckling again, I could hear the baby's happy lip-smacks under the modest cloth that veiled her breast, but her Bible was tucked in the crook of her empty arm, her eyes followed the characters, her lips moved softly. The cabin girl's eyes fell on nothing directly, but you could see she deprecated any religion that stopped her doing her morning duties, you could see that she only wanted to help, she was not ambitious, she wanted us happy, the flock of passengers in her care, she avoided the scorn and anger of the world, the furious intensity of this faith or that which made them fight wars, and obstruct her passage; she had only benefactions to distribute. With a smile that pulled hard at the lines in her lipstick, she hauled herself upright again and said, in automatic answer to my 'Thank you', 'Not problem, Miss. Please first erect the seat.'

Was the cabin girl's job one long sorrow and trouble? In some corner of some cubicle, wherever they could hide, she might steal an hour or two's sleep or gossip, but was it worth it when in a few minutes she'd be getting up again and struggling on? What did she feel about her work, which we always made her do again?

She fed us, we ate, we pushed it away, she had barely finished distributing the trays before she had to take it all back where it came from. Always conjuring things up, then accepting their destruction, whereas a writer's work was aimed at survival. (And I had survived. A small surge of joy.)

It wasn't easy, the world she knew, the eternal world of the servant class which Vanessa and I had hoped was ending. We had both vowed to do without servants! What a liberation

from their suffering! Who wanted them, sullen in some basement room not far enough away from one's own? Yet we had no running water till the 1930s, and at Asheham, endless chamber-pots, earth-closets, buckets. Our arms couldn't carry them. Without servants, Vanessa's and my work would never have got done.

Bowed down, they always were, with weariness, and how wearying for us to see their pain and hear their awful protestations of duty, the way they vowed they would never leave us, when all we longed for them to do was leave.

What should we have done? There was no answer; and the modern world seemed hardly any better. Our hotel had servants — the Wordsmiths Hotel, with its literature-themed rooms and bookish clients. Yet back up in the bedrooms were the same maids, somehow enduring the same duties, groaning faintly, on creaking knees because how else, pray, could you clean under beds? Was there any difference but the colour of their skin and the strange electric music mine sang to? She had to clean the bathroom, bleach the lavatories, take up mats, put down new towels ...

And who was to say if this African woman might have been a great poet, had she but had the chance? Might have given form to that hard, harsh life? Might have made each one of her peers a hero, and at last enlightened us about their story — a story as epic as any of ours? Who knew if one of them burned to do it, without the words, without the schooling?

That's where it came from, our shame, our awkwardness. Because, I think, one has always known it. We had the luck, and they did not.

Yet she sang along to that fizz of music, which must have been some kind of consolation. Perhaps this new century had given them hope, they had freedoms our servants never dreamed of, and though I didn't care for how they used their

freedom — that crowd at the Statue, so loud, so venal! — they had hopes that their children, perhaps, would be masters, and one had to accept that was no bad thing.

'What am I,' she might ask, or 'What is my life? What brought me from Africa to this strange place?' They had the luxury of questioning, of not just trudging down the path like dumb brutes. The difference between us was no longer so obvious, I told myself, sipping my morning cup of tea and imagining my next consolation, the coffee.

But the cabin girl continued her rounds as before.

VIRGINIA

'Look at the queues for the lavatories. I suppose one must go and join them. So international, the modern world. That woman in a sari, those Africans … You said Edward was an explorer. Which countries has your husband explored?'

ANGELA

'Exploring isn't like it was in your day. He has an ecological agenda …'

VIRGINIA

'But where?'

ANGELA

'So many places.'

VIRGINIA

'Do men and women share the bathrooms?'

ANGELA

'In which country?'

VIRGINIA

'Here on the plane, of course. I thought that was forbidden for Mohammedans? Don't bother to answer, I will go and find out.'

And with that, she was up, so I got up too quickly and dropped my book, while Virginia hared off down the gangway, disrupting people's breakfasts, tripping over their feet.

The truth was, I couldn't instantly remember the countries that Edward had been to. I always had my own books to write, so I couldn't really focus on what Edward was doing, whereas Gerda, being a child, had a little globe and marked his position with gobs of Bluetack.

Virginia had asked me early on about Edward. She fired off questions like a Catherine wheel. (Not always. She'd never asked about my novels. Or novels in general, by modern writers. There was only ONE writer who interested her. Or was I being slightly unfair?)

I told her how Edward began as a romantic. About me, about travel and nature. I left out the fact that he had been married, I spooled to our wedding in a blur of confetti. I went too fast, my words sounded hollow, and surely her sharp ears noticed it.

When we were first in love, before I got pregnant, he wanted to share everything with me, his love of wilderness, nights in the open. We fled the city and found each other on various unspoiled European beaches. But the sand-flies bit me, the sand blew in my eyes, and I grew tired of it, and he was disappointed. He was thinking about something bigger than we were – the fate of all humans, so he claimed – while I was obsessing about my comfort.

'You're a dreamer, Edward. I'm a realist. I want a husband and a decent bed.'

Perhaps it was inevitable that we would break up, but when I found out I was pregnant, I kept our daughter. So although we were apart, we shared Gerda. It took six or seven years for him to get a divorce, start making money, win me over.

He'd managed to get grants for his eco-projects; a research professorship, recently ended; and gigs on TV, because he was handsome. More recently *The Palace of Ice* gained a cult following, and the book which followed was a surprise success. Indeed he sold almost as well as me, though Gerda was enraged by the photographs of her, a blue bundle of clothes with a red round face. 'You didn't ASK me, Daddy!'

(In fact he had arranged it all from a distance, he was in the Amazon by then, and he claimed he had asked me to clear the shots with her ... if he did, which I doubt, I have no memory of it.) In any case, the book did extremely well, so I don't know what Gerda was complaining about. It was nobody's fault but Edward's that he'd put almost every penny of the money into this maddening new polar trip, because the grant wasn't big enough. In the end, people make their choices.

Seeing *The Palace of Ice* had stirred it all up. They pulled at my heart, those two little figures, struggling to put tents up in the gathering dark, laughing over mugs of tea in the firelight. Sometimes he gave Gerda the microphone, and her young, clear voice described stars or wolves – I was her mother, but I still marvelled.

Of course the split had been a wrench for Gerda. She loved her father, but she took my side, her sense of justice made her take my side, and besides, Edward had been away for three months and missed her birthday, except for a phone call. His postcard arrived over three weeks late, by which time both of us were furious. 'I'm afraid men don't remember birthdays,' I told her. Yes, she was becoming a feminist.

Oh, no. Virginia was struggling back along the row and calling out to me in clarion tones, 'Does the excrement fall on the heads of the people?'

'Virginia, please *sit down*.' I shut my eyes so I didn't have to see her.

VIRGINIA

I noticed that her eyes were closed. But I needed to ask her about the Balkans, and all the fighting everywhere else, and find out what she thought about it, for women were surely the pacific sex (though she herself could be aggressive!). I wanted to know if it had made any difference, my pamphlet *Three Guineas*, which nearly killed me. Half a dozen years of floundering and striving, and none of the men I knew liked it –

(not even Leonard – not even my love –)

I held back from asking for at least a second, just in case she was actually asleep.

'Angela, have you read *Three Guineas*?'

It wasn't my fault that she then spilled her coffee.

ANGELA (*to the man next to her*)

'*Sorry*, so sorry. Oh no, it's on your Bible, or Torah or whatever …'

I dabbed at him, helpless, with my paper napkin.

VIRGINIA

'Oh let the cabin girl bring a cloth. In any case, he's quite all right. I just wanted to know, have you read it?'

I allowed her time to stop flapping her napkin, then I continued with my theme.

'My thoughts about aggression were in *Three Guineas*. I hope it had … some influence.'

ANGELA

'Don't ask me at this moment.'

VIRGINIA (*generously*)

'I don't mind if you haven't.'

ANGELA

'Look, it's your fault I spilled the coffee.'

VIRGINIA

It was at times like this that one saw she had no breeding. One does not make a fuss about this type of thing. I allowed her time to stop flapping her napkin, then I continued with my theme.

'I hope *Three Guineas* had ... some influence.'

ANGELA

'What do you think it would have influenced?' (*In a furious whisper, to herself*) 'Fuck. Fuck. Fuck. Fuck.'

VIRGINIA

'It did make a certain stir, you know. Rhonda Cecil, who was hardly a radical, declared herself profoundly moved and excited.'

MAN WITH LOCKS (*strongly accented English*)

'It cannot be recovered. Wreck-èd.'

ANGELA

'Let me pay you for a replacement. I'm so sorry. I'm afraid I only have dollars ...'

There was a darkish stain on the smooth surface of his Bible, which paled slightly as the page buckled, only because it was penetrating deeper, boiling and bleeding, invisibly, beneath. The man was staring at me, dark with fury, and I, alas, was getting angry with him, and before we knew it, we would have a war on. I'd had anger training to deal with Edward, I was going through the mantra, *STOPP – Stop, Think, Observe*, get *Perspective*, *Practice* your techniques for defusing situations – but with Virginia yattering away on my left, I couldn't get the space I needed to *Practice*, I couldn't take the calm 'helicopter viewpoint' –

MAN WITH LOCKS
'You Americans think everything is money. Everything is not money.'

ANGELA
'All right, have it your way.'
 I folded my dollars back into my wallet.

MAN WITH LOCKS
'But our community is not rich. You Americans think everyone is rich.'

ANGELA
'I'm not American, for God's sake! Look do you want my money or not?'

VIRGINIA
'Lady Rhondda thought *Three Guineas* would have a great effect. Angela, dear, you are shouting, you know.'

MAN WITH LOCKS
'So give me the money if it makes you feel better.'

(*Angela grimly hands over the money. His hand stays outstretched. She gives another note.*)

VIRGINIA
'It's one of the books I am most proud of. I had such a struggle with *The Pargeters*, could it work as a fusion of fact and fiction? – but in the end, I separated the two, and the fiction part became *The Years,* which takes a family through several generations, and the wars come, and so much time passes …
 It was a best-seller in America, you know. And the part that

was intellectual argument I turned into a book of its own, *Three Guineas*.'

ANGELA
'I know!'

VIRGINIA
'*Three Guineas* had a genuinely new perspective. War and women's rights could not be disentangled. Because educated women are too rational for war – '

ANGELA (*incandescent*)
'Could you please shut up for *one* second, I am trying to sponge coffee off my good coral suit …

'Oh *fuck*, I didn't mean to say shut up, sorry! I will opine on every war on the planet, but now I just need a few moments' grace.'

VIRGINIA

Yes, Angela was a poor traveller. I refrained from pointing out how much harder it was when we travelled to Turkey by boat and on horseback. I gave her ten minutes or so to cool down before I asked my next question. 'Are we nearly there yet?'

ANGELA

'Well, we've come quite a long way. We've flown over Portugal, Spain, the Balkans – there's actually a little map you can look at – '

VIRGINIA

'Not at the moment. One tires of screens. Spain – is it still Fascist?'

ANGELA

Christ, she was so out of date! But yet, of course, I had no right to feel impatient. 'No, but they outlasted the Nazis. Franco was in power until 1975.'

That was what, three decades after her death. No-one ever thinks like that though, do they? 'This curse will go on thirty years after I die.'

When would I die? Was it really – real? That lives would be lived beyond my understanding? Gerda – a pang as I thought of her. She would be thirty, forty. How long would I know her? The loneliness of her going on, beyond my comfort, beyond my help.

How did we ever get so far apart? Why did I send my daughter away?

VIRGINIA

'You know my nephew was lost in Spain.'

He stayed behind, young, a sacrifice, and we grew older, and left him behind. His eternal youth became terrible.

Just a series of sunlit fragments – Julian laughing or explaining, his big hands waving, why we were all wrong – but as time went on, his hands clung, and hurt.

I will never know if Nessa recovered. It seemed to me she never would.

The year he died, even nature seemed poisoned. I barely left my sister's side. Night after night, summer and winter. The universe was nothing but brute confusion, its rhythms pointless, lifeless, aimless.

Then, the next spring, the garden urns, casually filled with wind-blown plants. Around them, violets, daffodils. My favourites, the sweet-sharp, strong-scented narcissi, stood looking straight ahead at nothing, because I didn't have the heart to enjoy them, didn't, as usual, bend to look into their eyes, so even the garden became hard and blind. In that year, Nature gave no comfort. There was no point, if youth had died.

(he was Nessa's hope he was our future)

53

In another universe, Gerda has landed. Yes, she feels lucky as they bounce, lightly, roar down the runway, come to a halt. She has made it to America! This is more or less as far as she has let herself think. As she plink-plonks down the metal walkway, other thoughts creep into the waiting void –

– this forest of signs: Arrivals, Transfers, Baggage Claim, Immigration Control – when she'd come with Dad, she clung on to his hand and he made all the hard decisions –

yes, the young self she was with Dad, getting piggy-backs when she was tired, trying out her rollerblades in Central Park – seven years old, Mum and Dad had just got married, life was brilliant, both her parents adored her –

where had she lost that Wonder Child?)

Gerda has a worry – thirteen-year-olds have worries, but she hopes fourteen-year-olds would not – that every day she is growing less brilliant, further from the toddler she's seen in photographs, pink and rosy, snub-nosed and sturdy, with carrot-red hair that shone in the sun, who, she was told, announced to the world as she was lifted out of the bath, not yet two, 'I'm a person.'

Is she becoming less of a person? Has the grownup world nibbled her edges?

Certainly not. She steps on to the escalator and keeps on going, overtaking other people off the same plane, trying to look like a person in a hurry. Dad had told her – what had Dad told her? 'Never take a case on an escalator.' But it's OK, she's only got a backpack.

Their trip to New York had been the best trip ever, but any trip with Dad would be the best trip ever. He had bought her a Swiss Army knife at the airport (this was before everything good got banned.) The hasp was red and shiny with a small Swiss shield. 'That shield will always keep you safe, Gerda.' He'd explained to her what each part did – the bottle-opener, the corkscrew, the file. The bit that she wanted to use the most was the gizmo for getting stones out of hooves, which seemed to promise an adventurous life (though she always meant to live with Dad, and Mum could live nearby with a washing machine, and come in to bin the pizza boxes). This pleasant thought carried her with her backpack safely down the moving stairs.

Dad's knife was sitting in her case right now, being whizzed towards her in Baggage Claim. She was feeling happy to think of it, though oddly, the case was otherwise empty, 1) because in general, Gerda didn't need things, once she had her book, and socks, and money, but 2) because she'd done magical thinking, which she knew in general was a Bad Idea ...

It had all happened at the very last minute this morning, she was leaving home, the cab was waiting – surely Mum would be delighted to pay for her cab? – when she remembered her phone, still charging in the kitchen, so sweating, panting, ran back up the steps to get it – saw the dirty knife and fork in the sink, and thought of her Swiss Army knife – Dad's knife! –

fetched it, stuffed it in her backpack, but stopped mid-stuffing, cos of course, it wasn't legal!

'It will always keep you safe, Gerda'

She nearly put it down, then the worry assailed her, if you don't take the knife, something bad's going to happen, if you do take the knife, the knife will save you,

and although she knew this was Magical Thinking she grabbed Mum's Prada suitcase to put it in, which was shell-pink, ditsy and elegant, with bits of glittering gold on it. She knew her mother would be angry about it, but it was the only case she could see, so she'd bumped it down the stairs in a frantic hurry and rushed out of the door to find the cab still waiting and didn't forget to double lock, well done Gerda, she told herself –

– but something was missing in the sequence, she realised as she stepped off the escalator, something struck her no, no, make it not true a cold sweat prickled from her neck, her back

had she forgotten it no she would never

no, no but yes, yes

had she got distracted, and forgotten her phone???!!!

Was it still plugged in to the kitchen wall???!!!

Gerda stood at the entrance to Baggage Claim patting all her pockets again and again, repeating the sequence, then varying it, her level of hopelessness slowly rising.

SHE COULDN'T RING MUM TO TELL HER SHE WAS COMING.

Mum and Dad were both suddenly far away. She stood very alone, shrinking into herself.

Baggage Claim was enormous and full of strangers. When you arrive, people should meet you – the thought popped angrily into her head. Which carousel would the luggage be on? She looked around for passengers from the same plane. No, not a soul. Then she saw a sign: LONDON. Most of them must have already gone.

Unwanted bags still circled sadly, dwarfed by the spaces left by luckier ones. They all looked slightly shabby and ugly. 'Look, they forgot us,' they seemed to say. Gerda watched their slow dance in gathering worry (Mum only bought that case a few months ago, she claimed to cheer her up when I started boarding school). But finally, a jolt of pink, and glory – at least she still had her mum's pet piece of luggage, at least Dad's knife would be inside. The catches and the 'P' flashed gold as she swung it, light as air, to the floor. She felt loads better, instantly.

Millions of people forgot their phones. It didn't matter, since she knew where Mum was. In a funny way, as she pulled out the handle which slipped like expensive silk into position, as the pink case followed her like a pink poodle or like a pink nut-shell with a rattling kernel, both her parents were with her now – not that she needed them, of course.

Gerda had googled public transport from the airport. She knew in theory where to go, where the airport line met the New York subway, but she havered, briefly, when she got to

ARRIVALS, and TAXIS seemed to be written in sunlight, big yellow taxis bearing her away, and after all, it was her mother's money.

Soon the yellow taxi was swooping her onward through the dazzling early afternoon. (Had she seen this – ordinary bit of it, with Dad? These roads didn't look American enough.)

'You did say Wordsmiths Hotel, Manhattan?'

'Fifty-fourth Street,' Gerda said, and felt better for the confidence of that, because streets had numbers, and she knew hers.

'Fifty-fourth and Fifth,' the man agreed.

Soon the towers were growing up all round them, and it was easily American enough. She saw a rabble of religious nutters with signs, bobbing. PRAISE, one said. HE IS RISEN. Briefly, it spoke to the cheerfulness in her heart. Gerda was excited; Gerda was afraid; Gerda refused to be afraid.

But what if Mum had gone out for lunch?

'Are we nearly there yet?' she asked the driver.

'You're nearly there.' Gerda swallowed hard. What if Mum wasn't pleased to see her?

In the stewards' hutch on the Turkish Airlines plane, trapped between the two cabins, the staff are hyper: they are nearly there. They are nervously devouring three uneaten breakfasts and some chocolates discarded by VIPs. They have been flying for ten hours; in ten minutes they will begin preparation for landing. The party of Israelis had not been too bad, despite the commotion in the gangways: at least the children had been no trouble. 'Better than British *çulsuzlar*,' said the chief steward. 'Imagine having thirty-two Brits. Whining children, shouting parents, having to lie that the bar has closed. If they fight a war again, they'll lose.' 'Why say that?' Süleyman objected. He had a cousin who lived in Enfield. One day he would go and stay with her, if he could get around the problem with the visa. 'We will never fight another war with the British,' and he helped himself to another croissant. It wasn't very nice, but his blood sugar was dipping, and it was a pity to let things waste. 'In any case,' the chief steward said, 'we beat them last time, thanks to the Father. In the War of Independence,' he told the two young women stewards, who knew nothing about history, so were idiots at the mercy of Prime Minister Erdoğan and his 'modernising' neo-Ottomans, who were actually sending Turkey back into the dark ages. 'And I never want to see you in a veil,' he told Amara. 'Atatürk died to get you women freedoms.' 'Leave her alone,' said her friend Maha. 'You're just another man trying to tell her what to do.' 'He's exaggerating,' said Süleyman. 'Atatürk died of cancer, didn't he?' 'He lost us our language,'

Amara said. She was vague about it, but someone had said so.

Now the chief steward became really angry. He allowed certain freedoms from the younger staff, but nobody should traduce the Father. 'And this means?' he asked her. 'You haven't a clue. You are just repeating what Erdoğan's mob say. It was the *written* language Atatürk changed, so Turkey could be part of the modern world. So other countries could understand us, and we weren't just lonely peasants on a hillside.' 'We weren't peasants,' said Süleyman. 'Who gave us the airport?' the chief steward demanded. 'Atatürk. Who gave us a constitution? Atatürk. Who gave us motorways? Atatürk. Without Atatürk, you'd have no job, you'd have been married at eleven, if anyone would have you. Now get back to the cabin and collect the trays.'

'I'm sorry, Sir,' she said, chastened. She loved the chief steward, who'd been kind to her, kinder, in fact, than her stepfather, who had tried to stop her training, but her grandmother had stuck up for her. 'I did not mean to insult the Father. Of course I didn't, we grew up loving him.' Yet he had lived so long ago. It was hard for her to imagine the 1930s, when her grandmother had been a girl. She couldn't grasp such a vast stretch of time. An eleven hour flight could feel like a lifetime.

They all fell silent, and just for a second, as the plane banked steeply into the sun and a diamond of white light cut into the cabin, the old leader seemed to be in the room with them, his great kindly head and refulgent eyes, reassuring them about the future: they need not fear the imams, nor Syria, nor America.

'Süleyman, you'll get fat,' said Amara. She was never down for long. 'Come and help. The Americans have spilled food on the floor.'

They did the gangway run together, a left and a right,

keeping pace with each other. Amara liked working with Süleyman. He told her things she needed to know, and she was not in awe of him. She wondered if he might not be normal, but at least he did not fancy her. He was a graduate; he knew things.

As they put away the containers of rubbish, she asked him, quietly, so the others wouldn't hear, 'Do you think it's true what some people say, that life was better for us before Erdoğan? Is it true there are lots of people in prison?'

He motioned, delicately, for her to be quiet, but smiled in a way that meant 'Don't worry.' 'Maybe things were better then than now,' he said. 'But life is for living. Things are good.'

She clicked the clasps of the containers shut and smiled at him. 'Life is simple.'

VIRGINIA

The will to live, that animal will. It carries one on, past so much despair. When my father died, it seemed impossible, the disappearance of the giant father, always behind me, sheltering, looming, for he loved my writing and believed in me. The keeper of the library, who opened it to me. I was desolate. Then the wound healed over. Second by second, minute by minute, day by day, loss became – less. His shadow shrank. I saw beyond him.

Could it have been the same for Leonard?

If my father had lived, I could never have written. His weight would have extinguished me.

ANGELA

'Virginia, have you got any rubbish? They are trying to collect our rubbish.'

Of course she didn't care about them. She was lost in thought, she barely looked up.

VIRGINIA (*passing a paper napkin*)

'I see you haven't solved the servant problem.'

ANGELA

'Virginia, please don't talk like that. The cabin staff are not our servants.'

VIRGINIA

'Of course they are. It's obvious. You sit in comfort, they are servants.'

ANGELA

'Virginia, please! Servants is not a word we use.'

VIRGINIA (*laughing*)

'That changes nothing. They are the servants, we are the masters – '

ANGELA (*protesting*)

'Shhhushh.'

VIRGINIA

'Oh, is it like the Jews? Are we not allowed to call them that?'

ANGELA

'We are not going to talk about it.'

VIRGINIA

'I start to think we were more free than you are … We talked about everything in Gordon Square. Never mind your scruples about "servants" and "Jews". We were always talking about buggers and semen.'

(*The young Hasidic woman beside her looks astonished, but then laughs.*)

ANGELA

'It's not clever, Virginia, honestly. You did ask me to take you with me to Turkey. You can't go on like this in Istanbul. You don't understand. It's a Muslim country.'

VIRGINIA

Her cheeks were getting very red again. Perhaps it was the change of life? It was clear she had no idea about Turkey, which seemed to us peculiarly free. Men urinated in the street; there were books devoted to copulation. We shopped for silver in the markets and I found a little charm, beautifully carved, of a man and woman in the act of congress. You could touch them, gently, and they performed. I still imagined, then, it would be my lot. I gave the silversmith fifteen lira.

Just when does the course of one's life become set? I might have been a milch-cow like Vanessa ...

ANGELA

'Virginia, put your seat belt on. The air hostess is talking to you – flight attendant, sorry.'

VIRGINIA

(Yes, they were obsessed with the names of things.)

Somewhere I lost it, that little silver charm. I looked out of the window, and there it was –

ANGELA

'Look! Quick, there's another plane – '

VIRGINIA

Like a brilliant silver needle, tiny – like a messenger, or the flash of a thought – a jet plane, was it, slender as a thread, fast as a minnow, sprinting below us – through blue, then cloud –

And then it was gone. And my life was changed. It was taken away, what I could have been. Those years of breakdown, after I married. Leonard was afraid, and left me alone, but part of me always regretted it. I could have been more of a wife, a mother. The window opened, and then it closed.

The beak flashed, and the fish were eaten. Before I knew it, I had grown old.

AMARA

'Please, Miss, put your seat belt on.'

ANGELA

'Ten minutes to landing in Turkey, Virginia. Are you excited? It will be so different from ... when were you there, 1906? And the second visit was – 1910?'

My Hasidic neighbour was looking at me strangely. But Virginia was less of an anomaly than he was. Both of them were relics from another time.

VIRGINIA

'The second time in Turkey was so different.'

The unthinkable loss after the first visit. My elder brother, my conspirator. I envied Thoby, but adored him, of course. He came with us to Greece on the way to Turkey, we rode and walked through the blue aromatic mountains, naming the gods and their transformations; he read us Greek, we drank that rough wine and I had too much and got a headache, but we plotted futures of fantastic greatness as the moon rose and fell and the crickets sang and the white vines of stars slowly faded into morning. That night I knew we would always be happy.

But I was the one who had the future. The gods demanded a sacrifice. Thoby's muscular back as he walked ahead. The illness must have already been inside him, breeding secretly, beckoning. The Furies saw the illness stirring, it signalled to them, and their nostrils flared; they reached out and touched him with their scaly fingers. Two spots of red appeared in his cheeks. The doctors could do nothing to save him, those grave old mummers with their hopeless nostrums.

The bravest, most beautiful of us was dead. They called him the Goth, but his death was not noble. He was incoherent, incontinent, he had wagered all on his intellect, but it wasted his flesh, his big, healthy, helpless body. Days after he died, Vanessa agreed to marry Clive, his dearest friend, I lost my sister as well as my brother, and she began another life as a mother.

(She went everywhere first: sex, childbirth. When I tried with Leonard, her probing questions forced their way into my intimate places and made me feel inferior. She placed her finger on her lips – no, Ginia, too much for you: I agree with Leonard, you can never be a mother.)

In the long view, was she such a good sister?

She is not here to answer me. She was dear to me. I must not grow bitter.

Oh, Vanessa oh, my Nessa

ANGELA
'Virginia? Did you say something?'

VIRGINIA
'It doesn't feel as if we're going down.'

ANGELA
'The pilot said we're in a holding pattern. Which means there's a queue of planes wanting to land. He also said there would be turbulence … we might have a bit of a bumpy ride.'

We were suddenly banking, horribly – one wing was making a bee-line for the ground.

VIRGINIA (*leaning across her neighbours*)
'All I can see is sea.'

ANGELA (*peering the other way*)

'The other side, there's a mass of black cloud.'

Then we straightened up. We were climbing again.

The flight attendants were checking that the overhead baggage containers were closed, and walking up and down looking purposeful, removing bags from the emergency exit rows. We must have been circling for twenty minutes; I was willing the plane to start to swoop down, but at the end of each curve, it climbed once more.

VIRGINIA

I realised my companion was nervous. Yet she was the frequent flyer, not me. I wondered: dare I reassure her?

Sometimes Nessa laughed when I tried to help her. She was never so dear as when she needed me.

ANGELA

Distraction, that was what I needed. 'Virginia, could you give me back *The Times*? I might do the crossword while we're landing ... "Domestic beast starts a phrase of poem in classical denouement" ... Eleven letters, begins with 'c'. Damn this pen. You're right, they're hopeless.' Was it the air pressure? I gouged the paper. Then I tried gentleness: twizzled it, shook it.

VIRGINIA

'Crosswords, to us, were an American craze.' (The answer to the clue was obvious, though ...)

1910. Over a century ago. The message came, and I had to go. Vanessa was miscarrying in Bursa, a boat trip away from Constantinople.

It was me she asked for. Roger wrote to me. And then I showed them what I was made of. I travelled alone, I travelled hard, I refused to fear heat, or snakes, or strangers, I went by

boat and bus and horseback and crossed Europe in less than four days. I found her lying in a darkened room. I became a man, off to save a woman – I was brave Gerda in my childhood book, my beautiful gold-and-green *Hans Andersen's Fairy Stories* that my father bought for me when I was eleven, Gerda, my favourite, who saved little Kay, a brave girl who saved a boy – Angela had named her daughter well.

Later I used that trip in *Orlando*. I was *Orlando*. A man-woman.

The pilot said 'Cabin crew, ten minutes to landing.'

ANGELA
The braying American was at it again, stopping me thinking about that clue. 'It's not their fault, they're just, frankly, at an earlier stage of human civilisation. But at heart, they are warm, simple people.'

'I wanna buy silver,' his wife complained, in a grating, whining, little girl voice. 'You gotta take me to the Bazaar, Howie. With you I know they won't get away with anything. You can come with us, Miss – I don't know your name.'

'Thanks, I'll be fine,' said the student.

The American bored on regardless. 'If you earn their respect, they'll be friends for life …'

'Do you have any Turkish friends?' asked the student.

Then we all gasped in unison.

VIRGINIA
'Catastrophe,' I said to Angela.

'What?' she said, anxious.

'Your crossword clue.'

ANGELA
We were going down, we were racketing down through

blinding yellow nets of lightning, bumping like a stone through black attics of cloud, floor after floor through a great broken building, electrics flashing to left and right.

VIRGINIA
'Angela, are you all right?'

ANGELA (*her hand shoots out, unthinking, and lands on Virginia's lap: Virginia clasps it*)
'Tiny bit bumpy, isn't it?'

VIRGINIA
'The sea voyage was so much worse.'

ANGELA
I valued her hand. I didn't want to lose it. In that moment, she mothered me.
 Ten minutes of fear can be a very long time. I was almost glad when she started talking, until I heard what she had to say —

VIRGINIA
'So what WILL happen at my conference? The conference, I mean. Not my conference.'
 (There is a collective groan and laugh as the plane tips and swoops, spectacularly.)

PILOT
'Cabin crew to positions for landing.'

ANGELA (*withdrawing her hand*)
'Virginia, I just want to get there.'

VIRGINIA

Now we plunged into another universe, a parallel universe of playful demons. Yes, I was ready, I felt excited –

It was the moment when darkness threatens, when if a feather alighted in the scale we would be cast down into the bottomless pit. One feather, and the plane, its back broken, would pitch us down into the depths – in the burning wreck, they might have found my bones, and who would they have thought I was?

I saw the body of the plane strewn over the city, perhaps in the wide green space in Pera, a broken, blackened insect of steel. They would remove our charred bodies. Later, picnickers might seek shelter there; lovers at night might lie on the gangways; a man with a goat might sleep in the galley, and a tramp creep up near them to ward off the cold. Then the roof would fall in; briars and hemlocks would blot out the seats, the lavatories, the eyes of windows. Grass and young plants would take root in blown sand, then brambles would flower and fruit above them, till some trespasser, losing his way in the park, could tell only by the fin of one wing, sticking up forlornly from a tangle of blackberries, that here once hundreds of people had flown, a plane full of people, their hopes, their plans, the families with babies, the couple holding hands, the young mother planning her next play for young people, 'Follow the ways of our forefathers' –

But a force was working that kept us flying. Angela shook her pen: the story went on.

ANGELA

'Oh God, oh God, oh God *save* us – '

(*They bump, hit, bump, bump-bump to a stop.*)

God. Thank God.

I am not religious, but at such moments, one calls on someone. A wash of relief left me exhausted. I loosened my seat belt and sank back to rest as the plane taxied towards its station.

We could have died. We were here, alive.

I thought of Gerda. And I thought of Edward.

What would they feel if I died in an air crash? Edward would suffer, and have regrets.

CHIEF STEWARD
'Please remain seated till the seat belt signs are turned off.'

ANGELA
No, he would never marry again. He might turn our house into a museum ... Yes, the Angela Lamb Museum ... Schools would bring parties to visit it ...

It was summer, the lawn was mown and all the roses were in full bloom. Edward, wearing the chief steward's uniform, was pushing a trolley of tea and coffee and selling duty-free copies of my books ... he could barely cope with the numbers. They poured down the gangways, unstoppable, jostling, with bags and cases and people treading hard on my foot, and flight attendants who tapped me on the shoulder and said –

AMARA
'Excuse me, Miss, perhaps you are dozing. Time to disembark from the aircraft. I'll get my colleague to help you, ladies.'

ANGELA (*jerking awake*)
'I'm not asleep.'

(*Takes stock of the half-empty plane.*)

'Virginia, why didn't you wake me? I must have been in everybody's way.'

VIRGINIA
'The Jews weren't bothered, they simply pushed past. And I took the opportunity to look at your map. Our hotel is in the heart of the old city.'

SÜLEYMAN (*to Virginia, not Angela*)
'Madam, please, let me carry your cases.'

ANGELA (*crossly, to Amara*)
'Actually half her things are in *my* hand luggage. It's very heavy. Can you help me?'

A minute later they were on their way. The two spoiled women – Americans, weren't they? – were almost the last straw for the flight attendants, blood sugar low after the eleven-hour journey. The praying passengers, the nappy changes, the kosher meals, the extra hand-luggage ... Now these American bitches couldn't leave the plane.

They found one last smile: 'Enjoy your holiday, Madam.'

'It's work, actually,' Angela huffed.

And then they were gone, and the plane was their own. Littered with plastic, paper-bags, blankets, newspapers, tissues – but their own. The crew smiled and drew a deep breath. Amara said 'I can't stand Americans,' and Süleyman said 'And I can't stand Jews.'

But the empty, disordered plane was in sunlight, the last strip of gold before the storm came, and Süleyman touched his friend on the arm and said 'You know I don't really mean it,'

and Amara nodded. 'I didn't mind the older one. She actually gave me a lovely smile.'

'Which one was older?' asked Süleyman. He was blind to the finer points of women, or maybe Angela was looking exhausted.

'We have to look after them in any case,' Amara said.

'Not for a bit,' said Süleyman. He was off until the flight back to New York tomorrow.

Time to go home, kick the nearest human and de-stress by stroking the cat.

Turkish people love cats: Americans, dogs.

VIRGINIA

I stood just inside the cabin door, dazzled by the light at the top of the steps, trembling before a new beginning. Through the open door the beauty of the world came murmuring, too softly to hear exactly what it said – but there were birds, who sounded like the same birds that sang in New York and in London, I didn't know exactly what species they were, there was deep golden light as I walked forward and all I saw was their wing-tips scattering like little black letters on the clouds' dark velvet – the storm through which we'd swooped was still alive above us, on the point of breaking. What did it matter if I didn't know the names of the birds, if their meaning, which was life, which was beauty, was plain? Air on my face. Fresh living air.

Angela still lingered behind me somewhere.

ANGELA

I faltered at the point when I landed with Virginia. I was, after a fashion, at home in New York, but in Turkey I was still a newbie. Yes, I had been there several times before, but I didn't have the skills to look after her. I had only brought her because she pleaded.

I trudged like a zombie through the queue for visas. The storm rumbled like a giant's borborygms through the airport roof above us. I didn't care, we were on the ground.

Virginia's big shining eyes were darting about, up, down, everywhere. I envied her vivacity – no wonder she had bounced

back from the dead. The visa queues were even longer than usual. Virginia tried to chat to the official, who smiled tolerantly but stayed silent. She was interested by such irrelevant things – the baggage carousel, a good-looking policeman.

Once we'd finally got to the cattle-drive of taxis, I slumped on the seat, gave the driver the address, which he failed to understand though I pronounced it correctly, wrote it down on a piece of paper, to humour him, and slept again, almost at once.

VIRGINIA

'So are all the taxis in the modern world yellow?' They looked exactly like the ones in New York. 'Angela? Did you hear me?'

The woman was actually asleep again! I hoped the driver had not noticed. Perhaps he would take advantage, and drive us by a roundabout route. I remembered the traders who robbed us in the market, though of course that was almost a century ago. Socks, shirts, curtain material, the Turks had got the better of us. It was half the price it would have been back home, but we expected it to be cheaper still …

Though it's true the shirts were beautifully stitched. Maybe they didn't rob us at all.

I sat and read my guidebook in the queer stormy sunlight, looking out of the window as the city unfolded. Strange red Germanic tower-blocks near the airport like Fritz Lang's film, *Metropolis*. I saw it with Leonard in – was it 1927? – *The Spectator* had just given me a positive review, we held hands in the dark, we were happy and excited … So Lang was right about the future. Or perhaps Turkish architects had seen his films – did dreams of the future have such power? Had today's young women read *A Room of One's Own*?

I stared through gaps in the dull buildings on the right at the dazzling dark of the Sea of Marmara, which I sailed across

in glory as a very young woman, so long ago, on the winds of the morning, as dawn came up over Constantinople, but now I just glimpsed its beauty through traffic, dark, blue-dark, reflecting the sky as great tree roots of lightning plunged into it and vanished. Angela slept on, and I did not try to rouse her.

My darling Vanessa. If I could, would I wake her? No-one was dearer to me than my sister – we could be here together again, hand in hand – and yet I had learned from the Hades of the laptop that her life after I died had been long, and hard, that Duncan loved boys into his dotage, that her goddess good looks grew dry and worn and our family sadness fell upon her like hoar frost.

I should leave her, then, exhausted as she was, to sleep all the ages of the earth away.

Gently the waves would break (maybe Angela heard them in her sleep); tenderly the light, which was a deep golden storm-light, the apocalyptic beauty before the fall, would touch the blue skin of her closed eyelids.

And as I groped for the thought, 'Why is everyone sleeping?' – I shut my guidebook, and drifted away.

Nothing broke their sleep, not even the storm, until, as they drove along by the water where men still stood with fishing-lines, there was a burst of car-horns, and their eyes opened wide.

Four western eyes looked for eastern beauty.

Here we are again, Angela thought, sitting bolt upright in her seat. Awake.

And Virginia thought: Constantinople. And then, straight away, rethinking: Istanbul. For she was starting to see that the names mattered.

PART THREE

Virginia in Istanbul

There's thunder in Istanbul, and thunder in New York. Thunder from the trains underneath both cities and in Istanbul also from trams above the cobbles. Blank sheets of lightning banging like migraine.

Turkey is doing very nicely, thank you. Its economy is on fast forward. Once the Turks wanted to join Europe, and the euro: for years they struggled to meet impossible targets of fiscal well-being (though the countries demanding them were deep in debt) and human rights (which they did not agree with, but found they did not have the right to refuse). Despite all their efforts, they were never accepted. And now that Turkey's economy is whizzing, while the euro limps from crisis to crisis, they are not so sure that they want to join Europe. They can trade with Russia, or the Gulf States, or China …

But the Europeans and Americans still come in their thousands to holiday here, they throng to the 'exotic' Old City or the 'cool' young streets around Istiklal, they queue in the heat to see what lies under the great red dome of the Aya Sophia or the blue-green citadel of the Blue Mosque with its pattern of domes like crusted shells and its tall, musical minarets, and they sigh at the skyline of the city at sunset, and exclaim for a day or two at the call to prayer, though after you have stayed in Istanbul for more than a few days you might start to hate it, the wailing at midnight and five in the morning. But if you stay longer, and begin to belong, you no longer hear it, unless you are the faithful, it's just one of the five, six, seven dimensions of one of the thousands of worlds that meet here, a voice that has

been calling for nine hundred years since Constantinople fell to Mehmet the Turk.

Though history here is much longer than that. Before the Turks there were the holy Roman emperors and the savage hegemony of the Christians, and before the Christians were the Pagans, and before the Pagans there were ... What?

Goat-bells. Human animals crouched on the shore at the meeting of two seas and three waterways, collecting wood at nightfall to make a fire. At a time when in New York, Manhattan – 'Manahatta' – there were only bears, and mammoths, and trees, and Central Park was a granite wilderness, and the rain fell everywhere, all over the world, and there were no borders, or written names.

On Fifty-third Street, New York – where a bookseller, Evri, with the headache he always gets before storms (who just snapped at a journalist on the phone, 'Of course people will go on buying physical books, why do you people?') sits staring at the taxis out in the road, counting them like golden beads on a string, not seeing a red-headed child peering in – and on Divan Yolu Caddesi, Istanbul, where the tourists are panicked by the thought of getting wet – yellow taxis are filling up with people: Turks in New York, Americans in Turkey, Yanks and Turks a long way from home, and the blue-black sky far above them darkens one more shade and pours down.

(In New York, Gerda's unhappy. She has saved half the chocolate bar she bought at the airport in case there is an Emergency, because Dad once said 'Always save half your rations when you are on an Expedition', but the uneaten chocolate in her pocket makes her hungry. And she's asked the taxi to stop, on a whim, 'I am going to buy my mother a present,' because she saw the bookshop, and she suddenly couldn't bear to reach the hotel,

just in case – just in case Mum isn't ...

'I can't park here,' the driver said. 'You can walk from here, it's only half a block,' pointing up the street, in a would-be reassuring fashion. Gerda pays him the money, and gets out, very slowly, cautious as a snail.)

In both cities, poorer people run from the thunderheads above in a last-ditch attempt to escape the rain, *It's here* – tangling up the runners as they put on a spurt, pitting the surface of the Hudson and Newark Bay and the swells of Bosphorus and Marmara the same – hissing past slates and bouncing back up again with terrible force from drains, turning streets dark, turning shoes, coats, gutters, bags, leaves, dust, stone – now everything's black.

(Fifty-third Street quickly turns into a river, and Gerda makes up her mind and darts inside the bookshop.)

Just a few bright drops of time are left for a hundred silver sardines on Galata Bridge, Istanbul. Scooped out by the veil of lines that trail from the blue iron parapets, they swim on bravely in polystyrene boxes. In plastic beakers, smaller fry bunch like flowers: sprats lie head-down in a collar of blood.

The rain hits Galata, the fishermen run, Ali picks up, drops, then kicks over his box, and a single fish slithers and buckets through the rails and leaps, leaps for the sea. Alive!

'The fish is very good here, Virginia,' says Angela, rubbing her eyes. 'You must try the fish.'

Virginia's eyes brighten. 'I adore fish.'

(In New York, the rain is battering the glass, there don't seem to be many adult books, and the dark-haired man at the till looks depressed. Gerda compromises with a large greetings card: there are plenty of witty ones, not all of them pathetic.

But she chooses one with two women, one of them looking more like a granny, captioned in silver ' I couldn't live without you. You gave me life. Mum, I love you.' Of course it is soppy, and she prefers the others, but she buys this one, which speaks her heart.

Then she slips into the children's corner of the bookshop. If her mother were here, Gerda would refuse to go there. But Gerda suddenly wants to be a child. She has finished *To the Lighthouse*, her brain is tired. Sitting at the table for crayoning, Gerda writes a message of love to her mother. Happy, she sets off again down the pavement; her two bags feel as light as birds, perching for luck on her left shoulder; the downpour is over: sun in the puddles. Nothing will go wrong. It will be perfect from the start. Gerda splashes pell-mell along the New York street towards Mummy, Mummy, Mum, Mummy.)

The hotel Angela picked is in Istanbul's Old City: Sultanahmet, not far from the Blue Mosque, the university, Aya Sophia, the Grand Bazaar. But some way away from the crowded main streets, with their belling of tramcars on steel tracks, their touts and pedlars on the lookout for the throngs of tourists from richer countries – 'Hallo! Speak English?' – selling everything from ice cream and corncobs to $10,000 carpets, which may be worth $1,000.

'It's very strange the way time passes,' says Virginia as they climb out of their taxi. 'And everything but us remains. We came by sea, before, in the very early morning, we came up on deck to see the dawn, and it burned on the golden domes and windows. My sister has gone. All of us have gone. But those airy domes are still standing, as if the past had waited for me.'

'Don't talk to me for a minute, Virginia, I've got to pay the taxi,' Angela says. 'Unless of course you've got the money ready? No, I thought not. Right, I'm doing it.'

Angela wishes, briefly but intensely, that she were travelling with Gerda. A young child, not an elderly one. Enough of the past. She longs for the future.

Yes, she needs a rest from Virginia.

59

VIRGINIA (*rings Angela's room, with deliberation, peering at the paper where she's written the number down.*)
'Hallo?'

ANGELA
I had hardly got there. I had not unpacked. She rang, making demands, as usual.

The hotel's wireless key didn't work. It was typical, typical, just my luck. I needed to de-stress with my email. But the phone rang before I could think.

'Angela! Is it you?'

'Obviously.'

'You see, I managed the telephone! I am getting the hang of the twenty-first century. I love my room! – so much plainer than the one at the Wordsmiths Hotel, but it's bigger. Whenever you're ready, I would like to go out.'

'Virginia, give me a minute. You're sure your room is bearable? '

'It's delightful. The window opens on the street.'

'Well close it at once. That's not safe.'

VIRGINIA
Naturally I took no notice. A bird was singing, there were people going home, women were laughing and calling to each other. It was small-scale, human. It felt almost familiar. The air was cool and freshly washed. My curtain moved like the sea in the breeze.

ANGELA

'Are you going to close it?'

VIRGINIA

'Mmm. Though I need some air. I remember walking through the streets, at sunset. From Pera, we saw over the Bosphorus …'

ANGELA

'I know, I know, but I've got things to do.'

I didn't mean to be short, but yes, I did know because of course, as ever, it was in the *Diaries*, that secret passage so many of us had crept down without her knowledge or consent.

And yet, the writing, the writing … what a loss if Leonard had obeyed her! Her description of Aya Sophia … As usual, when I really thought about her writing, my irritation with her vanished.

(Would I ever get the chance to tell her what her work meant? How she had changed possibility for all of us? I tried often to express my love for her work, but all it evinced was a glazed, distant look as if I were showing some kind of bad manners, and then I grew shy, and my words faded. Would she always see me as a glorified servant?

Of course, in her work, she wrote better than anyone of her time about the lot of servants; but her horror and shame about the life they lived – which she knew made her own life possible – sometimes came out in contempt and hatred. But the best of her, the best of her … she deserved to be remembered by the best of her.

I could not bear it if Virginia despised me.)

'Let's meet for supper. Seven o'clock?'

She said, 'But that is two hours away. I think I might go and stretch my legs.'

'Virginia, you cannot go out by yourself!'

But I could. I did. I unpacked my coat, my yellow coat that made me feel youthful. I had the Turkish money we'd changed at the airport. It felt like toy money, crisp and strange. Maybe I would go and buy presents with it. Yes, I had always loved buying presents!

(But then I thought, who for? And felt sad. No, never mind, live in the moment.)

I left the window open to air the room. I'm afraid it is a lower-class attitude, assuming all foreigners are thieves. The wind played lightly with the curtains, and through them I saw a veiled young woman emerge from our hotel with a bundle of laundry, so maybe she had been working here – she bent down in the street to play with a cat, a thin golden cat with a triangular head and delicately arching spine, her hand rose and fell, it was a kind of ballet, then another young woman crossed the street, she was waiting for her, the two embraced – a leaf blew in and caught in the casement, edged with a line of diamante rain-drops, and suddenly I was completely happy.

To be on my own. Alive. In Turkey. Laughing with pleasure, I went out into the air.

Gerda, half the world away, is marching on her Promised Land
– Central Park, where she was once so happy swooping on her
new rollerblades, out of control, towards her father, screaming
with joy, mad with terror. Gerda has eaten a hamburger (yum!)
with orange, pecan and maple syrup (yuck!) and one supersized
portion of fries.

One road to cross before she gets there.

But Gerda is fleeing unfriendly voices, truth-telling
voices, harsh and loud. *Retard! Moron! Dimmoid! Malco!* She is
summoning all her reserves of self-love against the self-hatred
that's out to get her. She isn't afraid, not really, not yet, because
she dare not feel the fear.

Mum isn't here
Dad isn't here

The men in the Wordsmiths Hotel had been kind. Yes, they
knew Angie Lamb and Mrs Woolf. They had left 'only the
other day'.

'They can't have done,' Gerda told them, flatly. (*They had
gone! Gone! Was it possible?*)

The younger man looked. 'Yeah, they checked out. The
English ladies. Both of them.'

The older man expressed admiration, tilted towards Virginia.
'Extraordinary lady.'

'Which hotel have they moved to, please?' Gerda had
struggled to sound normal but her voice came out squeaky,

like a bossy mouse.

'They never said. Just "Istanbul".'

(Istanbul! Not possible! Stupid hotel man has got it wrong!)
'No, she was actually going to a conference. My mother is
a writer. It's an … international conference.' But as she said
'international', trying to impress them, trying to sound cool,
Gerda started to worry, started to shake, could not shut out her
terrible fear. It had kept on coming for her, ever since she'd
landed, snaking towards her from the shallow water where she
stumbled on problems too big for her –

'Your mother did say she had a daughter.'

'I think it was the other one who mentioned you,' the
younger, thinner man interrupted.

Gerda was torn between feeling sad her mother hadn't
mentioned her and proud that Virginia Woolf, superboffin
writer of the supercool book she had been reading on the
plane, actually knew that she existed. But gone! Gone! She
must not cry.

The older man gave her a good look over, smiling and
frowning through gold-framed glasses. 'You better stay here
while we contact ya mother. She musta left her mobile number.'

'No, it's all right,' said Gerda, dry-mouthed, 'you can leave
that to me, I'll give her a ring.' If they phoned up to tell her
Gerda was here, Mum would have a heart attack!

'It's fine,' she said. Then she had started to gabble. 'I'm
actually eighteen, I've got her debit card, she told me to take
it, she knew I was coming.' (It sounded unbelievable; it *was*
unbelievable.) 'I'd better just book in here for one night.'

'We'll give her a call, any case.' The younger man was looking
hard at her now, taking in her clothes, which had hamburger
stains, her uncombed hair, her improbable bag, pink and gold,
an eye magnet, the equally impossible age she claimed.

'Take a seat, young lady, make yaself at home,' the older

man added kindly (that Angie was a frost, you have to pity the daughter), but Gerda had darted past the younger one, the pink case flying out weightless as a wing, calling over her shoulder 'Don't trouble my mother, I'm going to be on the first flight home,' as the older man shouted 'Hang on, don't go!'

Their last sight of Gerda was running through a cohort of Japanese book-lovers who were just arriving, making her look bigger and older than she was.

'How old is that kid?'

'She said eighteen.'

'I thought that Ginny said thirteen ... Coulda misheard her with that crazy accent. Still, I better ring her mother. Let her know. Or do you wanna call her?'

But at that moment, the Japanese commenced intensive communal check-in, and the phone call to Angie Lamb was forgotten.

VIRGINIA

The city was just as I remembered. It was steep, so steep, the street we were in, and the hotels were dark, wooden-fronted. Narrow passageways, roughly cobbled, plunged down, down to where the water must be. So many things were almost familiar.

The tremendous change was the great snake of traffic that bumped its way down the centre of the highway, where once we saw carts, donkeys, dragomen. But the same array of physiognomies that I remembered from before, streaming down the pavements on both sides of the street, pale European (though perhaps they were Circassian, the sultans had chosen Circassian wives for their beautiful white skin and red Russian lips, I had read in Melek-Hanum's autobiography), Mongol, with those high cheekbones and strange, slanted, intelligent eyes (when I made simple observations of this sort to Angela, she contradicted, or disapproved, but honestly, how can one make sense of the world if one never hazards a generalisation? It is part of the work of ordering particulars; otherwise one's totally at sea. But my thoughts weren't allowed in the twenty-first century). Strong thickset men with short beards or dark jowls who could have been Turkish, Greek or Italian, talking loudly as they strolled in pairs; a few with jutting beards and downcast eyes which flicked up, momentarily, at my yellow coat; women with luxuriant blue-black hair that fell like blackbird's wings down their backs; others in every form of veil, some thick and padded out behind like an eccentric kind of back-to-front nosebag, long, tight overcoats in pastel shades,

the belt pulled draw-string tight at their waist, plus high-heeled shoes and heavy eye make-up – after a bit I saw it was a uniform for grouplets of young women clinging together, I supposed they were religious, but why the heavy eye make-up? – then other girls in the lightest of head-scarves, and some with curled yellow-blonde hair and dark roots; and women who must be from Arab countries, black from head to foot, only the eyes showing, which made them look curiously guilty as I caught little flashes of hidden life. A pale hand came out of one shroud, suddenly, and cuffed a small boy on the head, a little modern boy in shorts and a T-shirt which I saw, as I bent closer, read SPIDERMAN; he had a red plastic gun in his hand with which he was prodding his small, veiled sister. There were men who were clones of those I'd seen in New York, in crumpled business suits, with bulging briefcases, watching passing women with abstracted eyes; other men in calf-length tunics, pyjama trousers, and small round hats: and as I gazed at all the faces, skin-colours, sizes, I thought 'This country could rise again, maybe there will be a new Ottoman Empire, for after all, it sits at the isthmus of the world, it looks east and west, it is Asia and Europe. With the power of contradictions, it can rule us all. Look how vigorously people stream down the street, they have finished a day's work but they are not tired.' I could hardly wait for supper, so I could tell Angela!

Surely there was more vitality here than in the richer parts of Manhattan, where frail young men walked their waisted poodles and the fashionable women went out without trousers, and when you looked closely they were thirty years older than their long thin legs and blonded hair. Two decades might have been scraped off their faces but it just made them fainter, they were being erased, and I thought of Manhattan with the exits blocked, crashes in the tunnels, traffic-choked bridges, and I wondered, would New York sink under the sea while the Turks

leaped up like a school of dolphins?

(Then I remembered Central Park. The fresh green leaves, the springy joggers, the Spartan glamour of some of the people, elegant, polished, unstoppable as robots, fit as greyhounds, determined to win. And the mesmerising power of the big corporations, the black buildings blocking the sun ... No, Americans and Turks might be evenly matched.)

I was walking downhill into the end of the afternoon. My yellow coat danced beside me in shop windows. Surprise! A young man outside a barber's with the same striped pole we used to have in London – maybe we borrowed them from Turkey? – suddenly stretched out his arm and said 'Hallo, lady. How are you today?' He had thick black hair and his eyes were slightly crossed, there was a cushion of flesh around his waist – but I saw his muscles underneath his red shirt, and the teeth in his smile were young and white, I evaded his arm and slipped past him, gasping – I had left him behind, he was in the past, or was he shouting after me? – I found I was patting & stroking my hair – I hurried on, dazed by the light, past the random poems of strange hotels – The Coliseum, *The Rose Bouquets* – & their charming amateur attempts at decoration: asymmetrical trees hung with orange lanterns, a wooden hotel with baroque Spanish casements, a tree-trunk snaked around with fairy-lights. Anything could happen on this winding, plunging street, whereas in New York, there was no room for error, the roads ran straight to the neat horizon –

– but none of that mattered, I was here on this planet –

– the yellow-pink evening illuminated the wide washed blankness above the city, sunlight glinted on the radial cobbles, the broken kerb-stones, a plastic chair; a brown hound sneaked the eyed beak of a fish; the mosque began its call to prayer and

the birds circled the chasm in the buildings through which the road ran down towards the sea – & all this had always existed in me, and I in it, and it would last forever – just round the corner it would soon appear, the vision of water I was longing for, the Sea of Marmara, so blue, it would be, now the storm had passed and the sun was out, and there would be fishermen, broad backs bent, their corded arms against the brightness –

But I looked at my watch, and it was half-past six. I would have to turn back, to meet Angela, and in any case, I saw Leonard frowning, 'Virginia, you are too excited.'

Walking back uphill – it was harder going up, and I was perspiring in my yellow coat – I found myself thinking of the cross-eyed barber. Yes, I would have to pass him again. And I felt – what was that strange feeling? But the red-and-white pole stuck up unattended, there were just two black tom-cats outside it, bristling, padding around one another like boxers –

Presents, I remembered, and dived into a shop with a little flotilla of red Turkish flags and something very blue in the window – but ah, it was all modernity – shimmering cases for telephones, fluorescent cigarette lighters. But there against the glass, a waterfall of light! Rows of small round white and turquoise eyes on blazing glass disks of cobalt blue. Yes, they were instantly familiar, they were charms against the evil eye, Nessa was pulling me by the hand through the hectic theatre of the Grand Bazaar, plunging through stalactites of gilt and bead-work –

(we had walk-on parts the brief play was over)

Then I saw the hat, on a pile in the corner. It was casual, youthful, nothing like the navy-blue swan of a hat I'd been forced to leave behind in New York; this was a happy, summery,

cream straw boater. I put it on, and in that dim corner, in that dirty mirror, I was twenty-four years old again! 'I'll take it, please.' A rush of pleasure. 'And two of the charms.' (They would bring good fortune. Writer's luck – one needed it.) An immensely old woman with a scored brown face took my money, wreathed in smiles.

So much to tell Angela! So much to see!

– But I could guess what she had been doing. The thing these modern people always did, switch on their machines and fret at them. If it didn't work she would be losing her temper, as she did in front of me in New York, in the restaurant of the Empire State Building. 'This fucking, fucking thing,' she said loudly, but she was annoyed when I started laughing. 'Virginia, you're embarrassing.' I was embarrassing! She was embarrassing!

While I was breathing in the evening air, Angela was tethered to her London friends, or worrying about her editors – (she had so many editors, her agent, first, then her publisher, then her American editor – did these modern writers not edit themselves?). She was a chained monkey, night and day, dancing to the tune of her accordion.

The laptop thing came with her everywhere, on her knee, like another baby, her real baby, now Gerda had flown. Perhaps it had always been her real baby. Had Gerda always felt alone?

Gerda is walking past the Plaza Hotel where Eloise lived in that wonderful book. She stops and stares, a laser beam of longing. Here a girl could live on her own, waited on by compliant adults, next to the park – skating rinks, cafes with caramel milk-shakes, hills, rocks. Where Dad had taught her to rollerblade (true, that was seven years ago).

It is only early afternoon. I am fine, thinks Gerda, I am wonderful. Yes it is a blow that Mum is not here, because the stupid cow has flounced off to Turkey. Yes, Mum told her pals in the lobby but didn't bother to inform her daughter …

But Gerda's subconscious is working overtime. *Had* Mum, in fact, mentioned Turkey? Why had Gerda assumed the conference was here? How on earth did you get from New York to Istanbul? Should she just give up her quest and go home? Would Mum be cross that Gerda had spent so much money – so much of *Mum's* money – flying over here?

Once again, suspicion is gnawing at Gerda, a heavy shark tracking her under the pavement, snapping its jaws at her hurrying toes.

Mum did tell me. Ages ago. She was really thrilled they had invited her.

Yes, it was an international conference IN TURKEY. How had she forgotten! Retard! GAY! DIMWIT! LOSER! (Though 'Gay' was sexist.)

Gerda is still walking unnaturally fast as she leaves the white fountains of the Plaza behind. She is smiling in order not to cry, and focusing on the positive. Her namesake in Hans Andersen

had to travel solo all round the world, probably for years, on a boat, in a carriage, on the back of a reindeer: therefore she, Gerda, can bear another journey. She has still got Mum's card, she can fly to Turkey – but where IS Turkey? And how do you get there?

Her courage falters. But look, she's at the park, and the driver of one of the be-plumed carriages winks at her as he pats his horse.

She's a pretty girl with curly red hair, but as he straightens up he sees she's crying, and a lot younger than he had thought, rather too young to be winked at, in fact, and he straightens his face into something paternal.

Soon the sun will be leaving the park.

(Gerda is crying because she has realised that without a phone, with no computer, she has no way of booking that flight. *Where is my mother? Why isn't she here? Why is she never where I want her to be? Why did both my parents go away and leave me?*)

Gerda stops and blows her nose quite long and hard on the brown paper napkin from the hamburger joint. She congratulates herself on having a hanky. She tells herself she is doing fine. She has come to the park because here she had been happy. After a brief walk, she'll check in to a hotel. Later this will seem like a Great Adventure. Even now it's an Experience, better than rotting away at school (but she suddenly remembers her History teacher, Miss Larman, who also taught Latin, and knew a lot, though she wasn't popular, but Gerda liked her because she was clever, and now she is gone, Gerda misses her. In fact, she misses – anyone at all.

Anyone At All who cared about her.

No-one At All was Thinking about Her.

Which is fine, because I won't Think about Them).

She walks on down into the park's green bowl, waiting to feel happy as she looks around her at knots of small children

playing in the playground, children with mothers, children with fathers, leaping and shrieking against yellow-green grass or queueing to play on climbing frames or see-saws, but after a second, she turns her head away, she has grown too big, she walks on towards the trees.

Though Gerda felt too big to go into the playground, other people watching her – other lonely people – see only a small, isolated figure with a silly pink case and bright red hair.

Virginia is musing on the Istanbul pavement, an interesting figure to a middle-aged tourist who jerks past her in a yellow taxi, seeing a tall, elegant woman with full lips and a cream straw hat. Certainly a woman of distinction, standing alone, waiting for someone. Actually, she is in a brown study, thinking of the blindness of each generation.

VIRGINIA

Angela doesn't see her own addiction.

And my generation? What didn't we see? What did the people who came after us say?

At that moment, I was nearly knocked down by a young man rolling down the street like thunder, pulling behind him an enormous cube of shadow that completely blocked the pavement. All I saw for a moment was darkness, and his angry face as he lurched to a halt, he was shouting at me in what must have been Turkish but what I could read were his eyes, full of hatred, I raised my hands to protect myself – then realised the cube was a mountain of rubbish, and stepped into the street to let him pass, saying 'Sorry, sorry, *pardon, pardon*', though why did I think my French would help me? – perhaps his face softened, but he had rushed on, and then there were people shouting behind me and a giant lorry had nearly hit me, its brakes squealing, then crunching metal, I covered my ears and hopped back on the pavement and a surge of adrenalin made me run, I knew for a fact I could not run, but as in a kind of dream, I was flying up the road, my legs were light and strong

as steel, I was hardly panting, I was laughing with pleasure as the lights danced past me in a coloured chain and people stepped out of my way, startled.

I stopped a block or so from the hotel. Blood coursed round my body, strong as a river, my cheeks were warm, my lips were warm. I hugged myself. I patted my arms. I thought, briefly, clearly, 'I love my body'. I had not felt that since I was a girl.

Why did I feel it then? And the answer came, as an owl hooted and the sun sank down below the roof-top. You were threatened by the angry refuse-man, then nearly killed by the passing lorry. You saved yourself. You were strong. You ran.

I wanted to tell Angela, but I knew she would tell me off for being careless.

Then I thought something else, quite clearly: *I do not want to write about it. I want to be here. Here in the moment.*

Being alive was all that mattered.

The birds were calling for the setting sun, wheeling in clouds above the busy city, looking to settle on the terracotta roof-tops. Surely they had let me out of the darkness so I had another chance to be alive?

One day, perhaps, I would meet this Gerda, who'd been sent away to school as if she were a boy. Angela talked about her intermittently, usually protesting what she was about to do for her: emails, money, holidays. She had red hair, she adored reading.

And Gerda writes, according to her mother. The young are interesting, and need our help. Tonight at supper I will ask about Gerda.

I had come back safe. I was nearly home. Then I looked at my watch and began to hurry.

Gerda saw her father on every corner. The pink suitcase, though light, was a nuisance. It didn't feel right on a walk in the park, and the wheels made a self-important fol-de-rol of chattery, stuttery noise on hard surfaces (and yet, Dad's army knife was inside, which he had told her would keep her safe, and Mum's gold bracelet was on her wrist, gleaming in the late golden sunshine).

Then she actually saw him – a tall, skinny figure with a quiff of pale hair like a ruff of feathers, fifty metres ahead in the last of the sunlight, an egret-father, yes it was Dad, a magical presence, *I have made him come by sheer longing,* a voice whispered in her ear, *it must be true, such things can happen* –

Bending over his bike at the turn of the path, yes, his red jacket, his big boots – but as she started running, he actually vanished; she looked again, he had disappeared, he had slipped away up through the dark trees.

She could feel the air cooling as she left the path, but through the trees, she saw the sun still glinting on the islands of granite that broke through the grass, and hope broke through, because there, oh joy, the red of his jacket, there, surely …

She started to run, and nearly stumbled on a grey rootball that clutched at her foot, and she broke her nail as she stopped herself from falling, but she mustn't lose him. Gerda ran on.

VIRGINIA

I was thinking too much, and hurrying too much, my good luck charms clutched against my body, concentrating on the mental map that had got me back where I started from, but I had not learned the basic rule for navigating Istanbul on foot –

ANGELA

'*Oh no! Look where you're going, Virginia!*'

I knew it was too late even as I shouted, I saw she had no clue, as she stepped into space, that the pavement she was on ended abruptly, with a two-foot drop down to gravel and dust. She was wearing a hat, which promptly fell off; she knelt quite neatly in the gutter, facing the hotel as if in prayer, a middle-aged woman in a yellow coat, the late sunlight picking up the brown in her hair, which definitely made her look younger than before.

VIRGINIA

'Hallo-o-o! What is the Turkish for "sorry"?'

ANGELA

'Oh, Virginia. I was looking for you. I should have known you'd wander off. Are you all right? Sure? There's blood on your knee. You *must* be careful! Turkish pavements can't be trusted!

'"Sorry" is "*Pardon*", as a matter of fact, though you don't need to say sorry in Turkish.'

VIRGINIA

'How clever of me! I said "Pardon" earlier.'

It was only a scratch, though she made a fuss, and insisted I clean up before we went out, coming back to my room as if she were my mother. I unlocked the door, we went inside –

ANGELA

'Aaarghhh! What's THAT?'

VIRGINIA

'Don't, you'll frighten them!'

Because, yawning like young lords on my bedspread, there were two small, lazy-looking, light gold kittens. They were – what were they doing? – they were eating something, delicately chewing, one at each end – Angela ran at them, waving her hands and yelling –

ANGELA

'Ugh, how disgusting, it's a fish. How on earth did they get in? Oh, you left it open – '

VIRGINIA

It was me she was disgusted with!

I did let her chase the kitties out, because I thought they might have fleas, but they looked so sweet, on my double bed, enjoying that peaceful meal together.

'They were doing no harm,' I said, unfairly, as she closed the window with a bang, and locked it.

'Virginia, I told you to close it – '

'I suppose I went out in a hurry. I'll tell you later what fun I had … What are you going to do with the fish?' I asked her, spotting it lying on the carpet. It didn't look attractive. Half-eaten and bloody. 'You'll have to open the window again.'

'Why is it my job to clean up your fish?' she shouted as she snatched it up off the floor, two fingers spraddled askew in distaste, and unlocked the window to sling it out.

'You've forgotten the tail,' I said. It glistened, small and mauve, on my pillow. She turned, very flushed, her eyes staring. She must have this sickness that came from flying, she had warned me about it: 'jet-lag'.

'But don't concern yourself, I will get it.' I pretended picking it up was easy, though in fact it felt slimy and unpleasant.

But after I had got rid of the tail, I admit I closed the window firmly. She helped clean my leg, she gave me a dressing, a small mean thing called a 'sticking-plaster', but I knew she was still cross with me, though she denied it. She was strangely unwilling to answer my questions ('When did these "sticking-plasters" come in? Why are they better than bandages? Perhaps you haven't got any bandages?') and seemed reluctant to admire my hat.

I wanted to share my happiness. 'Angela, I bought you a present.' I handed her the charm against the evil eye – 'This will protect you against demons – and critics!' – but the attention she gave it was perfunctory. 'Very pretty. Thank you,' she replied, and thrust it out of sight in the pocket of her suit, its blue eye sinking in a sea of coral.

'One day you will thank me for it, my dear,' I wheedled, smiling at her in my most charming fashion, and really I did feel fond of her, and didn't want her to be distressed. Usually it worked, but not that night.

'Lobby. Ten minutes. Don't be late,' she said, and went to her room to collect her phone (a smaller, more tyrannical version of her laptop, which 'ding-ed' at intervals to make her take notice). As soon as the door closed behind her, I rang reception for new pillow-cases. I didn't want my face to smell of raw fish.

Yet I held it in my mind for a long time, that picture of animal bliss in my bed. Their paired contentment on my pillows, their young golden bodies stretched long and slim, two small happy mouths with a kiss of sweet fish.

Afterwards, Gerda could never remember what gave her the courage to step off the path. Maybe it was just something inside her, her Gerda-ness, which had never been broken, the fact she Was A Person, always had been.

She came up through the trees, panting slightly, skinning her elbow on one of the tree-trunks as she turned around to free her case.

When she turned back, Dad wasn't there.

he wasn't there he had never been there

(her mother complaining 'You have never been there!' but it wasn't true, was it, Dad took me to America.)

She saw them, then, waiting for her. They were there, a gang of them, camped in the sunlight on the summit of the shining rock. Instantly Gerda's eyes were drawn to the tall strong girl with a mane of dark hair, wavy, tangly, staring straight at her, a strip of red tying back her curls. Muscled brown arms, grey shorts, tattoos. Round her were a crew of – who or what?

Words came to Gerda. Words from stories. Rapscallions. Ruffians. Shaved heads, stringy legs, hard and muscular as legs of horses, eyes like black pebbles you couldn't see into. Some were mixed race. Maybe all of them? Or were they – what did you call them – Gypsies? Rom, was it, you were supposed to call them? Tanned Gypsies. Or just – New Yorkers? She didn't know *anything* about New Yorkers.

Those shorts aren't grey. Those shorts are dirty, she suddenly realised. This she knew.

'Hey,' said the girl. 'Come here. I like you.' The others were sneering and pushing each other, but the dark-haired girl looked radiant. Happy to see her. Waiting for her. She had a kind face. Didn't she?

All round them, through the trees, the border of skyscrapers seemed to bend closer to hear what would happen. Gerda herself had no idea. But at least, now, someone was pleased to see her. The sun still felt hot up here near the rocks, and she realised it must be glinting on her bracelet, Mum's gold bracelet with the animals. She pulled her cuff down to cover it, but the girl's eyes followed every movement.

Had she insulted her? They stared at each other.

The dark girl pushed the boy crouched below her, quite gently. He didn't move. He was – leering at Gerda. She saw that one of his teeth was gone. He had a ratty, straggly beard, like a Muslim beard too thin to grow – perhaps it was a Muslim beard, though the tats on his neck were not a bit Islamic – and his eyebrows frowned above his eyes.

'What's your name?' The dark girl smiled.

Gerda wasn't sure she was ready to tell her. 'Are you American?' Gerda asked. 'What's *your* name, in any case?' She folded her arms to make herself bigger, and stood very straight, at the base of the rock, peering up at the sunlit troop of monkeys. She passionately wanted to be part of them, part of a gang, part of the park, but also dreaded them. They were united, she was alone, she was only thirteen.

'Nosy,' said the girl, quite pleasantly, 'arncha? I'll tell you though. I'm Lily Roberta. People call me Lil Robber, I don't know why!' There was a chorus of laughter and jeers from below her. 'Call me Lil,' she said, sweetly, then, and with sudden energy kicked out her foot, and caught the bearded boy hard

on the shoulder, yelling 'Fuck off, all of you! I want to talk to my friend here.'

After a frozen second, they started moving, but as they went, their eyes ran over Gerda, and she saw the bearded boy had a fleck of spittle at the corner of his mouth as he walked muttering past her, too close, and for a second she thought he would spit. But no, they all vanished like smoke through the trees. But were they really gone, or were they just waiting?

Gerda looked at her feet. Mum's ridiculous case, pink and girly and luxurious, everything she hated and was not. It was like having an enormous pink spot. She tore her eyes away from it. The skyscrapers on their side of the park were just tipped with sunlight, needle-sharp, and on the other side they had gone dark.

The rock still looked warm and bright. The girl came down from its summit towards her, and stretched out her hand to pull Gerda up. Red round cheeks, river-brown eyes, smiling eyes with snow-blank whites. 'It's warmer up here,' she said, and laughed. 'Now why do I think you've got nowhere to go? I'm right, aren't I?'

'Maybe,' said Gerda.

She made a decision. She stepped on to the rock, and took the hand that was offered her. As she reached out her arm, the cuff fell back and the gold chain bracelet caught the light. She saw the gold, and then the girl's bare feet, brown as a nut, but with painted nails, wild-strawberry-bright, in the same, sharp, unforgettable shot.

I am entering another world, she thought.

VIRGINIA

What I noticed in the lobby was the number of men. Most of them seemed to smile at me. Another world, a populous world, a world that seemed to welcome strangers. Hotel workers, I gleaned, quite soon, by their synchronised smiles as more guests arrived, their mild jockeying over errands. The men were all identically smart, in crisp white shirts, black ties, black trousers, gleaming shoes despite the dusty pavements. This hotel was half the size of the Wordsmiths Hotel in New York, but there were three times as many men working there.

One of them, I thought, was looking at me strangely, a small, stocky man with golden skin and a poised, balletic way of walking, his shoulders back, like an acrobat. I had watched him lift a case as if it was a feather. The lobby phone rang, and he answered. Now he was definitely looking my way. I was sitting by an enormous cactus. Perhaps it was Angela on the phone.

'Was that my colleague, ringing for me?' I asked him, and he mimed incomprehension, then came and stood quite close to me.

'Slowly, please. I have little English.'

'Telephone call? For me?' I pointed.

'You want to make telephone call?'

'No.' He was smiling at me very warmly. His face was jolly, like a smiling bun, lightly gleaming, and he smelled of lemon. His teeth were slightly stained, I noticed. I felt sympathy: my teeth were bad. 'Would you like Turkish tea?' he asked, and

before I could answer, he said 'I invite you.'

'Well – '

'It's free.'

'Thank you. I am just waiting for a friend.'

'I am Ahmet,' he said, with a small bow.

'I am Mrs Woolf. Virginia,' I said.

At that moment, Angela arrived. Without a word, she hurried me out into the night, though I half-raised my hand to wave goodbye to him.

'I was having a conversation,' I said.

She ignored me. 'Look where you're going,' she said. 'I am going to take you through the Hippodrome. I do not want you falling over.'

I saw no signs of a Hippodrome as we marched uphill past laundries and gift-shops, but her face did not encourage questions. I thought about Gerda. I hoped she was tough. I was starting to feel pity for Angela's daughter.

Men sat outside their businesses on plastic chairs, drawing deep on red-tipped cigarettes. They talked to their friends; their eyes idled. Many held small, curved glasses of golden liquid.

'What do they drink?' I couldn't stop myself asking. 'Tea,' said Angela. 'Turkish tea. Everyone here drinks Turkish tea.'

'That is just another generalisation.'

She looked annoyed. 'Never mind, it's true.'

Would I have got away with a riposte like that?

It didn't matter, I was happy again. Such a cheerful thought, that everyone drank tea, that Turkish tea could please everybody. In New York, I had been paralysed by the number of choices in every café, the urgency with which each young American spelled out his particulars: 'Large skinny decaf latte, three sugars.' Then when it came: 'No, I wanted it wet.' They were mad with choice, so it seemed to me. The bony walls of

the self were so thin that something essential might be crushed if a purchase did not reflect their whim.

Here things were slower, more communal. Cats and people wove about like smoke. I looked in vain for the golden kittens. The shops were small and all of them were open, although it was nearly 8 PM. Sacks and boxes spilled on to the pavement – it was untidy – it was human. Shopkeepers chatted to customers.

'The Hippodrome,' Angela announced. We were climbing up into a rectangular open space with an enormous mosque to our right. Above us, violet sky. Things flickered across. Owls, bats? Only a few people on the edges.

'This is where the Romans had chariot races,' Angela said. 'And there's the Blue Mosque. By day, it's crowded. We might go together.'

I thought, perhaps I will go alone.

'Aya Sophia's down there,' she waved vaguely, 'and that's the Topkapi Palace. Once we're sat down, we'll make a plan. There's so much you should see, Virginia. So little time before the conference. And of course, I need to finish my paper.'

At the far end of the Hippodrome, the crowds began. There were minor key bells and a scream of metal as a huge tram like an ocean-liner hove up the main street from the sea below, its bright windows crammed with people. We turned to follow in its wake. 'I could help you with your paper,' I said.

'I doubt it,' she said, 'it's … specialised.' Then 'Come to think of it, though, perhaps you could. Yes, a read-through would be useful.'

'If the paper's about me, I'm a specialist,' I said, and laughed at my wit, but she did not.

'You have to understand,' she said, and then ' – no, I can't possibly explain it.'

'What?'

'Oh, just something about the conference. Something about

the academics. Don't say you're a specialist.'

'I need to know about modern academics!'

She looked perplexed and cross, and the crowds pouring down the street were so thick we could hardly make headway, let alone converse. 'I know this will sound strange to you, but they won't believe what you say about your work.'

'Because – because I am dead?' It was obvious. 'Because they won't believe it's me?'

'No, nothing as simple as that, Virginia.'

When the trams hove past, the crowds squashed back on to the pavements, and elbows, shoulders, feet shoved us. I was surrounded, enveloped, by Turks, I had lost my edges, I was almost Turkish.

'It's because – some modern scholars think authors don't know anything about their work,' she panted, over her shoulder.

'That doesn't make sense. We are the ones who wrote it.'

'It's not about sense. Or sensible. Sense is considered to be old hat. Rather a dull, Anglo-Saxon idea. This is a concept. A critical concept,' she said. 'You can't expect to understand it, Virginia, so don't dismiss it before you do.'

'It's obviously ridiculous.'

'You see? I knew you would sneer at it. It's "The Death of the Author". It's – well, it's French.'

'But I'm the living embodiment of that. I'm a dead author,' I said, and started laughing again, because, really, it was quite funny.

'You don't know everything about your work. It's the intentional fallacy,' she said. 'That is a critical concept, too.'

'You mean we don't know what we're doing?'

She nodded. 'It's not what I believe,' she added. 'I just ought to warn you.'

'Our conscious intentions do not count? I see the influence

of Dr Freud.'

Her eyes were defiant, and slightly nervous.

'Then how can critics know their own intentions? Maybe, unconsciously, they want to kill us. Yes, of course. Then they have the power.'

'No, Virginia. That's just – glib. I hope you won't say that at the conference.'

With that she hared ahead of me, furious, her strong calves powering her on through the crowd, seemingly indifferent to whether I followed.

Odd how they hated a judgement from the past, these modern young people, so sure of themselves!

'Can we go on a tram?' I tried to change the subject. She pretended not to hear me. I said it louder, trotting to catch up with her.

'Not tonight, Virginia.'

'Why not?'

'No.'

Her job was mostly saying 'No' to me.

Soon she plunged into a net of bright tables in a small street entirely lined with restaurants. Black-and-white waiters bobbed in and out like magpies. A lot of the diners were speaking English. She sank into a chair, and motioned me to join her. 'Will you be warm enough?' she asked. 'Look, there's an outdoor heater thingy. They're not ecological, but they work. Edward would be furious! First, I need a bucket of wine.' Suddenly friendly, she smiled at me. 'I've got my notebook. Let's make a plan.'

We were two women, making a plan, this freedom to sit and eat and drink wine had become normal, all over the planet; all around us, younger women did the same thing. I liked the new world where this could happen. I wanted this moment of warmth to linger. 'Thank you. I would like wine, Angela.'

Lil and Gerda were drinking warm Coca-Cola. Normally Gerda would have shunned it, or rather her parents would have shunned it for her. When Lil held out the can, Gerda shook her head. Lil was astonished and indignant. 'Everyone likes it,' she said. 'Course you do. Try it.' To be friendly, Gerda had a sip. To her surprise, it was delicious. They shared a can, shuttling it to and fro. Gerda watched Lil's lips and teeth against the metal. She had big white teeth and her mouth was very red (*Mum says Coca-Cola eats your teeth*. Gerda took the can and sucked it down. This was another world, with different rules.)

From where they were sitting, on top of the rock, Gerda could see other rock islands through the trees, with little figures enjoying themselves, but as the kingdom of the sun shrank up towards her feet and the evening chill settled, they disappeared. Now it was just the two of them. Gerda knew she depended on Lil.

Lil revealed she was Danish. (My dad is half-Danish,' said Gerda, excited.) Lil's English sounded weird, the words were OK but the accent was a mixture of every accent you had ever heard. Quite quickly Gerda got used to it. Lil told her she lived in Central Park 'when I'm not on the subway, working.'

Gerda thought, 'She is not a ticket collector.' She knew without asking what Lil Roberta did. It was very exciting. Now she knew a thief. But her gold bracelet burned a line on her wrist.

'This rock is ours,' Lil Robber said, 'The birds. The shit.' (A bulky pile was covered with a violently blue tarpaulin.)

'Everything's ours. No-one will bother us. You sleep with me. Put that thing' (indicating, with a wealth of scorn, the pink case Gerda was trying to ignore) 'under the tarp.'

'That's kind of you, thank you,' Gerda said. It sounded very formal (Lil Robber's mouth dropped open) and stupidly English, and she didn't want Lily to think she was a twat, so without thinking, Gerda reached forward and kissed the other girl full on the mouth, and felt Lil pull away, and then kissed her again, and they stood on the rock like two gladiators, half-kissing and half-wrestling, and when they stopped, Lily was laughing.

'You're very full on,' she said. 'I like that. Come on, I'll take you on a tour of the park.'

'If I leave my mum's case, won't it get stolen?' Gerda asked. 'There's no-one watching it.'

'First, my people *are* watching it,' said Lil, grandly gesturing towards the trees. 'Secondly, no-one goes under that tarp.'

'Why not?' asked Gerda.

'Because it pongs.'

'What's in that box next to it?'

'Birds.'

'Why are they in a crate?'

'They're pigeons. Racing pigeons. They fell off a lorry.'

'You ought to let them go.'

'Who says so?' Lily jutted her brown jaw at Gerda, and after a split second of nervousness Gerda said 'The Great God Gerda,' and Lily chuckled and said 'Fuck off.'

It grew dark as they walked round the lake in Central Park. You could see the lights from the buildings on the edge, but the lake itself was huge and black, with strange cracklings and rustlings running like rats through the bushes along the edges. Lily told Gerda she was beautiful. Gerda was pleased someone else had noticed.

'We could swim in that lake,' Gerda said to her companion. 'I'm good at swimming. I've won medals.'

'Not tonight,' said Lil. There was a long silence. Their feet crunched on beside the dark water; a water-bird broke the surface with a splash. Then Lily asked, sounding oddly shy, 'If you stay with me, will you teach me to swim?'

'Can't you swim?' Gerda asked, astonished.

'You can't do loads of things that I can do,' Lil flashed back, instantly angry.

'I will teach you,' Gerda said, though she thought 'I won't be here long enough.' She was amazed to be here; Lily was a goddess; she was having the adventure of her dreams; yet somehow she already knew she would have to go back to the world outside, where she had Prospects, and Lil did not.

ANGELA

'Such a lot to do, so little time! Two days is all we've got for the whole of Istanbul. Where is the waiter?'

VIRGINIA

Two days left. She was frightening me. I felt that the end of the story was coming, and then perhaps mine would be over – but no, please, I wanted to stay and watch life unfold to the end of time.

All round us, people were laughing and talking, the brilliant light making the women's hair into swinging bells of bronze and jet, and some of them had children on their laps, and a man passed selling wind-up puppies – I realised something with a shivering force that made the hairs on my arms electric.

No, I had never wanted it.

I myself never wanted to die. The self I knew, the self I owned, that loved the sunlight on the spine of the downs, loved Leonard, loved my Nessa.

Of course I didn't want to die. It was just the illness, the cloud of darkness, something outside me, tracking me.

'Where is the waiter?' she asked, impatient.

'I'm happy,' I said, 'Happy to be here.' I wanted her to know what I was feeling. Maybe I owed everything to her. Without her, after all, I wouldn't be here – no, I might still be down in the dark – not that one always loves one's saviour.

'I'm glad,' she said, and she looked less cross. 'For me, of course, it's all quite stressful.'

'The Turks are nice,' I offered. 'They're very friendly at our hotel.'

'Virginia, this isn't New York. I know that there you had friends in the lobby, but here it isn't such a great idea.'

'Why not?'

'They will try to sell you something.'

'They tried to sell me things in New York. They were always suggesting one outing or another, some special deal they could book for me.' (In fact, we also talked about their families, and the young today, and how to write books. I even talked about her and Gerda. But yes, they did try to sell me things.)

'They will try to exploit you,' she said. 'I know. It's different here.'

I was looking at the menu. 'Things are cheaper. So I'll be cheated less.'

Her mouth was tight again. She waved at the waiter. 'Bring me a bottle of the house white.'

The waiter was just at the end of being young. He had elaborate hair to hide the start of baldness. 'Ladies,' he said, with a practised smile that managed to embrace us both. 'Lovely ladies. How else can I serve you?'

'Could you take my coat?' I asked. 'That heater above us is rather warm.' He performed the task caressively, taking his time to slide the collar from my shoulders, freeing each arm gently and slowly. I enjoyed the operation. I enjoyed his touch. 'Beautiful coat, beautiful lady.'

Angela looked affronted. 'Could you take mine?' she said sharply. 'Hang it where I can see it, please.' He removed hers, a little roughly.

'You see,' Angela hissed as he went away. 'They will even flirt with old women, it's disgraceful!'

ANGELA

As soon as I said it, I wished I hadn't. 'Not that you're an old woman, of course. I mean, we both are, if anything.'

Fortunately, at that very second the waiter returned with yellow wine, and the moment passed, she wasn't offended, but I cast a quick glance at our reflections in the big plate-glass window behind us and just for a moment I thought, it's true, I don't look that much younger than her.

I was tired from the journey, that was all. I was beaten down from travelling *with her*.

'Where are you from?' The waiter was asking. Or rather, asking Virginia, who was smiling too much as he poured her wine. 'I think must be Paris,' he pretended to decide.

'We'd like to order,' I interrupted.

She said she hadn't decided yet. I didn't care. I seized the menu, ordered for two, fish soup then the special. 'Please bring the water now, at once.'

VIRGINIA

I saw her demons were attacking her. 'I enjoy talking to people, Angela.'

ANGELA

'Turkish waiters aren't people, in that sense.'

VIRGINIA

I was the one who was supposed to be snobbish! I was the one who made generalisations! 'That's another generalisation,' I said.

ANGELA

'Virginia, don't be difficult. It's all right for you, but I'm very tired. I've got so many things to do.'

VIRGINIA

With that, her phone was out of her pocket. She laid it on the table, the veil came down, she was tapping the glass to bring her ghosts to life, she took a great swallow of her wine.

I felt rejected. I drank too. The golden liquid slipped sweetly down. '*Pardon*,' I said. She looked at me. 'You know, Turkish "sorry",' I reminded her. 'I'm sorry if I offended you. Don't start internetting, Angela. Let's make a plan before the soup arrives.'

ANGELA

As soon as Virginia had some wine, her mood became less quarrelsome.

VIRGINIA (*raising her glass*)
'Thank you for letting me come with you.'

ANGELA

When she was on form, there was no-one nicer.

At the next table, American students were swopping boasts about their travels. 'You haven't seen the Taj Mahal? I was there at 6 AM. That was kind of cool. It's the time to see it, as the sun rises. Course, it isn't open until later.'

'What's it like inside?'

'I couldn't hang around.'

'Macchu Pichu, that would be tops for me.'

Virginia was listening with half an ear. 'They must be very rich,' she hissed.

I inspected them. They wore jeans, T-shirts, which told me nothing, but their trainers did: bog-standard Nike. 'They're not,' I said. 'You see, everybody travels. Well, everybody young. That is, the students.'

'How do they afford it?'

'Some of them have loans. And travel is cheap. Their expectations are different. They "do" South America, all of them. It's normal to travel all over the globe.'

Virginia said, 'In our day, very few people travelled. I think most people, now, are rich.'

'I'd say the Great Wall of China,' said the girl. 'It's so … long. And kinda wavy.'

'How long did you have there?'

'Half a day.'

'You have to get on top of the itinerary.'

VIRGINIA

By the time we left the restaurant, our plans were settled, and Angela's mood had become benign. (Angela, of course, believed in plans. She was still young – I was a century older. Leonard had been the planner, not me. Yet nothing turned out as he thought in the beginning.)

We would go to Pera: just across the bridge from the Old City, it would be there still. ('Lots will have changed,' she cautioned me, 'but they can't change the sea. It's beautiful.') We would visit the Harem, in Topkapi Palace. We would go to Aya Sophia, of course. We would visit Scutari, for Florence Nightingale. And of course, on the third day, my conference. *The* conference, I corrected myself.

'Great, we have got ourselves organised,' she said, as we emerged on to the main street. 'And of course, I will need some time alone to practise.' 'Practise?' 'My paper for the conference, yes.' 'Two days isn't really enough, is it, for everything we want to do?'

ANGELA

I could hear the sadness in her voice, as if she was coming to the end of an outing, and perhaps she was, perhaps we both

were, for surely this episode couldn't last, and we wouldn't have much longer together – which would help me keep my patience with her.

GERDA

What's hard for a child is, you don't choose your parents. Specifically, you don't choose your mother, yet once you are born, you are landed with her, nearly all the time, for years and years, and you have to be good, you have to make her love you, because she's the one who gives you things.

It's better when you have two parents because one can make up for the defects of the other, which was what Dad did quite well, when he was there.

Being with Lil was a bit like that. I did like her, yes, but I was lumbered with her. Suddenly she was all I had got. I slept as close to her as I could.

I admit I told her a fib about my mother. Not really a fib, but not the whole truth. 'I ran away from this school like a prison. My mum didn't care, so I stole her money, and came to the other side of the world.'

Lil Robber just said 'It's cool what you did, robbing your mum to go round the world. If I had a mum, I'd do that.'

The trouble was, none of them did have mums. They smelled, this gang, in the middle of the night, sweetish, oniony, kicking and mumbling and snuffling around me. Moaning their way through small panicky dreams, maybe of terrible deeds they had done, maybe of terrible things they had suffered. Lil Robber smelled different, of chlorine and pondweed, because she washed 'most days' in the lake, although she never washed her clothes, just stole new ones when they got dirty, and her fantasy (in which I now had a role) was to wash, naked, like she

usually did, 'but sometimes people see me, and then I feel silly, cos I just climb out again like a moron, and it's slippery down there, so you can fall over'. Instead she would push off, 'like a fish, you get me', and go swooping away from them through the deep water, and not come back till they had all fucked off. 'You don't learn to swim all at once,' I said cautiously, as she was drifting into sleep, but Lily stiffened, and said quite loudly 'You told me you won actual medals, so you gotta be good at teaching it,' and I said 'Yeah, I hope I am, but you might be crap at learning, Lily,' and after a pause, Lil Robber laughed, and tucked her arm painfully tightly around me, and started snoring on my neck.

At first Beardy Boy pretended he was keen on me. He looked at me as if he was having horrible thoughts. But everything he did was like a test. He gave me chewing-gum out of his pocket but I could see what his pocket was like. 'Nah,' I said, but I held back from saying what I wanted to say, which was 'Urrghhhh, disgusting, I wouldn't eat that even if I was starving.'

(Which by the way, I was, pretty much.)

He offered to do me a tattoo, the next morning. It was the first thing he said as we were waking up. 'No,' I said, without even thinking. 'Why not, ya scared?,' he sneered, 'Ya soft?' And I was scared, and compared to him, I was soft, but I knew the others were listening, and Lil was too, to see how I'd cope, so I said 'Because your hand would shake. Because you look like you're always wanking,' and then Lily laughed, and I felt better, but he stared at me like he wanted to kill me.

So then it was just Lily and me. And I was dependent, as if she was my mother.

But I did choose her, and she chose me. So that was a bit of an advance on childhood. And I knew I had to survive on my own, because in the end I would get my parents back – I

thought I would, I had to believe it – but I had found out they would not live for ever. Most of these kids' parents were already dead.

I knew I was different, but in a way, as time went on, we would all be the same. We were the young, alone with the future, while the parents would slip away into the past.

Tour of Istanbul, Day One
1. *The Harem*
2. *Aya Sophia*

ANGELA
Yes, we were different generations – Virginia could have been my great-grandmother! But sometimes we did have fun together.

VIRGINIA
We breakfasted on the roof of the hotel, on a blazing Istanbul morning. The roof-top terrace was a skating rink for sunlight; a minaret soared alongside us, slender-necked, heron-like, looking upwards, then a tumble of reddish tiled roofs, then blue, blue, pearl and blue.

'What are we looking at, Angela?'

A sturdy guest enlightened us, setting down her teacup. British. Common. Northern. 'That's Sea o' Marmara. And over there, that's Golden Horn.'

Those names from long ago: poems, even in her strange dialect. We were gazing across the roof-tops to the blue and pink Sea of Marmara. Painted, as before, with pearl-white light, but it had become a thoroughfare. I remembered small boats like homing birds, dancing on the waves between the islands. Now the ships were flat and black and steady, a heavy, constant line of morse – the work of the world was getting done. In the distance, dove-grey-blue, the islands, the same islands I

had loved before, though we never landed, we just slipped past them, floating on a distant layer of sea-fog, catching my desire, veiled, mysterious, as if all the loved faces might be there, peering towards me, across the water … I shook my head. 'Let's get breakfast.'

But Angela pointed at the roofs nearby. Close-up, the view was less romantic. 'You see, there's still rich and poor,' she said. Rusting railings, burnt-out wood, broken roof-ridges where seagulls stalked, a muddle of forgotten white plastic chairs on a dismal terrace with broken pipe-work. A stone's throw away were the new hotels, small shining enclaves of sunlit breakfasters gazing out across the city. Travellers like her. Golden flotsam. So many people seemd to travel now, but did the money ever reach the poor?

(At least it was paying the men in the lobby. A surge of pleasure when I thought of them.)

We returned from the buffet with plates of spiced sausage. 'We arrived over that sea,' I told Angela. 'I'd hardly slept. I was so excited. We passed a pretty little tower – '

'Oh yes – I've been past it in a ferry. The guide called it – Leander's Tower, or The Maiden's Tower. You know, Hero and Leander. But the Turks call it something different, something like Kid, or Kin – '

'Kiz Kulesi,' said the same sturdy woman, sitting at the next-door table. 'Very fairmous. Yer can get it on tea-towels. Fridge magnets.'

'Are you from Yorkshire?' I asked. 'I haven't heard that accent for – a very long while.' (And indeed I hadn't: for a century or so.)

'Plenty of people talk like me back orm. Tell yer what though, I haven't eard one with a voice like you for decairds.' She stomped off into the breakfast buffet. I hooted with laughter. I couldn't help it.

'Virginia, stop offending people!' But Angela was laughing, too.

'Three days,' I said. 'I've only got three days, but that's what it took Jesus to rise from the dead. And I have already done that part!'

'Virginia, you might be surrounded by Christians.'

'I would like to go back to that tower. Adrian called it Leandros Tower. The Maiden's Tower, you said. I saw it when I was a girl, that first morning, when my heart was so light.'

(That day I saw nothing but golden bubbles rising row upon row on a dark green hillside. The domes were so airy, they were like glass. I was running from side to side of the deck, and Nessa told me I was over-excited, and one of the sailors kept pulling my arm and pointing – 'Üsküdar,' he said. It looked like a barracks with four tall towers, on the eastern shore, dark against the sunrise. 'Yes,' I said, 'Thank you.' But he wouldn't let go, he wanted to teach us. 'Florence, the lady, the famous English lady,' he said for the second time. 'Üsküdar.' Vanessa put two and two together. 'Oh he must mean Scutari, Virginia. The hospital where poor Florence Nightingale wore herself out.' Nearby there was a tower that seemed to float on the water, about three hundred yards from the shore. Was it a lighthouse, was it a boat? Because it seemed to move with the waves, or I did, dizzy with beauty and lack of sleep. 'That's charming,' I said. 'Does some princeling live there?' And Adrian, who had done some research, said 'It used to be the custom post. There's been a tower there for a thousand years.' 'Adrian, don't exaggerate' – we never believed what Adrian said. As the youngest, he naturally got bullied. 'I'm not exaggerating. It's famous. The Tower of Leander, where Hero lived. Her lover Leander swam the Hellespont to woo her, which even you girls must know about. One night it was too stormy,

but she told him to come, and her light blew out, and her lover drowned.' 'Wasn't that the Dardanelles?' said Vanessa. 'I'm sure you've muddled it up, Adrian.' 'It's not me who's muddled,' he said, and reddened, as poor Adrian so often did.)

'I love the story of Hero and Leander,' Angela said, as she stirred her coffee. 'Though why is it always the men who do the swimming?'

'We all swam in the sea at St Ives,' Virginia said. 'Thoby was best, of course he was. Not that it helped him, in the end.'

'I always wondered,' Angela said, looking out over the water to the far horizon where the blue islands hung low in the mist, 'did Hero let the lamp go out on purpose? I mean, I know the night was stormy, and she shouldn't have begged him to make the crossing – but what if it was worse than that? What if she actually let him drown? What if she thought about all the effort and mess of loving a man, and deliberately didn't replace the oil? And when the flame flickered out, just went to bed?'

'That's a terrible thought,' I said, and it was, but part of me felt – exhilarated. Women could be wicked, as well as good.

We were helping ourselves to water-melon. It was red and succulent, dripping wet. I thought, 'I will take another slice.' Briefly, my eyes met Angela's.

'So can we change your, what do you call it, schedule?' I asked. 'Let's say Scutari and Kiz ... What was it?'

'Kiz Kulesi,' said the Yorkshire woman, who was piling her plate with her third lot of rolls. 'I'm a teacher, see. I'm good at nairms.'

She was smiling now. I had a second chance. I never wanted to hurt anybody, though I hurt Adrian and hurt Leonard, and sometimes, I know, I laughed when I shouldn't. 'Most kind of you. Thank you,' I said.

Yes, I would meet Angela in Reception.

VIRGINIA

I put my new hat on; inspected the mirror; it looked – jaunty.
I took it off. But we were going for a jaunt! I put it on again,
and went downstairs. She didn't arrive. I wasn't perturbed, my
friend Ahmet was there from the day before, standing smartly
suited with two friends. They were talking, but he was pleased
to see me.

'Very nice,' he said, expansively, smiling meaningfully at me.
The other two men looked at him sideways.

'What, precisely?' He looked baffled. 'What is nice?'
I encouraged him. The man next to him was muttering in
Turkish, and his face was disapproving. '*Ayip! Ayip!*'

'Oh, hat,' Ahmet said finally. '*The* hat, I think is the right
way.'

'This hat? I bought it in Istanbul,' I said. Somehow I didn't
think he meant my hat.

I started to think – could it be? Perhaps he liked me as a
woman. Old as I am. Was it possible? Were tendrils of feeling
extending towards me, like tiny green vines unfurling in the
garden?

His colleagues didn't seem happy with him. Perhaps it was
wrong, as Angela would say, 'culturally', for him to talk to me.
Or perhaps it was the way he looked at me, for rather too long,
that his colleagues disliked. 'Kiz … what is the name of the
famous tower?'

'Kiz Kulesi,' he said with a delighted air. 'Yes, I can arrange
trip to this.' He tapped his forehead, as if advertising his brain.

'Do we take a taxi?'

'Very long journey by taxi.'

'Taxi and boat?'

'No, I take myself.'

I must have looked puzzled, for he mimed driving. Then he gave me an enormous smile. 'Maybe tomorrow? Or tomorrow of tomorrow?'

At that moment, Angela stormed into reception.

ANGELA (*loudly*)
'He's RUINED my day.'

VIRGINIA
Had I upset her by talking to Ahmet?

ANGELA
'He has that effect on me, every time. I'm doing fine without him, then he rings. Come on Virginia, let's get going.'

VIRGINIA
'Ah – I see – your husband.'

ANGELA (*storming towards the tramway on Divan Yolu Caddesi, with Virginia trying to keep up*)
'You probably don't see, Virginia. These things are different when you have children. I told you – did I? – he's in the Arctic Circle, he's on an expedition, he's always away – well the funding's run out, they've lost their grant, and he seemed to think that I – why should I?'

VIRGINIA
'Why should you what?' But she wasn't listening. 'Are you all right?' But I saw she wasn't. Her eyes were red. She had

been crying.

She tried to speak, but her voice tore. 'Gerda – Gerda – '

'There's a problem with your daughter?'

ANGELA

'Gerda will blame me. Children do.'

I'd been perfectly happy in my own sunny room. Then the phone rang, and it wasn't Virginia – I saw him in my head, as I stared at the phone, his faraway voice worrying like wire, a tiny figure dwarfed by all that ice, muffled in furs, his face a blank, he seemed to have turned into someone else – I knew even then that Gerda would judge me. She loved her father, always, blindly. Daughters are very hard on mothers.

I didn't care. I was angry too. A gross black spider ran across the floor.

'No! Not a chance! No, you bastard! You're *always* away! Don't dare to ask me! You've already taken money from our joint account! I know you have, so don't deny it.' I didn't say what I could have said – 'I never wanted you to go.' I switched off the phone and stamped on the spider, once, twice, and then it was still. That little fucker would run no more.

VIRGINIA

Her epic of complaint continued as we made our way through the Hippodrome, transformed by daylight into a market. The wretchedness of women through the ages filled my ears ...

But the day was dancing before my eyes – men with red-and-white-striped awnings on their carts selling roast yellow sweetcorn with a fringe of brown tassels, men selling chestnuts in pouting black skins through which the flesh of the nut glistened, men doing theatre with ice creams, juggling the ball of ice into the cone, bowing to the queue of squealing girls who were wearing wreaths of artificial rosebuds sold by

a man who sat on the kerb – to me the day was a holiday, but Angela, beside me, was voluble and blind. The seagulls wheeled overhead, so white, free-er than us, without human feelings.

'He thought that I would bail them out. He seems to think I'm a millionaire.'

'Bail them out?'

'Pay for them. Let him have the money to finish the journey.'

'I thought you were a millionaire?' I interrupted. 'I thought you were a best-selling author?'

'That's not the point, it's not the point, everyone's a millionaire these days – '

'*Really?*'

'No, but you know, all one's friends. In any case, he claims they need money to get the vehicles mended and feed the huskies and whatever research he claims to be doing –

'What is his research?'

'Oh, same old, same old, he's always investigating global warming, the ice-caps are melting, but are they, really? Virginia, do you mind not interrupting – the point is, Edward's always away. He's never there for Gerda and me. This time it's been three months already. He didn't need to go – '

'Why not?'

There was a pause. She looked uncertain, but she was too enraged to stop for long. 'Because, it doesn't matter, look it doesn't matter. He doesn't need work, there is plenty of money. I mean, I've got money ... In any case. The bastard only phoned to ask me for money. A lot of money. From our joint account, which he had promised he would never use. I had no choice, I had to say "No". There comes a point when you have to say "No". Otherwise women get exploited.' That last phrase seemed to give her confidence, but surely she knew her argument was muddled?

'You felt you couldn't afford to help him? – You said it was

a joint account?'

'Why are you looking like that, Virginia? Do you want to make me feel bad? It's all right for you, this never happened to you, I'm pretty sure Leonard never asked you for money, I don't suppose you had a joint account, we agreed it would be a cushion for me, in case he died and I needed it.'

She was crying in earnest now. We were waiting for a tram, and people were staring, not unkindly, at the weeping woman. To me it seemed she understood nothing.

'We both kept accounts,' I told her, though I did not much care to talk to her about money. 'I wrote everything down, like a housekeeper, money for ink, stamps, notebooks. The press did make money. We were a success. And after *To the Lighthouse*, I earned more than him. I think I preferred it, actually. My father tormented Vanessa and Stella, always blaming them for extravagance, even though we ate the same lamb for three days. Women must have their own money. But we had enough, Leonard and I, between us. I never wanted more than that.

'But it isn't, as you say, "all right for me." I'd give anything for Leonard to telephone one morning. And I would give him whatever he asked for.'

ANGELA

Sometimes she reminded me of Gerda. That knack of saying things that cut to the quick. '£40,000 he asked me for.'

VIRGINIA

'I suppose expeditions cost a lot?'

ANGELA

But £40,000! It was nearly as much money as we'd spent last year on the conservatory, after the monkey-puzzle tree fell on

the roof. It wasn't peanuts, whatever he said. I was sure they could manage, somehow, without it. Did they really need that many huskies?

Perhaps I was just trying to make Edward come home. Perhaps I didn't want to live without him anymore.

(*Not a word from him for nearly two months, and then he rings up and asks me for money.* That was the story that told itself, again and again, in my cramped, hurt, heart.)

I couldn't convince her. We both fell silent.

VIRGINIA

I hovered to one side of the queues in the Topkapi gardens. The people queueing looked hot and fretful, but the gardens were green, and it was spring. Angela, who was always in a hurry, tried to marshal me into the line, but I stood on the grass, and looked, and breathed. The tulips blazed yellow and red down the path: I thought of Kew, butterflies, summer; but there were two sentries in sentry-boxes, little men dwarfed by the size of the gardens, and two others at the gate of the palace, and when I looked more closely, both cradled rifles, holding them up like uncomfortable babies, a little too easy, too intimate. For where was the threat? In the sea of grass, there were deep purple pansies, and families sat talking, and children played. Over the wall, blue water, boats, and seagulls hung, indifferent.

'There are more flags than there were before,' said Angela, looking in the same direction. 'Why do they need to point those rifles? Terrorism, I suppose.'

'It reminds me of New York. The fuss before we were allowed to get on the boat that took us to the Statue of Liberty. Then at the airport the same. Are there really so many terrorists now?' The scene around me was peaceful, idyllic. 'In our day things were different ... we thought of

assassins and anarchists, not terrorists … though Conrad had some in *The Secret Agent*.'

ANGELA

I didn't want to explain to her, I had my own troubles to think about. I thought she had just wandered off, but in fact she had found the little coterie of guides who were walking up and down, touting their skills. Yes, she was growing more confident.

VIRGINIA

Choosing him was easy: he had good English. He was not bored, or beaten down. Soon we were all inside the palace. He told me that his name was 'Max'.

ANGELA

She believed him because she lacked cultural awareness. I asked him, what was his real name?

VIRGINIA

'You said we had to call people whatever they wanted.'

ANGELA

It turned out, his real name was Muhsin.

VIRGINIA

He was elderly but very handsome. Looked Russian, or Tartar. High cheekbones, golden skin, teeth so white that I suspected them, though many modern people had blinding white teeth. He laughed and said he was 'Mongolian'.

ANGELA

I think she had a crush on him. Though I admit he was good at his job.

VIRGINIA

Angela was slightly in love with him!

Lime catkins were hanging in the sunlight, bees were just lifting to life from the ground, the crows were watching us from the roof-tops – but no, Max was talking again, showering us with facts like pollen from the lime trees. 'The "seven hills of Istanbul", named after the seven hills of Rome … there were Pagans here, before Byzantium, then the Emperor Constantine … a Christian … long after the Romans in the west had fallen … Mehmet … in 1457… the Topkapi Palace you see before you was built only three hundred years ago.'

('Only three hundred'! He made me feel young. I have to admit I did find him handsome, though unlike Angela, I wasn't smirking, or running my hands through my shingled hair. I tried to concentrate, to do him justice, but I was distracted by the sunlit gardens. How old was I really? What did time mean?)

ANGELA

'Virginia, are you listening?'

VIRGINIA

– He was saying the best part of Topkapi was the Harem, but we'd have to pay another fifty Turkish lira.

'Of course we must see the Harem,' I said.

Angela paid up with a bad grace. She had many things to learn about being a lady.

ANGELA

This was the place of women. So we should have had a female guide. I did say that to Virginia, but she pointed out that there weren't any. Was she, really, a feminist?

VIRGINIA

His eyes glinted behind his round gold glasses; his teeth flashed; he was enjoying himself. I had thought the Harem was the realm of the erotic, I was looking forward to hearing about that, I thought Max would tell the story well – but he talked about history and politics. And so I had to imagine the rest from a few wide beds and elaborate bathrooms, white marble enclaves with anterooms. Yes, I glimpsed pairs and trios of women, semi-naked, langorous ...

ANGELA

Muhsin's narrative was all about power. The women were chosen from the slave markets, to avoid dynastic quarrels with Turkish families – Circassians, Russians, Ukrainians, Greeks – teenagers, separated from their parents, pretty children trained by the black eunuchs; then the 'best' were picked by the sultan's mother, and the first to give birth became the sultan's wife. As soon as they were women, the power games began. Everything was focused on the future of their sons. Some would inherit, others would die.

VIRGINIA

Their living quarters were ornate but sad. Elaborate landscapes to replace the real world. The gaolers must have understood what they craved, for the paintings on the walls and the golden furniture were of wild flowers, fruit trees, boats on the ocean, wide sunlit landscapes they would never walk in. Maybe it just sharpened their hunger. The stone was worn away by their slippered feet. Those window-panes; women must have pressed against them, eyes yearning up to find the sky, soft flesh rubbing the sills away. Lives which left no other imprint. And every summer too hot, I thought, but they could never stroll on a hill in the breeze, and week followed week, and every

morning the pattern of the sun on the wall would be the same, every morning until they were old.

Were they watching us and whispering, the ghosts of mistresses left behind?

Would they be glad, or envious, to see us – two free modern women, with a man we were paying to serve our needs?

'The only men allowed were the Sultan or the black eunuch. They had absolute dominion over the women's lives …'

Max was surely enjoying this a little too much.

ANGELA

Out of the blue, Virginia interrupted. 'Maybe the women were fucking each other.'

Fortunately Muhsin appeared not to hear. 'Virginia!' I protested, shocked, though part of me just wanted to laugh.

'*You* say "fucking",' she said, 'I've heard you. I thought it was normal?'

'I haven't said anything like *that*.'

'But you do say "fucking".'

'Well … only when I don't mean it.'

Muhsin, meanwhile, had ended his tour. Virginia gave him an excessively large tip.

I got lumbered with taking their photograph together. It was Muhsin who suggested it, when he realised he had read one of her books. Fortunately he was vague about dates when it came to modern literature! '*Mrs* – I've forgotten,' he said, enthusiastically. 'We read it at Istanbul University. Wonderful story about a party. Did you really write it? I would like very much a picture with you.'

Virginia was preening herself – I think that is an objective description '*Mrs Dalloway*,' I interrupted. I wanted to cut short the love-fest. 'She doesn't like photographs,' I added, but she didn't back me up; just smiled at him, so I felt foolish.

'Yes, *Mrs Dalloway*, exactly. Very famous book! Very famous author. Take my camera,' he said to me, peremptorily.

'I write novels too,' I said. 'I've written eight. I am translated into Turkish. We could ask one of these Chinese people to take all three of us. They've been taking photos non-stop, they are experts.' But neither Virginia nor Muhsin was listening, they had gone to find a spot where they would look photogenic. Virginia, true, pretended reluctance, and jammed her boater down over her eyes, wailing 'For heaven's sake get a move on', but when Muhsin begged her, she took the hat off, because he wanted her to 'look like the photo he remembered'.

I must be more short-sighted than I was, because I took several pictures, posing them so light would fall on Virginia's hair – lit from behind she looked particularly young, next to Muhsin's white head hers was golden brown – I swear I did my best for them, but when Muhsin checked the pictures, he said 'Where's Virginia?' I looked, but all I could see was him, the passage behind and a patch of darkness, and Virginia refused point blank to pose again.

VIRGINIA

She deliberately left me out of Max's photo. As I said, she was in love with him. True, I found him charming, and wanted to please him ... So I may have bent my rules a little, and this was her way of taking revenge. I suppose we were fighting over a man! It made me feel – amused, and young. I liked the new me. This was an adventure.

ANGELA

We said goodbye to him. He said it was an honour. I think that included both of us.

VIRGINIA

The tall trees en route for Aya Sophia reminded me of somewhere else – their gentle leaning, their high graceful arcs, the complex patchwork of colour on their bark, grey-green and eau-de-nil, in the sunlight – recalling something intensely hopeful – yes, it was the trees when I emerged from hell, the delicate pale giraffes of trees by the New York Public Library where my new life began. And there were crows: chattering ungainly, hopping and scattering over the grass, cawing at me. '*Kaar, Virginia.*'

(Were countries real? Were cities real? The birds, the plane trees spread all over the world?)

The leaves moved above us and above the tired tulips. Deep purple pansies blew in beds, an intense depth of colour with a dust of white weeds. Two yellow dogs slept on the green. Summer was coming – would I still be here?

'Time for the Aya Sophia,' said Angela.

But I couldn't stop thinking about the Harem.

Somewhere in the warm colonnades of Topkapi, on the side of the palace that looked over the sea, did the souls of the imprisoned women become birds, swooping in and out over the blue water? Had their suffering earned them a thousand years of freedom, like the children of air in Hans Andersen's 'Little Mermaid', set free from the green and gold book in my library?

(Could I escape too, from my old story? Could I ever recover my own desires? My own desires, which were stolen from me.)

ANGELA

'Was anyone allowed to say "No" to the Sultan?'

(I thought, it would be nice to be a Sultan. Whereas I had to be unselfish. Mostly. Was I? Edward claimed when he was

346

home he was always looking after me. Just because he's good at getting up in the morning! It's not much trouble making cups of tea.)

A line of crows stretched across the lawns. Big-headed, powerful, a living chain. Their black beaks rose and fell like hammers.

VIRGINIA

'I suppose – yes, but only if he loved them. If you want someone's love, you can't coerce them. My Leonard let me say "No" to him.'

Poor Leonard: those first years, we shared a bed. I felt no more than if I was a rock, and on my rock, he starved and suffered. But kisses: yes, and caresses, I gave, like swallows landing, then I darted away.

ANGELA

'I could say "No" to Edward, too.'

Though I probably said it too often. I was tired of course, I was a young mother. And then, an author ... maybe modern women are always tired.

VIRGINIA

'I had brothers ... difficult half-brothers. One couldn't always say no to them. It's a knack girls need to learn quite young.'

ANGELA

'Do you think those are normal crows, Virginia? I mean, are they the same as British crows?'

VIRGINIA

'Let's go and have a look. I'm fond of crows. One saw them in Sussex.'

Crows were allies, somehow – one always felt that. But as we approached, they broke ranks, and we saw the dark-grey of their bodies (not quite British) as their wings part-unfolded and they hopped and skipped sideways, tumbling ungracefully, only half-bothered, cawing harshly. Then two little boys in matching blue jumpers took their lead from us and ran at the birds, with their mother, who was veiled, calling vainly after them, and soon all the crows, with a loud batting of wings, had flown far away over the walls of Topkapi.

'It creeps me out, when he looks at me,' Gerda told Lil, 'the boy with the beard.'

'Tell him to fuck off.' Lil wasn't bothered. 'I tell him to fuck off all the time.'

They were walking in the sunlight with a huge grey deerhound that was there when Gerda woke the first morning. The golden-skinned girl claimed it was hers. 'I call him Wolfy.' Fortunately Gerda was OK with animals. She gave him the Three Musketeers chocolate bar she had half-eaten in the taxi from the airport, and the dog wolfed it, and licked her hand. She felt at home with him after that. Gerda got credit from Lil for courage as she walked along with her fingers plunged into the wiry curls at the base of his neck, which meant she had to hold her arm up. He was awesomely tall, with a noble head and oddly long, speedy hindquarters. 'The others are scared of Wolfy. You're not.'

It's not really true, Gerda thought to herself. The others aren't scared, or not very scared, and I am, slightly, but I'm hiding it. Lil made this up so she can think I'm special, so she has a good reason to feel what she feels.

The truth is, the feeling's about her, not me. Lil is lonely among all those Divs. She just needs someone she can have fun with. It's not really about me at all.

(But *I* like *her*. So is that about me?)

'He's not your boyfriend, is he?' Gerda asked. Suddenly it mattered that he was not.

'Boyfriend? *Him?* I haven't got a boyfriend. Why would I

want a *boyfriend*?' Lil said the word as if squeezing it in tweezers prior to disposing of it in toxic waste.

'Well, on your rock there's a lot of boys.'

'On the rock it's a different world.' Lil reached out without warning and grabbed Gerda's wrist, quite painfully tight, then let it go and interlaced their fingers. They walked along with the dog between them, a bridge of hands over giant Wolfy, arms too high to be relaxed, like a flying buttress on a church. Gerda felt awkward, glad and proud. Lil queened it over all of them, but she saw Gerda as an equal.

Somebody's noticed I'm special, thought Gerda. Someone from the other side of the world. 'Do you think life would be better if it was just girls?' she asked cautiously.

'Obviously,' Lil Robber said. 'But boys are useful to do things for us.'

Gerda suddenly remembered something. 'I went to an all-girls' school,' Gerda said. 'It wasn't better, it was actually awful.'

'That's *school*,' said Lil. 'School's awful. It's prison, isn't it.'

'Still you have to learn things,' Gerda said.

'School is prison for innocent people.' (Gerda thought: she's said that before.) 'I pity you for being locked up,' Lil added, but her face said something more complex, more resentful.

'One of the teachers was good,' said Gerda. Lil was so sure of her opinions, and Gerda needed to hang on to her own.

'That's like saying "I had a nice prison guard".'

'It's – all about your point of view,' said Gerda. 'It's an Assertion, not a Fact.' She could feel the mute force of Lil's anger. The Robber Girl couldn't answer her.

The dog was loping along by the lake, blue-grey-black against the blue–dark water. He had escaped their arch of hands, which had collapsed into a hanging garland that they swung, swung as they kept in step.

Then an army of crows landed in the shallows, splashing,

pecking at the brightness, chattering. Suddenly the dog leaped into the lake.

Lil rounded on Gerda, eyes blazing topaz, hands on hips, cheeks heavy and red.

'Now you got to get him back. Fact.'

ANGELA

I was watching our shadows as we walked towards the gates.
Did they look frail and elderly? Were both of us slightly bent
forward, from writing? I pulled my shoulders back and looked
at her. We had pitied the women of the Harem, but I suddenly
knew they wouldn't want to be us. No, they would have pitied
Woolf's childlessness.

VIRGINIA

'What are you staring at?'

ANGELA

'Nothing. I was wondering what the women of the Harem
would have thought of you, Virginia.'

VIRGINIA

'I would have been beyond their comprehension. And what
would they have thought of you?'

(They would have asked her if she had a husband, and when
she said 'Yes', they would have asked 'Where is he? And how
old is your child? She isn't with you?' They might have thought
she had missed the point.)

ANGELA

'Have I tired you out, Virginia?'

'Certainly not!' She struck out towards the arch more
energetically than before.

VIRGINIA

We walked over the gate's massive threshold, a great metal sill, burnished in the middle to dazzling smoothness by the endless passage of the little people, their shoes humbly passing and polishing. Thousands of shadows of the living and the dead. We are cotton-fluff: dandelion; we blow on the wind.

Aya Sophia glowed into view, its central dome like an enormous gold-tipped breast on a cream and pink, sprawled, stucco body.

New York is a man, I thought to myself, cool, straight, confident.

And Istanbul's a middle-aged woman. Watery. Supple. All tides and inlets.

ANGELA

'Of course the wives plotted against each other. It was politics, and that's what male politicians do – oh look at the queue for Aya Sophia.'

VIRGINIA

The queue stretched out in restless motion towards the flowerbeds and fountains of Sultanahmet Park, which rose and fell, rose and fell, bowing and aspiring to the Blue Mosque in the distance. A shifting succession of people crossed the bright expanse of paving-stones in front of the water, flickering and fading like the fountains.

ANGELA

So many people. Ants, midges. Why should I mind so much about Edward? Surely I would find another man.

'It wasn't a story of sisterhood, was it?'

VIRGINIA

'Sisters do feel rivalry.'

ANGELA

Now we were in the queue behind a young Chinese man who was doing a full Kung Fu routine to pass the time. He kept doing lunges, and shouting 'Ha', which was wearing.

'I never had a sister. I imagined I would love her. Were you really jealous of your sister? Did you ever, for a moment, hate her?'

VIRGINIA

'I didn't dare to hate her, you see. After Mother died, Vanessa mothered me. Even before, I ran to her for kisses. For me, Nessa always meant kisses. But we were both artists. Of course, I was jealous. Artists are always jealous of each other.'

ANGELA (*suddenly very earnest*)

'I hope you don't think I am jealous of you. I'm not, I promise. I admire you, Virginia. You're like my mother, honestly. All modern writers look to you. That's what you are, our foremother.'

I felt so hurt when she hooted with laughter. The sweating Chinese man paused mid-kick and looked at her sharply, but she was oblivious.

VIRGINIA

'It sounds like an ape, a foremother! No, it's ridiculous, I wasn't a mother, I had no talent for looking after. You can't foist motherhood on me.

(*More gently*) 'I never learned to look after children.'

ANGELA

'Do you object to followers? (*Cheering up.*) If you won't let us be your daughters, we'll just traipse after you, unacknowledged.'

(*She follows Virginia to the ticket office, which they have reached at last. They pick up guide-books. Virginia reads hers.*)

ANGELA

'I know quite a lot about it already.'

VIRGINIA

We entered the body of Aya Sophia through tremendous doors, twelve feet high. It was huge, and cool, full of light and people. It went on forever. It was a city.

'Who was Saint Sophia, by the way? I'm sure she must have been hideously tortured to deserve this kind of edifice.'

ANGELA

'Aya Sophia wasn't a person. It means "Sacred wisdom", Virginia.'

VIRGINIA

'*Sapientia* in Latin … Yes. Wisdom is female. I was never wise.'

The temple stretched above us, airy, colossal, essentially unchanged from a century ago, though the wheels of lights which hung from the roof were now electric, not candles. But far above the lights, reappeared like phoenixes, two golden mosaics flickered like flames – Mary the Mother gazed down at us, child on her lap, calm patient face, and I recognised her with joy and sorrow, the eternal absence I could never fill, the mother I always had to find again. When we came before, there was only blank plaster; the Christian murals had been painted out by Mohammedans who thought images were sinful. Atatürk, 'friend of history', had restored them, according

to my guide-book. People were gazing up, but thoughtfully. These were aesthetes, not religious enthusiasts. Watching them, one thought 'those wars are over'.

According to Angela, alas, they were not.

An American guide gave a loud commentary somewhere at the back of the church. 'This is the Omphalos. What we call the umbilicus. The spot where the child was joined to his mother at the beginning of the world. The Romans crowned their emperors in this circle. They believed that everything started here …'

Yes, the mother. But I had to escape her. All through my life, 'my mother', 'my father' …

I wanted to go up to the gallery where I had gone with Vanessa, when Aya Sophia was still a working mosque, so the women had to watch the men from above. 'Angela,' I said, 'come upstairs with me.'

ANGELA
'Where are the stairs?'

VIRGINIA
'There weren't any last time I came, just a sloping stone ramp that spiralled up sixty feet or so. Empress Theodocia used to drive up it in her chariot. Such a shameless display of power, to drive one's chariot right through a temple! I'm sure they've installed a lift by now.'

ANGELA
What followed was something I will never forget.

'RAMPA', it said on the notice. But when I looked right, I saw a sloping tunnel. As a girl, I could never use the underground. I asked a guide if there was any other way up, but she shook her head. This was it.

It was pinkish-grey, low-ceilinged, cobbled. It must have been there since Theodocia's time. Waiting for me for two thousand years.

As I stepped over the threshold, my courage failed. 'Does it go on like this? No windows?'

VIRGINIA

'It will be fine, you'll see. I just remember being young, walking up, with Nessa, arm in arm, and in a hurry. Not wanting to miss anything.'

ANGELA (*walks to the first turn, then stops*)
'Virginia, I can't do it. You go ahead. I'll sit and wait.'

VIRGINIA

'What's the matter?'
She was trembling, and breathing fast.

ANGELA
'Nothing. I'm going to try.'

I didn't want her to see my fear. I took a deep breath, made for the first turn, and rounded it, but it went on ahead of me, narrowing slightly, and no more windows, and would go on forever, no hope, I thought, and no Edward in the background to help me, and if I go on, I will never get out. As I turned and fled, I bumped into Virginia, and her body was surprisingly warm and solid. 'I can't,' I told her. 'I'm claustrophobic.'

And then we were together, back at the beginning. Virginia looked into me, into my fear, with those piercing orbs, without flinching.

'Perhaps I am afraid of being born,' I said. I tried to laugh, but my heart was beating, and a light breeze told me my skin was wet. 'My mother told me I was born too fast.'

VIRGINIA

And so I took Angela's hand. I helped her to be born, though I had never had a baby. I saw how she suffered, but for me it was easy. 'Step by step,' I said. 'Step by step, and we'll get to the top.'

Her hand was shaking, but she did what I said. We reached the first turn, and the last window. 'Don't look back,' I said. 'Trust me. If we just go on walking, we will get there.'

ANGELA

Step by step, she led me on.

VIRGINIA

I could feel the tension in her arm. She started to pull away and go back. I talked to her quietly, as if she was a child. Some nonsense, 'It's all right, good, you're doing well …' I no longer remember what I said. There was just my will-power carrying us, some womanly force that would make things happen, Theodocia's chariot, Nessa and I, driving us up towards the light.

ANGELA

I will remember her voice for ever. It was soft and low, a sweet murmur. It kept me going, like a golden thread, and the gentle pressure of her hand on mine. But another voice tried to drag me down. 'You've gone too far, you can never go back, you will burrow on through the dark forever.'

VIRGINIA

I could hardly bear her mute dependence, but I took the burden, I found a smile, my legs were strong, we went on walking. Suddenly there was a hole in the wall, I suppose an air-shaft, not really a window, and through it we heard the voices of children, sweet and clear and echoing. She stopped

for a moment – I thought she'd given up – but then I saw she was breathing, smiling.

ANGELA
'I'm all right.'

VIRGINIA
So we carried on up – only three more turns – the voices of the gallery were coming to meet us – and she was no longer pulling at me, but I kept her hand in mine to the end, and we walked together, free-er, faster –

ANGELA
And then we were out. The glory of it! Light, freedom. Light, light. The world all about us. She had brought me through it.

I felt as if I had been – reborn. I was laughing, crying. There's no other word for it.

'Thank you, thank you, Virginia.' I took her other hand and held it.

VIRGINIA (*laughing and pulling away*)
I thought she was going to dance with me! 'Please don't mention it.' Yes, I had helped her. Still, after a second, I broke away.

We went to the balustrade and looked down. Busy tiny people, wide hoops of light. Massive pillars supporting our world. 'This dome has fallen many times, I believe.'

ANGELA
'I'm glad you didn't say that before I went in the tunnel. Why did it fall?'

VIRGINIA

'Earthquakes. War ... human beings, always conquering things, destroying things. Warring religions, of course. Pagans, Christians, Muslims. British, French, Germans. It goes in cycles; build, demolish.'

ANGELA

'But everything here feels so – permanent. So monumental. As if nothing could change it. One moment, then another moment. Everything feels inevitable. I know cities fall. And civilisations. I can do it in my head, but I can't make sense of it, not physically, in my own human body. Which tells me this will go on for ever.'

VIRGINIA

'You see, I have been so far away. That place where all of us must go. And when I came back, they had all vanished. It was as if we had never been. New York had forgotten Roger, and Duncan, and Vanessa. They had all – flickered out. The images they meant to capture for ever were in the stacks, or sold, or lost. And the streets were so straight, and everything so new, and the sun so bright – it all felt – shallow. Why did they ever work so hard?

'Now the whole world looks like flats for a play.'

Of course it was different for Angela. She still had husband, daughter, a home, not that she'd learned to value them. She was clinging to the brightness of her last stretch of youth, she thought her choices would last forever, though soon a narrower corridor would take her. She dared not loosen her hold on space, she dared not loosen her grip on money. 'Are you ready to go down again?'

ANGELA

The way down was easy, just an ordinary staircase. By the barest margin, I had passed the test.

At the bottom, the sun poured through the great doors. Just for a second, we remained in darkness. She took one of my hands, and pressed it on the wall. It was a moment I will not forget. So brief, this sense of being one with her. What was she giving me, a gift or a curse? I could hardly hear the words she whispered.

VIRGINIA

'Only the stones. Only the stones. The stones remain, but we are just shadows.'

(Though just then, Angela was painfully real, probably because I had seen her suffer. One would have liked to say, 'Nothing much matters. So save your marriage. Give Edward the money.')

Gerda held Lil at bay for a second. 'Dogs are animals. They don't need saving.'

'Wolfy's different.'

'Why?'

'He might not come back.'

'Why not?'

'Because he doesn't know he belongs to me.'

'Well ... I don't have to get him back, but I will,' said Gerda, stripping off her trousers, shivering, but clenching her jaw so Lil didn't see it. 'Assertion!' she shouted over her shoulder as she splashed into the freezing water. *Miss Larman, help me now.* She had to go straight in, no messing.

Lil was laughing demonically on the bank. 'You've got a thong! I can see your bush!'

'You won't see me for – ' Gerda would have said 'dust', but just at that moment she vanished underwater as the bottom of the lake fell away from her, and for a moment all she saw was bubbles and weed, and she swallowed death, but then she was off, swimming straight and strongly over to the side of the lake where Wolfy's head was moving fast, the living point of an arrow of ripples, a dark triangle with a blue-white crest.

'Wolfy,' she called, briefly treading water, 'Wolfy, come here!'

Come on, you bastard, she begged in her head. *I've got to get you back or Lil will kill me.*

But Wolfy was not interested. He was swimming after birds. The crows had swooped away, laughing harshly, so Wolfy had settled for some inoffensive moorhens who half took off,

undignified, half-scooting on the lake away from the dog, three black and white flurries of bristling feathers, making for the green edge where they lived.

'Wolfy!' He was getting out now, on the East side, shaking white cloaks of water off him. 'Come on, Wolfy, I'm not going to chase you.' But his long hind-legs were powering him onwards, leaping and gambling through a haze of drops, and now he had found another dog, a little white poodle who yipped sharply –

'Wolfy, come *back*!'

Yipped and nipped. Wolfy barked twice, sadly, at his would-be lover and then, a thinner, more bedraggled dog, re-entered the water with a bark in her direction, a small, gruff sound that seemed to say 'All right, fair's fair, I've had my fun.'

'Good boy, Wolfy! Here I am!' Gerda did a leisurely side-stroke, waiting. Yes, he was arrowing back round the shore, working his way down the grey-green line, he was only fifty metres away –

And then, quite suddenly, he wasn't. Something strange was going on. His nose had gone up, he was bucking in the water, throwing up a spume of white spray – had something attacked him? – barking, frantic. Had he found a fish? Was he mucking about?

But the sound of terror is universal. 'I'm coming, Wolfy!' Gerda shouted. 'It's all right, I'm on my way.'

Then Gerda became 'a living speedboat', powering through the water so fast and straight she was just a narrow line of white spray –

Or that was the way Lil told it, later, with Wolfy half asleep at her feet.

They were sitting on the rock, surrounded by children, a circle of faces, curious, resentful, wondering why *they* weren't heroes, not like the new ginger intruder. Someone had set fire

to a pile of boxes.

'I'm telling you, she went like a rocket! Well, like a mermaid. Mermaids always have red hair – ' (it was clear that none of them questioned Lil's knowledge, which was all Assertion, and weak on Facts, but this time Gerda didn't point that out, though she heard a child whispering 'What's a Murmured?') ' – when she got there, Wolfy was almost drowned, he'd got stuck in the water-weeds down the edge, I expect there were water-snakes in there as well' ('It was wire,' Gerda interrupted) ' – I WAS COMING TO THAT,' Lil insisted, 'so she had to drag him free, didn't she, he's a big dog and he was panicking, and she couldn't put her feet on the bottom or anything, and then she saw there was like BLOOD on the water, and she had to get BARBED-WIRE off his leg.'

With that Lil held up Gerda's hand in the fire-light and showed off the red jagged line of blood. 'So she did all right, didn't she?'

There was a general, grudging noise of approval, and Wolfy, who had been welcomed back with a hamburger Beardy Boy had nicked from a stall, pushed his warm, greasy, hairy nose firmly into Gerda's palm. Under his eyebrows, Beardy Boy stared.

'He would have got free on his own,' he said.

'Beard's jealous,' Lil said. 'He couldn't do it himself. He can't swim, can he. He couldn't be a mermaid.'

'Mermaids are girls,' Gerda pointed out. 'Never mind, it's a beautiful word.'

'What is a Murmured?' the same child asked.

'A really good swimmer,' Lil opined. 'It isn't a boy or a girl, it's either. It has to be a hero when there's a chance. Even if it hurts itself.'

VIRGINIA

How it fascinated me: self-sacrifice, service. Angela wasn't feeling talkative. It was our second day, we were on our way to Üsküdar, the tram was screeching round a corner, a man got up and gave me his seat – she flashed me a look of irritation.

Üsküdar. Such a beautiful word, the Turkish word, so much softer than Scutari, not just a shield, a husky fullness, but with that strength, that 'd', underneath. Scutari where Florence Nightingale nursed. I longed to go there because of my mother. Florence Nightingale, twenty years older, was always a hero for my mother, though to us she seemed fabulously aged, a dragon, and because of Lytton, faintly ridiculous.

ANGELA

Virginia had no idea of the efforts I'd made to get her into Scutari.

VIRGINIA

Florence Nightingale's 'Letter to Cassandra' was so ... bitter. Yes, she was right, women's talents were wasted, women were imprisoned in the drawing-room, but raw pain does not make good writing. I preferred to use wit. Wit and lightness. Then the men can't laugh, or pity us.

ANGELA

She naturally left all the details to me. Because it was a barracks – the Istanbul barracks – the Turks didn't welcome just anybody.

You would have thought two respectable English ladies would not be suspected of being spies. But I had to fax a letter explaining our interest, and pages of our passports, and home addresses; even then their fax accepting us had only arrived during breakfast. To all this, she was oblivious. That morning, on the tram to the ferry, she was regal, as if everything came to her by right, and she got a seat, while I did not, and the Turk who gave it stared at her … I suppose Virginia always looked strange.

VIRGINIA

From the tram to the ferry, in the early morning, skies of pearl and rose, and no-one was on deck but we two and a family (I judged, from the way they herded together) of brutal-looking people in children's clothes – identical two-piece romper-suits with 'UKRAINE' written across their shoulders ('It's the name of a country,' Angela explained, 'They're not romper-suits, we call them "tracksuits".') They stared at us as if we came from space. The boys had matching blonde stubble on their heads. Why did they wear the name of their country on their shoulders? Strange that this world, so international, was still so eager to declare its loyalties. Or maybe they were 'terrorists'? Angela was tetchy, so I didn't ask her.

The barracks was up on the hill. The only way to get there was along a huge road. It felt raw and tremendous, with the narrowest of pavements, not at all like the avenues in New York, no traffic lights or pedestrian crossings, heavy lorries roaring and trembling past us, their burdens shaking at the cords, the wind from their passing flattening our clothes and blowing our words into nothingness. I was deafened, maddened, would we get there alive? Was this terrifying artery the meaning of progress? No room for error. If you stumbled, you died.

The drivers were blind, too far above us to see as we midgets scampered along by the traffic, heads down.

At last we turned left. Yes, there was the barracks. Three sentries stared at us, amazed, from their posts fifty yards up an empty road. We had to approach under hostile eyes. 'Smile,' said Angela over her shoulder as she preceded me with our documents. My mouth felt dry and dusty from the road but I tried, and to my surprise, a soldier smiled back. Men were definitely smiling at me more. Turkish men must be friendlier.

A soldier – he looked around fifteen, white teeth uneven in his mouth – escorted us into the guardhouse. It was bristling with soldiers, guns at the ready, who took the documents, removed her phone. How would Angela manage without it?

'Camera, Miss.'

I said 'I don't have a camera.'

Angela pretended not to hear, but the soldier asked again and she yielded – 'But I wanted to photograph the museum!' 'No photos.'

'There are a great many soldiers,' I whispered.

ANGELA

'They're just conscripts, Virginia. Probably students. Everyone has to go in the army.'

VIRGINIA

'Pity about the camera.'

ANGELA

'What's tragic is – I haven't got a single picture of you.'

VIRGINIA

'I believe it's all about where you point it?'

367

ANGELA

'I pointed it at you, of course!'

VIRGINIA

'Well don't look at me as if it's my fault.'

ANGELA

'All I'm saying is, you never come out. Perhaps you're moving – accidentally, I mean – just at the moment I take the picture?'

VIRGINIA

'The poor photographer blames her subjects. Though it's true I am a reluctant subject.'

ANGELA

'I might like to have a souvenir. Something I could show my daughter. I am proud to have spent time with you, Virginia.'

Then an officer arrived, middle-aged, slightly jaded, his tired smile saying he had done this before. A saloon car with a uniformed driver swept the three of us through the barracks. 'This is the north-east tower,' said the officer. 'Get out here, please, for Florence Nightingale Museum.'

VIRGINIA

What had I expected? One hoped to find … her. The actual woman. Florence Nightingale. Something more authentic than Lytton's sneering picture.

Alas, the museum was not a success. First, a room full of dreadful brown plastic soldiers, most of them not from the Crimean War. Models of guns, men in gaiters, gallant officers ordering charges. Our own officer – plump, balding, intelligent – kept disconsolately trying to please us, so one feigned interest, but it wasn't easy.

ANGELA

Not destined to appeal to the author of *Three Guineas*.

OFFICER (*ushering them past cabinets of nineteenth-century medicines*)
'I actually studied English Literature. I have read Graham
Greene, and *Great Gatsby*. Very good author, your Fitzgerald!'

ANGELA

'Yes, thank you.'

OFFICER

'Our professor said Graham Greene was a spy. Ha, ha!'

ANGELA (*nervous*)
'I definitely prefer *Great Gatsby*.'

OFFICER

'Yes, it's better. Through here is where she lived. Follow me,
please. Here are ancient bandages … But I think you English
admire him very much, Graham Greene?'

ANGELA

'No, neither of us like him at all.'

OFFICER

'This is Florence Nightingale's sitting room.'

ANGELA

The view from her room was dazzling. What she must have
seen every morning, on waking. Wide, wide across the river.
Two walls of the room were windows. There was a constant
coming and going of boats. She must have seen the injured
arrive, on groaning ships from the Crimea.

'The whole big world. She was part of it, here.'

VIRGINIA
'So this was what she fought to leave her family for.'
Escaping the tiny world of visiting cards. The middle-class harem, the prison in the parlour. But what did she escape to? Endless work. The harrow of service. Duty, like Mother.

OFFICER
'Florence Nightingale taught us modern medicine. Before she came, this was just a – what do you call it? Funeral place.'

ANGELA
'Cemetery?'

OFFICER
'She cleaned everything, and looked after everything, and soon, no more people die. We admire her.'

VIRGINIA
'My mother admired her, she was expert at sick-rooms. Some women are very good at looking after people. Not me.' (Yet I was thinking: duty. In a way, my writing was also a duty. I had to do it. It harrowed me.)

OFFICER (*laughing*)
'Not my wife either. Unfortunately. Every morning, I make the breakfast.'

ANGELA
'Virginia? You cared for me. When I was afraid. You cared for your sister.'

VIRGINIA

'Oh, but one knew it would not last forever.' (*Laughs.*)

(Yes, I had to write every day, thousands of words: duty, duty. Maybe, now, I was free at last.

Yet I had loved it more than life itself.)

ANGELA

'I read what people in your village said about you, after you, you know – '

VIRGINIA (*impatient*)
'Died.'

ANGELA

'Yes. Lots of them said that you were kind.'

VIRGINIA

'Re-a-lly? I'm sure it's undeserved …'

ANGELA

All the same, she did not look displeased.

Much bowing and smiling when we parted with the officer, and flattering remarks about English literature, which we were too ignorant to reciprocate. I told him I admired Pamuk, and Shafek, but I have a dreadful feeling I muddled it up and managed to say 'Shamuk, and Pafek'. At any rate, he looked blank, and said 'Very nice. Goodbye ladies.' 'Thank you, thank you' – then I muddled through a brief pledge of British friendship for Turkey. It felt like a pound of unwanted sausages. Why must I always try to please?

As we walked away from the Barracks, we swopped notes. Virginia asked why I had been so friendly, and I tried to explain that Turkish intellectuals liked the army because they

were seen as modernising, secular. 'They're not the same as the government. Nothing is like it is back home.'

'I understood the old world,' she said, as we walked. 'I grew up in it. Most of our friends were conscientious objectors. The army was the enemy. I was in my thirties during the Great War, which made us what we were, perhaps. But of course, I missed so much of the Second. And I'm trying to understand your world, but sometimes I think it's impossible. I'm just a visitor – a tourist – trying to catch up, but always failing. And without writing, does one really exist? Yet must one always live for writing?'

'Come on, Virginia, that ferry's leaving.'

ANGELA

I think she was trying to say something important, but I had to make decisions, time was running out. Now the afternoon began to unravel. She wanted to go to Kiz Kulesi – Leander's Tower, the Maiden's Tower – but I was sick of fake history, and hadn't I done enough for her? It was time to focus on the conference, which was coming closer hour by hour: in particular, what to wear. I fancied a sharp new jacket from Zara. It wasn't hard to overrule her, especially as she didn't know the modern city – (Kiz Kulesi was less than half-an-hour away!) – so I ushered her on to the ferry to Europe. 'I really do have to do some shopping.' She said 'I'll see Kiz Kulesi another time,' but she sounded as though she didn't believe it.

The seagulls squawked around the ferry, doing acrobatics in the headwind as we curved smoothly towards Pera. I started to feel high-spirited. Of course the paper would speak for itself, but I wanted my clothes to say 'Young, hopeful'. A flash of orange? Fashionable cobalt?

VIRGINIA

'So are we going to the Grand Bazaar?'

ANGELA

I realised I had just said 'shopping'. 'No, Virginia, just regular shops. You know, clothes shops, Next, Zara.' Of course, she didn't know. How could she? I started to explain, as we

disembarked, how the same chains were everywhere. In the modern world, shopping was easy. You could find what you wanted in Oxford Street, London, or on Fifth Avenue, or here.

Virginia took on her stubborn look.

VIRGINIA
'But of course, shops in Turkey should be Turkish. These "chains" you talk about, don't they imprison you? Why travel, if the whole world's the same?'

ANGELA (*puffing – the road up is very steep*)
'Wait till you've seen how nice the clothes are. And why shouldn't Turkish women have the same choice? Do you want to keep them in national dress?'

VIRGINIA
'No, though I think there are more covered women on the streets than when I came here last.'

ANGELA
'It's the religious government. Erdoğan's own wife wears a veil.'

But most people here, on the tiny road that led up to the main part of Istiklal, were tourists, not a veil in sight, people were buying in English or German from the garish stalls that lined the road: key-rings, cheap jewellery, juices, sweets.

Halfway up, I noticed something. Far more people were coming down. They did not look happy. It was almost a flood. We began to find it hard to make headway. And then I heard the noise, still distant, a vague buzzing muddle of shouts, sirens. Perhaps there had been a traffic accident.

The day, which had started fresh and blue, was heating up: orange, amber. I took off my jacket, pushed up my sleeves.

VIRGINIA (*pausing on the hill*)
'Are they hurrying to catch a ferry?'

ANGELA (*unwilling to stop*)
'Probably. You'll enjoy Zara. If you liked Bloomingdale's, you'll like this.'

Though would she, I wondered? Zara was cheaper, and Virginia seemed to enjoy spending money.

It struck me she might think me selfish to be buying clothes when Edward needed money. But this was work, after all. Youth, image, they did matter ... I knew I could never explain it to her.

Istiklal! Always a festival. Each time I'd seen it, it was never still – buskers and singers, armies of the young, teenagers, arms linked, four abreast – that sense of swimming in a human river, as if the whole city was going out. I loved the mysterious lateral veins, like the deep cut down to the Museum of Innocence, half a mile below, beside the sea, or the small dark opening to the silver market, where last time I'd bought wonderful jewellery, and yes, why not buy a bracelet for Gerda, to cheer her up when she came home? I looked round for Virginia. There she was, behind me, a stately but incompetent swimmer, chin high, telegramming a smile, but struggling, now, to stay afloat as waves of people buffeted her.

'Virginia! Virginia! Here! There's a little silver market, on the left.'

Yes, on the left. I was looking at it.

It all clicked into focus. And then I was worried.

For the traders were almost obscuring the entrance, deep in frowning, arm-waving debate, and then, quite swiftly, the debate ended. No, they were – what could they possibly be doing? It was Saturday, sunny, the usual crowds were out on Istiklal eager to spend money, but the Heliogabalus silver

traders were closing up. Pulling the heavy grille across, shutting the door of paradise.

VIRGINIA

A sudden shock – twenty yards ahead of me, men were spilling out of a big white bus: a smashed ink-bottle spurting dark stains.

ANGELA

There were white buses lined up like ambulances, and dozens of men were pouring out, not doctors or soldiers, yes they were police. Dozens, a hundred hard-faced men in navy-blue uniforms with bulging holsters, guns and coshes, and I heard the shouts, just out of our sight, and felt the tension, drawn tight like a string, as people stood in doorways and waited. Dark people, both resigned and nervous, talked to each other in low voices. Others were indignant, hands jabbing. All of them were Turks, I realised, not tourists, this was their area, they had to know, they would stay and watch and learn the worst, but the tourists were leaving as fast as they could.

On the other side of Istiklal's hill, maybe fifty metres ahead of us, were enraged or suffering human voices, and now I could no longer ignore them.

'What's happening? Speak English?' I asked a fat man with beads of sweat on his forehead, outside a café, frowning at the sun. At first he didn't hear me, he had other fish to fry, he didn't want to bother with the nosy tourist, but then he said, briefly, 'They stop us selling alcohol. They stop a lot of things. Religious people.'

'Who?'

He didn't answer, straining to see what was happening. Then 'Government'.

'Ah, thank you. Stop you selling alcohol? But it's a tourist city.'

'Yes, thank you, you are right,' he said. 'But religious people, they are crazy. They think everything is sin. They try to stop everything. No demonstrating. No discussing.'

'Dangerous?' I said, gesturing around me.

'Danger-ous?' he said, then understood. He laughed. 'Not for you, I think. For us, maybe. For the students.'

'Virginia, we have to get out. There's the conference tomorrow! I can't get arrested!'

'But look,' said Virginia, 'It's exciting.'

The police had lined up in a tight phalanx across the mouth of a small side road to our left. It was higher ground, which would lend them impetus. Their helmets were on, and their riot shields raised. A wall of faceless, shining plastic.

VIRGINIA

There was something in the air, something sour, I could smell it. A harsh male smell; badness fermented. Then my excitement changed to fear, a switch as sharp as milk turning. The police were covered in plastic & metal – no longer human beings at all – hiding their eyes, hands, faces. They had made themselves into a giant fist, pulled back taut to gather power. Still the angry, youthful, passionate shouts yelled on over the hill, out of our sight, behind the crowd – & the sun was too hot, and the sky overcast, a lid of thin cloud that kept the heat in. They were poking the ants, those brave, fierce voices. My anxious heart begged them to stop.

ANGELA

'We're going, Virginia.' I took her arm. She was staring at the police, eyes fixed, immobile. I pulled her away and we hurried back along Istiklal Avenue together, struggling to push our way through the crowd.

This time we noticed the silent protesters, standing stock still on the street like statues. No shouting, no slogans, just young people – students? – with serious faces, beautiful with the stern beauty of belief, holding magazines up in the air one-handed, raising their convictions to the sun like a beacon. They were spread out, singly, ten metres apart. Each one looked inexpressibly lonely. Why did that make me feel for them? Each one embodied their own courage. We could not see them as a mob like the policemen. This way, only one at a time could be arrested. They were brave enough to be taken alone ... I tried to remember each young frail profile, radiant and still as faces on a flag, though somehow I forgot to take a magazine.

Suddenly the shouting intensified behind us, there were whistles blowing, the sirens were closer. The pressure in the bottleneck increased, but now there was no hope of going forwards. And something fiercer was on the air. I knew, without being told, it was tear gas. Sour, oniony, catching at my throat. My eyes began to sting and water.

VIRGINIA

I have never liked being too close to people – the sweat of the herd about to stampede – & now that choking, chemical smell – I spotted a tiny passageway, I took Angela's hand – we were in this together, she looked at me surprised, her flesh was dry, hot paper – 'Quick,' I said, & we wormed our way free, into a deep cutaway with high blind walls.

ANGELA

Of course I didn't trust her to get us out of trouble – but I followed her, there was nowhere else to go. It felt dank in that passageway. Furious graffiti. We had no idea where we were going. But ten minutes later we were in a small square – not regular enough to be a square, just an opening-out, sun, the

backs of buildings, and a little café. Just what we needed. Here the air smelled sweet again. We frightened a fat pigeon on an outside table, peck-peck-pecking at a sticky red puddle.

VIRGINIA

'That was clever of me.'

ANGELA

'Yes, you did well. Do you think that's blood?'

VIRGINIA

We ducked inside. There was a 'bar', but with beautiful pink and lilac lights underneath it. The serving-woman had a head of wild curls and smiled at us, elaborately friendly, almost as if she had always known us, her gaze embracing us, enfolding us. We realised we were still holding hands after our escape, and let go with a small nod of mutual acknowledgement. 'There is music later,' she nodded at the bar. 'Come back later. American?' Two young women were sat close together, drinking beers, gently chinking glasses.

'No, British.' We ordered 'English tea.'

'Having fun here?'

She most definitely liked us. We smiled and nodded. 'Except for the riot. What's going on?'

'Oh Istiklal – there's always some problems. Nothing for you to worry, though. How did you find us?'

'We were just lucky.'

Her smile was delightful; tender, roguish. It almost felt as if she knew us, and was especially pleased we had come today.

ANGELA

'I suppose that's the end of any hope of shopping.'

VIRGINIA

We sat outside with our tea and two large pieces of apricot pie. Every so often, the waitress came out and smiled. At intervals, panting people came hurrying through from the direction of Istiklal; the waitress talked to them, her face briefly serious. At the next-door table, a group of three moustachioed middle-aged men in vests – what people now called 'T-shirts' – made flamboyant jokes and swam with their hands. Then they were joined by a tall, elegant woman, a redhead, with a careful coiffure. She had a raucous laugh that didn't go with her dress or her svelte silhouette, like a resting greyhound. The foursome sat and smoked and shouted. The kindly waitress seemed to know them well.

After a while there were no more dishevelled people hurrying through from our narrow passage. The sound of sirens and whistles faded away. This little courtyard felt like somewhere else, Italy perhaps, a theatrical world of sunlit laughter where police and rioters could not come.

ANGELA

The thing we had shared – fear, then relief – must have loosened Virginia's tongue, and made her daring.

VIRGINIA

'May I ask you a question about your husband?'

ANGELA

'Go ahead.' I was flattered. Most of her questions were about modernity, which made me feel like Wikipedia.

'I need some wine,' she said suddenly. I waved my hand, and the sweet girl came. 'Two large glasses of Turkish red.' Was it illegal yet? Evidently not.

'Cheers!' said Virginia, holding hers up to the light, and we

touched glasses, and she smiled at me. Virginia was almost a modern woman. She drank deeply, and then again. The group next door was louder than ever. The loud-voiced woman had a smoker's laugh.

Virginia's question was not what I expected.

VIRGINIA

'Angela – do you miss your husband? Physically, as it were.'

ANGELA

'Physically? Do you mean – you don't mean sexually, surely?'
She was blushing. She did mean sexually!

VIRGINIA

'Actually, I do, Angela. Yes.'

ANGELA

How could I talk about sex to *her*! She wasn't a girlfriend! She was ... Virginia! Famously chaste, traumatised! What was that passage in 'Professions for Women'? She said women couldn't write about the body.

'Why do you ask?'

'Oh ... I just wondered.' Her eyelids dipped, she took another sip, but when she looked up again, her eyes were mischievous. 'I have been having ... feelings. Feelings I haven't had for some time. Some time before I died, that is. One hadn't felt – desire – in ages.'

VIRGINIA

Angela looked as though I'd shot her. Stricken, that's the only word for it, as if I had somehow let her down. Or let myself down. A puritan! I thought. Yes, of course, these modern feminists are puritans.

But after a moment, she started to smile.

ANGELA

'Virginia? Are you really? – I don't know what to say. It's sweet. Put it down to coming alive again. It probably gives you all kinds of feelings. Nothing to be guilty about. It's not abnormal for – '

VIRGINIA

She stopped.

I knew quite clearly what she meant to say. 'Not abnormal for older women.' She didn't understand! I no longer felt 'older'!

'The point is, Angela, I find myself thinking – about the people I see in the street. And ... in the lobby. Turkish people.'

I didn't say that it was mostly one man, Ahmet, who occupied my mind. His dark-eyed charm, his currant-bun dimples. Whenever he saw me, that warm, flawed smile. Marzipan skin, sensuous lips. Under his smart work-clothes, his muscled plumpness.

All so very different from Leonard. A shiny berry, a wiry twig.

ANGELA

'There's nothing wrong with having these thoughts.' (Though Virginia was old enough to be my mother!) 'But don't, you know, be too friendly in the lobby. I told you before, they won't understand. They'll think you're, well – ' I couldn't say it. I couldn't say 'They'll think you're up for it.'

And then I did. 'They'll think you're up for it.'

VIRGINIA

My wine had almost gone; the blood was coursing through my

veins. 'I was wondering. I don't know what you think – After all this time, do you think I could …?' Perhaps I spoke louder than I meant. Would people hear? I didn't care. 'Why do you assume I am not "up for it"? If that is what you modern women say.'

ANGELA
'Virginia?'

VIRGINIA (*stares defiantly, says nothing*)

ANGELA
'*Virginia??*'

VIRGINIA
'I don't see why I shouldn't. I'm a writer. We're not supposed to shun experience. So many things I have never done. I can't be a Turk, or an American. I can never be a member of the working classes. One has to be born to it, don't you think? But for some reason – since coming back – one has felt … "I might, perhaps, like to try that." Try it again, as a new person. With a new person. Say, a Turk.

'Why are you staring? I'm not a virgin. Do my readers expect me to be a virgin?'

ANGELA
'A Turk? Not with a Turk, Virginia.'

VIRGINIA
'Why not?'
Angela's mouth had gone thin and cross. Then she laughed.

ANGELA
'You're teasing me, of course. I fell for it.'

VIRGINIA (*coolly*)

'No, I'm serious. I was never able to write about the body ... But that's not the point. I just – want to do it.'

ANGELA

'But, Virginia! Everyone knows ... It's just not you. You can't do it for research.'

VIRGINIA

'Maybe I've become a different person. Maybe I never was that person. Why can't I, you know, with a Turk?'

ANGELA

'Of course you can't, it's ridiculous. Turkish men! Impossible.'

VIRGINIA

The next-door table were definitely listening. Angela's mouth opened, then closed again. She looked flushed; confused; her shoulders drooped. It didn't take long for her to recover.

ANGELA (*gathering energy and volume*)

'It's just so stereotypical! Older woman, western, comes to Turkey for sex! It's a cliché, Virginia! It's ... orientalist!'

VIRGINIA

She pronounced this triumphantly, as if it clinched it. Her final '-ist' sprayed the air with saliva. 'Orientalist? Is that bad?'

 (She said it as if it meant 'murderess'. I was not familiar with the usage.)

ANGELA

She was smiling again, superior, maddening, her lips moving with unvoiced words, looking down that fine-cut nose at me.

Why did my opinions suddenly seem flimsy? She was arrogant! And ignorant! Yes, Virginia Woolf was *ignorant*!

Orlando suffered from the same kind of thinking. Romantic Gypsies. Sentimental fantasies. The East with a soft erotic glow. Perhaps I should add that to my paper. Perhaps I had always been too respectful.

'Of course you can't know about Edward Said, he was a brilliant thinker, a profound thinker, he revolutionised the way we write about the East. But you must see it's a stereotype, deciding to go to bed with a Turk?'

VIRGINIA
'Would you rather I had sex with – whom, exactly? A Belgian? An African?'

ANGELA
'Good heavens, here's Ray Kuyperman. Professor Kuyperman! Come and join us!'

VIRGINIA
' – No, I will sleep with whomever I want to.' But I had to break off. A tall thin man had materialised in the square behind us.

'Ladies!' he said, manifestly startled, almost as though we had somehow caught him out. 'Angela Lamb! What a surprise! Of course, you are giving a reading at the conference. And one of the plenaries, I believe. But – what are you doing here?' Rimless spectacles. Firm jaw-line. He gestured vaguely around the tables. One of our neighbours raised his hand, but Kuyperman ignored them.

ANGELA
'This is Virginia, a friend of mine. Virginia, this is Ray

Kuyperman, from the University of Witwatersrand. Which is in Africa, but actually he's Belgian. He lives in Brussels most of the year.'

VIRGINIA
'How convenient!'

DR KUYPERMAN
'You must be joking. The travelling is dreadful.'

ANGELA
'Were you caught up in the demonstration? Is that how you came to be here, like us?'

DR KUYPERMAN
'Pure chance, dear lady.'

VIRGINIA
He had beautiful manners, but under the surface he was agitated. The man with the longest moustache next door was definitely trying to attract his attention, but Kuyperman seemed oblivious. The red-head's beautiful cream silk scarf had fallen on the ground under their table. Something odd about her neck. Oh, and her hands, in flamboyant rings, heavy silver crusting the knuckles – but the fingers extended too far from the rings, and the nails, when they came, were square and broad. Those elegant legs. Those enormous feet! Of course, she was a man. Feeling shy, I looked away.

ANGELA
'Are you here alone? Why don't you join us later on? I have to go back and prepare my talk, but we'll go out to eat, I expect.'

'Professor!' A chorus, rather loud, almost jeering, from the raffish group at the next-door table. 'Academics,' he mouthed to us, 'I must say Hallo.'

We agreed he might call at the hotel at eight.

'By the way,' he said to her as he turned away, 'You are awfully like the other Virginia, as everyone must tell you!'

She looked at him – a long, noticing look – and smiled, but said nothing.

'Distant relation,' I said. 'Through Leslie Stephen's brother, the judge.'

'Really?'

VIRGINIA

'I am related to the judge,' I confirmed. (Quite true, he was my uncle.)

By now the homosexuals – for now I was sure – and the red-headed transvestite at the table next door were laughing openly in Kuyperman's direction. As we left, one made a slight, ironic bow. Why had he not introduced us to them? Was homosexuality still taboo? Kuyperman was evidently one, but who cared?

The crush on Istiklal had eased. The police-buses were still there, but the shouting had stopped. The young people holding up their magazines had gone. I hoped they were not inside the buses. A few policemen stood around, hard-eyed.

'He's distinguished-looking, don't you think?' she asked me. 'Who?'

'Ray. Professor Kuyperman. I'm sure he'd love to have dinner with you.'

Evidently she was match-making. Trying to divert my attention from Turks. Marching across the Galata Bridge, she explained his work.

ANGELA

'He's a well-known scholar. Loves your books, especially *Orlando*. I'm amazed they haven't asked him to do a plenary. His best-known book is *Quiddities: Denaturalised Concepts of Sex, Gender and Queer Love in Orlando*.'

VIRGINIA

'Good heavens.'

ANGELA

'I think he's single.'

VIRGINIA

'Quite.'

Back at the hotel, we went to our rooms. I thought with shame of my attempt to confide. She had simply refused to hear what I was saying. So modern women were prejudiced too. I was too chaste, I was too old, I must always be what I was before – so many boundaries around desire. Angela could not help or advise me.

So I'd have to find it for myself.

I would search for the long-lost secret garden I dreamed of when I was just a girl. Before what was hidden was stolen from me.

When Lil told the gang about Gerda's great swim and how she saved Wolfy from the barbed wire, she said not a word about what happened after.

The three of them were reunited. Gerda and Wolfy were both sopping wet, standing there shivering and dripping in the sunlight, hidden from view by the trees round the lake from the grownup world of robbers and killers. (Lil had told Gerda stories about things so terrible that Gerda only knew them from fairy tales. 'You've got to be careful. I'll look after you,' Lil had said.)

It was nearly midday. The sun was hot. Lil kept hugging Gerda's wet body. Wolfy was whining and licking his leg, but it was Gerda that Lil worried about. 'You'll have to get dry,' she said, protective. 'This is the Ramblers, this wood, it's famous.' 'What for?' Lil Roberta didn't answer her. 'I know a place that's beautiful.' She led Gerda, dripping, through narrow paths to a sort of greenhouse, but without any glass, a Japanese-y shelter that looked from a distance as if it was made of pale blue lace. 'This is the Ladies Pavement,' she said, proudly. 'It's a secret.'

'Pavilion,' said Gerda, reading the plaque.

'Same thing,' said Lil.

(But it wasn't, thought Gerda. Softer, fuller. She'd been to school. She loved 'pavilion'.)

Close up it was Victorian iron, like the conservatory in Gerda's home. The roof was darker, like mauve bluebells. Gerda suspended her wet blouse and jumper on the pale iron of the

verandah. At the front there was sunlight and a view of the lake. 'You're all right like that, it looks like a bikini,' Lil told her. 'I'll take my clothes off to keep you company.'

The three of them lay in a huddle in the sun, and slowly, as Lil stroked and kissed her, Gerda's goose-pimples subsided, and Wolfy's flanks stopped shuddering, and only after about twenty minutes did he stand up and snuffle, feeling left out.

'You stay and guard us, Wolfy,' said Lily. Then they forgot him: but Wolfy stayed.

They slept, that night, in each other's arms, on the fire-warmed rock, Gerda and Lil, by the broken crate with the pigeons in it, shuffling and ruffling and roucouling, and did not lie still until the other children, who Lil Robber had sent off to work, crept back, slowly, and they all slept together, a raft of bodies loosely patched and woven against the spring night with its chill dead wind, and whatever worse things the park contained.

79

VIRGINIA

Inside, of course, I was young as ever, but I evidently looked old to Angela. Thinking of Ahmet, I peered in the mirror. My hair, which had once looked straggly and grey, had a glow to it, yes, the brown glow of honey, my eyes were bright, and there again, my cheeks – surely they were pinker? And they were not hollow. They were oval, with roses. I ran my hands down the sides of my body. I wasn't fat; I wasn't thin. I was tall, wasn't I? Could I be – 'striking'? In fact, I had become what Leonard, with a wry smile, sometimes said of a passing stranger: 'a fine figure of a woman'.

It helped to explain the way Ahmet looked at me. But maybe all old women imagined that. Maybe he was just a professional flirt, and I was a fool, and Angela was right.

Suddenly, I heard her voice through the wall. Of course, she had gone off to practise her paper – her 'plenary', as she kept calling it. Why did she have to be so self-important? –

That was unkind. One didn't want to be spiteful. Angela had done her best for me, and slowly, I'd become fond of her. Despite her brassy air, she was vulnerable. She cared a lot about her little talk. Probably because I would be listening; she definitely wanted my approval. We had never really spoken about my work. I moved closer to the wall to listen for a moment.

'… elitist, snobbish … self-indulgent … art for art's sake …'

A small, cold moment of doubt. But it was obviously not me she was talking about. She must be comparing me to, say,

Katherine Mansfield.

'… stultifying … ivory tower … not relevant to today's … if ever …'

No, she was a fan of mine. She had told me so. It couldn't be –

It couldn't be – could it – that she hated me?

'… undeserved preeminence … *Mrs Dalloway* and *To the Lighthouse* …'

Yes, she was talking about me.

Of course, she had always hated me.

'… bloodless … anaemic … breath of real life …'

She had brought me back to life to give me pain.

There was a shudder in my bones, my heart. My stomach clenched tight against my ribcage.

I could not stay there, in that stupid modern room, alone with the menacing 'television' screen, its great blank eye peering down from the wall, laughing at me, staring at me, as I reeled from the spite hissing through the plaster.

(I had thought we were friends! Didn't she like me? My heart beat loudly. I was very afraid. For who in the world would stick up for me? Who in the world would be on my side?)

No, there was no-one. I was quite alone. No Leonard to comfort me, no Nessa to listen gravely, no Ethel to huff and puff on my behalf.

I went numbly to the wardrobe. Yes, something else. My brain started playing an old song, loudly, something by – what was her name, Greta Keller, that trembling alto with the giant bosom, 'So little time, my dear, and so much to do/ So little time to make your dreams come true …'

Yes, there was a feeling of the day speeding up, I was changing, swiftly, so was Angela, the stage-set slipped and slid around me. I stared at the tiny keyhole in the wardrobe, a detail snipped from a Dodgson fantasy that at any moment might

come to an end. My second chance at life on this planet, it had been so vivid, I had been so happy, but –

she hated me she wanted to destroy me

Suddenly I knew I must be dreaming, that terrible sense of things fading, thinning, of scrabbling to hold the scenery together, to keep out the darkness nibbling at the edges ...

Her voice, inexorable, through the wall: '... daughter of privilege ... patronage ...'

Gerda fell asleep happy, but when she woke, at 3 AM, she thought nothing could be worse than where she was, with one round, shocked pigeon eye staring at her in the moonlight through a crack in the crate that imprisoned it.

'Trapped like me,' Gerda thought. 'Lost like me. We will never get out.'

Where was Mum? It was all her fault. (How often had that thought come to her? It had polished its own special groove in her brain. *Mum's fault, Mum's fault, Mum's fault, Mum's …*)

Oh no, she remembered (which was worse), it's mine.

Gerda flung out her right arm in despair, and it was caught, hard, by a big cold hand. 'I'll have that if she won't,' a boy's voice said, his voice just breaking, greedy, harsh. He was pulling at her bracelet, which cut into her flesh.

'Stop it,' she shouted, 'Mum gave me that.'

Before she could breathe, a hand grabbed her cheeks. 'Shut up,' said Lil, 'or I'll stab you, right? And you,' she added, to the straggle-bearded boy, 'get away from her or I'll bite your ear off. Lie still,' she ordered Gerda. 'I need to sleep.' She flung her arm back across Gerda's throat.

Gerda couldn't help it, she started to cry. She tried to do it silently, but after a bit, her shoulders were shaking.

Lil sat up with a jerk and loomed over her. 'I don't like snivelling,' she said. 'What's up?'

In a whisper, dreading she might wake up the others, Gerda poured it all out. 'The truth is, I was actually looking for my mother … I did run away, that was true, and I did take her

money … but I came to look for her here, and found she was in Turkey … I've come to the wrong bloody side of the world … I've got to go to Turkey to find her … I've lost Dad too, he's at the North Pole … and I've lost my phone, well I left it at home, which is even more fucking stupid and dickish … without my phone, I will never find my mum – '

'You won't get any sympathy for losing your parents, we've all done that,' said Lil Robber. 'Lost your phone though, that's serious. But stop the fuck crying and I'll fix it. Long as you shut up and let me sleep, then I'll go out to work in the morning … It's cool what you did, all the same. Like I said, Gerda, if I had a mum, I'd run off to Morocco and find her, like you.'

'Turkey,' Gerda corrected, cautiously, feeling better now she had spilled her heart.

'Turkey's in Morocco, look it up,' said Lil. Wrapped in wisdom, she fell asleep.

VIRGINIA

Feel nothing, act. Do the thing you long for. I stepped blindly out of the sensible shoes and trousers I had worn for Scutari.

The dress, the dress —

(On, on, it hissed, the hatred spitting through the wall, the syllables even louder in the cupboard: 'over-precious ... narrow ... cold ...'

I was not cold! I was never narrow!)

I began to sing, anything, anything at all to drown out her lecture. 'Come let us stroll down lover's lane/once more to sing love's old refrain/come let us sing auf wiedersehen/auf wiedersehen again ...'

I had bought it in Bloomingdale's, and only worn it once, a classic shirt-dress in warm pink silk. It was knee-length, quite modest, with small pearl buttons. I slipped it on; it stroked my skin. But my walking shoes looked quite wrong. Time for the other Bloomingdale's purchase.

'... frigid ... withholding ... lesbian ...'

My feet slid into the taupe suede heels with marvellously seductive ankle-straps. Then I undid two buttons on the shirt, and rolled up the sleeves to look more ... relaxed. Lipstick, yes. It was unsettling. My lips, coloured-in, were very full — full lips were what men liked, Leonard told me. Leonard had not been averse to cosmetics, he had confessed to me one day. I was taken by surprise, as so often by Leonard ...

But his aching need. I had tried not to see it.

I could not give it. I failed to give it. The thing he wanted as a man. Because of my paramount need to say 'No'. When my half-brothers brought me their urgencies, their hot breath, their painful rawness, I could not say 'No', they were my elders, and I made the error from which girls do not recover: I gave more than I had to give. Leonard let me regain some part of what was mine, though it was just a chill vacancy. How often did I make poor Leonard feel foolish, though I offered love in a hundred thousand ways, I was full of pats and strokes and kisses … The other thing I could not do. He had been with prostitutes, I knew. He was a man of the world, with a man's desires, and I was ignorant, and wounded.

But now, it seemed, I had changed, I was ready. At 120 or so years old, something inside me had stirred and softened. I had been dead; I was alive again. Now I was ready to find a lover.

As I slipped through the door I still heard her droning. I would not let her hatred stop me.

On the landing one of the girls who served breakfast, still in her white headscarf, was delivering two cups of coffee on a tray. Her dark eyes widened as she saw me. When I looked more closely, she was very pretty. Yes, it was the one I saw on our first day, leaving the hotel with a bundle of laundry, putting her burden down for a moment to play with the golden cat on the street – then the other girl came over and hugged her. She looked genuinely pleased to see me, and that lift of the mouth, that blush of warmth was helpful, when Angela had made me feel lonely.

'Madam – ' she was going to ask me something, or offer me something, probably coffee, but I smiled and stopped her with a wave of the hand, 'I don't need anything, I'm just going out.'

Her face fell slightly, then she smiled again, set down the

tray and clapped her hands. 'Madam is very – lovely!' 'Thank you!' I sailed downstairs in my new high heels.

Thus it was that, when I entered the lobby to find Ahmet and a friend at the desk alone, and Ahmet looked up and said 'You are beautiful, Mrs Room 15,' I was not altogether surprised. His friend looked down sternly at the bookings, then briefly up at me, then down again.

Leonard had said it too. I was beautiful, yes. Why had I never felt myself so?

'I would like to know many words for this. "Lovely", "beautiful", is not all. Will you teach me English?' Ahmet asked. 'You should stay long time, and teach me English.'

'You surely learned English at school, didn't you?' I didn't mean to sound rude, but he drew himself up, though he would never be tall.

'I know many languages,' he said, proudly. 'I learn for myself, with my ear' (he pointed). 'Maybe I know more languages than you! But not well. I want to speak English like you, very beautiful.'

'Beautifull–y,' I corrected him. 'Yes, Ahmet, of course I will teach you.'

'Are you going out with your friend in Room 14?' Ahmet asked me, sounding oddly shy.

He knew all the numbers off by heart. Or just our numbers, perhaps.

'No.' I must have said it forcefully.

He stared at me. 'May I ask, where are you going?'

'Out,' I said. I didn't have a clue. Perhaps he could see it in my face. 'To eat,' I improvised.

'Alone?' he said. 'I, Ahmet, will escort you.'

' – But you're working.'

'On contrary, I have finished my working.'

His companion was muttering something in Turkish, but

Ahmet was totally focused on me. His eyes so brown, so like melting sugar, warm caramel, enfolding me, sliding lazily over the slopes and valleys of the coral silk dress, then back to my face. I bathed in his gaze. I smiled. I shifted. Deep under my dress, there was something electric.

Anticipation. A gathering. I was 120, but I suddenly thought 'It's what Nessa told me she felt at eighteen, while I listened dull as a stick or stone.' In those days I had no feelings to offer. Then later when we swopped stories of bed, she made me feel gauche, clumsy, a failure.

(Although she loved me, perhaps she was glad. At so many other things I bested her: in the competition for our father's love, for Father always favoured me; at words, which grew like grass from my fingers; at Greek, a country she never tried to enter; at parties, where she just sat like a hard black gemstone, absorbing light, while I glittered and rattled and ran on like water – so what if afterwards I was exhausted? –

But this. The secret heart of us. The womanly part, the making part, whence children, passion, the river flowed. There I was dead, and the river passed by, leaving me writing, dry, on the bank, while she struck out into the centre and swam, surrounded by men, admirers, in the morning; flanked by children, the water-babies I also loved, but could not possess; flesh in the sun, rosy, easy; once I had so longed for them; I waved across: was an aunt: was nothing.

Suddenly, now, I could be something again.)

I waited in the lobby while he got his jacket. The other man stood pretending to work but looking at me, every now and then, with an air I hoped was not speculative.

Then I knew it was, and began to enjoy it.

I crossed my legs. These American shoes were certainly not the most comfortable, but I saw his eyes were drawn to my ankles. Something about the tight little straps. When he looked

up, I smiled at him. At once his eyes dropped down, afraid, and he did a small, important frown. Yes, men had always been afraid of me. But Ahmet – no, he was not afraid.

A sweet, fresh smell on the air of the lobby. Ahmet emerged in a cloud of cologne. From twelve feet away, he was plump and short, but his smile was warm and sweet as a baby's, his eyes embracing, his manner tender. 'Give me the arm, dear lady,' he said. Out the two of us stepped into the radiant world.

Lil slipped from Gerda's arms when she was only half-awake, as the first rays of sun gilded the park, and the earliest joggers bounded to meet it. Before ten minutes had passed, she was back, panting, triumphant, smelling slightly of sweat. 'There you are,' she said, handing over a phone. 'Now book your plane quick, before they block it.'

Sitting on the rock beside Lily's deerhound, her hands still cold and clumsy from the night, Gerda started to do battle with the internet. There were flights today. Eleven hours in the air, if they had a seat. She would fly into Istanbul in the morning. She kept mis-typing the card expiry date, but in the end, she had entered all the details. A surge of joy filled her as the website told her to wait and not refresh her browser. Now there was nothing else she could do, by her own efforts, her own will-power, she could close her eyes and trust to fate –

If it all came right, she would get away, she could sleep on the plane, if they let her go, if she ever managed to leave the park.

That morning the light was beautiful. The gang looked more ordinary, less scary – sullen, sleepy, terribly young. One or two actually cried out in their dreams and the tall deerhound licked hands or faces, though Lily jealously kicked it away. It was her dog; it was her he must love, and perhaps she had no-one else to love her.

'Get on with it, quick, I've got to fucking lose the phone,' said Lil, who had watched most of the booking process over Gerda's shoulder in open admiration ('It's different for you. You

can do all that. I haven't got a mother with cards and stuff.')

'Waiting,' said Gerda, praying it would work, pouring all her hopes on to the paralysed screen, and in this strange world, hope was rewarded, and as Turkish Airlines finally yielded a seat, Lil snatched the phone out of Gerda's hand and disappeared into the bushes.

By 9 AM it was starting to get warm. The sleeping children were awake again, stretching and sniffing, hungry, resentful, openly curious about their intruder. Beardy Boy plucked briefly at Gerda's jacket, on the side of her Lil Robber couldn't see, and swinging round, Gerda knew he hated her. Trapped in his eyeball, in his red, mean eyes, she saw the Furies watching her.

'You got to leave,' Lil Robber said. 'You owe me swimming lessons, right? You will come back and see me, right?'

Gerda said nothing. She saw Lil knew that they would never meet again. 'Yes,' she said. 'And you'll come to me. If I need you, obvers. Blood sisters. And I'll come to you.' They looked at each other for a long moment, all the rest locked out, though Gerda half-heard Beard Boy making retching noises. Then he was rifling under the tarpaulin.

'Would you like your bag back, slag?' he sneered. 'Cos you don't get it, Mummy's Little Princess. Right?' he said, suddenly not so certain, looking to Lil for authorisation.

'Who asked you to speak?' she growled. 'Dick.'

For a moment, half a moment, they locked glances. Lil was the boss, but nothing was certain, the contours of the rock were sharp and rough, the dirty children surged about, looking wildly from one to the other, Gerda saw the bearded boy was a killer because he didn't have anything else to do.

'I'm giving it you,' said Gerda suddenly. 'Yes, you with the beard. Ugly Boy. I was always going to leave it behind.' There was a ripple of nervous laughter.

He was thrown. 'You can't give me nothing. Girly rubbish,' but he didn't know what to do next.

'Look inside,' Gerda said. He pressed briefly, roughly at the locks. No go.

He came crab-wise down the rock towards her then, muscular, scrawny, his old woman's beard blowing in the wind, wielding the glittery pink case like a club. Everything was twisted to one side, and his eyes bored into her, little black stones.

Gerda stood her ground, her heart thumping. 'Give it me, Feebleton, I'll do it.' She snatched it from him just before he hit her with it. The locks yielded. She took out Dad's Swiss Army knife. 'See, I told you I had something for you.'

'Yeah, she told you,' Lil affirmed. The tension in the group of watchers resolved. Most of them crowded round Beard Boy. 'If you ask me nicely, I'll tell you what it does.' But they weren't listening, they were all trying to touch it.

For a moment, at least, the group was distracted. But everything felt horribly dangerous.

Where was her mother? Did she think about her?

ANGELA

Of course, I was obsessing about my paper. After all that I had done for Virginia, I hoped that I could count on her. Ok, I may have been naïve. But I thought – assumed – Virginia had – what? Some sort of taste. Some discretion.

I read it aloud. It seemed pretty strong. As soon as I'd made a few edits to the text, I got it printed, down in reception. Did I really dare show her before the conference? That was the thing I was conflicted about. But my hunger was stronger than my caution. Obviously I longed to know what she thought.

The plan had been to dine together, with Ray Kuyperman joining us. I thought I was providing her with what she needed: safe, uncomplicated masculine attention.

Wrong premise. Wrong person.

First, she was not in her room when I called. I knocked twice. No answer. I pushed my paper under the door, then tried to get it back, and broke my nail. I was kneeling on the floor on the landing when the Muslim breakfast girl came past with towels. They're all Muslim, actually, I suppose, but she wore a headscarf, very slim, very proper. She stood watching for a second before she spoke.

'You look for your … friend?'

'I am delivering something.'

On the floor, I felt at a disadvantage. This was not a conventional delivery mode.

'I can help you? You look under the door for your friend, I think?'

'No, no.'

'She has gone out. She is, she looking, beautiful!'

I rose to my feet in a dignified manner. She smiled at me. She was very pretty, in a way the headscarf could not conceal. Her skin was pale, her teeth very white, her eyes jet-black. She said, 'I think you love her.'

'I like her, yes, of course I do.' Her English was quaint, perhaps she was a student.

'So you saw her go out?'

'Half-hour ago.'

The men down in the lobby set my mind at rest. 'Yes, first she waited, then she goes to eat.'

'She waited for me?' They looked at each other.

'Yes, maybe.'

'But she went out alone?'

They consulted again. 'Yes, but nice colleague show her where to go.'

'Somewhere safe?'

'Yes, naturally.'

'Oh, that's OK then. Thank you for that. This is, you know, her first time in Turkey.'

'No problem, we look after her!'

One of the younger ones was smiling too much. He had a wart in the middle of his forehead. The others looked at him repressively. Like the headscarf girl, he was trying too hard to please. But I did not mind it. Better than indifference.

Just at that moment, Ray Kuyperman arrived. Linen-suited, more chiselled than ever. 'Ray! I'm afraid Virginia's gone out.'

'Then we will eat *à deux*,' he said.

I admit I was not entirely displeased. Ray and I had often met at conferences. I liked his intelligence, his gracious manner. Let's face it, I also liked his good haircut, the elegance of his rangy physique, without the little pot that so many men had.

(But not Edward. *Edward*. The two-beat sadness. So far away. So far, so cold. What had I done? What had I done?)

Don't think about it. 'Ray, let's go.'

And I hardly thought about Virginia again until I came back, slightly tipsy, at midnight.

VIRGINIA

Now I am completely content. Here, now, in this pool of sunlight. The head on the pillow: the gentle breath. Cheek to cheek, skin to skin.

This is where it was, then. Happiness.

And where it is. A second chance.

ANGELA

Why did she have to do it *then?* Did she not understand how it mattered to me?

She let me down. She let herself down. She was not the great writer I expected her to be. She was – ungenerous to those who came after.

'Readers connote responsibility.'

She did not try to help with my paper!

Lily Roberta did a generous thing. 'I've got something for you. To help you, you know, on your travels round the world.' Her face, a rosy, barbarian face, a face, Gerda thought, of fruit and brambles, the eye-whites bright as the wild strawberry flowers that grew all over their London garden, was flushed for a second with generous love. Lil was holding out a subway card. 'Got it from the idiot whose phone I nicked.'

'Hey, why you giving her that?' 'No-o-oh!' 'I want that!' From the group around Beard Boy, there were mutinous cries. 'Man, she's really got the hots for her.'

Once again, it was all in the balance. For a second, Lil Robber paused. Then she said loudly to Gerda, so everyone could hear 'And what are you going to give to me? What is your favourite thing that you've got?' Gerda saw that Lil had to show her power. 'For real,' Lil said, looking deep into her eyes, 'Because I saved you and I love you, don't I?' She said the last bit very quietly.

Without hesitation, Gerda reached into her hand luggage and pulled out her book, *To the Lighthouse*. She handed it over, reverently, but Lily took it with an angry frown, looked at it briefly, then threw it on the ground. 'That's no use to anybody.' She eyeballed Gerda, about to lose her temper. 'Are you trying to cheat me, then?'

But Gerda stared back into the angry dark eyes. 'I wouldn't do that. I know what you did. Take my gold bracelet,' she said under her breath. 'It's gold, isn't it. From my mum. I didn't nick it, she gave it me. Snatch it from me. Then they'll be pleased.'

'Why should I give a fuck about *them*? No, you got to give it me.'

A ragged mixture of jeers and cheers went up from the parentless, awkward children as Gerda took off her bracelet, kissed it, and handed it to Lily. The morning light burned on the gold.

Lil Robber tried to put it on her wrist, but failed, and held it out towards Gerda, stern-eyed. Gerda fastened it carefully on the lean brown wrist.

'You know I'll sell it, but not yet.' Lily hugged Gerda tenderly, roughly, and took her face between her hands, then turned one hand so the metal of her cheap Goth ring tickled the softness of Gerda's throat. 'Now get the fuck out of here to wherever you're going. The end of the world. I'll meet you there.'

'See you at the end of the world,' said Gerda. 'You ought to free those pigeons,' she shouted, over her shoulder, as she ran into the trees, and Lil Robber shouted cheerfully 'Fuck OFF!'

After a bit, they stopped following her, the motley grey figures from the camp on the rock, curious about her, hating her, and soon she was back on the neat little path where sheeny-thighed joggers ran with well-kept dogs, going fast and straight in the direction of the Plaza, the world of Eloise, the world of privilege, where, in the end, Gerda has to live.

Yes, I'm an inside girl, mostly, Gerda thinks later as she goes through the doors of Rizzoli's Bookstore, which she spots by chance as she wanders south. *To the Lighthouse*, rather more dog-eared and dusty than before, is back in her bag, but she wants another book. There is an eleven-hour flight in her future.

'I want to read *A Room of One's Own*,' she says. 'By Virginia Woolf. It's very famous.'

The young man at the counter looks soft as a girl, with floppy hair falling over his eyes. Gerda is fresh from her nights in the park, newly hard, and ready to judge him.

'Oh yes, I know all about her,' he said. 'We just ordered a set of her books, as it happens. There seems to be a lot of interest in her.'

'It doesn't matter whether people are interested,' said Gerda. 'She's just great. It's just a Fact.' (Though she knows her history teacher would call it an Assertion.)

With the book in her bag, she slips down into the subway. She watches two people go through the turnstile before she dares to use her card.

It doesn't work once; it doesn't work twice – damn Lil Robber and her useless gift! – but on the third go, Gerda floats through, and is drawn, thanks to her magic pass, into the charmed, unstoppable system that will deliver her around the world, to JFK Airport, where she washes in a basin and drags clean clothes, rather squashed, from her bag – first time she's changed them since she left home. *Yay, Victory over the Cleanpolice!* – and yet, it's nice not to be stained and crusted – to Check-in where she no longer has the ridiculous suitcase to check in, through Security (good, no knife, she knows that Dad will buy her a new one), to Gate 32 of Turkish Airlines, to kind flight crew who pamper her, this sweet young girl whose red hair smells of soap, and a seat in which she reads her new Virginia Woolf with growing wonder, then sleeps like a baby; thus finally, bright-eyed and rested, to Atatürk Airport, Istanbul.

PART FOUR

Interzone

VIRGINIA

'It's not as if one had done this before. Of course I regret making you late.'

ANGELA

We were stuck in the frightful traffic in a taxi. The 'Welcome Session' would soon have started, and I should have been there, networking, not struggling to drag her out of bed. 'This isn't the time to talk about it.'

As soon as I said that, I regretted it, much as I enjoyed the high moral ground. Because I was longing to know what happened.

The sun through the window was painfully bright.

VIRGINIA (*with asperity*)

'Is it your paper you are cross about? I am just as cross about it as you.'

ANGELA

'It's irrelevant, we will probably be too late for it.'

VIRGINIA

I couldn't understand why Angela had pushed the thing underneath my door. Naturally I did not care to read such stuff. I had heard enough. What did she want from me? The woman should be ashamed of herself. I had returned it this morning without comment.

But I was also slightly sheepish. The last faint flutter of the Angel in the House. Then my happiness sent her flying off skywards –

No, I would never regret last night.

'Everyone's late, in Turkey. You said so yourself. So they will wait.'

ANGELA

She had a hazy, lazy look, as if all her contours had been blurred and softened; she was – softer? Larger? More material? The opposite, somehow, of that time in New York when she had shrunk and chilled and faded.

I sneaked another look in my powder compact. The light from above was unforgiving. My frown lines had deepened since all this began. My eyes were red from lack of sleep. I was thinner, surely.

How dare she look young?

'It was so – inconsiderate, Virginia! And I mean, to be late for your own conference!'

VIRGINIA

'Remember you told me not to say that.'

ANGELA (*raising her voice*)

'Stop – point-scoring. How did Leonard bear it?'

VIRGINIA

I stared at her. Those hateful phrases that I had heard through the bedroom wall. I thought – at least, I had come to hope, over the time we spent together, that she was an ally, a true supporter. She was looking old and tired this morning. I looked afresh at her dyed hair, her painted eyelids, her rouged cheeks.

The hate that lurks under the surface. Blade concealed in a cake of soap.

I covered my eyes, no longer laughing. The joy of the night before wavered. Too much black coffee. She had forced me to drink it. My nerves quivered, my skull-bones shook. Leonard protected me from too much coffee.

(Those murderous pages pushed under my door ...)

ANGELA
'Virginia, what are you staring at?'

VIRGINIA
I knew I must beware of her

I could feel such gladness, such peaks of joy, that was always the case since I was little

but never any safety
 no guiding rope

 Leonard, my rock, no longer there

I was slipping my bearings in time and space
 Nessa forbade me to get excited
Handy dandy, who was my lover?
 Lear was mad, but I dared not go there

Yes, they were back at the turn of the road,
 waiting for me with their cackling voices
'You are ours, child, now' there was no escape

they were here already there, in her eyes bright and
 tiny and terrible

the eyes, I perceived, of a consummate actress, there was a
Greek word but it skipped out of reach, a chorus of birds were
shrieking it, the taxi was stuck, its sides shrank inwards –

ANGELA
'Virginia, are you all right?'

VIRGINIA
I looked away from her, out of the window, I made myself
concentrate, look, listen –

No, just crows. The '*Kaar*' of crows. My intelligent friends
from two continents.

They flew like guardians around the taxi. Greyer, less
threatening than ever this morning, the colour of socks or grey
flannel trousers, they spoke no language besides their own, an
animal language sufficient to save me. '*Kaar, Virginia. Kaar, Kaar.*'

*I was animal too. I was sane. I had proved it. Like the birds, I could
mate, I could fly.*

I would brazen it out. I would not be afraid. Of her, of the
Furies, the sad blank void that yawned behind when I looked
at her, the lie in her mouth, the sharp cruel teeth protruding
under her orange lipstick

and I looked away again out of the window, at the sunlit world
outside the glass –

through cracks she had made in the city's bright surface, the
rosy roof-tops, the red-striped stalls, the blue of the sky which
had woken me earlier, cloudless, perfect, a perpetual moment,
my joy still glittered as it leaked away, liquid silver in the greedy
gutters

but a child came out and ran up the pavement, what flew above him, a kite on a string? through the hordes of adults with their heavy purpose – no, it was a swallow, in fact, it was two, two bold young swallows looping the loop, dipping, dancing over Constantinople – one of them rose till I could barely see it, hovered, oh where, with its *quivit, quivit*, then plummeted, my heart stopped, had I lost it

– no, crew-on-the-blue, there were six, a dozen, doing acrobatics as they cheeped and twittered, *chideep, chideep*, that silver again, the joy of that thin filigree music, and Angela looked up: even she heard them.

I would not be robbed. It could not be stolen.

Yes, I was not afraid of her. I looked again; she was ordinary. Cross, perhaps, but not unfriendly.

'Give me the paper. I will read it.'

The cab started again. She handed it over.

ANGELA

I watched her, staring down at my pages, or past my pages, was she taking it in? – her heavy mauve lids more languorous than usual, the orbs underneath them flickering sidelong. Some birds were squeaking like a midget violin, a hair of annoyance tickling my brain. And we stopped again.

Did I know her at all? Had all my reading of her books meant nothing? How much did we ever know anyone?

I'd thought all her characters were part of herself, that by adding them together, you came up with the author, a shifting composite, the details uncertain but the basic shape, against the light, constant.

Now she had thrown the book out of the window, like Becky Sharp and the 'Dixonary' – and I always felt uneasy with Thackeray's Becky, I loved her, yes, but she was so – selfish!

As I watched Virginia, her brow relaxed. After a moment, she started to laugh. 'Oh I see. I see … what a fool I am.'

Now she was nodding, and reading more swiftly. At least twice, she nodded. My anger dissolved, though my fear was still great. Her long artist's hands on my vulnerable pages.

But the taxi was jerking down the road again. We were rounding the mosque near the university. Still some time before 11 AM.

'Angela,' she said, looking up suddenly. 'Thank you. You defended me. But really – how heavy-footed critics can be.'

ANGELA

The question 'What happened that night?' must be answered. I can only tell you what happened to me. One day, perhaps, wherever she is, Virginia will tell it from her point of view.

What did I expect at the start of the evening? Not a lot. Fun and flirtation. Though I'd invited Kuyperman to please Virginia, I was half-relieved she was out of the picture. I had had the most exhausting day, beginning with the terrible row with Edward – then the ramp in Aya Sophia – then the riot …

Now the consolation of male attention. I was glad I had washed my hair. I decided to wear my Afghan coat, which made me look hippy, alternative, young.

(Was Ray … *possible*? I didn't see why not. He had sought me out at a conference before, he had praised my novels, albeit rather vaguely.)

Long before dessert, I was disabused. Over starters, he first mentioned 'Jimmy', who seemed to accompany him on long walks. I was going to ask him what breed he was, but by the main course, I knew Jimmy was human.

'It's a bore being categorised,' he said to me, 'and things are still a little touchy in Jo'burg, but I realised, of course, in retrospect, after I saw you and your friend in Ida's, that you were probably there for the same reason as me.'

'Which is?' A slight pause. It dawned on me. 'Oh, I see. No, she's … No. Yes, the cafe. Yes, *yes*.'

He carried us over the awkwardness. 'Jimmy didn't come with me, on this occasion, but we love Ida's, we always go.'

I felt obscurely cheated, though, as if he'd taken something away from me, and started laying into the wine. He wasn't even paying! We were going Dutch! I hadn't forgotten the conference next day, but by the time we left, I was no longer sober.

It was twelve o'clock. Virginia must be back. Prodded by the same unsatisfied desire for some kind of reward or recognition, a simple nod, a word of praise, I marched upstairs, bumping into the wall because the stairs were stupidly narrow, and knocked on her door. By now she would have read it.

I knocked again, a little louder.

There were noises inside. Laughter, movement.

Perhaps she was talking in her sleep. I did not want to wake the hotel. The landing light was very bright, so I could not see if her light was on.

'Virginia?' I called, quietly. I could definitely hear a creaking of furniture, two voices, surely, and someone coughed.

But Room 13 was directly adjoining. Probably the sounds were coming from there.

I took what seemed like the easiest course, though in retrospect, it lacked dignity, and got down on all fours on the floor of the landing to see if there was light under her door.

In that instant it opened, and I was exposed.

Kneeling on the landing like some kind of goat.

In the Afghan coat I had put on to go out.

What did I see? It's not easy to be clear, for I wasn't expecting the door to open, it was dim inside, I was hauling myself backwards and scrambling upright at the same moment – the figure who emerged was not Virginia, but the slim pale Muslim girl who'd seen me before, when I'd just poked my paper underneath the same door.

'Room service,' she said. 'I bring your friend tea.'

'I was trying to see if the light was on.'

We had both talked at once. We stared at each other. She looked compassionate, as if I were insane. It was the second time, to be fair, that she'd found me on the landing with my head jammed against the crack beneath Virginia's door.

Then I saw a large black shoe on her floor.

'Are you all right, Virginia?' I called.

'Go away.'

The voice that answered was fuzzy with sleep. Or perhaps tipsy, or *I* was tipsy.

'She is well,' the Muslim girl asserted, blocking the door, almost protective.

What was I to do? I was unwelcome. I had been assured that Virginia was fine.

Perhaps she was lying on the bed naked! I could not bear to see my hero naked.

When we'd shared a room, I never saw her naked (though was she my hero anymore?).

I shuffled away, backwards, defeated. I had missed something, I knew, I was sure.

'Thank you,' I said to the maid as I went, trying to reassert my authority. *Why had she taken her headscarf off?*

ANGELA

As I tossed and turned through the night before the conference, telling myself I must go to sleep or I would be too tired to give a good paper, a salting of details fell like snow, bright disconnected particles against the darkness.

1. The pale girl with the sooty lashes had lost her scarf, and had no shoes on. Of that I was sure. I was at ground level, I could not be mistaken.

2. Virginia was a lesbian. (As her husband summarised it, after her death.) When she talked about her 'feelings' for men, in the café, it was a smokescreen.

But

3. the shoe I had glimpsed on the carpet by the bed, sturdy, black and shiny, was a man's.

 Or a lesbian shoe? Did it belong to the maid?

But

4. the maid was small, and the shoe was large. What was going on? What was Virginia up to?

Then at four, I jerked awake with

5. a mind-boggling explanation. She had gone to bed with a woman and a man. But why was I shocked? I had read *Orlando.*

6. An innocuous explanation. The maid was a maid looking after a guest. She was a small person with very big feet. She had taken her shoes off out of respect. It was a universal Turkish habit. Devout young Muslims were not lesbians. Virginia was married for over three decades. Muslim women did take their veils off when they were alone with women.

And slowly the innocuous story gained ground. I berated myself. I was a horrible person. Censorious to boot. Why did it bother me?

7. Well, because I was losing my own husband. He was disappearing in a dream of ice. He was shouting, waving, but I could not hear him. And Gerda, too, her small mouth opening. The two of them on the same sleigh. I should have known they would gang up together.

8. Nightmare firmed up into half-awake conviction. As the night thinned in my lonely room, the light was fading from the poles, and I found my fingers were clutching the duvet, they were both together in the gathering darkness, they were huddled together, unimaginably cold, two tiny people on a blue-white field, they had called for help and I had not answered, and now they had turned their backs on me. I tried to hold on, but they slipped over the edge while I fretted in a half-life between sleep and waking.

Daylight had formed a blank shape on the mirror before I finally rolled over and slept. One hour later, the alarm exploded.

I woke up to one clear realisation. Of course I must let Edward have the money. It was partly his, in any case. I had gone mad. It was not too late. In the Arctic it would be the middle of the night, but I left him a long text with a short beginning: 'Sorry, Edward. Take the lot. The whole £40,000.

We can afford it.'

I felt a bit better once I had done that (though hopefully, he wouldn't spend all of it …?) Then turned my mind to the day ahead.

At 8.30 AM, as agreed with Virginia, I was up on the roof-terrace, frowning at the light, waiting for her. She did not come, but she still might. On balance, she was innocent.

Our taxi was ordered for 9.10 AM. I ate my eggs in agitation, pushing the tomato around the plate. I was due to talk at 11 AM, but the opening ceremony was at 9.30 AM. I started to feel convinced of her guilt. The toast dried my throat. My chair scraped the floor. I looked at my watch every other minute. Virginia was now a hardened harlot.

Modern women should be *professional!*

(Preferably not at sex, of course.)

As a woman and a feminist, she'd let me down.

By the time I regained our landing, I was raging. Only ten minutes till the taxi arrived. (And I'd given away all our money! I was poor!) Then I noticed something. Her key was in the door.

Could she have checked out?

Was she all right?

Was she fucking coming, as promised, to the conference?

In one furious move, I had turned the key, I was in through the door —

She lay there sleeping.

VIRGINIA

That happiness: they want blood for it. I never had it before, so I never realised. She knew I was happy, so she wanted me to pay. It reminded me of something, the look in her eye when she finally extricated me from the bedclothes. Who did she remind me of?

– Yes, long ago, the narrowing faces of our Bloomsbury relations when they spotted us coming, twenty feet away, with Vanessa in her new uncorseted dress that showed her body; we were laughing together, her hair was loose, and her lips were red, and she had been kissing all afternoon. They nodded to me, the most minimal nod, we were arm in arm but they refused to see her. And ever afterwards, they cut us dead. With her happy body she earned their hatred.

Now suddenly I am bare as she was. Now the hard glances will come for me. I have to be humble. (But I am proud!)

Ahmet. How did we choose each other? What miracle made what happened, happen? Happen, happen, happiness.

I will keep those hours till the end of my life – this second life, my happy life.

GERDA

Atatürk Airport was like New York except some of the signs were not in English.

I remembered Istanbul was enormous.

I remembered Mum telling me that. 'It goes on forever. You'd love it there. The whole world is in Istanbul, Gerda. One day, I'll take you.'

Yes, but she didn't. And I hadn't got a visa. I got to 'Immigration' and was sent straight back. A kind Dutch teacher saw what happened and showed me where to buy my visa.

'Tourist?' asked the officer, serious-faced, getting ready to put a stamp on my passport. I had the £10 in my hand, no problem, but a little devil made me say something else. 'No, I've come for the conference.'

'Conference? What conference?' He frowned crossly. His stamp hovered in mid-air. 'You are tourist, yes?'

'The *International* Conference.' Surely he would know. Then I could ask him where I had to go. But he'd lost interest, his stamp came down, he took my money and the queue moved forward.

As soon as I got into an internet café, I googled 'Istanbul' and 'international conference'. *Fuck, there were thirty-one million hits.*

'The whole world is in Istanbul, Gerda.'

How, in a whole new world, would I find her?

VIRGINIA

In the street outside Tash Konak, Ahmet had put his arm briefly around my shoulders, light as a leaf brushing my arm, the merest declaration that he would protect me, that I was with him –

And yes, I was. I was with a man. He walked like a dancer or a weightlifter, as if every step was slightly sprung, and his pleasure in my company was like a cloak of finest cashmere keeping me warm.

'What shall I call you?' he demanded, as we walked up towards the Hippodrome, passing a restaurant with globes of coloured light like a bunch of illuminated glass balloons. Everything was weightless as a children's party, for this one evening I would be someone else, a new person with different rules, and the breeze on my face felt deliciously cool.

'Ginia?' I said. 'It was my childhood nickname.'

'Pretty,' he said, 'very pretty name. Pretty like you, Mrs Room 15. From now on, I call you only Ginny.'

'No, Ginia,' I repeated.

He nodded, and then, with careful lips, said 'Ginny. This time I got it right!'

What did it matter? I was laughing. 'Ginny.'

We were veering up left past the carpet shops, which were still open, their soft dusty golds and faded roses spread out over crooked walls. I ate those colours with my eyes.

'You want?' he said, 'I can get discount,' but I shook my head.

'Ginny, you can take home with you.'

For one split second I was piercingly sad. No, I had no home to go to. I wanted this evening to move more slowly. If every moment could release its twin to shine in the mirror, *again, again* ... my temporary glory of looking-forward, the wavelet-crests of this shiver of excitement – each flamingo plume of sunset light which made even the broken pavement lovely – the rose-grey sand by the blue-grey cobbles – each circle of stones with its own tinct of blue, each last ray of sun touching differently – oh everything fresh & new & alive – I loved it so, could I not stay longer?

No, it would all shine on without me.

'Where I must go, I can take nothing with me.'

'Why not?' he asked, suddenly concerned, looking deeper in my eyes than the words suggested, 'they will roll up, pack it beautifully, Ginny. I will ask them now!'

'Slow down,' I said. '*Tout va bien.* Let's not hurry with anything, Ahmet.'

Of course, he was eager to choose a restaurant, his friend was the cook, 'All the fish is fresh,' but I said 'Let's wander,' and we wandered on, down towards the sea as the sun sank beneath it and the clouds, which were peony-pink, turned black. Night was coming, and the things of night, secret things, intimacies. As the birds settled to their night-time roosts, my arm began to feel right in Ahmet's, and our pace became companionable, though what I felt as his hip pressed mine was not entirely companionable.

Every couple of paces, it seemed, he stopped. 'You are beautiful, Ginny,' he said, once again. His breath was sweet; his eyes intense. He was staring at me as if he would eat me. Yes, once again, things were going too quickly, he was pressing too close, it was going too fast.

'There is something I want to do,' I said. I was surprised to

hear myself speak. It had always been hard for me to say what I wanted. Men's wishes were so strong, so immediate – but I refused to slip back into the past. 'It might be too late – perhaps it's too late – but you said – right back at the very beginning – you said you might take me to Kiz Kulesi. I would love to see it. Is it possible?'

No sooner said than he was leading me back in the opposite direction, towards his car. 'Of course I do this. Of course, for you.'

His car was parked on a perilous slope, so getting into it made me giggle, and after that, I relaxed again. 'Nice car?' he asked, as he drove me, expertly, through honking traffic to a massive bridge that carried us high over the water. 'Bosphorus Bridge,' he said. 'Nice driver?'

By the time we left the car, the sun had gone down. He had driven me from Europe to Asia! The last stage of the journey was a tiny boat that threw us hard against each other as we rocked wildly across the waves, we were laughing as the spray blew in my face, I shrieked once and then he copied me, Ahmet didn't mind playing the coward, we were both mock-whooping with fear and laughter as the magical tower grew bigger before us, Kiz Kulesi, shining white, tipped with light, pitching forwards, backwards as we righted ourselves –

The boatman tied up, staring strangely at us. Ahmet took my hand and helped me disembark. Close up, Kiz Kulesi lacked mystery; everything had been modernised. The floating fairy tower was no more. Inside, it was a tourist place, really – a little shop, a restaurant, a café. I did not need to be afraid of it: I had not needed to long for it.

'You know story of tower?' Ahmet asked me. 'Yes,' I said. 'Hero and Leander.'

'Hero?' he said. 'No, no hero. About princess, Turkish story.'
'Ah, another one. Tell me.'

'This, I promise, is real story. Poor – princess. King's daughter, yes? He try to keep her from any lover. He keep her here, in this tower. Many father here the same! Very bad!'

'Yes, Ahmet. But if you had a daughter – '

'No, I promise, I am not married.'

'Never mind. One day I think you will be. Then you will have to think about your daughter. Go on with the story.'

As he told the story, we were climbing the stairs, dark wood, narrow, to the upper floor.

'So he do it, like he wish, and only he visit. Then when she about to be woman, he bring her a basket of fruit in her birthday. He think "I have done it! She still, what you say, safe!" Then snake that hide itself in basket come out and bite it – bite her – until she die.'

'Very interesting story,' I said, out of breath, 'but I don't like the ending, Ahmet. Better to have a lover than be killed by your father.' (Those sad elders with their terrible needs, the flickering snake pressed down in the basket –)

But I wasn't going to think about that, I was a free woman who had skipped across the water, I was with a man I had chosen myself.

This was not the lighthouse. Getting here had been easy. We were noisy, the journey took less than ten minutes. This was not the Statue of Liberty, the light-bringer, the life-giver – I no longer cared about my father or my mother. We were here and now. I would live this day.

Yes, upstairs it was just a café, with a little bar and hanging lanterns, but we went outside on to the balcony and the fresh sea air shivered my skin and hair, and all round us extended the marvellous city, bank to bank and side to side, the Golden Horn, the Sea of Marmara, the bridges and boats that joined Europe to Asia, and everywhere lights were just pricking into being, golden networks connecting the living, along every

street they would be blossoming, couples and groups going out for the evening, clusters of faces on the dark like bright petals, and I thought 'How incomparable it is to be here – '

'Coffee?' he said. 'Or maybe wine?'

'Coffee.'

'Tell me honestly,' he said, with a smile, 'which is best story, Turkish or English?'

'The story of Hero is very old,' I said. 'Not English, in fact – Greek.'

'We don't like Greek.'

'To be honest, I don't like either story. In both the stories, the woman dies. In the Greek story, the woman kills her lover, maybe accidentally, maybe not, then jumps in the water and drowns herself. In your story, the father kills her. Couldn't we have a story where the woman lives? I think I think – only life matters.'

'I never think about this,' he said, dashed. For a moment, he looked genuinely grieved. Then '*This* is story,' Ahmet said, with a sudden smile as he took my hand, my cool white hand in both of his. 'Now, tonight, we make new story. You will see, Ginny. Woman – LIVES!'

And he burst out laughing, throwing out his hands to encompass the lights, the sea, the city, the glittering ferries going back and forth. 'The life is beautiful. We will be happy.'

Yes, he was very different to Leonard. Yet also similar, it struck me, as competently, coolly, he drove us back across to Sultanahmet, coming to a halt in the same steep road. Surely the car would run downhill backwards – but no, we were safe, the brake was on.

When we finally looped back to the restaurant he liked, he chose a table in a private corner: a potted palm tree protected us.

He told me he liked my eyes, my lips. 'Are you married?' he asked, adding, a split second later, 'Of course you must be married, it doesn't matter.'

'My husband died,' I said.

'Oh, sorry, dear.' He did look sorry. He looked long across the table, grave and tender. I admired his cheeks, round as a child's. They reminded me of toffee apples, of sweetmeats. I wanted to pinch him, I wanted to eat him, I felt that we could play together, and he would let me make up the game.

'And you,' I said. 'Are you sure you aren't married, Ahmet?'

'Not yet,' he said, almost scandalised. 'Too young,' he added, with a merry smile. 'Later I will marry. Many times, often!'

We laughed together. I definitely liked him.

Then he said, 'Of course, I am joking, I marry one time, and love her always.'

So then, naturally, I liked him more.

He asked me about my parents, my family. I told him about Thoby catching cholera in Greece. 'Very dirty country,' he said, with vigour. 'I am so sorry about your brother. If only he visit Turkey instead!'

One of his sisters had five children. I told him that I had no children. ('Too late now?' 'Yes, of course') – but my sister had two. 'You see, we were artists. Maybe that mattered to us more than life. I was a writer, actually.' Of course I could not tell him that I had been ill, the doctors' edicts, the whole messy saga.

He was a little afraid, I saw it in his eyes, when I said that I was a writer. What man on earth wanted a clever woman? *Only my darling. Only Leonard.* But Ahmet did not need to like me as a writer. 'I stopped writing long ago.'

The words expanded in my head.

'Because you make enough money?' he asked.

'No, because … that time is over.'

Virginia, you will write no more.

Somehow, it was enough to be here.

I said, 'I expect you're too busy to read?' I knew modern people rarely read.

'I have a degree in Tourism,' he said, 'from Istanbul University.' He said it as if it were a private joke, something faintly absurd and yet delicious, he said it with charm and irony – or else, he said it as a simple boast, but because I liked him, I saw what I wanted. I needed him to be lovable because there was love in me, longing to alight. I told him, 'You're better educated than me.'

'You did not go to university?'

'Alas, no.'

'It is OK, do not be afraid!' He was all smiles, all kindness. 'More wine?' he said, and filled my glass.

'You are a Muslim, Ahmet? But you drink wine.'

At once his face became solemn. 'No, never, except tonight.'

'I don't believe you!'

'Honestly!' But the smile with which he looked up from his wine glass was so full of laughter that the lie didn't matter.

Leonard always watched my intake of wine. Like everything else, talking, walking, seeing our friends, going to parties, drink made me excited, only more so. When I talked too fast, or laughed too much, he got worried. 'Time for a rest, my love.' I was his love. It was because he loved me, and yet there were rules, and I was unruly.

Ahmet did not try to stop me drinking. Ahmet actively encouraged it. But I did not find myself talking too much. Actually, there was not much to say. We were gazing at each other, content together, savouring the food, which we shared with each other – he fed me morsels delicately, neatly, on a fork (tiny plump roast birds in garlicky butter, saffron rice, buttery spinach the glossy dark green of laurel leaves, tiny grilled tomatoes like ripe soft rubies: I chose a steak, because

435

I rarely ate it, but it was too big for me to finish it, and he speared the remains and devoured them, boldly, though his eyes were on me, still fixed on me, and his strong white teeth and sweet mouth were waiting, his eyes declared they were waiting for me.)

Both of us knew that something would happen. But where? Much too soon, we were back in the street. The night had come down. Now the street felt chilly. We stood undecided. Ahmet cleared his throat. Once, twice, and then he spoke, as a small cream cat shot across the street, lit up briefly in the glare of some headlights: 'Would you please like to visit my home, Ginny?'

A second's silence, and then another. By the third, my hand was in his warm hand, and we turned towards each other, still on a slope so his face was slightly lower than mine, and the kiss, when it came, was not quite conclusive, my lips brushed the salt of his upper lip and almost bumped the tip of his nose, and then he took over, and our mouths met, hot, and two small warm animals licked and burrowed.

I don't really know if I liked it at first, but certainly he was different from Leonard, different from Clive. More like Nessa! Tender and wet.

I was a maelstrom, a storm of feelings. There were strange tingles underneath my dress. The cobbles seemed harder, the slope steeper as we walked uphill towards his home. He was walking faster than before, as if he had pressing reasons to hurry, and I did too, so I tried to keep pace, though I also wanted to savour each moment: stars through the branches of lemon trees, two pretty girls Ahmet barely glanced at. The thin soles of my shoes meant my feet felt unprotected, yet the heels clutched at my aching tendons. Soon discomfort progressed to pain.

'We are here,' said Ahmet. He pulled me closer. The house

was set back, in a snaggle of doors. I tripped on something – a dog, a cat? – and cried out. Instantly he hushed me. There was a sharp, animal smell. The only light came from the street. I realised I was a little afraid. He was searching for something – must be his keys – but his other hand was upon my breast, which he'd suddenly found underneath my blouse, pushing in boldly between the buttons. 'Very nice,' he said, as the keyhole yielded. 'Very nice breast. Very nice … nipple.' He said it 'nip-lay'. His accent made the word beautiful. My breasts felt strange, full and hard, like fruit.

(Fruit and flowers on a balcony, yes. Once when Leonard and I were young we were driving through France on our way to Spain and we stopped at an inn in the Pyrenees. Next day was hot, we decided to stay while a fault with the carburetor was fixed. We walked, as usual; had wine at lunch; read a little, then both felt sleepy. The balcony had an arbour of vines which made it like a nest, underneath: white stars of light pierced the greenness; when we got used to the dark, we saw the grapes, great purple clusters with a bloom of sweet dust. Leonard picked some; the bench was inside but the maid had left its striped seat to air, beside a dry pot of geraniums, and a ray of sun found the silk of one flower, a brilliant purple, bruisable. We sat down together, like children in a tent. We started eating. We were hazed by the sun from our morning walk. More sunlight found us; it was circling south. Suddenly I felt my breasts were aching. Thinking, unthinking, I told Leonard. He bent and kissed them, fed me a grape, felt my nipple, and it swelled in the heat underneath his fingers, and without planning it, we tried it again, the thing that had not gone well for us.)

The hall light went on. It was harsh on Ahmet. He looked a little like a plump schoolboy. Inside, his house was surprisingly respectable; big stuffed sofas, antimacassars, a general air of fancy dress. But the light died almost instantly, he lit a large

candle, we were back in mystery, there was fire in his eyes, two perfect flames, and I looked more closely, and saw myself, tiny, the reflection of a full, unfamiliar face.

'So beautiful,' repeated Ahmet. He pressed very close. That smell I loved, of vanilla and lemons. 'Would you like Turkish tea? Would you like lie-down?'

But I did not intend to lie about it. 'I like you, Ahmet.' It was so easy! 'I like you a lot. I want – to kiss you.'

And then we were kissing in the flickering light. New odours: candle-wax, musk, cinnamon. Noises from the street: barking, engines, faintly the goat-bell sound of the tram, the melancholy call of cool mountains in Europe, but I was warm, here in Istanbul, there was not a scintilla of doubt in my body, and I, or the wine, swam in the moment, smelled it, savoured it, vowed to remember.

(That day on the balcony. We'd tried this before, but there was still the faint hope that it would be different, the dazzled blank hopefulness of wine and sun, I would let Leonard do it and everything would change, if he were different, could I be different? – and which came first? We were chicken and egg, awkward, tense-thighed, a tight flurry of feathers, my blouse on the ground, the sawing sound of his dusty panting, the warm hard stone which softened none of his cockerel force, this had nothing to do with my own dear husband, and his eye shone, desperate, staring, mad, and then it was over, and I had felt nothing, just hard dry friction and loneliness.)

I don't recall how we reached Ahmet's bedroom. I know that I had slipped off my shoes – the pain so sharp, the relief so sweet. I think he took me by the hand. 'Bedroom,' he whispered, as if there were listeners. This time he did not put a light on. It smelled of him, and of something – earthy, not unpleasant, not socks, surely? He opened the window. The night rushed in, sweet as beginnings, fresh and cool.

Gently, Ahmet sat me on the bed. I stretched out my fingertips and found the wall. It was obviously only a single bed, but that was good, we would be close together. In any case, I dared not stay overnight, Angela would notice, Angela would worry!

(In retrospect, yes, I had forgotten my conference. But that was tomorrow, this was the present, I could not think about the morning.)

There was just a great hunger I knew he would fill. He was doing something odd by the side of the bed, kneeling on the rug, gently parting my knees. There was a tickle in my throat; was he a dog? – but no, I liked dogs, my satin-eared spaniel, the panicky urge to cough left me as my elegant shell-pink American undergarments (thank God! my old ones had been blunt white cotton) were lifted away like a silken veil, and I had no time to feel shy or worried, my nakedness felt the faint breeze in the air – a millisecond later, Ahmet was there, and my hands reached out of their own accord and pulled his dear head with its wire-fuzz of hair (round as an infant's, I thought, briefly), towards the lost place at the heart of me, and my secret part was no longer empty, my lips, my openings were made complete by the hot rose of his working mouth, he was kissing me at my deepest centre, it pulled and called and gathered me, there was a warm vortex, growing, glowing, low down in my back a congestion began, I was drawn down into my deepest body, my head, my belly, my thighs were all one, something was radiating out through my core, up through my stomach, spine, ribcage; my eyes were closing, my lips parting, it was lifting me up, no choice but go further, I pressed against him, my hands urged him on, oh more, higher, the peak, oh go on –

and a broadening wave of silent laughter broke in my body, glossy, muscular, rolled from my toes up to my shoulders, it

found no limits, surged on and on, and somewhere a long croon of ecstasy began, somewhere in the room a cat's voice unspooled through octaves of sound, a cat in bliss – and as it abated, the ebb-tide of blood warmed every abandoned cell of my body, finally freeing, unfastening me –

'Shush, Ginny, shush' – his voice, breathless.

I realised the deep-throated sound was my own, a ribbon of happiness thrown from nowhere: my body singing its own lost song.

In a split second, the man was inside me. I was the sand as the sea pressed in, he entered me as the waves rolled onwards, he waited, kissing me, 'Beautiful woman, *seni seviyorum,*' and the more he kissed me, the further he came, and soon we were rocking in time like a boat, was I the boat and where were we sailing as we swayed together in the cinnamon night, 'I love you, Ginny, *tim eyot,*' and I didn't know, was he laughing or crying? the waves grew higher, he was brave, he was desperate, at the height of the storm he was my sailor, I held and stroked him, his back, his neck,

gather – gather – no otherness –

I thought, in a tear-drop of light, my Leonard –

and with an explosion of helpless noises, a broken, happy, almost childish sound, he lay inside me on the distant shore.

Briefly, I think, both of us slept.

I woke unhappy to jerking and banging. A woman was shouting outside the room, or maybe a little further away. Ahmet must be pulling his trousers on, I heard his belt buckle hit the wall and coins were falling from his trousers.

'Who is it? What's happening?'

'I think – is Mother.'

'Why is she here?'

'Because she live here. But she is supposed to stay with sister. I think they have another quarrel.'

'What shall I do?'

'I don't know.'

'It must be all right for you to have … girlfriends.'

Even in that crisis, I enjoyed the term. I wasn't dead, nor old: I was a girlfriend. But as I said it, I knew it wasn't true. It could not be all right for him to have girlfriends, and if Mother saw me, it would be worse still.

'No, not all right.'

'How does she know I'm here?'

'Maybe we leave something in drawing-room?'

'Oh God, I left my shoes in there.' Not that I'd be able to get them back on.' My feminine, painful, American shoes.

'Is OK, I tell her I clean them, for hotel.'

It transpired, in the end, that all Mother wanted was a kindly ear for her tale of woe – the sister's lies, the thieving nephews. There was a side-door via a neighbour's garden. This house was only a block from the hotel, though our roundabout route had made it feel much further. He was very insistent that he should come with me, and I equally insistent that he should not.

The shoes remained a problem, and we only solved it once we realised we had similar size feet.

Which is why, at half-past eleven that evening, I was stomping – a verb I had never used, a verb for negroes, a verb from jazz – I was stomping, feeling both proud and foolish, downhill through a back street in Istanbul, under the stars, under a winking moon, born up by drink and by my warm, calm body, in a coral dress and shiny black men's lace-ups.

And yes, I was singing. 'They're singing songs of love, they're all for me ...'

The night of love was not yet over.

ANGELA

10.45 AM: we arrived united. In fact, she seemed in a very good mood.

The architecture: Ottoman grandeur. Young dark-eyed people smiled at us, in twos and clusters; notebooks, backpacks. Not like the English; few were fat.

I forgot, or forgave, the panics of the morning now I had what I needed, Virginia's blessing. I was not an academic, but I took enough pride in having had an academic training (first generation in my family, so it mattered) to want to make a good impression. Academics didn't always like novelists. Especially conference-going hybrids like me. As the first plenary speaker, I felt exposed.

But, yes, Virginia's good opinion mattered.

Even the opinion of this modern chimera, from whom I could never gain any credit. One quote from Woolf on the cover of my novel! ... No, she would never bother to read me. To be fair, I had never seen her reading. Or writing, when it came to that.

It was odd, affecting, this perilous friendship. It was in itself and for itself, no-one knew about it, it could end any second, I had no photographs or messages.

(So was she – could she be – just a projection? No, I protested, *it could not be true. She laughed, she ate, she frequently crossed me, my Virginia Woolf was definitely human.*)

Professor Melike was excessively delighted to see me, boring through the crowds with clipboards and coffee cups to

seize me by both hands, and kiss me. A pantomime of elaborate relief. Of course, the traffic jams, terrible, yes, but they had sent the car, yes, never mind, she hustled us towards the hall for a sound check. I tried 'This is a friend of mine …', she barely blinked, but as we strode up the stairs, she heard 'distant relative of Virginia Woolf's,' and stopped dead, causing chaos behind us, people collapsing like a house of cards, to shake Virginia's hand and make her welcome. 'An honour,' she panted as she hurried us on.

We were in the great hall. Marmoreal cool that promised heat in the afternoon. Through the pointed window I saw a swallow. Melike summoned the sound engineer. Ah, the microphone, a black beetle on a stick. I told him the contents of my breakfast, as usual, biting back the desire to add 'but I could scarcely eat a mouthful, because Virginia had not got up.' The lectern was too big and imposing. They would see my face like a tiny rubber ball, balanced on a tower of shiny wood. Never mind, today I needed protection. My hangover was bouncing lightly in my head.

The audience began to arrive. The staff came and sat at the front, as usual. The students flooded into the rows at the back, got out their mobiles, and started texting. I was introduced to my introducer, and then to the head of department, or dean, who would be introducing my introducer, and then to another even grander book-end, possibly the warden or vice-chancellor. Everybody looked terribly old and solid, except for the students in their distant youthfulness, their hands and fingers flickering like wings and their laughter silvery as the swallow's.

Gerda – a stab of missing her. Two weeks to her birthday and the end of term.

We stood on the stage like awkward relatives arriving for our own funerals. Virginia tried to make her escape before

the obligatory photographs, but Professor Melike insisted she stayed. As the cameras flashed, the whisper spread among the little cluster of nodding grandees: 'distant relative ... lawyer ... Stephens.'

My stomach was tightening. I wanted this over. I took a brief overview of the hall. Good attendance. At the back, the young. In the front few rows, some familiar faces. There was Ray Kuyperman, smiling slightly. And no – oh no – that familiar figure, Moira Penny, somewhat paler and more startling than before, her hair in two braids of vivid magenta. Dr Moira Penny, the academic who at one stage was such a fan of my work, but who in some unfathomable way I had hurt and disappointed. The critical study of my work she had planned had long been stalled, and I hoped, aborted. I turned away before she caught my eye. (Didn't Moira write about Virginia Woolf? Good, then she wasn't here stalking *me*.)

The audience settled. Most of the stage party left and assumed positions in the front row, leathery and awkward as seated turtles. I put on my glasses. The vice-chancellor tapped his microphone and made a thunderous rumble of sound. There was miming between him and the sound engineer, and audience laughter as the latter rushed forward and tripped on the steps up to the platform. My glasses felt hot upon my nose. At last, the introductions had begun.

The students started texting again after a brief pause of static hope. There was praise for the organisers, the university, Professor Melike, the introducer. Some of what was said gained a ripple of applause; I heard the phrase, 'intellectual freedom'. Finally the introducer praised me, in a fancy-footwork Wikipedia shuffle in which all the grammar was pointlessly inverted to add an air of originality (I wrote the entry, I should know): '... Iceland Prize ... best-selling ... ground-breaking ...'

Yes, it was me. I was gurning horribly. The flying fingers at

the back had stopped moving.

I thanked everyone as briefly as I could. My glasses lighted on Virginia's face. There she was, sitting on her own. She had wandered away from the academics. I was going to deliver my gift to her. I had long loved her. I would defend her. None of the rest of it mattered, finally. I had never been able to say what I wanted; never told her why I loved her work; never quite had the in-depth discussion that I had always longed to have. What would remain of us was love. But the light fell strangely; her face was a blank.

And as these split-second thoughts flew past and I raised my pages to begin, I saw Gerda sitting in the middle of the room, the middle of the row, the centre of my vision. The room around her faded; she was the only one.

Of course it wasn't her, it was an illusion.

No, Gerda was there. Her sheaf of red hair, her round pale face, her lips half-open, she was mouthing something I could not hear. I could not take in what was happening. She was at school, surely, in Hertfordshire, England, four or five hours' flight time away. This was a red-haired doppelganger.

No, it was her. That turn of her head. I was going mad. It could not be Gerda.

Yes, my daughter. My love for her.

But the hall was waiting. They were staring at me. A little ripple of unease. I must go on, I must give my paper. For a moment everything blurred with tears. Had I ever given enough to Gerda? I thought: I will make this talk for her, it must be for her, not Virginia. Gerda's thirteen, on the cusp of adulthood. She will help Virginia go into the future.

Strip out the theory, talk from the heart. I clutched the lectern, and then I began. The first page will do, I thought, then cut it.

'This conference is yet another tribute to the power

of one woman, Virginia Woolf, whose record of human consciousness lit up the borders between self and world. Who showed us doubt, and ambivalence, and the fluidities of sex and gender. Whose witty, flashing prose, in the diaries, makes other diarists look like plodders. Who was male and female, old and young.

'Such brilliance comes with a cost, of course. It may throw others into shadow. It may cause envy from the less successful. It may breed hatred as fierce as love.

'By her own contemporaries Virginia Woolf was seen as modern, as well as a modernist. By those who came afterwards, however, she has sometimes been seen, or rather misrepresented, as reactionary, elitist, snobbish, self-indulgent. It is astonishing, actually, that one woman made so many people so angry.' (*A flash: how often she has made me angry, since coming to life in the reading-room.*) 'Including those who have barely read her. Perhaps it is her face: aristocratic arrogance complicated by vulnerability. If you prick her, you know she would bleed – ' (*or fade, dwindle, disappear. That day in New York when she had nearly vanished, after finding all the bookshops were closing down.*)

And then I was off on my catalogue of haters. It took me ten minutes to get through the roster.

'... art for art's sake ... stultifying ... ivory tower ... not relevant to today's ... if ever ... undeserved pre-eminence ... *Mrs Dalloway* and *To the Lighthouse* ... bloodless ... anaemic ... no breath of real life ... daughter of privilege ... patronage ... precious ... narrow ... cold ... frigid ... withholding ...

'I think we can see, when it is gathered together, that this is so much spiteful nonsense – often promulgated by male critics – '

Remember to smile.

I looked up and smiled. But the audience were looking depressed and sober. Gerda's face was flat, uncertain. I was not having the effect I wanted. And indeed, as my words came back to my ears, I suddenly realised what I had been doing: replicating hatred, despite myself. (*Why had I gathered so many quotes? Was it my own shadow side? Did part of me feel something like hatred?*)

Turn it around. *Turn it around!* Get out of the shadow! Find the light!

My body. Somehow it knew what to do. My hands were crumpling, tearing the pages, they were falling on the floor, big flakes of white ash. My eyes moved from Gerda to the young at the back. They had not given up. They still looked to me for something. I didn't know them, or what to give them, but Woolf, surely, was for everyone, if I could find the words to say so.

What could I surmise about the students? Only two – no three – of the girls were covered. There were boys, as well, a minority, but again, three or four had Islamic beards (no, they were just beards, don't call them Islamic, facial hair is not a religion. Beards were signs with plural meanings.) Fifty, no a hundred, one hundred and fifty young. They were here for me, still interested. They were not inspired, but no-one was texting. If I found the right words, I might make this work.

'You girls' – I meant Gerda – 'you brave young women.' (*How had she got here? She had always been brave, she was never afraid of worms or beetles.*) 'Virginia Woolf had a message for you. I believe you study *Mrs Dalloway*, but have you read *A Room of One's Own?* Who has?' There was a little ripple of self-conscious giggles, and then a very few hands went up, apart from the lecturers near my feet, who instantly sprouted a self-righteous forest. One of the hands at the back belonged to one of the male students with bushy black beards.

Then a familiar little hoot of laughter. Yes, Virginia had put her hand up, a long white hand, a goose-neck waggle. When she saw I had seen her, she dropped it again.

There was another hand in the middle of the room.

Gerda's hand was so high she was almost bursting, thrusting her plump arm out of its socket.

Had Gerda read *A Room of One's Own*?

It was extraordinary, but must be true. She was always difficult, but rarely a liar.

– But where was I? I was thrown off course.

– Suddenly I thought, don't talk about gender. Gender divides before it joins. I'll come back to it. There are other things to say.

'*Mrs Dalloway* – your set text, I believe? – in so many countries, that's the one they choose – is a wonderful book – stylistically, structurally – but it is a book that is focused on a certain party, certain individuals, a certain class. It stays, finally, in the early twentieth century, and in London, England, very far away. To some of you, I think, it must seem rather old-fashioned.' (I looked up for corroboration; at the back, some guilty smiles and nudges. I didn't look at Virginia.) 'Why should you be interested in Virginia Woolf? Yes, she came to Istanbul in 1906, as a young woman of twenty-four, and again in 1910, when she was twenty-eight – but her Constantinople was a very different city.

'*Mrs Dalloway* herself is a great fictional creation – as are Mr and Mrs Ramsay in *To the Lighthouse*, Miss La Trobe in *Between the Acts* – but she is, deliberately, defined by her limits. She is creative, but only socially. She makes theatre in a private house. She is bodiless. Physically, she 'fails' her husband – the suggestion is, she doesn't like sex – sex with a man, in any case.

'It's tempting to see her creator like this. How many of you, consciously or not, have superimposed Virginia's face on *Mrs*

Dalloway's privileged body? When she sets out to shop, did you see Virginia? That elegant neck and long delicate nose?'

A little laughter, a few nods, but I certainly had a long way to go. I had to dig deep inside myself. What did they want? How could I woo them?

'I want to invite you to see Woolf more widely. She is a great writer because she is neither Clarissa Dalloway nor Mrs Ramsay. The fact is, she can be anybody. She has Keats's "negative capability" – in her, others can find their lost voices. That means, my voice, your voice' (*I was pointing at the front row*) 'your voices' (*now I was reaching out to the back*). 'I believe we can all find our lives in her pages.'

'Politically, culturally, you are at a crossroads. You live at the heart of all the twenty-first century's conflicts. Your quarrel isn't with New York. There are close relations, politically, between America and Turkey. Your Prime Minister Erdoğan is apparently exactly what America wants him to be. A free market capitalist: isn't that what we are all supposed to be, today? Yet Erdoğan is a devout Muslim. So is it over, religious conflict?

'You cannot look at the great rose-red dome of the Aya Sophia without seeing the fight between the faiths, the endless struggle for religious dominance: the heartland of the Christians, taken by Muslims. I have travelled, for this lecture, from New York, and I've thought a lot about the two cities. New York has its skyline with the absent twin towers, brought low by Islamist jihadists. Both cities wear the scars of religious conflict.'

(My eyes dipped briefly to the row of lecturers. A mixture of expressions: interest, puzzlement. Melike's eyebrows telegraphed: *a little off message*.)

'The Turkish government – correct me if I'm wrong – has strong links to religious orthodoxy, and was formerly supported by Fethullah Gülen, the banned Islamic leader.

And America takes pride in its own religious faiths. Obama must be photographed singing Christmas carols; evangelical Christians attack the teaching of evolution in American schools and universities. Sometimes it's as if the world is going backwards, as if we all modernised too fast, and now religion's rushing in through the back door, which we were all too busy to close. Here you are seeing, a little more each day, Atatürk's Turkey becoming Erdoğan's: secular Turkey veiling itself.

'Religion means authority. Religion means people have to behave. First, no alcohol, then no sex, then, perhaps, no other freedoms.

'Clarissa Dalloway didn't like religion. "Love and religion!" thought Clarissa … how detestable they are!" She was afraid of the brute power of both, their appeal to our instincts rather than our brains.

'On the way here, on the plane from New York, I travelled with about thirty orthodox Israelis. It felt as if we had gone back in time. They were binding their arms with leather straps, praying in the gangway, facing the east, all of this on a modern jet-plane flying over the Atlantic at five hundred miles an hour. I overheard a very young woman explaining her philosophy: "Follow the ways of our forefathers." This is going back to the Old Testament, the most conservative, warlike part of the Bible! It's as if God is making a comeback, everywhere, in all his forms – as if secular democracy has been too taxing.

'I always remember what Virginia Woolf had to say about the Old Testament of the Bible. In one of its books, the Book of Job, a man is relentlessly tested by God. She said, "I read the book of Job last night, I don't think God comes out well in it."

'She used her wit and her sceptical intelligence. And this is what she would expect of you young people, you lucky group who attend this university, one of the best in Turkey.

A university education teaches you to think, as well as feel. It teaches you to criticise.

'But in Turkey, I hear, academic jobs and money are increasingly going to the religious. And what are these new "crimes against Turkishness"? The same kind of insults are flung in New York: dissenting academics are called "un-American". So is it wrong to criticise your country?

'Virginia Woolf criticised her country. She wrote a great tract against the folly of war, *Three Guineas*. It's witty, truthful, unpompous, passionate, a book none of her usual male admirers had time for: they found it "shrill", an embarrassment. She talks about war-making, and its illusions. She sees war as the sport of men, so perhaps it's not surprising men did not like it. Even her husband did not like it much.

'Woolf did not risk imprisonment, as you do. I have seen you young people protesting on the streets, and I know what perils you incur when you do. But she risked men's sneers, she risked male scorn. For a mind so unarmoured, it was like braving acid.

'You need no-one to teach you to be brave. But you can find your lives, and your struggles, in her pages.'

I looked up. They were listening, now. Gerda had colour in her cheeks. I came out from behind the lectern and stood with my feet among my torn and crumpled pages, so they could see the whole of me. I had a body, so did they.

'Which is one great gift literature offers, when we aren't just studying it for exams. To find ourselves – new parts of ourselves, or parts of ourselves not fully expressed. To find ourselves in others. "Our unacted parts", Woolf talked about. How books can free our other selves.

'"We have other lives, I think, I hope ..." I am quoting, some of you will know, from Virginia's last novel, *Between the Acts*. A short, generous-spirited book that reinvents art as something

for everyone, for villagers and landowners, for rich and poor. You have these divisions in Turkey too: between those with an education, like you, and your contemporaries who could not afford it; between the city and the village. Art, Woolf says, can be a village pageant. Where even the audience play their part. As you do now, my audience.' I found Virginia, I smiled at her. 'Art, she says, unites us all. All of us need to play, or sing.'

I could not make out if she was smiling back. The sunlight had washed out her face again. Suddenly I could not see her at all. (But then, I was walking around the stage; obviously she must be behind a pillar; or else it was problems with my contact lenses.)

'Most of you here are younger than me,' I said. 'Your country's population is young. I want to come back to something I began with, something important to you young people. Sex and gender in Virginia Woolf − ' (As I said it, I thought about *my* Virginia, the day before, when we'd fled the demonstration and sat in the café near Istiklal. She'd tried so bravely to talk about sex, and I had been deaf, and fobbed her off. *You fool, you thought she was too old for it.*)

' − which is important to us older people as well,' I added, in time to raise a few wry smiles from the lecturers in the front row. 'Virginia Woolf came to Istanbul − Constantinople − as I said. She was twenty-four: young and inexperienced. She found a city of domes and minarets, yes, but also free women on the streets, some of them veiled but taking their veils lightly, throwing them back to look in the shops, not what she had expected to find. She found a people who did not envy or copy the people of London or Paris, people who were happy in their own existence.

'By the time she wrote *Orlando*, in 1928, nearly everything here was different. The First World War had changed the maps, and in Turkey Atatürk had come to power and was dragging

Turkey into the future. But because *Orlando* is set in the past, Woolf was free to work from her memories.

'What did she imagine? A place of transformation; a place where anything could happen. There are Gypsies; there are secret assignations; you can sleep for days without being woken; you can escape from the city into the wilds. Finally, you can change, if you want, if you dream the right dream, from a man to a woman. Her hero goes to bed a man: three days later, he wakes up a woman.

'She imagines a city without fixity. Unlike New York, where Woolf never went, it is not a city of right angles and rectitude, a city with a rigid matrix. Orlando's city is all being and becoming, not one where categories fix us in the past. It is not orthodox, or puritanical. Long may your city remain free, and fluid.

'We know that *Orlando* was dedicated to Vita Sackville-West, Woolf's lesbian lover. Yet we know how much Virginia loved her husband. It's a book that says: we can be male or female. We can find the male and female in ourselves. We can have lovers of either sex. Heroes can be men or women. Writers can be women or men; they can be happy as either, and happy with either.'

(There was a shuffling going on in the front two rows. Oh, it was Moira, she had shouted something, she was waving her hand, obviously indignant. I had touched on a nerve, I managed to ignore her but part of me heard it, all the same: 'Literature's not about happiness!')

'I admire this novel greatly,' I continued, 'and yet, I still don't think it is her greatest achievement.'

'Remember she was born to privilege. Her father, Leslie Stephen, editor of the *Dictionary of National Biography*, was one of the best-known public intellectuals of his day. She grew up doing no domestic work, in a house that was run by servants.

Yet somehow, in *A Room of One's Own*, she steps completely outside herself; outside her class, outside her time. For me, the end of *A Room of One's Own* is Virginia Woolf's greatest achievement, because it links us, the lucky ones – me, your teachers, each one of you students, everyone here in this room today – to all those less lucky human beings of the past; our mothers, grandmothers, great-grandmothers; those women whose chances, and hopes, are over. In perhaps her greatest act of creation, Woolf's imagination lets them live again. She says they can be redeemed by us. That through our lives, they can come back to life.'

I stopped to catch my breath, and take stock of the room. Yes, I could feel it gathering. We were together. It was warming, melting. I looked for Gerda; yes, she was there. I still couldn't see Virginia. Time to produce a clincher.

But I was suddenly blank; I felt alone. I needed others; I needed Virginia.

Keep their attention. You can't fail now.

And then a hand went up from the floor. Two-thirds of the way back, so not a lecturer, but she looked too old to be a student. I fell upon it, a temporary respite. Her face was worn. Greying hair, a cheap jacket. Could not wait till the questions at the end.

'Yes?'

'I am sorry for ask, but please, can you read it for us, this text, *Room of One's Own*. I have no English books. Here they are very expensive. I like very much what you say, and I want – how to say – I *long* to read it.'

The room was quiet, attentive. It took courage for the woman to say it. By an irony, I had prepared a long quote, but it was on the last page of my written paper, the paper that I had decided not to give, and I'd torn it up, thrown it down on the floor. I dared not fumble through the mess at my feet.

'I had intended to read a passage, yes. But, a small problem. Can any of you help me – Professor Melike, one of your colleagues maybe? I don't seem to have it with me. It's the passage about Shakespeare's sister.'

The front rows rustled and muttered, uncomfortable. Shrugs of apology, raised empty hands. OK, this was going to end in bathos. *Not the end of the world*, I told myself – but yes, an opportunity lost. I smiled an apology to the brave questioner.

'No joy at the front? Sorry about that. I think I will end there, and take questions.' I stepped back from the lectern. I waited for applause.

But there were feet, loud feet on the wooden steps that led up from the hall to the stage. Fast heavy feet. I looked up, startled. Red hair, flashing like a squirrel in the sunlight. Pale face, Gerda's beloved face. Her shoulders were pulled back, soldier-style. She smiled an unnaturally wide, scared smile.

'Gerda! Darling, what are you doing – '

'It's Ok, Mum. It'll be all right. I've got it, see. I will read the passage.'

I thought: my God. I thought: this is great. And then: what if Gerda reads the wrong bit? 'I'd better do it sweetie, thank you.'

But gently, firmly, she pushed me aside. She was bigger than before, taller, older, but she was still just a teenager, *my* teenager, my lovely daughter – rash, buoyant, terrified. She smelled of chewing-gum, fear and cheap soap.

She touched the microphone. A thundercrack. The audience was open-mouthed. Melike was frowning, speaking over her shoulder, half on her feet, was it an incident?

'I am her daughter,' she said to the hall, one pale finger pointing in my direction. 'It's OK, I'm not a nutter. I've got the book. Now I will read it. It's brilliant, actually. You're going to love it.'

There was a wave of friendly laughter.

Then she began. Her voice was nervous, at first, yes, she went too fast, but as she spoke, it steadied, strengthened; the words carried her, the words became her, they walked confidently, gracefully through the hall, they were Virginia Woolf, alive and with us (*where was Virginia, I thought, briefly?*) – they were Shakespeare, too – and Shakespeare's sister.:

> I told you … that Shakespeare had a sister; but do not look for her … She died young – alas, she never wrote a word. She lies buried where the omnibuses now stop, opposite the Elephant and Castle. Now my belief is that this poet who never wrote a word and was buried at the cross-roads still lives. She lives in you and in me, and in many other women who are not here to-night, for they are washing up the dishes and putting the children to bed. But she lives; for great poets do not die; they are continuing presences; they need only the opportunity to walk among us in the flesh …

Her clear young voice rang out through the hall. I searched the rows. *Yes, but where was Virginia?*

> This opportunity, as I think, it is now coming within your power to give her. For my belief is that if we live another century or so – I am talking of the common life which is the real life and not of the little separate lives which we live as individuals – and have five hundred a year each of us and rooms of our own; if we have the habit of freedom and the courage to write exactly what we think …

The common life which is the real life; yes, we made up a whole, somehow, we tiny atoms of human life, in the longer view we were part of one another …

... if we ... see human beings not always in their relation
to each other but in relation to reality; and the sky, too,
and the trees or whatever it may be in themselves ... if
we face the fact, for it is a fact, that there is no arm to
cling to, but that we go alone ... then the opportunity
will come and the dead poet who was Shakespeare's
sister will put on the body which she has so often laid
down ...

Through Gerda's mouth, those magnificent words. I prickled
with tears. They have laid down their bodies, our mothers, our
grandmothers. Lorna, my mother: I missed her still, with her
frail dark roses, her frightened eyes, her ready laughter, her love
of books, her painful pride that I became a writer, though I
knew she would have liked to write herself. Somehow Virginia
had spoken for her, this young working-class woman who
might have crossed her path, for they had both walked on this
earth together. And yet she also spoke to Gerda, Mum's grand-
daughter, who could travel the world, who might write stories
we could not imagine, strange shapes, marvels, new forms of
life that would escape from bookshops.

'Drawing her life from the lives of the unknown who
were her forerunners, as her brother did before her, she will
be born ...'

Had Virginia left the room? I still could not see her. Would she
mind Gerda reading her words, in an accent so very different
to hers?

'As for her coming ... without that effort on our part, that
we cannot expect ... But I maintain that she would come if
we worked for her, and that so to work, even in poverty and
obscurity, is worthwhile.'

The clapping broke round us like the sea. It was for Gerda,
for Virginia, for me, for whatever had brought us all together.

The students were clapping furiously, lifting their hands above their heads: the staff, at the front, more contained, more modest, but Professor Melike was looking happy. Suddenly a warm hand pressed into mine. Gerda was taking a bow alongside me. She hissed, 'Mum, was that all right?'

'Perfect, darling. Now I'll have to take questions.'

'I'm off, it's OK.'

'*How on earth did you get here?*' But the applause was starting to settle. 'Never mind, tell me later. Don't go far. Do you hear me?'

'*Latahz.*'

Gerda was backing away, she kissed her hand, like a physical pain I watched her grow smaller as she clattered down the stairs again. Then, with relief, I spotted Virginia. Had she been there all the time? Had she heard my daughter?

'Thank you,' I told the microphone. 'Now I am happy to take questions.'

The usual silence, people watching each other. 'And please – I want questions from the students. Don't let your teachers take up all the time!' Slightly sulky expressions on some of the faces in the first two rows, student laughter at the back.

I scanned the room. Who would start us off? My God, Gerda was heading for Virginia. She was stumbling along a row of smiling faces. Now she and Virginia were sitting together. Something caught in my throat to see it. Yes, there they sat, she had dared to join her, my child's red hair by that familiar face, and their lips were moving, they were talking to each other. Virginia was whispering to Gerda!

Then the youth with the beard at the back raised his hand. A microphone was ferried to him like a baton. 'I have read *A Room of One's Own,*' he said. 'This is only for women, or for men?'

The expected hostile Islamic question. 'Not just for women,'

I said, robustly. 'No, she is writing for everyone. It's important that men share the work Woolf is speaking of. For women to flower, men have to help.'

But he was looking indignant, shaking his head, beckoning the microphone back again. 'You don't understand,' he said, pointing with his free hand to his chest. 'I love this book. I love Virginia Woolf. I am, I am already helping!' Smiles and laughter from the students around him. I saw that he was popular. Yes, I had misunderstood. It was the beard. I felt myself flushing.

'Sorry,' I said. 'Er – I didn't see where you were coming from.'

Another hand at the back, this time a girl – or was it a boy? She had short hair. Her English sounded slightly American. She spoke clearly and slowly. 'Virginia Woolf talks about a man turning into a woman. She thinks she is – androgyne.'

'Androgynous,' I corrected. 'Go on.'

'But in real life – we can't. Parents don't let us. The society don't let us. It's just the dream, isn't it?'

'I know what you mean,' I said, though I didn't. But I heard the anger in her voice. 'Biology is still destiny, up to a point. But the dream is helpful, isn't it? And when we are reading or writing, we surely can be both male or female – even if we still can't be at home?'

It wasn't enough. How could it be? She had given back the mike, but she was whispering to the girl beside her, voluble, articulate, indignant. One day, maybe, her thoughts would be a book. Her own book, not mine or Virginia's.

Another student hand went up. A handsome boy with thick black hair, beckoning the mike with a confident flourish. 'It's not true men can't be girls, in Istanbul. There is transsexual district, in Pera. If you are brave, you can operate!'

He was drowned out with laughter, but hung on to the microphone. 'No,' he said, 'it's not a joke. For us, maybe. But

it happens. Virginia Woolf can do it with words, she is lucky. Other people need doctors. Or better laws.'

Some people were nodding. The room felt alive. A shimmering movement ran over the faces. My contact lenses playing up again. I blinked, refocused. There was a breeze. Did it matter that we had strayed from the text?

Yes, a hand sticking up at the front. Oh no, it was her, that familiar face, five years older, thinner, more ravaged. Moira Penny, half-struggling to her feet, the woman who had screamed at me like a banshee one morning in a café when she felt neglected. A terrifying scene I would never forget. I had realised that day, in the acid sunlight, as her face fell apart into cubist hatred, what toll is demanded for admiration.

(*Had Virginia ever felt the same about me?*)

She beckoned the microphone with a white hand, spectral, bony as the claws of a bird. What would she say? I could not stop her. That hair, that dark, chemical red, thinner now, plum-dark, almost purple, such a cruel contrast to Gerda's bright mop.

She rose in her seat, listing away from upright. She was ill, I saw, she had to cling on to the chair in front of her for balance, she was hopelessly crooked, but then I had a split second of doubt; was it the room, was the room off balance? The curtains in the long windows were blowing, bellying out and then retracting.

I found I had retreated behind my lectern, not consciously, but I needed protection, I held on firmly to the polished wood. *I have done my best, she cannot hurt me.*

'Professor Moira Penny,' she rasped. (*She had attained professorship. At what cost? For God's sake, at what institution?*) 'Thank you for your ... series of remarks,' she began. She made it sound like 'silly remarks'. 'You spoke about Virginia Woolf almost as if you knew her.' (*Well I do know her,* I thought, *as it*

happens.) 'This is a very *subjective* approach. For the students listening, it may have been surprising that *there was a complete absence of theory.*' She was getting louder; the microphone squeaked, a painful sound like a giant bat, and her clothes were dark against the sunlight that flooded through the gaps in the curtains. 'Forgive me if I *missed anything*, but I did not notice a *single citation!*' Louder still. She was becoming shrill. Professor Melike was turning round. Moira Penny loomed black behind her. 'I myself have written extensively, *close, detailed* analysis, on *Orlando.*' Pause. I noticed her hand was shaking, which explained the fretful, jittery backdrop of small explosions from the microphone – or was that thunder, outside the window? 'One would have thought it almost literally *impossible* to speak about Virginia Woolf at the present moment without referring to the collection of papers I both edited and contributed to last year, called – ' There was an anxious pause as she stopped, pulled a face – no, worse, it was meant to be a smile, her lips pulled back from her teeth, her tongue – and hauled up a gigantic plastic shopping-bag, in which she rooted, and retrieved, at length, a slim volume which she held close to her eyes – '*Liminalities and a Reading of One's Own: Confusions and Elucidations on the Threshold of Woolf's Room.*' She nodded, satisfied, and looked around the room, as if the title had proved her point. But she had not finished. She raised the microphone. A sudden, agonising burst of howl–round, sudden as a thunderstorm. For a minute, the whole room seemed to shake, people looked startled, it was all going wrong, some of the students were giggling. She looked straight at me. A sudden scream, the violent squawk of a roused macaque. '*Why do you always ignore my work? Why do you mock me and abuse me?*'

The room paused, electric, horrified. I felt dizzy. The audience spun. I did not know what to say to her. I have always been afraid of hatred. I opened my mouth. No sound came

out. I stared, dry-lipped, across the room. Perhaps it was true. I had not cited. I had abandoned my written draft, which made many nods to academics. I had trusted the text, Virginia's text, and tried to please the audience. Yes, I was a crowd-pleaser. Her furious face said she saw through me.

'I – I don't know how to answer you,' I said. 'Perhaps I spoke as a writer, not a critic.'

'WHAT DOES THAT MEAN??' she screamed at me. She was hanging on to the mike for dear life. Professor Melike was standing beside her, trying to wrestle it away. Moira mimicked me in a monkey squeal. "I speak as a writer, not a critic." WHY DO YOU THINK WRITERS ARE BETTER THAN CRITICS? Why do you think you're better than me?'

'I don't,' I said. (Though maybe I did.)

Then I saw my Gerda was waving her hand from the middle of the room, and calling something. I heard '... the microphone?'

With a little grunt, Moira lost her grip, and Melike staggered backwards, the mike in her hand. It was ferried backwards over rows of heads to the one where Virginia and Gerda sat together.

'*She*'s got to say something,' Gerda said, once the mike was in her grip. She passed it across to Virginia. There was a brief semi-struggle between them. Virginia was trying to push it away, but suddenly she smiled, took it, stood up.

'Mrs Woolf,' she said, in her extraordinary voice, low, murmurous, amused. The room, already turbulent, rippled again, a kaleidoscope quake like the start of a migraine. 'Make what you like of *that*. I am happy to be a distant relation. Two things. First, I liked the lecture. And, of course – I liked the quotation.' A short laugh at her own wit, which was rather lost on the audience. 'Secondly, though, there should be no difference between a writer and a critic. I am a writer and a critic. Virginia Woolf was a writer and a critic. Criticism, in

my day, her day, was no different to good writing. It wasn't hard to understand. I have to admit – (Professor, I'm sorry, I've forgotten your name, the woman at the front who spoke so – *loudly*) – the meaning of your title escaped me. Why would one write about "*Confusions*"? Perhaps I misheard. Was it "Confucians"?'

She sank down, smiling at her own pun, and passed across the microphone.

Gerda had it. Gerda stood up. 'I admit I am only fourteen,' she said. (*The liar!*) 'So I don't know nearly as much as a professor. But surely writers came first. If there weren't writers, there wouldn't be critics, 'cos they wouldn't have anything to write about. That's all I wanted to say.' Abruptly, she sat down. Almost as quickly, she bounced back up again.

'I forgot, I want to say something else. Which is about *young* people. I'm young obviously. And so are all these' (pointing to the ranks at the back of the room). 'I don't want to diss Virginia Woolf, because I think she's wonderful, and also, with her being here, it would be rude. But there's one bit of *A Room of One's Own* I disagree with.'

(I was getting anxious. My daughter's ego! At primary school, the teachers would take me aside and tell me they couldn't stop Gerda talking.)

'It's the bit about Mary Carmichael. She is the made-up "young woman" in *A Room of One's Own,* in case you haven't read it, who is supposed to be the next generation of writers. Virginia Woolf makes her quite good, but not *that* good. Well just because she's young, that doesn't prove it. Mary Carmichael might actually be a genius. Even if she's only a teenager. And the same goes for all these Turkish students, the girls. No-one knows about them, because I expect they write in Turkish – well only Turkish people know, that is – or maybe no-one knows at all.' (*Gerda, you're talking much too fast!*) 'I'm not just

saying that *I* could be a genius. Whereas Virginia says, it could take a hundred years before a woman writer was really great, which leaves out *her*, who was already great, the greatest writer, maybe, I've ever read, but then, as I said, I am only fourteen – and to be honest, thirteen, fourteen in two weeks. It didn't take a hundred years at all. It's already happening. It's already happened.'

With that, thank God, she sank down again, and yielded the microphone to a steward.

'Time for maybe one more question,' I said.

A hand was waving by a pillar at the back. A girl. Hang on, two girls, two hands waving. I blinked and stared. No, just one. I was having problems focusing. Could it be that the whole row had got their hands up, waving like a field of young corn? As the hands waved, the audience was blurring; stirring, now, like waves on the sea. I felt very hot, as if I were melting. Was it the menopause? I had to hang on, but I signalled to Professor Melike. 'Is it possible to open more windows? … Yes, there are questions at the back?'

Only one hand, only one question. A girl student with an intelligent frown, raven-black hair, a computer on her lap. 'Virginia Woolf, she was rich, she had – what do you say, connections, publishers. How do we do what she did? For her, I think it was more easy.'

An inspiration. 'Do you write?' I asked. 'I think you want to write yourself. How many of you,' I looked along the rows, 'how many of you students want to write?'

Hands unfolded, slowly at first, then a growing series of notes, like music, pale minims of faces with their stems of arms. I looked at them. They were beautiful. So many of them, a harmony.

Energy, a flurry, in the middle of the room. The worn-looking woman who had asked the first question had her

thicker, older arm in the air. She was mouthing something I couldn't hear. Then I lip-read it, or imagined it. 'Not only students', she was trying to tell me.

'Sorry,' I said, 'Not only students. Anyone here who wants to write.'

And yes, not far from the woman, there was Gerda, strong white arm jostling the air.

Not much more than a child, but she needed to write. Virginia sat stock still beside her.

There was a ripple, a slow stirring breeze that came from somewhere closer to the stage. Was it the windows that had been opened? No, the front rows were pushing up shoots, the lecturers, the research assistants, who toiled in libraries, who sweated over footnotes, who laboured with passives, 'It is sometimes asserted ...', 'It is believed ...', their hands were moving, their fingers uncurling, loosing their tension, opening up like flowers, they were smiling at me, a little shyly, maybe, but they were alive, their eyes were shining –

I was staring out at a room that was a forest. Sun poured in through the windows on the right, the filmy white curtains blew like water, the living things were unfolding in their seats, they were stretching and moving, free at last, there were small cries and laughter and delight as they looked around them and saw what was happening, the hall around them swam and shifted, they turned in their seats and found each other, some were embracing, two were kissing, then another two, the students were rising to their feet, girls at the front of their section were dancing, oh girls with garlands in their hair, those circlets, sun-lets of red and white buds I'd seen on sale in the Hippodrome –

Now Moira Penny was on the move, like a fluttering bat in her blue-black garments, but she was making, aslant, for the window, she knelt in the wall of white sunlight, she raised both

466

her arms to the wash of heat, she laid down her pain, she was young again – '

They no longer needed me – did they? Were they still waiting for an answer, or had they found it in each other? What had I got to say to them? I had asked the question – who wanted to write? – and the seed was stirring in everyone – but what came next? What could I tell them?

The student with the laptop thought Virginia was lucky. *'Virginia Woolf, she was rich ... How do we do what she did? For her, I think it was more easy.'*

I looked for Virginia. Would she have an answer? And I saw what I had not expected. She sat isolated in the middle of her row. Gerda had left her, gone to dance with the students, the garlanded girls in their youthful roundels, off with the raggle-taggle-gypsies-oh ...

Virginia sat alone. She alone was unmoving. Yes, a stillness at the heart of the hall.

The sunlight pinned her to her seat. Her face was like a photograph, the sun so sharp she was black and white, her lines erased, a perfect portrait, marble-pale twin of that famous profile taken of her as a very young woman. No-one surely, could fail to realise. This was Virginia Woolf to the life. Yet animation had drained from her. She was motionless, she was stiller than paper.

A brightness on her cheek. With a great effort, she raised her hand. As if she was lifting lead through water. She was – yes, she was trying to speak.

I tapped my microphone for quiet. The noise it made went on and on, a thunder-roll of sound in this luminous room, this sunlit ballroom of dancing bodies, and they went on moving, weaving through each other, and the whispers darted around like swallows, splitting, spinning and finally joining in a joyous place where everything was known, 'It's her! Yes! Virginia

Woolf! Virginia Woolf is in the house!'

And the room fell silent, at last, for her. This was the room, the room she had asked for. This was the room she owned and ruled.

She did not stand; she did not, could not. She was straining to speak. It would not come.

I remembered the voice with which she'd first spoken, in the New York Public Library, hoarse, broken. I thought, 'She's leaving us again. Oh stay, please stay and answer them.'

On eddying currents, the mike reached her, a tiny dark boat, buffeted, it was in her white hand, so pale, so thin. Rumbles of thunder around the room. Outside the window I saw lightning flashes, and inside the room, but perhaps that was motion, the interweaving of limbs, glances, a shimmering in and out of focus, the wing-tips stretching and hovering.

We all heard her when she tried again. Out of the silence, it broke into being, her breaths, she was breathing, we heard her breathe, Virginia Woolf breathed hard for us, Virginia struggled to stay alive. Then the relief of her first words. 'My friends – ' But those drawling vowels, so narrowly formed, so definite a badge of the class she had come from.

No, she was more than her voice, her presence. Virginia was everything that she had been. But I thought: *Virginia is going home.*

'You are my readers. Thank you, friends. Some of you, readers who would be writers. You are the minds I spoke about, the writers of a hundred years later. What do I have to say to you?

'The young woman questioner thought I was lucky. And I admit I had great good fortune. Who is to say what I would have written without my father, without Leonard, without servants. What would I have written without money? Five hundred pounds and a room of my own?'

Wrong message, Virginia, I thought, anxious.

'But I tell you this: I *would have* written. Somehow I would have found my voice. I would have found a way to be heard, published.' (For a moment, there, her voice strengthened. In my memory, that was when her voice was strongest.)

'And so must you. And so will you.' There was a pause, or a fault with the power supply. Perhaps it was to do with the weather, which was crackling merrily around our heads. 'The young woman beside me tells me that now it is easier to self-publish, but some of you feel ashamed to do this. Remember, nearly all my books were self-published.

'What else can I say to you?' A longer pause. Her breath laboured.

'The light is on you. It is in this room. You are in the sunshine which, while it's here, feels as though it will last forever.

'There is only one kind of luck for writers. There is the room. This sunlit room. I entered in the early morning. Before my evening, I had flown again …

'Write while you're here. Write while you can. Write for your time. And for each other.

'Maybe because I missed my evening, I've been allowed to slip back again … the absolute glory of a moment's sunlight …'

Slower, quieter. Each word grew fainter, stretches of space between the stitches. Breaths so light the words were gossamer, silver.

'But I am only a visitor. I ached to write … But for me, that's over.'

We spun like planets around her star, so far away now, so barely here. More gulfs of light in the walls of our world, faces like petals, shining, falling, I tried to clutch at my text, at texture, space was splitting into thousands of threads, a thunder of feet, someone near, was it Gerda –

'Write,' Woolf managed. It was a whisper. 'Your turn now ... I shall write no more.'

My eyes were going. A cascading migraine shook the room into a deck of cards, a brilliant shuffle of hearts, diamonds, the jacks and queens were revolving, cartwheeling, Virginia's image stayed for a second, translucent, hanging over our crumbling building. Moonrise over the Sea of Marmara, a white fingerprint, fading, flickering

The room split apart, the set dismantled

The universe fissured.

We fell through the air –

– The plane soared on above the earth, the flight staff stumbled down the cabin, replacing cushions, picking up toys, Virginia Woolf was thrust into my hand –

Yes, I was holding 'Professions for Women'.

A flight attendant waved a mobile. God, it was mine. I reached out to reclaim it.

Yes, the plane, the storm, the shock

the blind white flash as we spiralled down

 I struggled to collect myself.

Put the phone back in your pocket.

Something was there, obstructing it. I pushed, impatient, but force got me nowhere. I loved my coral suit too much to risk tearing the pocket, so I stopped and explored its satin crevice. Something small and round and solid. I pulled it out. It was a brilliant glass disk, a shiny bull's-eye with rings of cobalt and lighter blue, on a cord of gold silk. Sky: sunlight. Life was sunlight. And then it darkened. And shone again. Maybe the universe split every moment. Minute changes of light or viewpoint …

Yes, it was Turkish. I had seen one like it. It was a charm against the evil eye. I stared at it: it stared at me.

We have other lives, I think, I hope … we live in others. We live in things …

The eye gazed through me, intense as a peacock's.

The air beneath us was still unsteady. The intercom crackled, the pilot came on. 'Sorry about that, ladies and gentlemen. As you may have noticed, we were struck by lightning – ' Relieved laughter ran through the cabin, followed by a crescendo of clapping.

Yet something about it was not quite right. The seat felt flimsy; the walls were half-painted.

Gerda was sitting in the seat beside me, and beyond her, a triangular presence, a cone of shadow – *no, a woman*.

Virginia herself was on the plane. Relief rushed through me. I had not lost her.

Angela, Gerda, Virginia, side by side in another world. If time had split, which fork were we on?

There were many worlds, many universes. Maybe we never die entirely.

Now Virginia hoots with laughter. She and Gerda are making up rude rhymes. And then she stops. And then she looks.

A grave thin man comes down the gangway, rubbing his eyes with a trembling hand. Leonard is weeping. He has seen his wife. He cannot speak, but he kneels beside her, takes her blue-veined hands in his. 'Virginia … Virginia … I think there has been too much excitement …'

'Leonard, I am well again.'

'They are all here, darling, all our friends… Lytton is busy with a steward.'

We live in others. We live in words.

Somewhere beyond the thin skin of sky that trembles between the different stories, I hear voices, and there is dancing …

Taksim Square is flush with faces, a rainbow flag, red carnations. A Kurdish poet is giving a reading in three languages; women listen. Far away in dark Manhattan, towers flower like Judas trees, bright-coloured people waving from windows. Staff pour out of the big hotels, shedding uniforms like snow. Crows hop past: '*Kaar, Virginia.*'

Through the old world, through the new world, through Constantinople and Istanbul, through Manahatta and new Manhattan, through Harlem and Brooklyn, Sultanahmet and Taksim, the people surge, weaving new stories.

We live in others. We live in words.

We fly on, on, towards the turquoise statue who always recedes into the distance, Liberty with her crown of thorns.

Monumental, foolish, hopeful, she holds her beacon up towards us.

Acknowledgements

Virginia Woolf is an overwhelming presence in modern English literature, especially for women who write. We who come after have to cope with her genius. Woolf was an inspiration to me when I read *Jacob's Room* aged eighteen, long before she became a central author in my 1980 doctoral thesis, supervised by Dr Vivienne Wylie and Professor David Lodge. I hope this novel will be seen as a twenty-first-century love letter as well as an act of cheek, an attempt not to be afraid of Virginia Woolf. Though most references to Woolf's real nineteenth and twentieth-century life are based at least loosely on her writings or on the biographies, her thoughts and feelings are mostly my imaginings. The passage on pages 437–438 is a complete invention. No-one can know what happens between two people. The same is true of Woolf's love for her sister Vanessa, and of her thoughts before she died. In the end, this Virginia is a phantasm, one of Thackeray's fictional 'puppets', always and only my own.

I have been greatly helped with this book by my friends. First among them must be Dr Mine Özyurt Kılıç of Istanbul, author of *Maggie Gee: Writing the Condition-of-England Novel* (Bloomsbury Academic), who helped me to understand a tiny amount about her country. Professor Barbara Goodwin, perennial first reader, and Dr Robin Jared Lewis, New Yorker in China, also read and commented on this manuscript. Thanks to my writer friends Hillary Jordan and Khaled Al Khamissi and to the El Gouna Writers' Residency at the Hotel Mosaique, Egypt, which gave me time to begin this

novel; to Abdullah Al-Kafri, Kadija Sesay and Victor Sugbo; to the librarians in the Berg Collection of the New York Public Library; to Anna Raverat, for shared writing time in Manhattan. Dr Sarah Dillon and Dr Caroline Edwards inspired and organised the real-life 2012 St Andrews international conference about my work where I lurked at the back of the room, palely foreshadowing my imaginary Virginia Woolf attending the fictional international conference about *her* work in this novel.

Dr Lyndall Gordon, author of the ground-breaking *Virginia Woolf: A Writer's Life* (OUP), encouraged this project at a very early stage. Dr Alexandra Harris, author of the beautiful short biography *Virginia Woolf* (Thames & Hudson), very kindly read and advised on parts of the final draft of this book, in less than ideal circumstances. All mistakes are, of course, my own.

My beloved daughter Rosa Rankin-Gee, author of *The Last Kings of Sark* (Virago), allowed me to plagiarise a few of her sayings and her adventurous spirit for Gerda, and read an early draft. My equally beloved husband Nicholas Rankin, author of *Churchill's Wizards* (Faber & Faber), saved me, sustained me and read me at various moments. He also took me to New York for a birthday present, and it was on that trip, in the New York Public Library, that the book began.

The British Council inspired my love of Turkey when they invited me to do readings in Ankara and Istanbul in the 1990s. Since then there have been many other working trips. My thanks especially to Jonathan Lee and the authors, both British and Turkish, who were such good company in spring 2012. The staff and students at Istanbul University have encouraged and challenged many of my ideas: special thanks to Professor Dr Esra Melikoğlu, who kindly invited me to Istanbul in 2011 for a plenary at a conference very unlike the one in this book; the fortuitous eruption of the Icelandic volcano trapped me

there for long enough to nurture this novel. Thanks also to Dr Mehmet Ali Çelikel, Dr Seyda Inceoğlu and their students for inviting me to Pamukkale University in 2013.

Professor Moira Penny, who implodes during the conference in my novel, was the heroine of my first novel, *Dying in Other Words* (1981) and had gone downhill sharply by the time she came back in *The Flood* (2004). Angela Lamb was a teenager in my second novel *The Burning Book* and a self-centred writer in *The Flood*.

Thanks to Dr Tracy Brain and to colleagues and students at Bath Spa University who heard my first public reading from the novel, and encouraged me. Thanks also to Katharine Reeve and Professor Steve May who generously gave me the time the book needed.

Most of all I would like to pay tribute to the enduring courage and professionalism of my independent publishers, André, Salwa and Lynn Gaspard. Thanks for the warm encouragement and loyalty of my agent Karolina Sutton and my editor Anna Wilson, and for the keen eye and logical brain of Sarah Cleave who brought this manuscript to publication.

My Animal Life

'A wise and beautiful book about what it feels like to be alive – I really loved it' Zadie Smith

'*My Animal Life* is full of riches ... Highly recommended for all aspiring writers' Bernadine Evaristo

Maggie Gee's journey started in a small family in post-war Britain, when love, ambition and good behaviour looked very different.

At seventeen, Maggie, who had 'never had a boyfriend, never had sex and never had a job' went, totally unprepared, to Oxford. From the 1960s onwards she was living the defining events of her generation: the coming of the Pill and sexual freedom, and tremors in the cosy British layer-cake of class and race.

In the 1980s, Maggie stumbles into the literary world, falls in love, gets married and has a daughter. Writing with remarkable honesty and grace, Maggie explores the questions that matter most: success and failure, sex, death and parenthood; our animal life.

'Exceptionally brave ... a wonderful book' Claire Tomalin

'A fine, honest, complex portrait of an artist's mind' *Independent*

'Read this vivid, minutely observed memoir' *Telegraph*

'Sensitive, honest, courageous, stylish' *The Times*

Memoir • 978 1 84659 090 0 • £8.99

My Cleaner

'Elegant, humorous and surprising, this is a classy performance.'
The Times

'This is one of those rare books you want to begin again
Instantly, safe in the knowledge that it is quietly wonderful.'
Telegraph

Ugandan Mary Tendo worked for many years in the middle-
class Henman household in London, cleaning for Vanessa and
looking after her only child, Justin. More than ten years after
Mary has left, Justin – now twenty-two – is too depressed to
get out of bed. To his mother's surprise, he asks for Mary.

When Mary responds to Vanessa's cry for help and returns
from Uganda to look after Justin, the balance of power in the
house shifts dramatically. Both women's lives change
irrevocably as tensions build towards a startling climax on a
snowbound motorway.

'An intelligent and satisfying read' *Sunday Times*

'Like Margaret Atwood, Maggie Gee has always been prepared
to tackle contemporary ideas on a grand as well as a domestic
scale … A moving, funny, engrossing book.' *Observer*

'This beautifully observed, intelligent and moving novel is
one of those rare things – a small, carefully wrapped surprise
that gets better and better with the unravelling.' *The Scotsman*

Fiction • 978 1 84659 008 5 • £7.99